AMBITION

ALSO BY NATALIE KELLER REINERT

Pride
Courage
Luck
Forward
Prospect
Home
Flight

AMBITION

A Novel

The Eventing Series
BOOK ONE

NATALIE KELLER REINERT

FLATIRON
BOOKS
NEW YORK

AMBITION. Copyright © 2013, 2024 by Natalie Keller Reinert. All rights reserved. Printed in the United States of America. For information, address Flatiron Books, 120 Broadway, New York, NY 10271.

www.flatironbooks.com

Designed by Gabriel Guma

Library of Congress Cataloging-in-Publication Data

Names: Reinert, Natalie Keller, author.
Title: Ambition : a novel / Natalie Keller Reinert.
Identifiers: LCCN 2024038917 | ISBN 9781250384980 (trade paperback) | ISBN 9781250384997 (ebook)
Subjects: LCGFT: Romance fiction. | Sports fiction. | Novels.
Classification: LCC PS3618.E564548 A83 2025 | DDC 813/.6—dc23/
  eng/20240906
LC record available at https://lccn.loc.gov/2024038917

Our books may be purchased in bulk for promotional, educational, or business use. Please contact your local bookseller or the Macmillan Corporate and Premium Sales Department at 1-800-221-7945, extension 5442, or by email at MacmillanSpecialMarkets@macmillan.com.

Originally self-published in 2013 by Natalie Keller Reinert

First Flatiron Books Edition: 2025

10 9 8 7 6 5 4 3 2 1

The Eventing Series is dedicated to all the readers who
have helped make Jules a legend, and to the horses
who carry our dreams.

1

A SHADOW FELL over the barn aisle. I walked to the barn door and inspected the sky: there was a big black thundercloud out there, promising the usual afternoon storm. But this summer had already been full of lies and false hopes, and I didn't trust the clouds anymore. I didn't trust anything anymore, except for Dynamo.

"Yeah right, Florida," I muttered, turning back to the barn aisle, and my horse. "I'll believe you *after* you send me a rainstorm, not before."

Dynamo peered over his stall guard at me. He had been hanging out in the stall door since we'd arrived, enjoying the breeze from the fan set just out of his reach. His chestnut forelock blew back between his ears, giving him a cartoonish look. But his nostrils were flared, and that was no joke. My horse was hot. Everything was hot.

It was a bad day to get on a horse, and yet here we were, waiting for our ride time, on what could very well be the biggest day of my life. We'd get through it, the way we'd gotten through everything life had thrown at us so far. I hadn't pushed and pulled to get into the Athletic Charities for Equestrians auditions so that we could cop out for a little *weather*.

But at the same time, I had my doubts that the Floridian climate was on my side today. The temperature was off the charts for June, the mercury near one hundred degrees, and the torpid air sat heavily in my lungs. All afternoon, I'd been waiting for the drumroll of fat raindrops on the steel roof, but the clouds seemed to be hovering just out of range, keeping their cool breeze and their refreshing rainfall selfishly to themselves. What a day to do it. I sighed, hot breath on hot air.

On our applications, the ACE committee asked, "What is one word you'd use to describe yourself?"

On mine, I wrote: *Ambitious.* I could have written a lot of things they might have liked better: "conscientious" or "generous" or "diligent." But I didn't see any reason to lie about myself. I was here for the same reason I'd gone to every event and horse show since I was seven years old: to win.

A deep nicker brought me back, and I felt my heart lift as my horse pressed his chest against his stall guard, looking for my attention. If Dynamo had to describe me in one word, I think he'd say "pushover."

I let him wiggle his lips along my shoulder, tickling my skin. His whiskers were soft, his muzzle was gentle, but his breath was scalding, carrying a damp heat from deep within. Horses run hot.

Like dragons. Big, cuddly dragons.

"If I had to describe you in one word," I murmured to him, "it would be 'adorable.'"

He tucked his nostrils against the nape of my neck and huffed deeply, settling in for a long cuddle.

"Sweet baby," I murmured, cupping one hand over a fluttering nostril. "I love you, but we're both too sweaty for this kind of affection. Can't you be cute in your own space?"

He pulled back a little, and snorted in reply.

"I know," I agreed, nodding at him. "You're ready to go out there."

New barns meant something exciting was going to happen. He might be warm in the barn, but he wouldn't care what the weather was like once he was out on course; Dynamo's primary interests, after hay and grain and Starlight mints, were open fields, huge logs, and the freedom to go flying across them, leaping everything in his path.

Dynamo and I were pretty much in agreement on those points. Nothing in the world was better than galloping a cross-country jumping course.

But of course, eventing was about three phases, and cross-country was only one of them. "Three days, three ways," the old saying went, and before we could go cross-country, we'd have to prance around a dressage arena, and get around a show-jumping ring without knocking down any poles. Here at the ACE audition, we'd be doing all three in just an hour, and the stakes were much higher than the usual competition for a fifty-cent ribbon.

We were the last team on the audition schedule, which meant we had to watch all the others go before us. The horses and their riders left the barn in solemn pairs, through air that grew thicker with every hour. I had a sinking feeling that it would be worst of all for Dynamo and me.

The last ride, putting our ride time in front of the judges' panel in the very middle of this hot afternoon—what kind of luck was that? None at all, or just bad? It was a toss-up. Personally, I'd always thought of myself as having pretty bad luck, and it looked like Dynamo shared it with me.

I ran my hand along his neck, under his mane, and he leaned back against me, asking for a good scratch.

"Here you go, buddy," I murmured, watching his left ear tip down to catch my voice. I dug my fingernails into the short, coppery hair of his muscled neck. "A massage for you."

His skin was already damp with sweat. I hated that I shared my bad luck with my good horse. Me, I must have done something wrong in another life. Something predictably horsey. If we are the same person born again and again, then I probably wheeled and dealed and lied and stole to get my paws on some big chunk of land or a particularly fine piece of horseflesh. I surely earned my champagne taste, my beer budget, and this afternoon's oppressive weather in another misspent life. But what did Dynamo do to deserve this?

We're a team, I reminded myself, running a finger down Dynamo's jagged white stripe. It ran from his forelock to his nose, a bright path between his dark eyes. When my finger got to his nostrils, his upper lip wiggled and he lifted it, trying to catch my fingertip between soft lips. I smiled despite myself, thinking: *Whatever I did, I'd do it all again. I* will *have horses, and I will* be the best, with *or* without luck on my side.

"We'll be fine," I whispered to Dynamo. "You're a Florida-bred, and so am I. We can handle a little June heat, can't we?" And I kissed him on the nose.

"You love that horse," a male voice observed.

I jumped. "What?" I asked, spinning around.

Beside me, Dynamo took a cautious step back. The source of the voice smiled at me from a few stalls down: a man, all curled up with his feet on his tack trunk, flipping through the pages of a local equestrian magazine. I recognized him from the past few months of eventing; we were competing at the same level. Pete Morrison was waiting around for his audition, the same as I was. He was gunning for the ACE grant and sponsored horse, the same as I was. And his ride time was the one before mine.

He said, "That's so nice to see. I feel like half the riders here are just going through the motions with their latest sales horse."

"Well . . . Dynamo's not a sales horse."

"That's what makes us different from everyone else, then," he replied, smiling.

I didn't know what to say to that. He seemed ridiculously calm, considering the prize on the line for one lucky winner today. Cash and a horse. It had everyone on edge—except, apparently, for Pete Morrison of Briar Hill Farm.

And that annoyed me.

The thing was, Pete Morrison didn't *need* this grant, or a big-time horse with all its bills paid. This grant didn't have the power to make or break his career, the way it did for me.

Everyone knew that Morrison came from eventing royalty. His grandfather rode in the Olympics back in the 1960s and was considered one of the greats of the sport. His grandfather's farm, right here in Ocala, had produced champions for years. Since he'd arrived back in Florida last year, Pete had been based at the family farm, so as far as I could tell, he already had it all. That was exactly what I didn't like about him. Not that I knew him personally. But I was pretty sure I knew enough.

I'd had to bend a few rules just to get my foot in the door today, so excuse me if I wasn't interested in being chummy with an eventing trust-fund baby.

But I had to admit, his wide smile was the most welcoming expression I had seen on a human face all day. To say nothing of his chiseled cheekbones and smooth, suntanned forehead, running up to a tousled head of dark ginger hair.

"I mean," he said, when I didn't respond right away, "I can just see you guys have a tight relationship. It's nice. You're not in a hurry."

Not in a hurry? *Not in a hurry?* Boy, this guy had no idea about me.

Although he was right about one thing.

"Yeah, I do love my horse," I admitted, a little embarrassed by the fact. Loving Dynamo broke my rules. My first riding coach taught me some tough lessons about falling for horses. Not born rich, but you still want to be a professional horse trainer? Then you have to get realistic, in ways that wealthy riders do not. And that means horses come and horses go, always for sale and never for keeps.

Despite this, I had been in love with Dynamo since day one. He would always be my horse. Not a sales horse, not a project horse, but mine. And that's why I was here, trying for this crazy grant. The promise of an upper-level horse for a year, corporate sponsors to pay the bills, was exactly what I needed to get ahead. If I could get ahead with *someone else's* horse, I'd really have a chance.

I just needed a chance. Before what little money (and luck?) I had ran out.

Dynamo shoved his nose against my arm, and my hand automatically went back to his neck, to his scratchy place. He stretched out his upper lip in contentment as my fingernails went back to work.

"He's the boss, too," Pete Morrison observed. "I know how that is." His smile widened.

He was so *cheerful.* Like he wasn't going out to ride for the judges in less than an hour, with the sun baking down on us and the thunder fading in the distance, our last hope for shade and a breeze melting away.

"Most of the riders here are just trying to sell and trade up to the next horse," Pete Morrison continued, apparently missing how much I needed him to go away and leave me alone. "I could never give up Regina. I've had her since she was three years old and didn't know anything but how to run very slowly around a race-track." He laughed and put down his magazine, running a hand through that wavy mop of auburn hair, nearly the same color as his horse's coat. Every now and then, he had the tiniest accent. An English or Irish trainer growing up, probably. That sort of thing rubbed off, and having the old country accent was good for business in the horse world. New money loved old accents. "Your guy is a Thoroughbred, right?"

"Yeah, he raced, too. Didn't win anything." I shrugged. "Like most of them."

Pete tickled Regina's nose and she nipped at him. "Yeah, my girl, too. Never saw anything but dirt in her face. I think it taught her all her ornery ways."

"I saw her refuse a warm-up fence at the horse park back in April," I recalled, cheering up at the memory.

"If I don't set her up for a fence perfectly, forget it," Pete said ruefully. "Sometimes I think she'd rather be a dressage horse."

"She *does* always win the dressage." My annoyance flooded back. Dynamo didn't win the dressage. Ever. He made up for his middling dressage scores with clear jumping rounds. After all, that's what we were really showing up for.

The jumping. The galloping. The adrenaline, the feeling of being truly and wholly alive.

"I ought to throw her tack on and get rolling," Pete decided, glancing at the time on his phone. He hopped off the tack trunk and gave the watching mare a big, smacking kiss on her nose. Regina pinned her ears, outraged, and pulled back, ducking into the privacy of her stall. He watched her fondly. "My beautiful witch," he said.

"Typical mare," I said, suppressing the urge to roll my eyes.

Pete nodded. "She knows her own mind. I really respect that in a woman." He led her out of the stall and tied her lead rope to the stall bars.

"Have a good ride," I said, the four words like an eventing passcode.

Pete smiled at me. "Thanks."

I walked back to Dynamo, who was back to nursing his fan, and leaned against the wall. This awful waiting was getting to me now. My heart rate was starting to ramp up. I watched Dynamo's forelock blowing in the breeze from his fan, wishing it could make time pass more quickly. All the way past our audition, past the week of waiting to hear who won, and maybe past summer, as well.

Pete walked his mare by a few minutes later, saddled and bridled and booted and wrapped. Everything he had looked identical to my gear. That was something special about our sport, I thought. As English riders, we'd been trained in the same nuances and traditions that had been taught to horsemen and horsewomen for centuries. We could trace our riding style back to kings and emperors.

Maybe I didn't like Pete, but at our core, I supposed, we were basically the same people.

He gave us a cheerful wave. "Good luck to you!" he said, and sounded as though he meant it.

Regina gave us what looked like very deliberate side-eye.

I watched him walk outside and mount his mare, still cheerful.

I didn't understand how he could look so upbeat and excited about the audition. I almost suspected him of trying to psych me out. Or was he just that nice of a guy?

Possible, but Pete Morrison was the only male applicant this year. And considering that there was only one male applicant last year, too, and that prominent eventing patriarch Damon Knox had publicly stated that there weren't enough young American men riding, compared to the hordes of horse girls dominating the sport at every level, and that Damon Knox was the head of the ACE committee, and that last year, the only male applicant won the ACE grant . . . No wonder Pete was so happy. Statistics were on his side. The publicly biased judge holding the purse strings was on his side. The eventing gods were on his side. And he knew it.

I shrugged, adjusting the knot in my neck, the collar of my fitted navy riding jersey, the chip on my shoulder, and went back to Dynamo's stall to get the big red horse saddled up. We would be next. I'd have him looking show-ring ready for those judges.

Twenty minutes later, Dynamo was standing with his chest against the stall guard, brushed, bandaged, and tacked. Every hair lay perfectly in accordance with the next, the swirls and whorls of cowlicks red and gold like the grain of polished wood. His fox-colored mane was brushed flat against the muscles of his arched neck, length kept a meticulous four inches long from ear to withers; his thick tail flowing like a waterfall before coming to a precise blunt ending halfway between his hocks and his fetlocks. "Banged," it's called, the way the English do it. Another pretty tradition.

Like my horse, my look was traditional, with updated fabrics and a few colorful touches we get to enjoy as eventers—the "wild ones" in English saddles. The reins looped over one arm were nylon knitted with rubber, for grip; my snug-fitted helmet had a navy-blue cover with a small false brim—in case a bad fall took me headfirst into the dirt, where a brim could be a liability. My hay-colored hair was tucked up inside it. I fastened the button closures on my show gloves, which looked like leather but were actually some kind of high-tech, grippy material. My long-sleeved riding jersey in navy, tucked neatly into my white show breeches and my bridle-leather belt, was actually cooler in the sun than a tank top. My polished black dress boots were the most traditional thing about my outfit: real leather, and understated to the point of being plain. Really, all of it was. I liked that about our show attire: the most beautiful, showy thing about our turnout was actually the horse himself.

Also, I couldn't afford anything fancy or custom.

Just as we prepared to leave, Pete Morrison walked back in, with a low-headed Regina dragging behind him. She was sweaty, her sides heaving. Her hind shoes scraped along the concrete floor. Pete gave the mare a pat on the neck and smiled at me as he approached. "All done," he said. "Thank God."

"Your horse looks knackered," I observed.

"Hot out there," he acknowledged ruefully. "Good luck." Again, he sounded like he really meant it, but maybe it was part of his all-around-good-guy schtick, the way he got clients and students and girls. Forget his warm smile. These guys on horseback were all the same: they had a groom at every farm. Just because Pete Morrison appeared genuine didn't mean he was any different from the rest.

I'd worked odd farm jobs to make ends meet here in Ocala and had spent enough time around breeding stallions and long-suffering mares to recognize peacocking and showboating, and I wasn't interested in being courted, however casually, by another stud colt. There was too much li'l ladying going on in the horse business. Too much swagger and men walking into the barn crotch-first in riding breeches that were entirely too tight. Something about being with horses made women more understanding and empathetic, at least that's what all the self-help books masquerading as horse books seemed to suggest, but they just seemed to make men more macho and chauvinistic. I suppose it was tough on their egos that both sexes competed on equal footing in equestrian competition.

We looked better in riding breeches, too.

2

THE DRESSAGE ARENA sat on top of the hill. Over the white fiber footing, blindingly bright beneath the midafternoon sun, I loosened Dynamo's muscles by putting him through his paces: circles and serpentines, voltes and half-voltes, halts and changes of gait, while the judges sat, rather less than regally, atop a picnic table along the rail. There were three of them, and the one in the middle with his head bent over his clipboard was Damon Knox, the one who worried me the most.

Beyond their picnic table, catching Dynamo's eye every time we passed, was a big oval jumping field, dotted with the kind of expensive, whimsical jumps—butterflies holding up orange-and-black-striped rails, two wishing wells spanning a false brick wall—that top events can afford to put out for their show-jumping phase. My jumps back at home were spindly, plain, with peeling paint or not painted at all. It was a reminder that there was significant money behind Longacres and the ACE grant I was here to win. This was a rich person's game I was trying to play.

Well, that's why you're here, I reminded myself. *For the money.* Just like everyone else.

Well, except for Pete Morrison. I shook my head to get his smiling face out of my mind. *Focus.* I looked at the jumps for something else to think about, and Dynamo tugged at the bit, trying to convince me that we should go play with them. My horse was like a little kid, hoping to skip the boring flatwork part of the school day and go straight to recess.

I felt the same way he did. It would be so fun and easy if the only thing we had to do today was hop some fences. Show-jumping fences—the kind that fall down if you hit them—and cross-country fences. The kind that knock you down if you hit them.

That was where the real fun waited: the cross-country jumps farther down the slope, opposite the stable where we'd spent the day waiting. Down there, I could see the railroad ties and telephone poles, sculpted by chain saw into their own forms of rustic art, that comprised the cross-country course. The stone wall out there wasn't painted rocks on a sheet of plywood—those were real stones, held together with real mortar. And the water complex had a particularly formidable drop. Once your horse was leaping over the fence in front of it, you were soaring six feet above the pool of water below.

I had to look away from the water hazard, actually. Maybe it was just the heat, but that jump looked particularly difficult today. Enough to make me feel queasy. But it would be fine. Big jumps, little jumps, whatever was out there, Dynamo and I would take them on and show the judges what we were made of. Cross-country jumping is the heart and soul of eventing, the reason why we work so hard. So maybe feeling dizzy, a little weak, wasn't the best setup for a cross-country run. But there was no turning back now. *In Dynamo I trust.*

I brushed the back of one hand against my forehead, trying

to sop up some of the damp, but my gloves were already soaked through with the sweat from Dynamo's withers and neck. All I accomplished was introducing a salty prickling into my eyes. Great. Burning eyes, trembling spine, and a little upset stomach just for good measure.

"Dynamo, *you're* not feeling the pressure, right?" I asked softly. "It's just me?"

He moved forward into a trot with a nose-clearing snort, and I had to smile. Despite all my misgivings and what was probably the start of heatstroke, Dynamo was ready to carry me through this audition with his usual style. Now it was my turn to help him along. I drew in a deep breath and let it out as a long sigh, hoping the motion would stretch my diaphragm and back, and tilted my pelvis so that my seat bones would sink into the saddle, feeling Dynamo's very spine.

There's a moment that I'm sure must be the entire point of riding dressage (the Olympic sport that takes decades to master yet, unfairly, puts the masses to sleep), a moment when your muscles flow into your horse's muscles, and you cease to sit as a passenger on his back and find yourself floating, buoyed by his impulsion and glorious strength. Whoever first felt it—a Roman cavalryman, a French knight, a Bedouin nomad—they must have been instantly, hopelessly addicted. They would have devoted the rest of their life to finding that feeling again. It is that sort of sensation. It is a moment of achieving perfect balance with a four-legged creature of speed and power, and I had never felt it so strongly with any other horse.

What was remarkable, though, and what I thought would impress the judges, was that while I could find perfect balance and enlightenment with Dynamo, he was not a natural dressage horse.

Dynamo was born with unbeautiful gaits: he lifted his knees

too high at the trot instead of swinging forward from the shoulder; he had a long back and a natural tendency to let his hind legs trail after him at the canter, instead of bringing them up beneath his body to create a springing, catlike bounce with every step. All his mismatched parts required a particularly long warm-up to start flowing together in the tightly-sprung-watchworks precision needed for a competitive dressage test, and for the first ten minutes or so of any warm-up, few onlookers would have believed me if I told them he was capable of upper-level movements. But he *could* do them. I was counting on the judges to watch our warm-up, and see the transformation I created.

We'd completed our first round of warm-up, and he was already moving better. We were almost there. But the heat was starting to tell on him. I could finally feel he was moving properly, with his hind legs underneath himself, pushing himself forward with his hindquarters instead of pulling himself along with his forelegs, but all that hard work under the blazing sun had his veins bulging from his neck, and sweat rubbed into white foam along his neck by the reins, the bridle, even behind my legs where I'd been constantly pushing, lifting, coaxing his abdominal muscles to rise up and bring his back to meet me. He was ready now, moving at his best, and I halted to give him a quick breather before we began riding our test. I let the reins fall loose and he turned his head; I could see the red rims of his flared nostrils, and I knew then that we didn't have much longer before he was courting heatstroke, too.

And then I realized that the judges weren't sitting quietly with their clipboards anymore.

The three of them were waving me over, flagging me down with all sorts of gestures: flourishing a hat, brandishing a notepad, waving their arms. For all the motion, it took me a surprisingly long time to notice them. I suppose I was absorbed in working Dynamo, but perhaps it was also that I was already so overheated that my reaction times had begun to crawl, neurons firing sluggishly, brain literally fried.

And then for a breathless, horrified moment, I thought, *They know.*

"*Over here, please!*" Damon Knox shouted.

Feeling like I was headed for the executioner, I nudged Dynamo into a trot and we jogged over to the arena rail. A few strides before we reached the group, I squeezed my fingers closed on the reins and sat deep in the saddle, pushing Dynamo with my calves so that his forward momentum ran straight into the firm hold I had on his mouth, causing him to rock back and halt beautifully and square, a leg at each corner, like a general before his troops. It was time to show off what we had. Just in case I was about to be escorted off the property.

I gave him a quick pat on the neck, and felt the heat of his wet skin. He was broiling. "This will be over soon," I whispered. "Good boy."

"We're going to make this brief," Knox said. Tall and traditional, in breeches and damp polo shirt and a faded ACE ball cap perched on his bald head, Damon Knox had been making and breaking penniless riders for ten years. I'd been gearing up for this audition for just as long. I stared at him breathlessly, waiting for the sword to fall.

"It's too hot," Knox said.

I blinked.

"We're risking your health and your horse's with this weather." He glanced up at the yellowish sky, and as my eyes followed his, I realized the thunderstorm was still hanging around, the one that had stubbornly refused to budge and let loose its pent-up rain and wind. It was nearby, white edges of cloud trailing toward the treetops. There was a slow growl of thunder. Knox said, "That was a good sample of your dressage. Just jump a couple of warm-up fences, then do the jumping course that we posted in the barn this morning, and we'll call it a day."

I was relieved . . . dizzy with relief, actually . . . and then I was *furious*.

So it was all going to come down to a ten-minute warm-up in the dressage ring and a show-jumping course? Was he kidding? Everyone else had ridden for nearly an hour, showing off their dressage prowess, their cross-country bravery, their show-jumping discipline, and I was going to have to show I was worth twenty thousand dollars and a new horse by doing just a third of all that?

I felt something crumple up inside of me. The years I'd spent prepping for this day, the qualifications I'd amassed, the glowing realization that this would be the year I'd be competing at a level high enough to apply for the grant, the last-minute gut checks when unexpected obstacles were flung in my path—and it was for *nothing*. Hot weather and Pete Morrison were going to take me down.

Because obviously, they were handing the whole package to Pete Morrison. He'd ridden right before me, and Damon had probably told the other two judges they could get out of this heat quickly if they just blew past my ride and awarded the grant to Pete, the way he'd wanted to all along.

My hot face somehow grew hotter at the idea, and it felt as if I was simply going to burst into flame with the rage of it all.

And I thought: *No.*

I might have been disappointed for half a second before the

anger took over. That was how I'd always coped with watching other people leapfrog ahead of me. And it *worked*. Resentment had always carried me farther than jealousy; despising my enemies had always been more sustaining than envying my competition. These are the true lessons you learn in high school, when you spend all four years of it mucking out after your classmates' horses. I was used to being excluded, but I would never accept it. If I just rolled over and took it when people told me I wasn't good enough, I wouldn't be sitting here right now.

And as long as I was still sitting in front of these judges, my horse ready to go, then I had a chance.

I hardened my jaw and loosened it again, realizing my tension carried into Dynamo. As soon as he felt my anger spark up, his back went flat and his head came up, losing the elegant, arch-necked stance that was so important in dressage. I could fight for this with everything I had, but if I slipped in my own composure, Dynamo would go around the arena like a plow horse after a long day in the fields. I had to go into battle shod with ballet slippers, easy and light on the ground, on my horse, on the eyes.

And I'd show them that I was brave enough and fit enough to take on the heat.

I spoke up so all three judges could hear me. "I think we could manage the whole ride. We're locals, you know. We were both brought up here in Florida."

Damon Knox's face clouded, and the two women beside him narrowed their eyes.

I saw my mistake instantly; their faces said it all. It was too hot for anyone to ask a horse for anything remotely strenuous. They'd just shortened the audition out of consideration for the horse. What sort of person *was* this Jules Thornton, anyway?

Knox was a snowbird from Virginia. His horses were already back up north; he'd be gone as soon as this audition was over. No Florida summers or Virginia winters for his home-bred, unraced Thoroughbreds; he shuttled them up and down the coast, chasing the perfect weather. He raised his eyebrows at me, clearly questioning my sanity, my humanity.

I could deal with his distaste, because I already knew he was team Pete Morrison, all the way. But when Ronnie Gibbs, sitting to his left with a huge sun hat plunked on her head, spoke up, I withered a little inside. Ronnie had been a world-renowned rider before a pelvis-shattering fall at Badminton Horse Trials in England ended her career. She rode with the kind of fearlessness that some people called recklessness, and I'd always looked up to her. Now she coached and taught clinics and was generally inspiring, with a voice that held the kind of carefully rehearsed, encouraging tone that kept hopeless riders coming back again and again with their wallets open. "You have the right spirit," she said in that very tone. "I'm very impressed with your spunk. But we have to be careful of what's best for our horses, don't we? After all, they should always come first. Without them, we're nothing."

My toes curled up in my boots at her pony-book platitudes. I hadn't been seen as brave and ambitious and worth a second look at all. To Ronnie, to all three of them, I was just a headstrong girl who couldn't take advice and didn't put her horse first. I couldn't come back from this; cruelty to horses was the eighth deadly sin, and the most grievous one of all. But I had to try. I hadn't *meant* it that way!

"I'm sorry," I said meekly. "You're right. I guess I'm so used to the heat that I didn't really realize it was worse than usual. I just got excited about running through that water complex, that's all." I said it as folksy and girlishly as I could. It didn't even sound like me.

Ronnie's lips curved into a smile that made her face pucker as though she'd bit into a lemon, every last inch of her skin sliding into a thousand wrinkles. She'd spent a lifetime in the sun, squinting across arenas and fields. "It's natural to be excited," Ronnie said kindly. "I like the water complex best, too."

I had the uncomfortable impression that she was speaking to me in the same voice she used for Pony Club seminars.

D-level Pony Club seminars.

The ones for eight-year-olds, who were *literally* riding ponies.

"Do you know the jumping course?" the other woman asked, rather more sharply. Kathy Britton, a respected owner and amateur rider who had gotten to the international four-star level all on her own (being wealthy helped), was tall and thin, with a drawn, bony face. She had propped her elbow on her knee and her chin on her fist, from which one perfectly manicured thumbnail emerged, tapping at her teeth while she studied me. I was mesmerized by the cherry-red lacquer on the nail for a moment, gazing at it while I tried to understand what sort of horsewoman had the time to maintain nail polish and cuticles. The rich sort, with people to do her dirty work, probably.

"Ms. Thornton?"

I tore my eyes away from her manicure and plastered another *what an exciting day!* smile on my face. "Yes! Yes, I know the course."

"Go right ahead," Damon Knox said, his voice taut, like he was done with me already. "Give us a circle and salute when you're ready to start."

I nodded and picked up the reins again, nudging Dynamo into wakefulness. He was sluggish as we moved off from the rail, and I gave the bit a jiggle in an attempt to bring his head up and get his attention back. But I could feel my own body rebelling against my demands as much as my horse was. Dynamo was lop-eared and low-headed as we trotted into the jumping arena, and as I turned him toward the first warm-up fence, a low vertical with a single pole, his gait stuttered a little, as if he couldn't quite believe what I was asking of him. Jumping? *Now?*

I couldn't quite believe it myself. And a part of me, deep inside, wondered if we should just trot out of the arena, right past Damon and Kathy and Ronnie and back to the barns. Pack up, load up, and head home, and let *that* be our statement about the weather. Maybe we could impress them by simply leaving.

But that was a stupid gamble, and anyway, the knowledge that we'd been set up for failure with this mini course was so upsetting that I couldn't really think straight. All the rage and resentment and the constantly thwarted ambition, always simmering, finally boiled over in me, and I bit down on my lip and swung my right leg, the one that the committee couldn't see, jabbing my horse hard in the rib cage with the blunt tip of one gleaming little spur. I only wore tiny Prince of Wales spurs, and they were meant to refine the requests I made with my legs, not hurt my horse, but still, it must have been a surprise to Dynamo, because he lurched forward.

He broke into a canter twenty feet before the fence, and sprang over the jump with the fluidity and power that always marked his jumping. As a jumper, at least, my horse was a natural, and after he had learned to carry himself efficiently in the dressage, the extra spring in his step and thrust in his hindquarters had earned him at least another two feet of jumping ability.

I let him canter in a circle and then brought him back to the other fence, a big square oxer, the front and back rails at least three feet apart. He pricked his ears and rounded his back, looking at the fence with a hint of a spook in his step. "Are you kidding?" I hissed, and gave him another jab with my hidden leg, sending him forward in a crooked leap.

Dynamo straightened himself a stride out and launched over the fence, and I closed my legs and huddled over his wet neck, my hands on the crest of his mane, my chin close over them. I always did have a dramatic jumping style, born of learning to jump on the dregs of the local stock auctions, whatever little beast my old trainer brought home for two hundred dollars or less. Those horses either didn't know how to jump yet and threw themselves at jumps with gusto, or they already knew they didn't like jumping and threw themselves *away* from the jumps with equal gusto. Either way, I learned to get out of the saddle and clutch mane for dear life. I'd never have made it as a pretty girl posing in the hunter show ring, but in the jumper ring, getting over the fence is all that matters.

Dynamo took a slight misstep upon landing, the rhythm of his stride in doubt for a split second—which can be a long time when you are perched atop an airborne horse—before he managed to catch himself, rebalance, and carry on. I sat still, poised just above his withers, with my weight deep in my heels, lodged in irons hanging tautly from the stirrup leathers, all 130 pounds of me dangling from the two steel bars in the center of the saddle, allowing him the freedom of his back so that he could help himself.

I hoped the judges were getting all this. It wasn't about the horse, after all, it was about how I got the horse around the course. This audition was about me. And why I deserved more good horses. Even better horses.

We made one more sweeping turn around the top of the jumping arena before I turned him back for another warm-up fence, where I was hopeful that I wouldn't have to poke him with a steel spur to convince him that he needed to jump. I needed him to regain some of his usual pizzazz and enjoy his job. "I know it's hot, baby," I told him, and his ears flicked back languidly at my voice. "But we really only have to be out here for another ten minutes or so. Help me out here."

His strides did not increase in strength, but the tempo remained even. He was the best horse—he always tried for me. Even when the air was too wet to breathe and his skin was too soaked to let him cool, even when his nostrils were extended to their red-rimmed utmost, even when his flesh was searing hot to the touch, he gathered his hindquarters beneath his body and shoved himself on, stride after stride, with the bounce and grace of a puma. It was my job to help him, so I put my leg on and gave him my hands to lean on.

I glanced to my right as we cantered along the rail, and found myself making eye contact with Pete Morrison, who was watching us from about fifty feet away, his bathed and dripping mare grazing beneath an oak tree. He gave me a thumbs-up, and as I turned my eyes back to find the path to the next fence, I felt a resurgence of anger. Spoiled rich white American male, spying on me while his good mare dried out after their audition, their *full* audition, while I would get only a third of the judges' time and attention. What was the point of any of it? He was going to win; Damon Knox probably hadn't seen anyone else's name after he ran his finger down the list of finalists and saw *Peter*.

I shook my head, regardless of how odd it must have looked to the judges. I wouldn't let him win. I put down my hands and waited for the fence ahead.

Dynamo took the tall vertical in perfect balance, his breath shuddering from his lungs in a great fluttering snort as his hooves connected with the ground again, and I immediately reined him up in a dancing halt, dropped my right hand to my thigh, and nodded a salute to the judges on the picnic table. They nodded in return. I brought back my right calf, touching Dynamo slightly with the tip of my spur, and he bounced forward into a bright, eager canter. The jumping had gotten him keyed up despite the heat.

And me, too. This was a second wind: this suddenly high, heady feeling, drunk with delight and passion and driving will all at once, to feel myself one with my horse, rocking back and forth with his swinging stride, my eyes tingling with the sharpness of salt dripping from my forehead. We drove toward the first fence, a confection of saw-sculpted wooden flowers holding up a four-foot-high series of pink and yellow poles. There was a sudden burst of wind, the reluctant storm that had hovered so tantalizingly nearby all afternoon, a hot wind like the gust from a convection oven, like the desert of Dynamo's forebears, and the whole heavy structure seemed to wobble before my eyes.

Not just mine; Dynamo's ears pricked and suddenly seemed to be directly under my chin as he leaned back in alarm. Despite course designers' continued efforts to make fences look more and more outlandish and alarming, there is one unwritten rule: jumps don't move.

Dynamo's strides faltered; I sat down in the saddle and pushed, hard, with my seat, forcing him to match my own motion and keep moving forward. Horses' bodies mirror our own; pelvis to pelvis, chin to chin, elbow to elbow, our weaknesses become theirs and our determination dictates their decisions.

And that is what happened.

Dynamo plowed forward despite his misgivings, right up to the very base of the fence, and then gathered himself up and launched upward. His hind hooves had not yet left the ground when the second gust of wind came bursting out of the cloud, my very own little black rain cloud that had followed me since birth, waiting for this very moment, and mowed down the pretty wooden flowers and sent the pink and yellow poles scattering. One pole caught Dynamo in his perfectly even knees, aborting his flight, sending him downward face-first. One standard of wooden flowers crashed into my left leg before sliding down my polished boot and across Dynamo's ribs. A blossoming red rose appeared on the bleached white of the saddle pad, dark and oxygen-starved, as the wooden flowers splintered on his side.

Did Dynamo flip over because his head hit the ground and broke his momentum? Or did he stumble as his hind hooves tried to gain purchase on the rolling poles beneath them, like scrabbling on steel rollers, sending his hindquarters up into the air? Whatever caused it, he was up before I was, tripping and falling and lurching, dripping blood from a half-dozen abrasions caused by shattered poles and fragments of flowers. I lay where I'd fallen, face in the dirt, clay in my mouth, mane between my fingers, tears in my eyes, until Pete Morrison was on his knees at my side.

3

"YOU DIDN'T REALLY fall off," my mother said the next morning. "The fence fell on you. That's completely different."

"It doesn't matter when there's no do-over," I said impatiently. I had a crick in my neck from trying to talk on my phone and muck stalls at the same time, and my elbow felt like I had shut it in a car door. I must have landed on it after Dynamo fell. I was lucky that was the least of my injuries. Last night, Dynamo had some heat in the suspensory area of one foreleg. It was gone this morning, but the creeping fear remained: we both could have gotten seriously injured yesterday, and for nothing. "I don't complete the audition, I fail, Mom. I lose. They're going to give it to Peter fucking Morrison, just watch."

"Stop cussing like that. You sound like a stable hand. You're running your own barn, act professional."

"I *am* a stable hand right now. What do you think I'm doing? I'm mucking out." I was impatient for the conversation to be over.

Phone calls from my mother were just opportunities for us to realize how much we didn't understand each other. She thought I should be building up a big riding lesson business to make money for one nice competition horse of my own. But I was in the horse business to ride, not to babysit. I trained horses, competed them, and sold them, and that was the business.

"Laurie would have had a kid in there mucking out," my mother pointed out. "She always had you doing it. She wasn't doing all that work. She was teaching, making money."

"Laurie liked kids. I don't. I like being by myself."

"Well, doesn't seem like you've improved much for yourself since she was out riding her horses while you were in her barn mucking her stalls. Except now you have to pay the bills, too."

I couldn't argue with that, as much as I'd love to. I flicked manure into the wheelbarrow with a practiced twist of my wrist. The expert at work. "I have an event to be ready for in two weeks, and that's a chance to showcase my sales horses before the season's totally dead. So my bills will get paid, thanks for worrying about that."

"And when are you going to ride these sales horses?"

"I'll ride in the afternoon today. It's fine."

"Oh, when it's ninety degrees and sunny? That seems smart." Her voice took on its nasal, sarcastic quality, which I associated with pretty much every foolish decision I'd ever made, beginning with the time I'd bought a plastic horse model from a girl in second grade for my entire life savings. What could I say? Yes, I was saving for a real horse at the time, but that model horse was so shiny and it was right there in front of me. Well, I had a long history of foolish equine-related decisions, and every one of them could be chronicled in my mother's special tone that she reserved for my stupidity and my stupidity alone.

I can't even describe the knife edge it took on when I announced my plan to buy a farm with my college fund.

"Listen to me, Jules—I heard Peggy Barlow is selling a nice lesson pony. I can give you her number. You really need to think about it."

"Wait, how do you know about something like that?" My mother wasn't involved in the horse business. How was she still in on the feed-store gossip, after I left home and took the horses out of her life?

"One of the girls at work told me. Her daughter rides with Peggy. That lady, she's another one making a fortune teaching kids. I'm really disappointed that you won't even consider it."

From sarcasm to disappointment. We were almost to the angry hang-up. Which would come as a relief, because everything hurt and this phone was getting hot. Along with my temper.

"Mom, I just can't deal with kids right now, okay? I'm not a riding instructor. I'm a trainer. They're not the same thing!"

She clicked her tongue in exasperation and I knew the conversation was over. "Jules, you think you know everything. I don't know why I even offer to help."

There wasn't a bang or anything to mark the end of the call; angry, explosive, cathartic, phone-shattering slams just don't happen anymore. She pressed the red button on her phone, and that was that. It suited my mom, but I wished for something more emphatic, to really let her know how she made me feel. I wanted a real phone, so I could slam it down after shouting, "You don't *get me*, Mom!"

I sighed and slid the phone into the back pocket of my threadbare cut-offs. The silence of the barn echoed around me. The horses were outside, enjoying a little freedom before I brought them back in for shade and the manufactured breeze of their box fans. I loved my barn best when it was occupied: twelve little horsies, neat and tidy in their boxes, heads poking out to watch me while I swept up the aisle, nickering their encouragement each time I disappeared into the feed room, ears pricked with their eternal hope for surprise grain or bonus hay. It was like living in a snow globe, or a magazine advertisement for a stabling architecture firm; it was like the fairy-tale existence I had always imagined.

But right now, the reality of life with horses was very much in my face. A hay-, dirt-, and manure-strewn barn aisle. Eleven dirty stalls (and one half-cleaned one). A hay pallet that was discouragingly empty of hay. A low rumble from the west that signified the Gulf of Mexico was already stirring with plans to flood my riding arena and ruin my carefully plotted training calendar.

Sometimes, I was very much afraid that my mother was right.

I didn't have enough money to be in the horse business, that was the simple truth. It didn't matter how many people told me that showing horses was a rich person's sport. There wasn't anything else for me to *do*. There wasn't anything else I cared about.

It had all started with a visit to a friend of my grandmother's. She lived deep in the backcountry of South Florida, on a ranch carved out of swamp and Spanish moss. I was five years old, and the only thing I remembered clearly was the shadowy, spidery barn, and the horses drowsing inside. I don't think I'd realized horses weren't just cartoons before that moment. Seeing them in real life, being offered a ride, filled me with helium. Five years old, hoisted horseback for the first time, I reached forward, grabbed that horse's shaggy mane between my fingers, and refused to get down. I stayed in that stock saddle until it was time to go home.

My parents caved after two years of horses, horses, horses every third word, and paid for riding lessons at a local barn. All through elementary and middle school, I rode once a week, bouncing around a ring for an hour on a bored school horse, and that was supposed to be enough. When it wasn't, I managed to find ways to work for riding lessons. My riding instructor, Laurie, knew a good thing when she saw it. I was willing to do anything at all to ride for an extra twenty minutes. She dangled rides on half-broke ponies in front of me in exchange for barn chores, and I snapped up every chance to climb onto her auction finds and rodeo rejects. As a working student, I scrubbed out drains, cleaned out gutters, mucked out stalls, filled in holes in the pastures, cleaned saddles—whatever it took. There was no time for anything else. Only horses.

I didn't have the money to ride *good* horses, but I was willing to risk life and limb and scholastic expulsion to get on any horse I could. And so I happily agreed to ride outrageously bad horses: horses who bucked, horses who bolted, horses who flipped over, and horses who lay down in the dirt when they were tired of working. But all those bad horses made me a supremely confident rider, able to stay in the saddle through just about any display of dangerous behavior.

Working at the riding stable ate any social time I might have had, and I didn't care. There were no parties, no dates, no prom nights. I wandered through my school years drawing windswept manes and pricked ears onto the brown paper covers of my textbooks, and, as soon as I realized no one was going to notice or care if I wasn't sitting slumped in the back of the room, I started skipping class to strip out stalls instead.

My happiest hours were spent in the saddle, with brief time-outs when some auction bronc managed to get me out of it. I always got back on. Laurie loved me for it. "I can put you on anything and in six weeks I have a lesson pony," she'd brag when she showed me off to friends. I'd shrug and blush and go get on another horse. I didn't know what else to do.

No one else at the barn loved me, of course. I was a working-class kid in a rich kids' world. Laurie financed her dressage and eventing career by teaching kids to ride on the auction ponies I had taught some manners, then selling their parents very expensive push-button show horses. Osprey Ridge catered to extravagantly wealthy girls, and by the time we were teenagers together, the lines had been drawn. I was on one side, the hired help, and they were on the other, making my life difficult.

Those girls delighted in nasty little teases like throwing their horse's sweaty tack in the dirt so that I'd have extra work to do in that night's cleanup, or "spilling" a drop of shampoo into a water trough I was filling so that I had to spend twenty minutes rinsing out the ensuing foam volcano that came frothing over the trough's edges. I was never ashamed to throw horse manure into a wheel-barrow in exchange for some saddle time. But those girls thought I should be, and they did everything in their power to let me know that I wasn't like them. I wasn't good enough for them.

All of which, in turn, made me more determined than anything to be the very best. If you can't join them, beat them and rub their noses in it. The horse show ribbons that I managed to bring home were strung up along the school-horse stalls for months. They grew flyspecked and mildewed, but I didn't care. I didn't need the ribbons in my bedroom where no one could admire them but me.

Those girls laughed when I brought home Dynamo, too. They didn't laugh so hard when we won our region's Novice Level Championship two years later, or the Training Level Championship the following year. By the Preliminary Level Championship, most of them had gone off to college. I won anyway, for fun. With any luck, they were still checking in with the eventing blogs or reading *The Chronicle of the Horse.* I smiled very broadly for the camera with every win.

I went on making my dreams come true, while they were off studying or going to frat parties or whatever it was college students did. My grandfather had left me college money—the only stroke of luck I'd ever had. And I knew exactly what I wanted to do with it.

Of course there was a fight. I had been arguing with my parents about college for two solid years. They wanted me to go to school—anything would have pleased them at this point. Equine science, veterinary medicine, business administration . . . *anything.* But I told them that Dynamo and I had something special, something that couldn't be put on ice while I wasted time at college.

Instead, I took the money and bought a farm.

Green Winter Farm, my own little ten acres, a dryish patch of land on the outskirts of Florida's horse country. My own (used, slightly dented) dually pickup. My own (used, slightly more dented) horse trailer. My own barn, my own paddocks, my own double-wide trailer. Or *manufactured home,* as the real estate agent put it. But who cared if it was a metal box? It was a place for me to sleep. I would have taken a stall in the barn for a bedroom if only to have my own farm.

Green Winter Farm, where it would all begin: my name in lights, my magazine covers and my shiny medals, "The Star-Spangled Banner" playing in the background as the flag was raised on high. This was it.

And here I was, in Ocala. Broke. Down on my luck. Jaw set with determination.

With ambition.

* * *

Iworked in silence for a little while longer, dumping wheelbarrows into the bin beneath the old ramp of the loading dock. Once this had been a broodmare barn on a much larger breeding farm, and the loading ramp, covered in grass and fenced on either side with crumbling wooden rails, had been for the huge semitrailers that were used to transport racehorses and high-end breeding stock around the country, or even, in this case, from one section of the farm to another. I didn't have such fancy transportation for my horses, though. Just the four-horse trailer parked out along the edge of the parking lot, waiting for the next event. Which wouldn't be anytime soon, I thought regretfully, wiping sweat from my face with the front of my tank top. It was too damn hot. I really shouldn't even be training in this weather.

But there was no time to spare.

I just had to be careful and watch the horses.

And myself. I had nearly ended up in the back of an ambulance in all the confusion at Longacres yesterday. I blushed to think of it: the way that Pete Morrison had held my wrist, checking my pulse, calling over his shoulder that my skin was cold, and I was going into heatstroke.

"No, I'm not," I'd hissed through numb lips. "Give me my horse!"

"Shush now, take it easy," he'd instructed softly, leaning over me as if he needed a better look, and I wasn't so far gone into heatstroke or shock or PTSD to not notice what shockingly blue eyes that man had, brilliant as the sky at that magic hour just after sunset. I stilled for just a moment, arrested by his touch and his gaze, and for a moment I wasn't thinking about horses at all.

Ugh. Here I was mucking out a stall, surrounded by manure and soiled shavings, and I was the most disgusting thing in it. How could I even think things like that? Lying there in the dirt, with my riding helmet unbuckled and sweat trailing muddy rivulets down my dirty cheeks, gazing up at that entitled shoo-in for the award I wanted, I needed, while God only knew what was going on with my horse . . . looking at him like some kind of lovestruck Juliet . . .

Well, that *was* my name.

Another reason to be angry at my mother. I stabbed at a pile of manure with fresh outrage. Why would you name your daughter after someone who fell in love with the wrong person and died heartbroken? It was like she had been wishing bad luck on me. *I already have quite enough on my own, Mom,* I thought as I finished up. Setting the fork to one side, I took down the dirty water buckets and staggered down the barn aisle with them, wishing that Monty would just finish his damn water instead of dunking all his hay in it, and dumped the water out in the parking lot.

The empty parking lot.

I stood and looked at it for a moment. It was a vast expanse of gravel and white sand, built for all the employees who had once worked here, for busy days full of feed deliveries and farrier visits and horse trailers pulling in and out with new mares for breeding season. When the real estate agent had left me to walk around and imagine my life here, I had thought this lot would be perfect for my thriving business to come: plenty of room for clients to store their horse trailers, plenty of room for their SUVs and luxury sedans when they came to see how their horses were doing. Room, too, for my working student to park when she lived here, working in the barn for room and board and riding lessons.

I'd pictured someone like me as a teenager, only adult—a pal and a coworker and a protégé all wrapped up in one. For a few months, Becky had really felt like that person.

Nothing sat in the parking lot now but my trailer, crouching off in one corner, and my truck, pulled up close to the barn. The few clients I had with horse trailers took their rigs home, to ferry around their other horses. The SUVs and luxury sedans had never materialized. And my working student, Becky—well, she was part time and didn't even live here anymore. Which was why I was doing the stalls instead of riding this morning.

I sat down on one of the railroad ties that lined the parking lot's edge. It was another hot day, and I was sore from yesterday, and dammit, I deserved a break, didn't I? A very brief one. I could hear thunder in the distance. I might have to dodge the lightning bolts and ride in the rain, if it came to that. With an event in two weeks, and no real hope of winning the ACE grant, I was back to my original game plan: win everything I entered, wow everyone, and get new training clients through sheer hard work. Simple, right? I'd only been trying for two years to get this pro-trainer thing right.

"That makes you two years closer to your first big win," I told myself.

A lizard raced across the railroad tie, paused at my leg, and looked up at me. We had a moment of eye contact. The lizard considered me, blinking slowly.

"You can cross if you want," I told the lizard. "Don't let me get in your way."

The lizard turned around and skittered off in the other direction.

I tried not to take it personally. Maybe the lizard thought, as Becky did, that I was a dangerous human only masquerading as an animal lover.

I chewed at my lip, remembering my return to the farm yesterday. The way Becky had looked at me, as if I'd betrayed her just by going to the audition. The way she had eyed the dirt on my breeches, the scrape on my face, and her lips had pursed, as if she was holding back a smirk. And then she had given Dynamo a long, assessing look. She'd seen the sweat on his haunches, the hollows above his eyes, the flecks of blood on his sides.

She'd unwrapped his legs while I brought in my tack. "There's a little filling here," she'd announced, kneeling beside him and gently touching his lower leg, feeling for heat. She gave me an accusing look. "What happened? Cross-country accident?"

She'd love that, I thought. Exactly what she'd predicted.

"We fell at a fence in the grass arena," I'd said. "Or—the fence fell, in the wind, right as we got to it. So we kind of all fell together."

"Dynamo fell?" She stood up, looking as if she wanted to fight me.

"Yeah. It was ugly," I admitted. "But it wasn't anyone's fault. The weather was crazy. The wind—"

Becky shook her head in disgust. "The wind," she repeated. She looked at me as if I was something she'd scraped from the bottom of her shoe. "I knew this would happen."

"You knew *what* would happen?" I demanded. "You could have come with me, you know. Other people had their grooms with them. I could have used some moral support."

Becky snorted. "Moral support? Yeah, right. You shouldn't even have gone, and you know it."

"I did what I had to do," I told her. "And if you had such a huge problem with it, you wouldn't still be here."

She picked up the hose and started to fill a wash bucket. I went into the tack room to wipe off Dynamo's sweaty saddle and bridle. The conversation was over. In Becky's mind, it had ended nearly two months ago, when she'd told me not to enter.

She appeared again later, in the doorway, as I was tipping saddle pads into the washing machine. Her nose was still wrinkled, as if I smelled. "I put a sweat on his leg," she'd said. "Wrapped the others. And gave him a liniment brace."

"Thanks." I attempted to smile, to pretend we were still friends, the way it had been when she had first come to work for me. "I'm sure he really enjoyed that."

Becky nodded stiffly. She leaned against the doorframe for a moment, an unusual moment of relaxation for her. Her ponytail was coming down and her straw-colored hair was falling around her tan face. We looked a lot alike. At shows, we'd been mistaken for each other. For a while, we'd thought that was cute. "I love that horse," she blurted. "He's so grateful for everything you do for him. When I was running the sponge over his withers, he was reaching around to try and groom me back."

"He loves having his withers rubbed, doesn't he?" I smiled, trying to keep the moment going. "He had a hard life before I got him. I think he really is grateful for every little thing now."

"That's why you shouldn't take advantage of him." Becky's voice turned frosty again. "He gives and he gives and he gives for you. He'll never tell you no. He'll kill himself for you."

I took an involuntary step back, as if she'd come at me with her fists. "I'm not taking advantage—"

"You keep pushing him. He's not going to be a five-star horse, Jules! When are you going to stop? You know what Sandra said, you two aren't ready for Intermediate level. She only rode at the Pan Am Games for Canada, I would *think* she's worth listening to."

Becky was never going to stop flinging Sandra Holborn in my face. As if she was the only riding coach on the planet. The only person in Ocala who had competed at the five-star level. Hardly. This was the epicenter of eventing in America. I'd just chosen poorly when I'd gone to get my ACE endorsement from a five-star rider, as required.

"I'm not asking Dynamo to be a five-star horse," I told Becky. That was mostly true. I was looking for another horse to leapfrog me to the uppermost level of the sport. That was supposed to be my ACE horse. "And what happened at Longacres was caused by the *wind*. Not by Sandra freaking Holborn saying that we weren't good enough."

"But eventing at Intermediate level is bad enough, and I *know* you're thinking Advanced is right around the corner. When you *know* how hard he has to work to get over those fences. And when you pull stunts like this today, taking him to this audition ride where you weren't even supposed to be, in this crazy heat, and look, what a surprise, he comes back injured—"

"He has a little heat above his ankle, Becky, he's not *broken*—"

"Not today." Becky shoved away from the doorframe, obviously finished with me. "I have to go."

"They haven't eaten supper yet," I protested. She wasn't going to help me feed?

"I have a paper to write." She turned away, and a few moments later, I heard her car rattle and whine to life.

I'd stood there for a few minutes, alone in the tack room. *Again.* Her accusatory voice seemed to roll around the room, bouncing off the saddle racks and the storage bins stacked against the water-stained walls. *Where you weren't even supposed to be.* Was she ever going to let that go? It wasn't even a relevant argument tonight. Dynamo's tumble was due to the weather. The eventing gods, stirring things up. Nothing to do with my experience in the saddle, or his training.

Just plain old bad luck, the kind I always had.

"And I'd never take advantage of him, *Becky*," I muttered, closing the lid of the washing machine with a bang. If Dynamo didn't want to do something, he'd tell me. We had a closeness, after our years together, that Becky couldn't even begin to imagine. And if

Dynamo had to work a little harder to get over the biggest fences, I had no doubt that for a little while, anyway, we could pull it off. Not forever. But just long enough to get the horses that I needed, the owners that I needed, to make our masquerade become the truth. He *could* be a five-star horse if I helped him along the way, and stopped when he said it was time.

For Becky to imply that I would hurt Dynamo, or purposely push him too hard? I shook my head. She was insane. Rude, and insane.

I blinked up at the sky, imagining a day in which we'd gotten around those jumps with our usual fluidity and everyone stood and cheered. Damon, Ronnie, Kathy, Pete Morrison, Becky—in this fantasy, she'd actually gone along to support me—they all agreed I was the next big thing. The most amazing rider to burst onto the eventing scene in decades. They couldn't give me money and horses fast enough.

A wet nose broke into my daydream. "Hello, Marcus," I cooed, wrapping my arm around a chubby, tricolor beagle. "Did you sense I'd stopped working for five seconds, little munchkin?"

Marcus leaned into me. His short coat was cold on one side, from sleeping on the concrete barn aisle for the past two hours. My dog's idea of supporting me was to nap nearby. He loved it when I took a break, which wasn't very often. It freed up my hands to rub his ears. I stroked his silky hound-dog ears with both hands, while he licked his nose with pleasure.

We sat and baked together. The parking lot shimmered in the heat. Beyond, the line of scruffy turkey oaks that blocked the highway from the farm swayed gently in a humid sea breeze, their tough little leaves rattling, a sound that to my ears had always promised rain. I heard a whinny from the paddocks behind the barn, and a high-pitched squeal in reply. One of the mares must be in season, and Passion, the brat pony I'd taken in as a sales horse, was *all* about that.

The whinnies reminded me that horses had to be ridden, that a barn needed cleaning, that there was still work to be done; I wouldn't be able to sit here all day, much to Marcus's sorrow. But before I got up and got to it, I decided, I'd run through a few affirmations to make the universe understand that I was a force to be reckoned with.

"I want to fill this parking lot up," I said aloud, my voice spooking the lizard, who had finally settled nearby, sunning on the railroad tie. He went scurrying into the nondescript bushes that grew scraggly and untended against the barn's front walls. "I want flowers here. I want twenty horses in the barn. I want a working student who gives a shit and shows up every day and doesn't leave until the work's done. I want sponsors' names on my saddle pads and owners with nice horses who pay their bills on time."

Okay, that last part of the affirmation might just be a pipe dream. "I'll accept just owners with nice horses," I assured the universe.

Thunder rumbled somewhere in the west. Were the eventing gods answering me?

If they were, they were probably telling me that girls who sat around making affirmations instead of getting their horses ridden weren't girls who made it to the top.

"I'll take that as a sign to get to work," I assured them hastily, and I hopped up, giving Marcus a farewell rub around the ears.

Marcus looked at me with his huge hound-dog eyes, letting me know he was disappointed with my work ethic, and then went toddling off in search of shade. I watched him settle against a stall door, and let my gaze rove down the messy aisle. No, you know what? I wasn't going to finish the barn right now. I was going to *ride,* right now, while I could. I'd do the damn stalls later, while it was storming. I'd work right around the horses if I had to.

Because now, while no one was showing up, while no one cared, what difference did it make if the barn was spotlessly clean? I had to get attention, and mucking stalls wasn't going to get me any attention. Showing horses, and winning, was going to get me attention. And clients. And sponsors.

Step one: ride.

Step two: win.

Step three: clients.

Step four: fame.

Whatever it took.

I rubbed my elbow one more time and then headed for the house to change into boots and breeches.

4

ELEVEN O'CLOCK AT night was an ungodly time for a horsewoman to be awake.

The green numbers glowed at me from the kitchen, shimmering and ghostlike on the microwave display. I narrowed my eyes at them. 11:02. Absolutely brutal.

I hadn't been up this late in months. It was enough to make a girl cry, thinking about how little sleep I was going to get. And how exhausting tomorrow was going to be. A Monday, which meant Becky was in classes all day, which meant I had all the barn chores and all the riding to get through, yet again. She'd been around all weekend and even though she worked quietly, disapproving of me with her every move, it was a blessing to hand off all the dirty work and simply ride my horses, one after another.

But even with a full day ahead of me tomorrow, I couldn't go to bed now. I was waiting for my phone to ring. A new horse was on the way, bouncing across the dark Florida roads in the back of a shipper's van, and even if I hadn't had to sit up waiting to settle him into the barn for the night, I'd be too excited to sleep.

That day after the audition, I had gotten up from an unhappy place, sitting there on that railroad tie looking at my empty parking lot, with a dirty barn and twelve dirty horses behind me. I had announced to the universe that I was going to ride horses, show horses, and get a whole roster full of clients. And the universe responded. The phone rang that evening, while I was icing my sore elbow, with an opportunity.

Now, a week later, my elbow didn't hurt anymore and the opportunity was on a horse trailer, heading my way. He was running late, sure, but that wasn't really for me to question. I just had to wait it out. I'd waited this long.

I watched the time tick closer to Monday morning.

The phone call had felt like a prize for getting through that long day. When I saw the number on my phone screen, I nearly dropped it in shock. I'd given up on this particular horse. His owner and I had gone back and forth so many times. But maybe the eventing gods weren't done with me yet, because she called up with her credit card number ready and the shipping company information confirming a delivery around 6 P.M. the following Sunday. I'd nearly collapsed with happiness. This was a *very* good way to make up for the ACE debacle.

Maybe I was out of the running for an upper-level horse with all expenses paid, but this horse had all the hallmarks of a future competitor.

I went inside for the night so optimistic that I thought I might experiment with sleeping in the next day, but it turned out that wasn't ever an option, even though Becky would arrive around seven o'clock to start morning feeding.

"Come on, man," I muttered. The clock read 11:06. The minutes were dragging past, but they'd be galloping by like racehorses once I crawled into bed. Like my horses would be in less than seven hours.

I had twelve horses just outside my window, and one of them thought he was an honorary rooster. It was the pony, of course. Mornings for Passion meant galloping up and down the fence line of his paddock, neighing continuously, as if the end of the world had come and he didn't want anyone to sleep through it. Enthusiasm like that was contagious, and by six thirty my poor little double-wide would be shaking with the rumbling of hooves outside.

The horses knew who was in charge of this little asylum, and it wasn't me.

Outside the living room windows, lightning flickered in the eastern sky. The storms had arrived right around feeding time tonight, and stuck around for hours. The horses were inside; I'd boosted their hay ration to make up for the enforced stall time and they were going to trash their stalls, but I thought maybe it would be nicer for the new horse if he didn't have to spend his first night in an empty barn, anyway.

If he ever got here.

Part of me wasn't surprised the horse was so late. I tried to squash that part of my brain down, but there was definitely a small, defiant voice trying to be heard over all my optimism, and it was repeating, over and over, that this horse was going to be trouble.

Not the horse, to be fair. The horse himself sounded perfectly acceptable, an off-track Thoroughbred who had been loafing in a paddock for six months, going on little hacks and trail rides, jumping crossrails, learning not to lean on the bit or run away, that sort of thing. No bad habits, no tricks, no vices. Just your average ex-racehorse in many ways, but also a particularly good-looking horse with a lot of raw talent that seemed to reach out through the computer screen. I'd first seen him two months ago, right around when I was getting my ACE application together, and I'd momentarily forgotten how much I wanted that ACE-sponsored horse, how much better for my career that would be than *another* green ex-racehorse to train and bring up through the levels. I tried to remind myself that if I wanted a horse who only knew how to run around a racetrack, there were plenty of them on offer for under a thousand bucks right here in Ocala.

But they wouldn't look like *this* horse.

You want me, the gray horse cooed through still photos, and I couldn't help but agree. I could barely take my eyes off him.

I *really* wanted this horse.

It was his owner who concerned me: she seemed like she might be a bit of a crazy woman. She cold-emailed me based off a web search, asking if I knew of any eventing trainers in Florida who could take on her off-track Thoroughbred. Confused—did she think I was some kind of trainer matchmaker?—I had emailed her back assuring her that I was an entirely capable eventing trainer who would love her retired racehorse in my barn. She replied asking about two trainers with Olympic credentials, and Peter Morrison. I stared at the screen for a moment, then hammered out another reply, as diplomatically as possible, explaining why I was a great choice for her horse.

For the next two months, I answered her persistent emails as she teetered back and forth between going with an established star and going with me. Becky thought she sounded like a difficult client, but by this point, Becky and I were on the outs, so I ignored her. But when Lacey Wright, my only student besides Becky, began asking me for weekly updates on my "crazy lady," I knew there was a real potential the horse's owner would turn out to be more trouble than her horse was worth.

Lacey couched everything in good-natured insults, as usual: "Does your crazy lady still think that training horses requires a gold medal and a shit-eating grin? Because you don't have either, so I don't know if this is going to work out."

I really liked Lacey, which was why I gave her riding lessons. I hated teaching, but she was worth it.

"I'll have both," I told her, "if I just bite the bullet and accept the crazy ladies into my program."

"Is being rich worth the drama?" she wanted to know.

I shook my head. "No, but avoiding bankruptcy is."

As the weeks went by, my crazy lady's questions veered more off the rails. She grew concerned that summer would be too hot a season to start training her little pasture puff, who currently lived in Michigan. Maybe, she suggested, in a long and rambling email that touched upon hurricane season, midwestern blizzards, and the sugar content of corn, it would be better to leave off and start talking again in September.

Well, I don't know, I wrote back, thinking of my bank balance. *You don't want to leave this too late. The eventing season really starts in Florida in September. He won't be ready for the winter season if he doesn't start work this summer.*

I wasn't about to let this fish off the hook!

Finally, I landed on an argument that stuck. What if he came here just to get used to the climate, and I could babysit him until some Olympic medalist was selected to continue his training?

And she went with it. Finally! She made a decision, she made the transportation arrangements, and I did a happy dance in the barn aisle even though I was exhausted beyond belief.

I looked at the clock: 11:12.

He'll be here soon, I told myself. *You can settle him in and go to bed.*

But my brain wanted to work out the details, again and again. He was coming just to acclimate, sure, *but!* Once I had the horse in my barn, I could really ramp up the case to leave him with me, despite my lack of Olympic medals (and shit-eating grin, to Lacey's point). And while my mental state would not be improved by having a crazy person for a client, I had made certain promises to myself, and I was planning on keeping them. Not to mention that in my current impoverished state, I couldn't really turn down any business. The results of the ACE grant were due to come out on Friday. The next feed delivery was due on Thursday. I wasn't counting on a positive bank balance for the weekend. Not that the check from ACE would have arrived before Friday at five, anyway, but I didn't expect to win it—even if a tiny part of me was hopeful we'd done *something* to show what a tough, valiant, promising horsewoman I was.

A very sleepy beagle came out of my bedroom, feet dragging, and looked at me hopefully with big brown eyes. "I know it's past bedtime, buddy, and yeah, I'm guessing Pete Morrison's dog probably gets to go to bed on time," I told Marcus. "My mother gets to go to bed on time. Becky always goes to bed on time. Even Laurie can. But we sit up waiting for the horses of crazy people, so that we can pay the next feed bill."

Marcus sighed and clambered up onto the couch next to me. He was a very loyal beagle, but sleeping on the couch must have seemed ridiculous to him when there was a perfectly good queen-size bed just sitting empty in the bedroom. He curled up next to me and put his warm head on my thigh. His dark eyebrows lifted as he looked up at me. *Come on, Mom.*

"If I get into that bed, I'll never get up," I said apologetically.

Marcus closed his eyes, done with me and my inexplicable behavior. I stroked his ears, reflecting that he smelled vaguely of manure. That was fine; I probably did, too.

My phone buzzed. Marcus opened his eyes again, aggrieved. It wasn't easy being my beagle sometimes.

"Finally," I muttered, and picked the phone up. There was a hissing of static and some mumbled noises that sounded as if they might be derived from the English language, from which I deduced that the van was at the front gate. I pressed the 9 button, which would open the automatic gate, and pushed myself off the couch with both fists. Marcus slithered down, hoping that we were headed for bed at last. Well, he was about to be disappointed again, poor little guy.

I was forever disappointing my dog. It was worse than disappointing my mother. Marcus, at least, always seemed to hold out hope that I'd surprise him and do something right.

I poked my feet into the pair of blue flip-flops by the front door, then considered that I didn't know anything about this horse and kicked them off, opting for the neighboring pair of Wellingtons instead. Closed toes were always safer. Wellington boots and denim cut-offs, Florida horse farm chic. I was sure the van driver had seen much worse. I went banging out the front door, leaving Marcus behind so he didn't end up under the truck tires, just as the tractor trailer appeared in the driveway, headlights illuminating the steaming surface of the parking lot.

The driver hopped out of the cab, pulled down a ramp, and unloaded the horse in front of the barn. He handed me the lead shank without ceremony, the horse's head swinging from side to side as he tried to figure out where he had landed after the long ride.

I handed the lead right back. "I need to check him over first."

The driver scowled and shrugged, simultaneously.

Protocol's a bitch, I thought without sympathy, and stepped back to look over the new guy. Only an idiot would accept a horse without making sure he hadn't been damaged in transit.

What I saw was enough to wake me up thoroughly, and forgive the van driver the late delivery. This was a good horse.

A very good horse.

A show-stopper.

Tall and iron-gray, with the white rings of dapples spread like snowflakes across his body, the Thoroughbred was the image of the classic sport horse. He had a short back, a gorgeous sloping shoulder, and straight legs with plenty of bone. A gracefully arching neck. An elegant head, lightening from gray to white, with a ramrod-straight profile and intelligent, bold eyes. Even in the dim light from the streetlight over the parking lot, his quality and athleticism were obvious. I had known from pictures and videos that I'd be getting a good-looking horse. But he was one thousand times more impressive in the flesh.

If I could get this horse going, if his mind was as good as his body, I'd have something really quality to compete. I could quit lamenting the likely loss of the ACE horse. Give it to Pete Morrison, fine. Just give me this horse.

And then I could *beat* Pete, and everyone else, in a few years.

Two problems, of course, which came crowding into my brain—he wasn't *definitely* mine to train, and I hadn't yet seen what was under the shipping wraps. I had to be certain that he was in perfect health after such a long journey. My eyes wandered down his legs as I walked in a slow circle, studying his every angle. "The bandages have to come off," I finally announced. "Hang on."

The driver sighed, as if this was completely unusual. I wondered if he was new to equine transportation.

The horse's fat shipping bandages were sagging in tired loops below his knees, which meant that no one had bothered to reset them during the journey. I bit my lip and kneeled down, hoping no damage had been done by the oversight, picked the shavings from the Velcro tab, and set to work unwrapping. Even the pillow bandages beneath the standing wraps were disgusting, stained through with manure and urine, but a horse person gets used to these things. I was more concerned with what was underneath. Sagging bandages, pulling unevenly at delicate tendons and ligaments, can be disastrous for a horse. The lacy structure of the lower leg is as perfect and fragile as a snowflake.

But running my hands down his warm, sweaty lower legs, steaming from the heavy wraps and the Florida night and the heat of the road, I felt only hard tendons and joints beneath tightly stretched skin. No puffiness, no swelling, no bumps or lumps. He was fine. I sighed with relief as I slowly straightened up. That was one hurdle cleared.

I took one more look over the rest of the horse, and then signed the bill of lading that the long-suffering driver silently held out on a clipboard. The horse ducked his head and pawed at the gravel driveway. In the barn, Passion whinnied, a high-pitched shriek, and the new horse turned to gaze up at the barn with wide eyes, as if he hadn't realized there were other horses nearby. He neighed in return, setting off the rest of the crew. A choir of whinnies echoed through the night, and I was grateful that I didn't have any nearby neighbors. From inside the van, there was a thumping of hooves and a few answering neighs to join the chorus.

"How many more do you have to deliver?" I asked through the cacophony, as the driver rubbed a big hand across his bleary eyes.

"Three more. To three different farms." He gave me a sideways grin, as if forgiving me for being a crazy horse lady after all, and then stuffed the lead shank back into my hand. I watched as he stomped off, slammed the trailer doors shut, clambered into his truck, and pulled out. Then I turned to the horse, giving him a gentle clap on the neck. His name, I remembered, was Mickey. Well, I thought, looking again at his magnificent build, he was no mouse, that was for sure.

"Mickey," I said experimentally, and then sang out *"Mick-eeeeeey,"* but the big gray horse just stared at the barn, more interested in the prospect of meeting new horses than new people.

"Mickey Mickey Mickey!" I tried one more time, but he wasn't paying me any mind. I gave up and led him into the barn, pausing in the doorway to flip on the lights. Twelve heads looked over their stall doors in astonishment, twelve pairs of eyes blinking in the sudden brightness.

"Here he is," I told them. "Lucky number thirteen."

Mickey stared at the other horses for a long moment, looking to his right and left to take it all in. I saw his sides tremble a little, and took a small step away from him in case things got physical, but he seemed to internalize his stress. No spooks, no bolts, no bad reactions at all. Just a flutter of the nostrils. Brave.

Passion shrieked his earsplitting neigh again, and then kicked his stall door for emphasis. Mickey watched him impassively for a moment, and then shook his head, snorted, and put out a foreleg to paw the aisle.

"That's a nasty habit," I chided, and gave him a little smack on the muscle of his forearm. Mickey swiveled his left ear to me, then stopped pawing and stood still. I waited, and the horses in the barn waited, and Mickey waited, until I realized that all of us were waiting for someone else to do something, so I just walked Mickey into his stall, took off the lead shank, and came out again, shutting the lower half of the Dutch door behind me.

I had plenty of empty stalls, but the one I had prepared for Mickey was right between Passion and Monty. It seemed like a safe space. Passion might have been a little demon, but he wasn't tall enough to bother Mickey over the stall wall, and Monty was just a nice young man in every respect. I thought he'd be a good babysitter for a nervous ex-racehorse.

But even the quelling influence of a friendly companion seemed unnecessary now. Mickey was entirely unmoved by his new sur-roundings. The big gray horse did a tour of his stall, rolled in the fresh shavings until he was covered from ear to tail in golden curls, and then set to work demolishing the pile of hay I'd left in the back corner.

I watched him for a moment with satisfaction. A horse this level-headed could be a real pleasure to train. If he could move well, and if he could jump well, I might be sitting on a really top-notch prospect. "And that's why you never turn down a client, no matter how insane they seem," I told myself, and nodded my head for emphasis. The horse flicked an ear in my direction and went on eating his hay. He was probably used to crazy people who talked to themselves.

My phone rang as I was walking back to the house. I looked at the screen: EILEEN—MICKEY'S MOM. Of course. Time to pay the crazy-lady tax. I put the phone to my ear.

"This is Jules," I announced, as if I didn't know who was calling.

"*Jules,*" Eileen breathed into her phone, her voice squeaking with anxiety. "Has Mickey arrived? I couldn't wait any longer to call!"

I was already at my front door, slipping off my muddy boots. A tree frog jumped from the gutter to the porch, nearly scaring the life out of me, but I managed to keep my voice nonchalant. Frogs were a fact of life, like owners. "Just got in. I'm watching him in his stall," I lied.

"What's he doing?"

"Eating hay." I quietly swung the storm door open and slipped into the house. It was marvelously cold inside. I probably would not be in the terrible financial shape I was if I would just turn down my air-conditioning a notch. Marcus gave me a rapturous greeting, scrabbling up my legs. *"Down!"* I whispered, hand over the speaker. He slunk back into the bedroom, fed up.

"Really? *Really?* He's not upset or anything?"

"Not at all. Such a good traveler. You have done a really good job with him, Eileen. He's in beautiful condition and seems absolutely bombproof. He should be easy to get started when he goes into work."

I'd barely handled the horse. But a little flattery wouldn't hurt. And he did seem bombproof. He'd walked off that van and into his stall with scarcely more than a quickening of pulse.

"Oh Jules, I'm so *relieved*!"

"I'm sure. Shipping a horse is scary. But no worries." I threw myself down on the couch. "So I'm going to head to bed, but I'll be getting up to check on him regularly. Make sure he's drinking water and his manure is normal and everything."

This, at least, was the truth. It wasn't too far-fetched to imagine that if I ignored him all night, he could be dead by morning. Colic after a long trip was common enough, and accidentally killing horses really wasn't part of my long-term client-relationship plan. I'd have to go and check on him, despite the fact that it would further shatter my sleep schedule tonight. I added "stall security cameras" to my long mental wish list of future farm items. Imagine if I could just roll over in bed and squint at a monitor to make sure everyone was okay, instead of trudging out to the barn once an hour. Oh! The sleeps I would sleep!

I managed to get her off the line with that promise, and a second promise to call her in the morning with a wellness update, and finally, well past midnight, I crept into bed.

And I did get up every hour—almost. I forced myself to set my alarm. I was up at one thirty, and again at two thirty, disappointing poor sleepy Marcus, who trailed dutifully behind me with a martyred look in his half-closed eyes. Every time, I would flip on the overhead lights, just to see the same, slightly confused horses in various states of nighttime horse activity: nosing through their shavings for the last wisps of their night hay, passed out snoring in the center of their stall, snoozing upright with their ears at half-mast, heads hung over the stall doors. Everyone perked up at my appearance—*Early breakfast? Extra hay?*—and grumbled and kicked their doors when I left. Their body language was pretty easy to interpret. *Bitch.*

The stalls would be extra messy in the morning, I just knew it. Payback, equine style.

Mickey seemed interested in me every time, though. He came over to say hello, nuzzled my open hands, blew his nostrils at Marcus, and generally impressed me with his good nature.

After each visit, I climbed back into bed, closed my eyes, and saw him there. Mickey trotting, Mickey jumping fences, Mickey at the ferocious, famous Head of the Lake obstacle at some future Kentucky Three-Day Event, leaping down into the water, our eyes already locked on the next fence. He was a dream, that horse: every girl dreams of the perfect dapple-gray steed. I fell asleep with my head full of him.

Even so, when the alarm rang at three thirty, I wasn't exactly leaping out of bed. An hour ago, Mickey had eaten his hay, drank a bucket of water, and dropped a few piles of manure. There was even a wet spot in his stall, which meant he'd just had a nice pee. His system was working perfectly.

I looked again at the red numbers on the bedroom clock. I was so goddamn tired. The horse was fine. He wasn't going to colic, or he'd have done so by now. He was a good boy, a model citizen, an excellent traveler who was not at all fazed by his new surroundings.

Ah, screw it. I slapped off the alarm, reset it for a slightly cheating six fifteen, and sank back into my pillow, a relieved little beagle curled up against my back.

5

I WOKE UP less-than-fresh after the last three hours of sleep. But almost immediately, I was hopping out of bed, excited to get out and see the new face in the barn by the light of day. "My big horse, my big horse," I sang, pulling on a pair of old barn shorts, stained with hoof oil and molasses and heaven only knew what else. The horses heard my footsteps on the hollow floors of the double-wide and started shouting for their breakfasts. Marcus padded after me into the kitchen, wagging his tail, ready to go out and get busy doing beagle things. I gave him some kibble and sipped at what was left of yesterday's coffee. It was a grand perfect *wonderful* morning. A new day, a new horse, a new chance to win this game on my own terms.

The storm door slammed behind me and we were out in the humid morning, dewy grass sparkling in the sunrise. The eastern sky was gold and pink; the western sky was piled up with distant clouds, thunderstorms over the Gulf of Mexico. They were beautiful now; towering heaps of white gilded by the innocent dawn. They'd be trouble later. But that was for future Jules. For now, I turned into the center aisle of the barn, ready to greet my twelve—no, make that *thirteen*—eager children.

"*Good morning!*" I sang out, and they whinnied in reply, a glorious happy sound that lifted my spirits as high as those thunderclouds. No matter how tired I was, feeding horses their breakfast always made me feel loved and wanted and needed. I counted their adorable noses, each in their place. Everyone where they should be, everyone where I'd left them the night before, no broken stall doors or piles of manure in the aisle to indicate a runaway or an escape artist. Everyone had been good little boys and girls after I'd stopped doing my hourly night-checks. I smiled, full of good will toward men, and horses, and beagles. I strode into the barn with the confidence of a schoolmistress who knows that she is loved and that all of her pupils will ace their exams.

And then I saw the puddle. And I stopped.

The horses stared at me, ears pricked, licking their noses and working their jaws in anticipation. A minute passed, and another, and their eager expressions darkened into confusion. It was breakfast time, and I wasn't making any move to feed them. Dynamo nickered encouragingly. *You can do it!*

Darling Dynamo. I'd do it the moment I could move my feet again. But first I had to get past that ominous, dark-colored pool just outside a stall door. Whose stall door? Who was in the box next to Monty? Suddenly, I couldn't remember the order. Then Monty began to fling his head up and down, his classic *pay me attention* move, and the horse in the next stall was revealed.

"Mickey," I squeaked. And then, louder, "Oh my sweet Jesus, what did you do?"

All of the horses looked at me with the same perplexed expression, Mickey included. He was probably wondering what sort of place he had come to, where there wasn't any breakfast. He nickered, and the other horses took up the chant. The barn fairly rumbled with the songs of hungry horses, and still, I stood there, my fingers tingling and bloodless, my feet rooted to the concrete floor. This was bad. This was *bad*.

Mickey's eager face was red with blood.

I knew I had to get myself together. I had seen nasty wounds before. But this one was so visually appalling, I thought I must be entering some sort of shock. The cap of red spilling down over the new horse's bright-white face, the gluey blood congealing on the ends of his eyelashes, making him blink owlishly, the pool darkening on the concrete in front of his stall door. And the horse's expression, the greatest contrast of all—he wasn't concerned with anything but the lack of grain in his bucket.

Indeed, I was the only one in the barn who had a problem right now with Mickey's face. Marcus was positively drooling at the sight of all that blood. My heart was thudding in my ears, my mouth was dry, my fingers were trembling—this was *bad,* Jules, *bad,* I kept hearing. Very very *bad.* It was going to be impossible to hang on to this client now. I was going to lose this gorgeous horse, all for an extra hour's sleep. If I'd just gotten up at three thirty and done night-check, if I'd just gotten up at four thirty . . .

It still might have happened. But it might not have.

"And Becky won't be here today," I remembered aloud, the horses' ears flicking to the sound of my voice. Mickey whickered gently, encouragingly. He didn't know me, but he obviously had confidence in me, that I could figure out how to get him his breakfast. He'd seen other humans do it before. It couldn't be that hard. "It wouldn't be," I told him, "if I wasn't in so completely over my head. Why'd you go and do this? You were going to save me, Mickey."

I closed my eyes. This wasn't happening.

Passion shrieked in protest, and the rest of the barn followed suit. *No napping on the job, lady!*

I shook myself out of my inertia, stepped carefully over the blood on the pavement, and reached up for Mickey's halter, tugging it gently to bring his head closer to me. He responded by shaking his head, hard, to clear the red goop from his eyelashes, splattering me all over with blood. Good thing I had nowhere to be today. If I went to the feed store like this, the clerk would call the police. I looked like the prime suspect in a hatchet murder.

Of course, my work uniform on mornings like this, when the barn chores were my problem, was not anything that a few quarts of horse blood could ruin. These clothes were already long past the point of destruction. I shrugged it off and put my hand on his forehead, atop the whorl of hair between his eyes, and willed him to be still so that I could get an idea of what was going on under all that mess on his poll. He picked up his head, resentful, interested only in his missing breakfast. Down the aisle, Dynamo kicked his stall door, and Monty followed suit. "Good God," I hissed, rubbing Mickey's forehead, sending a gentle shower of gray and white and red hairs onto my chest. "What did you do to yourself, horse?"

Mickey pulled away to look at his rowdy friends.

"Whoa, Mickey-Mickey," I whispered, gently touching his cheek, sliding my hand toward his ear. "Let me see." I worked my fingers through the thin hair, wondering what was missing. Something was off about his face.

Farther down the barn aisle, Daisy whinnied her pretty neigh, and the others joined in all over again.

I slipped my fingers behind Mickey's ears, gently probing the wound behind them, and sighed with relief when I encountered flesh immediately below the clotting blood. The whole thing seemed to be just a big abrasion—he was missing skin, for sure, but there weren't any gashes, and it wasn't anywhere near his skull or spine. Perhaps I could get through this. I closed my eyes and breathed thanks to all the deities in the universe, but mostly the eventing gods, who were capricious and easily angered.

I stepped back, my fingers red, and took one more look. I looked around at the red drops decorating the floor, the stall door, the fronts of the stalls, *me,* and thought slightly enviously of my working student's quiet, gore-free morning in an air-conditioned classroom, reading Jane Austen without a care in the world. She probably even had a latte on her desk.

Then I looked back at the horse, and I shook my head.

"I'll take care of you, sweetie," I told Mickey.

Mickey eyed me beseechingly, blinking red tears. *Breakfast?* I smiled at him. "In a minute, bud."

And that's when I realized what was missing.

His forelock.

There was no forelock falling between his ears. With all the blood, I hadn't missed it . . . at first.

My heart stopped beating for one long second.

Then I peered past his head and into the blood-strewn shavings of his stall. When it comes to equine CSI, I'm an expert. Spend enough time with horses and you'll learn to make short work of the crime scene. Their behaviors are all too obvious after a few years in the game. And Mickey's case was easily solved. I blew out a breath, cursing myself, my barn, and ponies everywhere.

The clues were everywhere, and they all pointed to a crime of

Passion. The pony, that is. A gap in the stall wall that hadn't been there last night—a streak of red on the top of the jagged hole left behind—and a wisp of white clinging just below that. The forelock.

So here was what happened: Mickey kicked his wall, probably because Passion was goading him through the boards. Then, later on, he stuck his head through the gap to see where that little devil on four hooves had gone. The horrible pony probably came after him with yellow teeth bared, and in his panicked exit, Mickey would have whipped his head right out of that narrow space, not very cleanly, leaving behind the skin on the top of his head.

And his forelock.

I leaned back again and looked over at Passion, who had his chin resting on the stall door. He was watching me with round brown eyes. Anyone who didn't know him would have thought he was cute. "You tried to bite him, didn't you?"

He gazed back at me guilelessly and let out a shrill whinny. "You are an awful nightmare creature," I told him. But he only pricked his ears and worked his jaw. *Hint, hint, I'm hungry*. That's the problem with ponies: they don't care. You can't chastise a pony. They have an extra empty stomach where their conscience ought to be.

I shook my head. I had to get a hold of myself. I was a professional. I could handle this.

First things first. The best place to start is at the beginning. Et cetera, et cetera. I gazed at the blinking, red-capped horse before me, and he whickered once more. It reminded me that as disfiguring and awful as the injury looked, it was actually only a scrape in an awkward spot, and there was no point in trying to clean it up when he was hungry. "You're right," I told him. "Breakfast, coming right up."

In the feed room, I set to work, slinging feed into buckets with mechanical precision, angling the big metal scoop so that I could accurately send grain from the storage bin into the buckets I had lined up in neat rows across the floor. Call it a horsewoman's party trick: I have always been very good at throwing grain.

Marcus watched me from the doorway, hound-dog eyes melting and sorrowful, hoping that I'd miss a throw so he could lick up the spillage. I tried to tell him beagles shouldn't eat horse feed, but he believed everything was food for beagles.

Slopping feed without thinking is truly a gift, especially if a person enjoyed berating oneself as much as I did, because I now had ample free space in my brain to consider what a fool I was to stick a horse next to Passion, or even to allow Passion to stay in my barn for another moment, or, really, to ever have accepted Passion into the barn in the first place. He wasn't valuable as a boarder, and ponies were a pain.

The truth was (I uncapped the bucket of electrolytes), I had simply been trying to fill the barn up, get another client on the books. I had a bad habit of doing that (I sprinkled neon-pink salt over the feed buckets), and the fact was, I was probably a terrible businessperson who would never make a dime at this game and end up losing everything. Cheerful thoughts like that were the fuel of my days (I took down the tub of vitamin E and selenium).

To put it in the bleakest and truest of terms: Passion was a black pit of a trainee. His owner paid the bills, but the profit was to be made on my commission when he sold. And he wasn't going to be sold anytime soon.

That was because Passion was an attractive pony but an unpleasant ride, with the wide-jowled face and swaggering attitude of a gelding left a stallion a few years too long. I'd made a staggering misjudgment in taking him as a trainee. The other trainers knew better. Everyone knew Leighann "Your Dream Farm Awaits" Anderson, Ocala's most successful real estate agent. Everyone knew her daughter's pony. Everyone knew he was an equine criminal.

Nobody else in this town wanted him.

I'd have to take him far afield to get rid of him, and in the meantime, he was still a monster to handle and a devil to ride.

"Stupid," I muttered aloud, taking down the bee pollen. I couldn't find room in my budget to buy Flintstones multivitamins for myself, but the competition horses got local bee pollen, exquisitely expensive, to guard against allergies.

Ugh, I'd been so excited to land Leighann Anderson as a client. Sell Passion the pony for enough, I'd thought happily, and maybe she'd send me another horse. A better one, one I could train and sell on my own terms. One thing about Ocala, the most unexpected people were always buying investment horses. The last time I took my truck to the dealership to have it serviced, one of the salesmen took out his wallet to show me photos of his Thoroughbred foal. A person couldn't seem to live in this equestrian wonderland without needing to dip their toe into the pool of equine investments—and more than a few had decided to dive in headfirst.

And it hadn't been the most ridiculous notion in the world, that I could fix a deviant like Passion. I capped the bee pollen and went for the kelp-derived micronutrient powder, green and smelly. Not everyone could ride ponies, but wealthy parents were willing to pay a premium for the good ones. So if I ever did figure out how to settle Passion down into a packer pony, and schlepped him to a horse show down in South Florida where no one knew him, I'd succeed yet at my little plan.

Good ponies were good money. The caveat, of course, was

having ponies around the farm. The first thing I would do as a big-name trainer, I thought, stacking the buckets and carrying them into the aisle, to the audible delight of the horses, was turn away all pony business.

I dumped feed into Mickey's bucket first, watching his lips decide if he wanted to eat the oral tranquilizers, breathing a sigh of thanks when he decided to go for it.

I gave Dynamo his feed next, glancing over the stall door at the now-tight foreleg that had been warm and swollen after the ACE audition. He was fine and ready for the next event. *Sunshine State Horse Park, here we come!* I was looking forward to the chance to debut Dynamo at Intermediate level, especially since the main competition had all gone north for the summer. By the time everyone got back in fall, I'd be ready to ride rings around them all. And if I got to train Mickey this summer, too . . .

One good horse was a start. Two good horses was a real chance.

I took the buckets to the wash rack to rinse them clean, thinking all the while that Pete Morrison probably had *three* working students, and was already riding his horses while the day was still cool. And then I wondered why I was thinking of him at all.

Just an enemy, I decided. Just one more mortal enemy to add to the list of people I was dying to beat. And my day would come. I just had to keep working. I could never stop working.

Dreams were exhausting that way.

It took a full hour of scrubbing with Betadine and Ivory soap to clean up Mickey. He was very cooperative, although the oral tranqs did not seem effective enough to keep his head low. He was a tall horse, I was a short woman—it did not always work out. So I went for the acepromazine, gentle and efficient for a little naptime. With a small cocktail administered, Mickey dropped his head and closed his eyes, hanging from the ropes of the crossties while I worked the red bubbles into his scalp.

Afterward, the soap and iodine bubbles sponged away with warm water, I eyed the nearly empty bottle of ace with apprehension; just one more drug to add to the grocery list for the next vet call. Jim Dear's ulcer medicine was nearly gone. The Regu-Mate for Margot's endless PMS was running low. The few pills left in the bottle of bute rattled ominously whenever someone had a low-grade fever or a swollen bug bite. I always seemed to run out of everything at once. My vet bill was going to be crippling this month.

Mickey turned his head slowly and regarded me through long white eyelashes.

His ears and a long stripe running between his eyes were a comical shade of pink, stains left over after the iodine and Ivory soap finished blending their suds together. The more lurid pink of the missing skin between his ears looked like a bright winter cap on his snowy coat, but it was more evident than ever that this was a completely superficial wound.

And the scarring, I hoped, would be minimal. He was so light-colored already that if the hair grew in white, it would not be noticed. If there was any sort of mark, he could be shown in a fly bonnet to cover it up—they were back in style. He would look lovely in navy blue, to match my barn colors.

As for the forelock . . . I sighed at the bald patch where a thick lock of mane should have half covered his drowsy eyes. That *had* to grow back. I considered clever braiding techniques that might draw his mane forward, to fill in a sparse forelock at horse shows . . . and of course, the fly bonnet would fall in a V between his eyes, obscuring the disfigurement.

But . . . I shook my head at myself. Time to be real. I wasn't going to be the one showing him. Eileen had been nice enough to say she would consider me as his trainer, but, seriously, who was I kidding? I couldn't even keep the horse under my barn roof for twelve hours without his inflicting serious cosmetic harm upon himself. An obsessive and overprotective owner like Eileen was not going to take this news well, nor forgive it easily.

Mickey sighed and licked his lips meditatively, working his jaw as a relaxed horse does. I put my hand on his neck, still damp from the scrubbing, and then leaned my forehead against his warmth.

"I need you," I told him, closing my eyes against the twisting knot in my stomach. "I need a horse like you so goddamn bad. All these stupid packers and adult-amateur horses that will never go past Training level were making me happy enough, and then you get here for ten seconds looking like a goddamn rock star and screw it all up for me."

Or I screwed it up for him. I didn't know. I felt a prickling in my eyes, but I squeezed my eyelids together and waited it out. I was too busy to cry.

It was getting hot already, and everyone needed turning out. Everyone except this guy; he would have to stay in and sleep off his hangover. He sighed again, then blinked, picking up his head just a little to look to his left and out to the empty paddocks.

"You're too cute for words," I told him, and he pricked his ears at my voice with as much energy as he could muster. "I can't keep you, though, so no hard feelings if I don't spend a lot of time on you," I told him, but I was really talking to myself. Resolving, then and there, to have as little to do with this gorgeous horse as I possibly could.

I'd turn him out, I'd clean his stall, I'd mind his wound, I'd pick his hooves—but other than that, until he was more than a layup on basic board, I wasn't going to spare him a second glance. I had a rule about falling in love with anyone, human or horse: don't do it, not allowed.

I was going to focus on what I *did* have: my little kingdom, my ten acres of hopes and dreams, and make that into the best, brightest version of itself that I could.

And if I got him in the end, so much the better.

6

BY THIS TIME it was past eight o'clock, and the tropical day was just warming up. I could see the baking waves radiating above the wet paddocks, warping a flock of white ibis as they made their way through the puddles, digging long red beaks into the earth beneath. Another brutal Florida summer was simmering us all, cooking us within our skins. The horses in their stalls were already dark with sweat, and my tank top was soaked through.

But I didn't really mind. It could be managed; days like the one at Longacres were rare. We had sunny, humid mornings and stormy, liquid afternoons, and when things hummed along according to schedule, you could manage well enough. I had grown up here in Florida, running around outside under the summer sun and the vicious lightning of the rainy season, and so the mugginess just felt normal to me.

Horses were another story. They were cold-weather creatures, children of Siberia. Even the Florida-bred specimens like Dynamo tended to overheat when the midsummer mercury soared into the nineties and the humidity was nearly enough to liquefy the air. To say nothing of the lightning risk. I hated seeing them outside, long-limbed, four-legged creatures standing on shoes of steel, when the thunderstorms that characterized Florida's six-month rainy season began.

Every year, the Ocala community swapped stories about lightning strikes—horses touching gates with their noses, horses standing under oak trees, horses grazing peacefully in an open field. Big farms with large herds had to take the chance every time it stormed. While it was hard to manage when everyone was turned out and a surprise storm blew in, I was determined to keep my horses inside during lightning, although it often meant risking my own life chasing after them in the paddocks . . . and heavy workloads in the morning if they stayed in all night, pacing endlessly in their stalls.

After last night's storm kept them inside, they were demanding freedom. I'd kept them waiting while I was playing doctor with Mickey, and now they were over it. Bangs, kicks, slams, whinnies, and neighs echoed through the old barn. Even mild-mannered Dynamo was rattling his buckets together as if he was doing a sound check before a bongo concert, and sweet, gentlemanly Monty was pawing at his door, rattling its rusty hinges dangerously.

"The natives are restless," I told Mickey, and he waggled an ear in response. Figuring he was too drunk to cause much trouble for himself, I left him alone with his thoughts and went into the tack room for a handful of lead shanks. "Let's get you nerds out of here," I told the barn, and got a chorus of whinnies in response. *About time, lady!*

Time was of the essence if I was going to make it through a Becky-free Monday morning, and I was already an hour behind.

When Becky had come to work for me, bright and eager and ready to show off her horsemanship skills, it had been the start of something beautiful. She moved into my guest room, she contributed to the Diet Coke fund, she watched reruns of *Friends* with me, although she did not think Ross and Rachel should have stayed together and this was a bigger problem for me than I could ever have admitted to her. And, significantly, she was around on mornings like this, when a horse was loose or a pipe had broken or there was a colic—someone to do the chores while I took care of the emergency.

I missed that version of Becky—the friend version—as much as I missed her help on the days she took classes. Now that Becky thought she knew so much about me, now that she believed I was a liar who was willing to do anything to get ahead in this business, I was on my own in more ways than one.

She'd have done the same thing, though. If she had a chance like the ACE grant and the only thing standing in her way was the approval of *one* trainer, she'd have done the same thing I did. Like I'd told her on the drive home, I'd just chosen the wrong coach for my evaluation lesson. There were dozens of other trainers in Ocala who would have happily signed off on my application. The fact that I'd only saved enough money for *one* lesson was unfortunate, but not insurmountable.

But she didn't see things the way I did, and a week after she decided I was a phony and fool, she announced she was moving out of my house and into an apartment forty minutes away near Gainesville, because she was going to back to school part time. She told me she'd keep working for me part time. She didn't ask me if that was okay. She didn't ask me if I was going to hire someone else to replace her. The condescension got on my nerves. Nothing grated like pity.

I could always tell when someone was looking down at me. I had a lot of practice in that department.

"I'll be here four days a week," she'd said coolly, after announcing summer-term classes were starting in a few weeks and she'd officially be in school Monday, Tuesday, and Thursday. "You can manage without me the other three."

"What if I can't?" I'd argued. "I hired you for six days. You can't just change your hours to suit yourself."

Becky shook her head. "Someone has to keep an eye on you, Jules," she said. "If I don't, you'll just keep hiring and losing working students until everyone in Ocala knows that you're full of shit. And I don't even want to know what might happen to Dynamo."

"I didn't hire a babysitter," I'd snarled.

She looked at me for a moment. "Is that the best argument you've got?"

And with that, Becky went to pack her bags and move out of the second bedroom in my house. I lost my roommate, my friend, and my helper. I was left with a stranger who thought I was full of shit, who wouldn't leave me for good because she didn't trust me to do the right things by my horses.

That was infuriating enough on its own.

But the thing that really pissed me off? Becky wasn't going back to school to do something useful, like equine science, or pre-vet med, or even business management. I could have used an assistant who was ready to take on the challenges of selling million-dollar horse syndicates around the world.

No, she was doing an English degree.

And that *really* stung. She felt that getting a completely useless piece of paper was preferable to working for me full time. What was she going to do with an English degree? "What about horses?" I challenged her. "What does English have to do with horses?"

Becky blinked at me. "If there's one thing I've learned working for you," she said, "it's that this is not the life for me."

So on top of everything else, Becky felt bad for me, which was awful in its own way. But despite saying that she didn't want to be a professional horsewoman anymore, she kept coming back. And I didn't quite believe it was all to keep me from making terrible decisions. No one really cared about me *that* much. I believed that deep down, she still needed to be around horses.

And just as deep down, late at night, I was afraid she was right about me.

Obviously, during the day, I knew she wasn't, and she was just one more person to prove wrong.

I pulled the other two mares out of their stalls, organized them to one side of Daisy, and used a tack trunk to jump onto the tall chestnut mare bareback. I nudged her into a slow jog as soon as we got out of the barn, and took the trio down the mulch lane that ran between the individual paddocks, all the way to the big turnout at the end of the row. The three mares were a trio of witches who couldn't be trusted with my nice quiet geldings. They spent their turnout time in a series of popularity tiffs and lunchroom quarrels, like the cast of *90210,* while the geldings just wanted to stuff their faces with grass. So the mares went out back where they could misbehave together without disrupting the rest of the farm.

True to form, they started bickering before I could even get the gate closed behind them, and I was spitting sand out of my teeth courtesy of a bucking bay mare named Louise as I trudged back to the barn, still trying to reschedule my day, still flipping through a mental calendar that was refusing to budge. How did I fit it all in and not work until nine o'clock tonight?

At last I had to concede that it *couldn't* be completed—some things would have to go undone. I was fighting an uphill battle trying to keep thirteen horses and train nine without full-time help, and I was starting to slide down the hill. Schedules and to-do lists were nice, but keeping horses was a series of disasters.

Back in the barn, the remaining horses nodded at me over their stall doors, their heads silhouetted against the brilliant white-gold of the sun gleaming through the far end of the center aisle barn. The barn sat at the foot of a driveway that spread into a wide gravel parking area, camouflaged from the lonely rural highway beyond by the cluster of scrubby turkey oaks, their hard leaves bleached by the sun. My farm sign leaned slightly, the post sinking into the soft sand, next to a crooked mailbox bristling with yesterday's bills, addressed to the unfashionable western Marion County backwater town where I had made my stand. There were millionaire addresses in horse country, but mine wasn't one of them.

Not yet.

I was going to put this forgotten little farm on the map. If not today, tomorrow. If not this week, next week. I was going to put my name, the name of the working student from Punta Gorda, Florida, who never got to go on trail rides because she was too busy mucking stalls, up in lights. I was trying out the every-ten-minute affirmation plan, reminding myself I'd get to the top of the heap if I just kept climbing. It was all I had to go on.

And after all, last week I'd affirmed myself right into Mickey. As long as his head healed up, I was still on track to score his training contract.

I popped open the sticky latch on the nearest stall door and slipped on the waiting horse's halter. "If not today, tomorrow," I told Jim Dear, a bright-eyed little Thoroughbred gelding, and he nodded in apparent agreement.

We walked out into the morning, and a soft breeze fluttered

across the paddocks, stroking my hot cheeks with a feathery touch. The horse at my side lifted his head and breathed in deeply, then whinnied to the mares. They neighed back, and suddenly I had one of those heart-stopping moments of pure joy, of horses and sunshine and the unbelievable realization that this was all mine, this was my life, it was *happening right now,* and things could only get better, as impossible as that seemed in this moment.

Oh, Becky. Missing this morning because you didn't believe in me. What a waste. She'd never be a horsewoman. Because if there was one thing I believed about the horse business, it was this: If you had a plan B, then you just didn't have enough passion to be the best.

S oft breezes and singing horses aside, the barn work wasn't going away. With everyone out in the paddocks and the barn empty, I took stock of what *must* be done. What could be ignored? The bloodstain on the concrete outside Mickey's stall was not one of those things. Marcus kept licking at it. I loved my dog, but he could be really gross sometimes.

It ended up taking the better part of a bottle of bleach and the destruction of a nice corn-straw broom, but after half an hour of hard labor, I managed to mellow the bloodstains down to a slightly darker patch of pavement, something that would just look like spilled hoof oil if anyone noticed it. I wiped my forehead with the front of my shirt, exposing my sweaty sports bra to exactly no one. Occasionally, it was convenient to be so utterly alone in the workplace.

Next, I leaned into Mickey's empty stall and eyed the damage. I was no handyman, and I didn't have the time to try and wrench the broken boards out of place, but what I could do was patch them up. It wouldn't be the prettiest fix, but it would be safe.

There were spare boards in the rusty garden shed behind my double-wide, and after screeching at the giant spiders who lived in there and usually kept me out, I managed to get a few boards into the wheelbarrow, push them back up to the barn, and nail them over the gaping hole in the stall wall. Then I stood back and admired my work. It looked a bit awkward, the extra wood nailed over the original stall wall, but who was looking? It was just me here anyway.

I dusted off my hands, walked into the barn aisle, and stopped short when I realized that I had left Mickey tied in the wash rack while I cleaned and did minor construction work for the better part of an hour and a half. I slowly turned, half expecting my sobered-up new tenant to be long gone, his broken halter hanging from one dangling crosstie.

Mickey, standing politely in the wash rack, craned his neck around the wall. He nickered, as if he'd never been so pleased to see a face in the entire world, and nodded his head, swinging the crossties like jump ropes.

"You're darling," I told him, dizzy with relief. "And wide awake, I see." He was practically on tippy-toes, his ears pricked in anticipation. I put a hand on his dark muzzle and felt his nostrils quiver against my palm, breathing me in. He didn't really know me, but he seemed happy to make my acquaintance again.

That was nice, considering the bulk of our time together had consisted of me giving him an injection and then scrubbing his head wound with iodine. A very forgiving horse, in addition to being good-natured and gorgeous.

"You're a problem," I sighed, running my other hand under his dark mane. "A big beautiful heartbreaker."

Mickey very delicately took his left foreleg, the one farthest from me, and reached out. He let it hang there in midair, leg half-extended, and regarded me with melting brown eyes. I had to laugh. "*Someone* taught you pawing was bad!"

He put his hoof down again at the word "bad."

A heartbreaker, seriously. I had to get my head on straight. This wasn't my horse—yet. I tapped him on his nose. "You want out? Fine. You can take your happy butt outside and nose around the hay out there."

Mickey nickered again in response, a throaty, deep murmur of interest, and I had to smile. I had a thing for horses that talked back.

In the tack room, I found a mesh fly mask that covered the head and ears and wriggled it over his nose like I was pulling on a pair of pantyhose. I poked both ears into their individual nets and let the elastic edging snap into place well behind the raw flesh of his poll, which I had adorned with neon-pink fly-repellent ointment. Then I smeared his pink nose with sunblock. The sun in Michigan would never have prepared his skin for the UVs outside my barn.

"You look ridiculous," I told him approvingly, and led him out to the front paddock, right outside of the barn, that I had kept empty for him. Right across from Dynamo's paddock. I considered the little field a place of honor. Closest to the barn, closest to my ministrations, always on my mind.

The big gray horse lurched away from me as soon as I unclasped the lead shank, breaking into an airy, elegant trot as he launched an investigation of his new surroundings.

There wasn't much for him to see.

There are incredible vistas in Florida's horse country: gorgeous rolling hills crowned with ancient live oaks that have been cutting out their gnarled corners of green grassland for hundreds of years, their spreading branches draped with beards of gray Spanish moss. There are miles of black-board fences cutting through emerald fields dotted with shimmering horses, broodmares grazing as their foals dance around them, all in a haze of heat rising up around them to a sky of incomparable blue. That was the Florida dream. It was real, if you could afford it.

I lived along with the rest of the other half, with the latecomers and the less-than-wealthy, who wanted a piece of the horse-country pie but who couldn't afford the seven-figure prices. (Or eight, or nine.) The outlying country surrounding Ocala's heart was more typically Floridian, from the sandy pine forests to the palmetto scrubland. The far western side of town held a dry slot of scrubby land that couldn't support pasture without a lot of help. The hopeful horsemen who bought out here often spent three times what they had expected to in hay and fertilizer, fighting against a microclimate that the real estate agents never mentioned. The 99 percenters of the horse world, fighting uphill to hold on to their hardscrabble hopes and dreams.

Green Winter Farm was neither too dry nor too wet in a good season, but neither was it the verdant wonderland to my east. We still got our share of storms and flooding—after last night's three-hour deluge, the sandy depressions around the water troughs and paddock gates were ankle-deep with black water. And there was always enough standing water *somewhere* to support a lively mosquito population, so, we had that going for us, I guessed.

Maybe I got the rain and the bugs, but I didn't have the vistas from the "Visit Marion County" postcards. All ten acres of my farm had been cut out of one vast expanse of pasture, and except for the nice live oak in the little hollow between the barn and the house, and the sparse stand of blackjack and turkey oaks across the parking lot, guarding some unused space against the front property line, there were hardly any trees at all, just one long gentle slope of grassland, slipping downward from the south to north, a contradiction of my mental map of the world. A little prairie of my own, walled to the north by a stand of plantation pine trees that stretched, in my imagination, infinitely toward the wastes of the empty northern peninsula, to the south by the cracked asphalt of a two-lane county highway, wandering indiscriminately westward toward the swamplands that would eventually block hopeful tourists from the Gulf of Mexico's uncertain shorelines. To the east and west, my only neighbors were cattle and a few cow horses, wandering overgrown fields like living memories of the ranchland Florida of yesteryear.

Mickey wasn't looking for views, of course. He was looking for trouble. But the only interesting things in the paddocks were the little three-sided run-in sheds set against each back fence. He snuffled greedily at the scents of horses who sheltered here in the past before squealing, spinning, and darting across his little quarter acre of space at a full gallop, his tail flagged and his head high beneath his clownish net cap.

I admired his movement for a few minutes, waiting to be certain that he would turn at the fences and not, in fact, run right through them (you'd be surprised), and then went back into the barn once I was satisfied with his respect for boundaries. I thought I might be able to steal thirty seconds to pop open a Diet Coke before my student arrived for her riding lesson. I wouldn't let myself look in the filthy stalls or at the bedding and manure dragged across the barn aisle by the hooves of the horses I'd led to turnout. I couldn't do anything about it right now, so I'd deal with it when I could.

Marcus followed me into the tack room and right up to the battered old fridge, so I tossed him a carrot. He sighed with pleasure and took the prize to his bed under the saddle racks, where he would carefully gnaw it to bits without ingesting a single speck, leaving a pile of orange slaw I would have to sweep up later.

I was just downing half the soda can, sitting the wrong way on a broke-back office chair in the tack room, when I heard the sputtering of a barely functioning car rambling up the gravel driveway, and I rolled my way over to the door. My blue dually looked lonely out there. Its only regular company was Becky's boring beige mom-sedan, missing today, and the approaching car, a falling-apart red hatchback.

The vehicle was a picture of equine bohemia, the ideal equipage for the dirty horse hippie. The sticker on the back window proclaimed EVENTERS DO IT FOR THREE DAYS, the radio antenna was fastened into place with orange baling twine, and there was a bridle hanging over the passenger seat headrest, slapping regularly against the window with every bump in the lot. I winced as the snaffle bit rapped against the safety glass with a rhythmic *clunk-clunk-clunk,* but the window somehow survived the onslaught. Like the rest of the car, it had been through a lot and probably thought that it was kind of pointless to die now.

The hatchback came skidding up beside my truck with a hailstone of gravel pebbles. Almost before it had been thrown into park, the driver's side door was flung open.

A girl my own age with a long dark braid climbed out and spread her arms wide. "I'm here!" she announced. "Let's get this party started!"

I peered past her, looking into the car. "Lacey, is that my good Edgewood bridle? Because I will *kill* you. I've been looking for that thing all week."

"I took it to Quarter Pole to get the noseband restitched," Lacey said, putting her hands on her hips. "You were gonna look like crap out there with a bum noseband. I can't ride for no bum trainer."

"You can't ride, period."

"Shut it, nag." Lacey stuck her tongue out at me.

"Whatever." She lived to torment me. Lacey was my only student outside of Becky, although she was more best friend/bratty sister than dedicated acolyte. She'd come from Pennsylvania to get a tan and ride horses, she liked to say, and so far she had the tan and every now and then I let her ride a horse. But her day job was at a coffee shop in Gainesville. She could've done *that* in Pennsylvania, she complained. She wanted to ride horses all day, every day, like she thought I did, so when she had time off, I let her muck stalls in exchange for extra saddle time.

Lacey leaned back into the car to retrieve the bridle. She straightened, tossed the tack over her shoulder, poured out half a can of Diet Coke that had probably been her breakfast, and skipped past me into the barn, flashing me an unrepentant grin as she went. "This place is a shithole!" she announced from inside. "You should try mucking stalls once in a while. I hear it's all the rage at the big farms now."

I shrugged and decided to beat it for the house for a few minutes. She could figure out where her lesson horse was and tack up all by herself. I needed something more than Diet Coke—my stomach was starting to remind me that sometimes pouring acid and sugar substitute into it wasn't the best idea without some sort of padding, and I was having visions of a cup of yogurt and a few glorious moments of air-conditioning. Lacey went on shouting, because Lacey thought shouting was the best way to cheer me up when I was in a mood. She thought her shouting cracked me up. Sometimes she was right.

"Holy God, what the *hell* is that? You have a horse out here with a pink head!"

"That's Mickey," I snapped, spinning around. She wasn't going to make fun of my Mickey. "The Michigan crazy lady's horse? He tore up his head when he took apart his stall last night. That's Swat on his head."

"Swat! I swear to Christ I nearly freaked out when I saw a horse with a pink head. I thought he was some kind of crazy albino or something. Like maybe you got into color breeds. Like next week we're going to be riding paints or something. In Western saddles, with diamonds and rubies on them. You finally decided you just have to be fancy. I knew this day would come. Can we wear blue eyeshadow when we show? Like, *sky* blue. Not regular blue."

"Just tack up Margot, will ya? I'll be right back." My stomach made a threatening grumble. *Yogurt.* I set off for the house, a hop and a skip away, but a world apart in terms of temperature. It was positively tropical out in the sun.

From the barn, Lacey went on with her stand-up act, all alone.

"Her stall's empty—I have to go get her? Oh my God. Are you for real? She's in the back pasture, isn't she? Jeez. Just once, you can't keep her in for me?" Her voice climbed to top volume, chasing after me as I traipsed off to the house. I ignored her. It was the usual rant, but Lacey knew the score—if Margot didn't get out for a nice roll and a few bucks, she'd take it out on her rider. And Lacey hated riding a bucking bronco. She was a decent rider, just about ready to start eventing at Novice level, but equine aerobatics were the chink in her armor.

On the way to the house I paused, turned back to look at Mickey where he could be seen in the gap between the barn and the house, and took a picture of him with my phone. He was the image of contented bliss, grazing in a green paddock, and it was a relief to see him so calm and happy. I wished I could be so calm and happy, but my heart was suddenly thudding in my throat.

Because, as I just remembered, I still hadn't called his owner.

7

CALLING OWNERS WAS one of my least favorite things in the world, even when I had good news. Now, calling about an injury? *And* I was calling my crazy lady? At least I was in the air-conditioning. I rubbed my bare foot against Marcus, who had sprawled himself belly-down across the cool linoleum of the kitchen floor, and dialed Eileen's number.

The phone didn't even get the chance to ring. Not a single time. Her breathless voice was on the other end immediately, as soon as I placed the screen to my ear.

"Yes? Is Mickey okay? Is everything all right? Did he eat his breakfast? How are *you*? I'm so sorry—how are you this morning? I just have been *so* worried . . . You understand, I'm sure."

There was no doubt that she cared about the horse, anyway.

I gulped down my nerves, put a smile on my face, and let loose with a burst of enthusiastic exclamation points, hoping to match her own keyed-up energy with equal measures of cheer and reassurance.

"Eileen! Hi! We're fine! Mickey is fine! I meant to call you but you know! It just gets so busy!" I paused for breath and she went gushing on in my momentary silence. Which was fine—ebullience was never my strong suit.

"Oh, of course! Oh, you must think I'm silly, but I just worry so much about him! I'm just so fond of him!"

Of course you are, I thought. *But you know he's too nice to keep as a pasture pet.* That was a tough lesson I needed Eileen to learn if we went into a partnership with Mickey. Being too fond of investments was never a good idea, according to Laurie.

I shifted the hot phone against my cheek, wishing I'd put in my earbuds in preparation for a lengthy conversation, and gazed out the kitchen window at the action in the paddocks. Lacey was trying to catch Margot, but Margot was avoiding being caught with her usual panache. The mare kicked out as she took off running. Lacey ducked and only narrowly avoided decapitation. I bit back a snort of laughter. She put her hands on her hips as the other two mares then joined the party, ears pinned and tails flagged, flinging mud from their hooves as they wheeled and galloped around the paddock.

Mickey was watching curiously, his head high, one hind leg cocked as if he'd been caught mid-nap. God, he was beautiful. I knew I was already obsessed with him. I loved seeing him standing out there in my field, and it was so easy to pretend he was mine, as he stood on my grass, wearing my fly bonnet. While his real owner went prattling on and on about heaven knew what. I checked in, heard "he likes to pick up his right hoof before his left hoof," and tuned her right back out again.

Lacey caught Margot, immediately looping the lead rope around the mare's neck so that Margot couldn't escape before the halter was fastened behind her ears. It was a nice move. *That's what I need in a working student*, I mused. *A little common sense without the attitude. That'd be a welcome change.*

If Becky ever left, Lacey would be on that job like a hungry horse attacking his dinner.

"Carrots," Eileen announced, cutting through the noise in my head.

"I always have carrots on hand," I said, hoping that's what she was talking about.

"He likes the organic ones, with the tops?"

"Of course," I agreed, trying to imagine a reality in which I could afford organic carrots to give to horses.

Eileen must have it good. I tapped a fingernail against the lid of a soda can, thinking. Such a doting mommy could come in handy. She'd be more likely to take an "only the best will do" approach to training . . . Which could be a lifesaver if I managed to score his training contract.

Nice new tack could be shared, expensive supplements could be carefully split with one or two other horses who needed a little extra oomph . . . Dynamo came to mind.

Hardscrabble to the core, I could always think of a way to stretch pennies—stretching someone else's dollars would be *cake*.

And then I noticed the silence in my ear.

Whoops.

"Right, Jules?"

"I didn't quite—static—" There was no static on digital lines, was there? What the hell. "The connection out here can be so iffy."

"Oh, you live right out there in the country, don't you! That's so nice! Mickey will love the fresh air! His last barn was so close to the highway—" And she was off again.

I forced myself to smile, baring my teeth, so that my voice, when I made small agreements and *mm-hmm*s, would be cheerful and sympathetic. Someone once told me that expressions could be heard through a phone call, and that I sounded as sour as a lemon. That someone being my mother.

"You understand, don't you, Jules? The way it feels to have him so far away? But this is his time to shine, so I can't get in his way—"

"Oh, I understand completely! He's your baby! And horses do take so much time and effort. He's really doing quite well but"—I took a deep breath, *here we go*—"you should know he gave himself a little haircut this morning."

"Haircut? I don't—"

"I'm sending you a picture right now." I took the phone away from my ear and swiped back to my photos, looking for the one I'd taken of his head, fresh and shining with ointment, when I'd finished with all the cleanup work. I kept talking to the distant speaker, voice raised. Marcus sighed as my elocution interrupted his nap. "Scraped his head on the fence in the paddock," I lied. "I was so surprised. You *do* have wooden fencing at your farm, don't you?"

"Um, no, actually we have wire mesh . . . ." Her voice was tinny coming out of the speaker.

"Well, actually, that might explain it." I forced a hollow laugh and went on fabricating a story of equine bad luck. I wasn't about to tell her my stall walls were being kicked apart by rampaging ponies. "Silly boy put his head under the top board to reach for the horse in the next paddock and then whipped it out again. Quite a scrape but nothing serious. Get the picture yet?"

"Oh—oh *God* . . ."

So she had it. I put on the lightest voice possible. "That's Swat, all that pink, just fly-repellent ointment . . ."

"Is the vet worried?"

I hesitated for just a moment. I only called the vet when I absolutely couldn't treat something on my own, and I was confident that I'd done as much cleanup and dressing of Mickey's scalping as necessary. But somehow I didn't want to tell this nervous Nancy that I wasn't seeking professional attention for her darling pet. She could either blame me for the accident, and expect me to cover the vet bill, or she could assume that the horse might have done something so idiotic anywhere, and that the vet bill was her responsibility. She already had the upper hand, since I wanted her business. Would she take advantage of that? Would she set the stage for the rest of our business relationship by telling me it was my fault? Sure, I had a boarding contract to protect me . . . but that wouldn't help me in the trainer wars.

If anyone else got this horse, I'd have a breakdown. I'd never had one before, but I was pretty sure this would be the reason for one.

If Pete Morrison got this horse . . .

I couldn't even think about it.

The silence was roaring in my ears. Eileen was waiting for me to speak, perhaps growing the tiniest bit impatient, probably wondering what the hell kind of hack she was dealing with here. I bit my lip, agonized, and then went for the simplest of lies. "The vet hasn't actually gotten here yet—"

"Let me know what the vet says. You can add the bill to my account, can't you?"

"Yes, certainly." Oh, the relief! Bless this woman! I smiled at the phone so broadly it hurt my cheeks, and then pulled up the picture of Mickey grazing in the paddock and sent that to her, as a sort of reward. That had gone so well! No blame *and* a free vet visit. A couple of the horses needed their annual Coggins test pulled and I hadn't felt like paying the sixty-dollar trip fee until I absolutely had to. Now I wouldn't have to. I was actually coming out ahead on this.

While Eileen squealed with pleasure over the sight of her four-legged son in the green Florida grass, I thought about calling my mom next, just to gloat a little.

And this, Mother, is why I don't need a college degree to run a horse farm.

D r. Em, my beloved vet and the enabler in all my DIY veterinary fantasies, showed up about an hour later. It was another one of her wonderful qualities—she always seemed to be nearby when I needed her. Which, considering I lived in the back of beyond compared to most of the Ocala equestrian community, was just plain magic as far as I was concerned.

"Show me the amazing scalped wonder-pony," she said in her transatlantic drawl, climbing out of her big SUV. Dr. Em had grown up in Alabama and then went to university in England. Like every vet at the Phillips and Donovan Equine Hospital, she wore a bridle-leather belt with a brass nameplate, only her nameplate read DR. EMMA JACKSON, MRCVS instead of the usual "DVM." It looked very fancy, as I reminded her every opportunity I got. She usually grinned and told me to stuff it, sounding something like Scarlett O'Hara imitating a Cockney maid.

Along with Lacey, Dr. Em was one of my favorite people in the world, and without her "Oops, there are too many pills in that bottle! Save the extras for a rainy day" prescriptions and those "We won't tell anyone about this, shall we" stitches, I would have been out of business a long time ago. I even had her personal cell number, with permission to call it instead of the official office number, if I was truly in trouble and out of cash. If a visit didn't happen on the office call sheet, it didn't happen.

There were times, usually while I was holding the lead of a horse while he had a gash sewn up, when I thought I owed Dr. Em everything. Vet bills had shattered the dreams of far more solvent businesswomen than me.

I went splashing through the steaming paddock to catch Mickey while she opened up the drawers in the complicated shelving unit that took up the interior of the SUV, filling a bucket with meds, latex gloves, and cotton balls and toting it all to the wash rack.

"I never need this stuff when I'm here," she admitted a few minutes later, poking at Mickey's pink scalp with a gloved finger. "You've done a lovely job. Plenty of other farms wouldn't even have had his head washed up. But I better have a look-see." Dr. Em scrubbed away at Mickey's head, rubbing away all my morning's hard work. The pink-coated cotton swabs grew into a little candy mountain behind her. Marcus investigated, suspecting sugar, then wrinkled his nose and moved on to clean up some manure in the dressage arena. "So what else is happening around here?"

"Same old. Had a buyer call me about Virtuoso, but she never showed up. The usual. Sunshine State Horse Park is coming up to close out the summer events. I'm taking Dyno Intermediate this time."

Dr. Em whistled. "That's exciting! Those are big fences, girl!"

Dr. Em had evented before vet school took away her free time. She often proclaimed that she would have time to ride again someday, but her work schedule was basically on call, twenty-four/seven/three sixty-five, so I thought it was a bit optimistic of her.

"Yeah, it's such a tiny step to Advanced after that. We'll be ready to step up in no time. Get my name out there." I glanced out the barn aisle toward the paddock where my chestnut Thoroughbred grazed. I was powerless against the urge that struck me a dozen times a day, to just make sure that he was still there, that I hadn't dreamed him up, that he hadn't disappeared into a puff of smoke. I took in his muscular lines hungrily and felt safe again—for a few more minutes.

"Dyno's a nice sound horse. You take care of him and he'll take care of you." She added still more cotton to the pile. Dr. Em was a messy vet. It was perhaps her only fault. "You getting out any, like I suggested?"

Second fault, actually: her desire that I acquire a social life.

"Um, no, I haven't had time," I replied warily. She didn't have another no-chance guy lined up, did she? Dr. Em had actually tried to set me up with several people, mostly racehorse trainers, but I knocked her suggestions back every time. I wasn't interested in dating, let alone someone with horses, who might try to tell me what to do with *my* horses.

She swabbed away, grinning. "I hear that. But come on, you should really go out once in a while. More to life than horses and all that. I had a date last weekend, believe it or not. It's nice to have someone buy you dinner and to wear clothes that don't have horse-hair all over them. You should try it."

It did sound nice. Especially the part where someone else bought me food. I tried to imagine getting my work done and getting cleaned up and driving to town for a date and potentially even staying awake past ten o'clock. Nope. I couldn't see it happening. And anyway, there was one glaring fault with every man I might meet in Ocala—his job. "I'm not going to meet anyone in this town who doesn't have horses."

"Nothing wrong with guys with horses," Dr. Em said, grinning down at me from her ladder. "You run into Pete Morrison yet? He's worth seeing."

Seriously, she was in this guy's fan club, too?

"The one who probably kicked my ass at ACE?" Sure, it wasn't official yet, but better to just accept it now. "I've seen him."

"You know he's only just back in town; grew up here, apparently. You should see his spread over in Reddick. Gorgeous farm. And as for him—delicious! I'd forgive him a trip fee or two." Dr. Em laughed and climbed down, wiping her hands on her jeans. "Wound looks good. I don't foresee any problems. We'll do a tetanus just because. And sorry about the Swat. I probably owe you a jar of the stuff now."

"No problem." I brushed it off, even though she'd washed about ten bucks' worth of ointment off his head and it would all have to be replaced out of my own pocket. It hurt my wallet, for sure, but she would make up for it in other ways. She always did.

Dr. Em jabbed Mickey with a tetanus booster, then doled out a few packets of SMZs, the current drug of choice for fighting infections, and then she doled out a few more—loosies that had broken out of a package. Good ol' Dr. Em. "Mind if I have a Diet Coke?" she asked, scribbling quantities into her iPad. This visit was on the books. Mostly. "Only I didn't have time for lunch today."

We adjourned to the tack room for caffeine and a quick rest, leaving Lacey to put away the horse.

"So, about Pete Morrison," Dr. Em began, once we were seated and sipping from cans. "I must admit he has mentioned you."

"What?"

"I was at his place just this morning for a check on that mare of his. Nice, when she wasn't trying to bite a chunk out of me. I got the call to come out here next while he was standing next to me. He asked after you and I said we were friends." She smiled. "As much as anyone can be friends with Jules Thornton."

"I'm ignoring that," I said. "Anyway, why would he ask about me? After trade secrets?"

"He thinks you're interesting," she said, raising her eyebrows. "I think he might even go so far as to find you attractive. He said you and your horse had a beautiful connection."

"He probably wants my horse, not me."

"He has horses," Dr. Em pointed out. "Very nice ones."

"You can always have more."

"I think he'd like to see you again. In a less horsey setting. He *might* have asked me to ask if you'd see him. If you wanted to."

"I don't." Although I did appreciate his saying I had a beautiful connection with my horse. I pressed down an urge to ask if he'd said anything else about me.

"Oh-*kay*-eee," Dr. Em singsonged. "But he'll be disappointed!"

"He'll get over it." I couldn't believe we were having this conversation about Pete Morrison. *Any* conversation about him was too much, but this was just absurd. "I'm not interested in dating my competition, if that's what you're suggesting."

"Oh, please! Competition has nothing to do with it. You're in the same sport and someone's always going to have to beat the other one. Maybe next weekend he wins. The weekend after that, it could be you. Whatever the eventing gods want to happen. Anyway, I could introduce the two of you. Properly." She looked excited. Dr. Em had a formidable matchmaking side. "Jules, you know he's absolutely gorgeous. You've seen him! His hair is dark red, like a liver chestnut's, and he has this amazing tan and a great body . . ." She trailed off, clearly taken away by the very thought.

"So . . . date him yourself?"

She laughed. "Oh Jules, he's like thirty years old. He's too old for me."

"You're five years older than me!"

"Yeah, but I'm not dating anyone over twenty-nine." She drained her Diet Coke and crumpled the can, tossing it into a feed bag I had designated as the recycling bin. "Actually, I'm not sure he's any older than either of us. But he acts like it. And I like a little bit of a social life. Dancing, crazy stuff you don't like. I go out and get wild whenever I can get rid of this damn work phone. Pete? He's like you—he's wedded to his horses. No life whatsoever. You're perfect for each other. You could ride and muck out and order pizza and fall asleep on the couch and call it exciting."

That actually sounded fantastic. She was good. But I held firm. I had rules. "I'm going to have to pass. I'm sticking with my no-life-whatsoever plan for a while—that includes dating."

I set down my Diet Coke and stood up, indicating that I didn't want to talk about it anymore. Any of it. Dating. Social life. Someone to ride out with and to muck stalls with. Not that all of that didn't sound very attractive. Who wouldn't want a gorgeous redhead to fall asleep on the couch with? But Pete Morrison? That entitled son of a . . . no. I shook my head.

Dr. Em got up and headed out the tack room door, effectively washing her hands of me. "You're nuts. Now, what else needs doing?

I have six more appointments this afternoon, and then I have twelve whole hours with my work phone turned off. I'm going to put on some dancing shoes tonight. So no emergencies from you, got it?"

Lacey helped Dr. Em with the overdue Coggins tests, holding the halters of the horses who needed their blood pulled and finding their files in the office binder. Horses couldn't leave the farm without a negative test on file, ruling out equine infectious anemia—a disease with no cure—so I'd been playing roulette by letting a few of them expire. While they were collecting samples, I started throwing tack on one of the youngsters. Despite the messy barn, I had to get some riding in before the day disappeared. It was already clouding over—the afternoon thunderstorms waited for no man.

"Lacey—I need you to finish stalls after your next ride!" I called as I led the first horse out to the mounting block, not waiting to hear her gusty sigh from the office. I *did* hear Dr. Em laugh. "Thank you!" I added, knowing that the tack room was receiving an earful of how much I owed her. It was fine. We'd work it out later.

Despite the approaching weather, I managed to get about twenty minutes each of decent work onto the Twins, as I had nicknamed the pair of Dutch Warmbloods in the barn. The youngest horses in the barn, the Twins had the same sire, but different mamas. Their breeder had sent them up from Myakka City for me to start under saddle. Aware of the considerable depth of her pockets, I had basically given away the farm to get the Twins in my barn, offering the breeder a break on board and taking extra-special care with their training. I was hoping she'd be so impressed she'd send other babies my way, and tell other breeders what a wonderful job I did with all her youngstock.

Word of mouth was the only advertising I could afford, with my budget. If it didn't work, I had sunk my time and money into horses that weren't mine. Not the best, but I wasn't working with a lot of options here.

And they were nice enough to ride, anyway, so it wasn't the worst thing to lose money on. Like so many warmbloods, bred for obedience and pretty gaits, they were pleasant to work with.

Twin One (real name: Avril) did have a nervous disorder when it came to butterflies—the sight of a fluttering insect batting its pastel wings past her nose was enough to send her into a quivering panic, and midway through our ride I had to sit deep in the saddle and try to calm her with my own steady breaths while she snorted and stared at one of the fluttering monsters making its unhurried way through the dressage arena.

Twin Two (real name: Sam) was slightly more complicated. He was unaffected by butterflies but was afflicted by such laziness that I was already forced to carry a dressage whip and give him a solid whack on the haunches to get him into a trot. That really wasn't what a whip was for—I carried a dressage whip to tap gently, as a polite request for a horse to move their hind legs over or add some impulsion to their movement. But nothing else got Twin Two moving. It was astonishing to me that a four-year-old youngster who knew basic cues and understood leg and seat pressure was so completely uninterested in moving forward. I was actually growing concerned that Twin Two wasn't going to amount to anything at all in life. Unless I could find something he was interested in, he was turning out to be a very expensive, very tiring trail horse.

Riding the Twins first meant I might not get in a ride on any of my competition horses before the weather turned, another annoyance settling in the pit of my stomach as I swatted Twin Two around the dressage arena. But miraculously, the weather held off, and if the lightning was a little closer than I would have liked at times, I managed to get through both of the Twins and was getting ready to ride Dynamo as Lacey finished up the stalls around five o'clock.

She eyed me warily as I pulled out his tack—Dynamo did not share a bridle with anyone else, and he had his own saddle pads and girth cover, lest some vulgar sales horse give him cooties. "You're going to ride Dynamo in this weather?" she asked, leaning the empty wheelbarrow against the wall in the alcove where I kept the tools. She picked up a broom to sweep up the shavings that littered the aisle, and a cool gust of air sent a whirlwind of old bedding spiraling past us.

"I *have* to ride him," I said impatiently. A little lightning wasn't going to change the competition schedule. "We have a training plan to keep up with."

There was a rumble of thunder so deep it shook the windows in the tack room and rattled the bottles lining the washing machine. Lacey looked at me significantly.

I felt my jaw tightening. As much as I liked Lacey, I was tired of being told how to ride my big horse. I'd had Dynamo for years before I'd met either Becky or Lacey, taken him from Beginner Novice to Intermediate basically all by myself, but apparently they both had big opinions about how often I rode him, how much I asked of him, and in what weather I did the asking.

"I'm just saying that thunder is really close," Lacey said, noticing my mood.

"The deeper it is, the farther away it is," I told her.

"That isn't true."

"It could be."

Turning my back on Lacey's reproachful gaze, I picked up a lead rope and started for the paddocks, their grass poison-green beneath the dark, boiling clouds. Ears pricked, eyes bright, Dynamo watched me come.

8

IF I COULD have wrapped Dynamo in cotton wool and rubber boo-
ties to keep him safe, I would have done it in a heartbeat. I would
have put him in an oversized horse-head helmet to protect his
skull, sheathed his legs with impact-resistant Kevlar boots. And a
steel breastplate for his priceless heart.

As it was, I watched him like an anxious mother watches a
firstborn child.

It was my greatest fear that Dynamo would do, as horses always tend to do, something self-destructive, like hook his leg
through a fence while pawing at someone who was annoying him
in the next paddock, or choke on a daisy he hadn't expected in his
mouthful of grass, or trip on an anthill and fall down and break his
scapula. You know, the idiotic things that ruin athletic horses every
day. I couldn't risk him, not for a moment. I couldn't lose him.
Dynamo wasn't the answer to everything, but for now, he was my
big horse.

And there was this—he was my one great love. On summer nights, when the horses were out to take advantage of the sort-of-cooler temperatures, I could gaze out my kitchen window and see him there, his white blaze glowing electric in the blue moonlight, and feel my heart swell, my throat close, my stomach do a slow flip in the sheer terror of loving someone so much.

Maybe Dr. Em and everyone else who thought I needed another human in my life didn't realize that my heart was full already, full of Dynamo.

My big horse, my chance, my champion. My ladder. And when I had climbed as high as he could take me, I'd put his bridle aside and let him grow fat and happy on the grass of his paddock, while other, stronger horses took on the heavy lifting.

"Dyno . . ." I called now, as I walked into the center of his paddock, his leather halter slung over my shoulder. "Dynamo . . . *cookies . . .*"

The big horse turned and watched me warily. He didn't like to be caught. It was the last remnant of his bad old days, whatever they were. I didn't know his history, but it couldn't have been pretty. I found Dynamo six years ago, when I was still in high school, waiting to go through the ring at a livestock auction in south Georgia. It wasn't the kind of place you'd expect to find a classy horse. And he hadn't looked like a classy horse.

There's no telling what happened to Dynamo, only that he had to have been strong to have survived it. When I first saw him, he was a scrawny scarecrow, with more skin fungus than hair—only his mangy tail and the thin fuzz on his legs gave away that he was supposed to be a red chestnut. His mane had been rubbed away by his crazed scratching, fighting the itching of parasites, infections, and assorted insects that had taken up residence there. He was a ruin, ready for slaughter, if only he weighed enough to be worth the trouble.

But one thing was starkly apparent about this bucket of bones: his skeleton was the frame of a Thoroughbred. When I stepped forward, grabbed his halter, and flipped up his upper lip, I saw exactly what I had expected—a blue tattoo strip of letters and numbers.

Once we were safe at home, I'd given the tattoo numbers to the Jockey Club and received his official identity in return. The tattered wreck on his way to slaughter was a chestnut gelding registered as Don's Dynamo, sired by the great racehorse Dynaformer. But the apple fell pretty far from the tree, because his race record was anything but a champion's: pulled up before the finish of his one and only race, then disappearing from racing's radar. After that, who knew where he'd been? A racehorse only had a record at the racetrack. Where he went afterward was a matter of fortune, and the conscience of the people who held his future in their hands.

Dynamo's people had not had any conscience worth mentioning. That first day that I saw him, there was no indication that he'd been carefully bred from the bloodlines of champions. He stood in the corner of the little sale pen with a number chalked on his hip, and when he went through the auction ring he was trembling from fear, from weakness, both. He was worse than a broke-down nag. He was a wreck wobbling on his last legs.

And now . . . now he was a magnificent gleaming chestnut *beast* of a horse. On sunny days his coat had a metallic copper sheen, his mane was thick and his tail was full. You'd never know to look at him that he'd been thrown away. And while he had a few hang-ups left over from his old life, like being ear-shy, they were mostly small, manageable things.

Except for being caught whenever he was turned out in the paddock. That was taking a long time to fix.

The first few months after I brought the sick, shivering horse home, I had to spend every evening sitting in the paddock, waiting for a chance to snag his halter. Laurie was sympathetic and encouraging. It was great, she said, that I had taken a chance on such a damaged horse. We would learn a lot together, and be closer partners because of it. But, she'd gone on, my horse had to come *last*. I was her working student. I took care of her horses, and the boarders' horses, for the privilege of riding lessons and, now, keeping Dynamo on the farm. And work came first. (School came a very distant third, after Dynamo.)

And so every evening, after the rest of the barn was fed and watered and tucked in for the night, I went out into the whining mosquitoes and the singing frogs of the hot Florida night and coaxed Dynamo's head into my hands. I still have the scars from the mosquito bites, a scattering of purple dots on my forearms, to remind me of those interminable evenings in the field, watching the sun sink, the stars come out, and my horse evade me as if I was the kill-buyer he'd dodged at the auction.

I'd bought him hoping to resell him for a profit. He'd only cost me two hundred bucks in the auction ring, after all, a nice investment of some leftover Christmas and birthday money that hadn't already been appropriated by my mother as repayment for new riding boots I had needed before the holidays. The slaughterhouse truck was full already, thanks to a contingent of two-year-old Quarter Horses from a bankrupt breeder down the road, and the broker didn't bother to outbid me for such a skinny wreck of a horse.

One advantage of buying a skeleton, though—I could see how those bones fit together. And Dynamo was put together very, very well.

I thought I could put weight on him, school him up nicely to jump little fences, sell him to an adult amateur or maybe a good kid.

I'd make a few thousand, put some aside, and buy another. Horse-flipping—it's like house-flipping, only much more interesting, and much more difficult to make a profit. But training horses was what I knew. And by this point, I'd been riding sales horses for most of my life. I wasn't worried about getting attached to this one, just because my name was on his papers.

I even had a plan for the money I'd make when he sold: a truck. The other girls at the barn were already getting cars from their parents, and the barn parking lot after school was glittering with luxurious status symbols. Ashleigh Cooper even got a vanity plate with her Oldenburg gelding's name on it: FRITZ. (I used to call him "On the Fritz" because he was a dingbat who spooked at shrubs when I was leading him in from the paddock every afternoon, but Ashleigh only rode in the shrub-free jumping arena, so it wasn't a problem for her.)

My parents weren't buying me a car. The gulf between myself and the other girls at the barn was widening.

Just once, I didn't want to be the poor girl. Just once, I wanted to be part of the gang, instead of the girl who cleaned up after them.

And I would be sensible, of course, if I had the money. I'd buy a nice, useful truck, something that could haul a horse trailer or carry a ton of hay back to the barn. A truck that was gorgeous and new, though. Something to show off.

And a *horse* of my own. Dynamo was my key to fitting in.

Or, that was how I'd seen it when I'd looked him over in the auction ring and raised my hand to bid my two hundred dollars.

But I'd underestimated how damaged Dynamo was. I hadn't expected the depth of his inner terrors—the way his skin would shiver and tremble at the slightest touch, the violence and deter-mination in his dark eyes when he flipped over in the barn aisle to escape the bridle slipping over his ears, the mindless exhaustion he'd work himself into as he tried to escape humans in the paddock, a ring of white gleaming around his eyes, foam gathering on his sweat-darkened body.

I used to go home and cry, my pillow over my head so my parents wouldn't hear me. It was the only place I allowed my despair to show, though. No one needed to know I was in over my head, that I'd invested in a horse that would ultimately be a mistake. And then one day I realized that Dynamo wasn't a mistake. He took a cookie from my hand and chewed it calmly, without jumping backward. His hot breath spilled over my skin. He looked at me without that flighty, panicked look in his eyes. And I felt something more profound than relief, something that went beyond the investment in time and money.

I felt a connection with him.

After that, things started to change.

Little by little, he came around. He let me brush him without shuddering at the touch. He tolerated—*just*—having his ears touched, so that I could stop taking the bridle apart just to get it off and on him for every ride. He stopped darting to the back of his stall when I came to do morning turnout before rushing to school, hay in my bra and mud on my boots. Instead, he waited, ears pricked, eyes quiet, while I carefully buckled the halter far behind his ears and led him out to his little square of grass and sand.

But once he was turned out, all bets were off.

And so after I frantically got through the little herd of troublesome projects that my trainer handed off to me, my nights slowed to a crawl. Instead of sitting in a saddle, proudly working on my very own project horse, I would sit on my heels in the center of his paddock. It was the smallest one the farm had available but still a good half acre in size. I would glance at neglected homework, turning the pages gingerly, but really watching Dynamo, monitoring his worried circuits of the fence line. He *wanted* companionship, he *wanted* to come into the barn and be with the other horses, perhaps even the humans. But every night, he had to overcome all the demons that told him it was dangerous.

Every night, when he finally gave in, was a moment of sublime triumph that boosted me through the next evening of waiting.

So much waiting. Long minutes turned into longer hours that first month with Dynamo, my heels prickling beneath me, finally falling asleep, so that I had to sit down in the scrubby grass and take my chances with fire ants. But the thrill I got when the horse would at last make his way to me, and place his nose along my back, to snort and snuffle through my ponytail, was worth any amount of pain. And about a million bug bites.

This was more than riding a horse, leading a horse, grooming a horse. This was more than anything I had ever done with a horse before. And all the rules I had set for myself, the lessons Laurie taught me about hardening my heart and seeing every horse as an investment, grew steadily more and more irrelevant. At least, where they might have applied to Dynamo. He wasn't just any horse anymore. He was *my* horse.

As I brought along Dynamo, slowly and painstakingly, fighting for every inch of ground I gained, my dreams of big profit evaporated. The scars a horse can carry within are not easily healed. Dynamo was raw and barely trained, a bolter and a bucker, with the fits of temper like sudden summer storms that are peculiar to certain high-strung, intelligent, nervy Thoroughbreds. Our entire relationship was based upon our mutual trust. Everything he gave me, he gave because I learned how to ask him.

He taught me more than any sales horse, any lesson horse, any packer pony ever had.

And because of that, I owed him everything I now had. The farm, the horses in their paddocks, the clients (barely) paying the bills—I owed it all to the lessons Dynamo had taught me about the nature of horses, the science of giving and taking, the art of asking and granting.

Now, I held out my hand, fingers outstretched, to reveal two small brown horse cookies in my palm. Dynamo looked over, ears pricked, head high, copper forelock draped over one eye. He was breathtakingly beautiful. I was reminded sharply, as I was every time he made one of his regal poses, that he was everything to me. That I didn't need anything or anyone but Dynamo in the end.

That someday, we'd show them all.

This afternoon, though, it would just be nice to catch him before we got stormed on.

His inclination, as always, was to turn to the fence line and canter in a big circle around me, evading the human in his space. But it was just an act at this point, a bad habit more than any actual protest, and it wasn't long before his whiskered nose was in my palm, grabbing roughly at the cookies, and I was slipping my hand very carefully around his neck with the strap of the halter, buckling the headpiece well behind his ears. His ears were still a sore point, and at this sensitive juncture of capitulation, touching one would send him racing backward in long frenzied strides, his head too high for me to reach. And we'd have to start the whole silly routine all over again.

Lord knew I didn't have time for that. The skies were lowering, growling, setting us up for an evening of lightning strikes and monsoon rains.

Back in the barn, Lacey was still sweeping up the aisle, creating an unholy pile of manure, shavings, cotton balls, latex gloves, and plastic syringe wrappers. Dr. Em had outdone herself today with the sea of litter left in her wake.

"Thank you so much," I began contritely, leading a gentled Dynamo into the wash rack and clipping the crossties to his halter. "I can't tell you how much you saved my life today—"

"Oh, Dyno-*saur*," Lacey crooned, ignoring me completely. She planted a kiss on the little white spot between his nostrils and made an exaggerated smooching sound. "Him's so *cuuuuute*!"

"Stop that," I scolded, but we all talked to the horses this way. We talked to them like they were great big babies. Because that was exactly how they behaved.

"Let me groom him," she said, abandoning the broom, and darted into the tack room. She reappeared with Dynamo's personal grooming bucket, a little plastic tote filled with his favorites: a soft horsehair body brush, a delicate polishing cloth, a few assorted tail combs and hoof picks. He never tolerated a rough or hard brush on his body, and misusing even the gentlest brushes could send him into a black mood, swishing his tail and flattening his ears. I stepped back and let her get to work, reflecting that this was an excellent time for another Diet Coke. Riding the Twins had soaked my sports bra and tank top through. I felt like I'd fallen into a very hot pond and just splashed around in it for a little while.

"What are you going to do with him today?" Lacey was grooming him as I had shown her, keeping one eye on his expression and ears, watching for temper tantrum cues, her body a careful distance from the sideways reach of his hind legs. When she groomed his hind end, she pressed her body close to his, so that if he did kick, he couldn't get up enough momentum to hurt her. It was second nature at this point. No one had been kicked in months. "If you're jumping, I want to come out and watch."

"We'll do a little course," I agreed, retrieving my cold can of soda from the tack room. I overturned a bucket and sat down, happy to rest my feet for a few minutes. "Something quick, before it storms."

I took a long swig of soda and listened to the thunder. The bottles on the wash rack shelf rattled with its vibrations. Lacey shook her head and went on sweeping the polishing cloth across Dynamo— she'd never let him go out with a hair out of place, even if there was no one to see him but the two of us, even if she didn't want us to go out at all. She was so good. I was so lucky to have her as a student.

As a friend, too.

I'd never had many friends. There hadn't been time to make friends at Laurie's barn. It was nice having Dr. Em come by; she was a good pal. Although if she kept playing matchmaker with me and Pete Morrison, we were going to have a problem. I closed my eyes, wishing I hadn't thought of him. Visions of Pete, his head tipped close to that grumpy mare of his, floated through my mind. He held out his hands and Damon Knox handed him a huge check and the reins to a gleaming horse.

I snapped my eyes open again and made myself focus on my own horse, standing right in front of me and gleaming just as much as Pete's imaginary horse.

"You make him look like a million dollars," I told Lacey, and she smiled at me. Then she threw the cloth back into the box and went for a hoof pick.

"Almost ready," she said. "He needs his mane pulled before the event. Do you want me to do that later?"

"Sure," I said. "Not too short, though. I need something to grab if things get crazy out on course."

Lacey laughed. "You guys? You won't have any problems out there."

That was the kind of confidence I needed in my corner. I wished Lacey had been with me at Sandra Holborn's the day we'd gone for our evaluation.

We'd had one or two pacing hiccups, but ultimately we jumped everything and no one died.

And then she told you that you weren't ready.

I drank down the dregs of my soda, its acid bitterness cold in my throat. No one knew about that part but me. And Becky.

It was one ride. A moment in time. Sandra didn't know about the other times we'd handled jumps like that with no problem at all. I had the qualifications; we were fully certified to compete at Intermediate level. I didn't need her signature to compete; so why did I need it for the ACE audition?

Whatever. It was over now. I forced myself to think in the future, not in the past. I pictured soaring over the jumps and bounding down the drops. I awarded myself first place, and watched the ring steward place a big blue rosette on Dynamo's browband, gold-spangled and fluttering in the breeze. I thought of Pete Morrison watching me from the sidelines, raising a hand in salute as we cantered around the jumping arena for our victory gallop, and I blushed. Luckily, my face was already red with heat.

"You feel ready for those Intermediate fences?" Lacey asked, like she was reading my mind. She was brushing out Dynamo's tail carefully, avoiding pulling any strands loose. A rider's chief vanity is their horse's tail.

"I think so, yeah," I said. "I mean, yes. Nothing out there is going to scare us." Confidence was key. If you stopped to think about the madness out there on the cross-country course, you'd stick to the show ring, where the fences fell down when you hit them.

On the cross-country course, hitting a fence could send you head over heels. And Intermediate was the level when things *really* got salty, preparing horse-and-rider teams for the challenges of the Advanced level.

And that's where we were heading. It was all up there at Advanced. All those big capitalized words . . . The United States Equestrian Team. The World Equestrian Games. The Olympics. The world. Someday, I'd have it all. And with every horse I got going, it would get a little easier to scale these levels.

"How big are the jumps at Intermediate again?" Lacey asked.

"Three foot nine," I answered.

She looked at me. "And how wide?"

"Like . . . five feet," I said, fudging a little. The *tops* of the jumps could be about five feet wide. A jump with a ditch in front could be more than seven feet wide.

Lacey fiddled with a knot in Dynamo's long ginger tail. "You've schooled that?"

"Of course I have. Multiple times. With coaches. It's going to be fine. I have the go-ahead, from experienced trainers, to do this. You have nothing to worry about," I added, appreciating her concern. "I'm not going to get hurt."

"I'm thinking of Dynamo," Lacey said.

Of course she was. "He's fine."

"Can I groom for you? Or is Becky doing it?" Her voice was flat as she changed the subject.

"You're so jealous of Becky," I said with a grin. "Just admit it."

"Puh-*leeze*. No, I'm not."

"Come on, Lacey," I teased. "Be honest. You want her job. You want to work for me for free. You wish you were so lucky."

"I already do work for you for free," she pointed out, holding up the tail comb for illustration.

"And do I charge you for your lessons?"

"No."

"All right then. See, you're actually my working student already. Just part time."

"I want to be full time," she said. "Can't I move into your house and follow you around like a little ghost?"

"I mean, you can," I said. "I would never turn away a personal ghost, obviously. But Becky works here four days a week and she's not leaving anytime soon."

"She doesn't even like you."

I blinked at Lacey. Was it that obvious to everyone? "Did she *tell* you that?"

"No, but I hear the way she talks to you." Lacey flicked Dynamo's tail toward me. "Like she always thinks you're making the wrong choice."

"Maybe I am," I said. "Did you ever think of that?"

She snorted.

"I'll be ready for a second working student before too much longer," I said confidently, and downed my soda. "Things will get better. This place is about to take off. When I have twenty horses, you better believe I'll have enough work for two people."

"Yeah, I bet." Lacey disappeared into the tack room and returned with my jumping saddle, settling it gently on Dynamo's dark blue saddle pad.

"But in the meantime, Becky is my groom at events," I pronounced with finality. "She knows what she's doing, and she wants to be there."

And she knows about Sandra Holborn's signature.

"I'm coming too," Lacey said. "You can't stop me."

9

THE DAYS LEADING days leading up to the Sunshine State Horse Park's Summer Horse Trials flew by in a whirlwind of wet arenas, stormy afternoons, and muddy horses.

On the appointed day of the ACE announcement, I waited for the email and read it without much surprise. After much deliberation, the award would go to Peter Morrison of Briar Hill Farm, Reddick, Florida, etc. etc. The money, the horse, it went to the man who already had both. There was an addendum personalizing the rejection letter, thanking me for my hard work and wishing me all the best in future endeavors.

The press release was what made me angry. Every rider was listed, and they put me down as "Juliet Thornton." Who told them my real name was Juliet?

But the disappointment and irritation were quickly swallowed up by the knot of terror and anticipation I carried around in my stomach as the event weekend drew closer. Suddenly, it seemed nearly impossible to distinguish one day from another. If I hadn't been crossing off the calendar days with big black Xs, one after another, on the eventing calendar that hung over my tack room desk, I couldn't have said whether it was Monday or Tuesday or Saturday.

Intermediate is coming, the calendar whispered. *Are you ready?*

I thought I was, but now the reality of it was bigger than I'd expected. Schooling cross-country wasn't the same as jumping a full course.

The last few days before the event rushed past with their own challenges. Monday meant that Benny Anderson, the old racetrack blacksmith, showed up in his Cadillac Escalade and his shiny belt buckle, opened up the back hatch to reveal enough tools and equipment to build a rocket ship, and set about sculpting Dynamo's flat, shelly feet into something resembling a decent set of hooves. Benny was an old-style, unreformed redneck, dismissive of girl trainers and disapproving of any horse that wasn't good for chasing cows, but he made a living by tacking racing plates onto young racehorses and he often remarked that doing my quiet sport horses was like a paid vacation. For him, maybe—I was the one who had to stand there and hold them all day long. Benny didn't trust crossties.

Tuesday was dry and hot, the atmosphere thick and unforgiving, and though I prayed for clouds, rain, torrential downpours, anything to break the heat and shield me from the sun as I rode horse after horse in the sweltering arena, every hopeful little cloud simply shriveled up in the pitiless blue sky. That night I took a cold shower, turned up the air-conditioning, and sat under the living room vent until my fingernails turned blue. Marcus went to bed and wiggled underneath my duvet.

Wednesday night I finished chores late, working alone (Becky had a paper due and left early), and afterward I sat out on the porch, watching the sun sink into pink and green clouds some-where west, beyond the sandy hills of Levy County, beyond the swamps and the clapboard shanties and the fishing piers out at Cedar Key, where people were living a different kind of Florida life. I drank cold coffee from a midday pot, waiting for some pro-spective boarders to arrive from Orlando. The sun sank beneath the distant tree line, and the frogs began to sing from their pop-up ponds, the flooded patches in the corner of every paddock and in the ruts of the driveway. Their song was deafening to my ears, but not to Marcus's. The beagle began to snore beside me. Venus glinted in the heavens, a mosquito whined in my ear, and no one came.

I went inside, emptied a packet of ramen into a pot of boiling water and poked at it until the noodles were cooked, then went into the living room and turned on the weather. Marcus woke me up an hour later, baying his hound-dog howl from the porch where I had left him.

"We're so sorry," the woman in the parking lot was saying re-peatedly, slamming the door on a shadowy BMW. "The traffic was just a mess. We left Orlando at five . . . that was our first mistake, I guess."

"There was an accident and the turnpike was shut down," the man continued, pocketing the car keys. "We learned a lot about back roads."

"You must be Maggie and Dave," I said, and smiled as warmly as I could. I waved away their regrets and slipped bare feet into my Wellington boots. Sure, it was nine thirty at night and I wanted my bed, but if they were bringing me money, I would give them the tour without complaint.

There was an appreciative silence as they looked around the grounds, which were damp but spotless. I could say this for people who showed up after hours: they saw the barn as it was meant to be seen. If they visited during the middle of the day, civilians from the world outside horses could be easily excused for thinking a barn was a shithole. Hay and shavings and manure everywhere, sweaty horses being walked, annoyed horses banging on their stall doors, sweat-foamed bridles heaped on top of dirty saddle pads heaped on top of errant wheelbarrows . . . a war zone. But if they came at night, they would find a picture-perfect representation of classical horse-keeping.

I watched them blinking at the gleaming expanse of shining barn aisle and thought I should schedule all my barn tours for after five o'clock in the winter, and after seven o'clock in the summer. I should make that a thing.

The couple explained, in halting words and with the sort of innocence that showed that they knew they were novices and were just hoping I wouldn't cheat the life out of them, that they had imported two youngish Hanoverians from Germany, and wanted them started in jumping and made into solid amateur-level horses that they could both show.

"Do you guys have riding experience?" I asked. Thinking: *Gold mine!*

"I do," Maggie said eagerly. "I rode all the way up to college. Hunter-jumper."

"Kind of," Dave admitted, less enthusiastic. "With my cousins and stuff, during the summers. They had a farm in Indiana . . ."

"So you're going to be taking riding lessons while your youngsters are up here being trained, is that right?"

They looked at each other as if they had been hoping this wouldn't come up. Dave pursed his lips a little; Maggie blushed. "Well," Dave said after a moment. "Maggie here is pretty experienced—"

Maggie put her hand on his arm. "No, I think she's right, Dave." She looked at me. "We'll take riding lessons," she promised. "From the best trainer we can find."

Sensible girl. I liked them very much.

I invited them in to celebrate the deal with Diet Cokes, the champagne of equestrians. We sat around the kitchen table until nearly ten o'clock, discussing the finer points of show jumping before a mystified Dave, who was clearly getting involved with horses just to please Maggie, and then I produced boarding and training contracts for the two Hanoverians, who had a few more weeks left on their quarantine.

They looped their elegant, expensive signatures onto my home-made documents, adapted from a workbook of equestrian legal forms I'd checked out of the Marion County Public Library, and after handshakes and back-slaps they went back out into the night, leaving me up too late on a school night, alone with Marcus, who was snoring on the couch.

I looked over the training contracts, popping open a beer to counteract the late-night caffeine. Signed documents were always nice.

And daunting, as well. Two more stalls filled, but two more horses to ride. I didn't have the time in my day. I needed *help*. I thought again of Lacey, who had been out four more times since she'd asked if she could work for me full time. She had been going out of her way to show how useful she was, handing me a new horse to ride as soon as I came into the barn with a finished one, cleaning stalls between groomings and bathings. She was stellar. And she was fun to have around. But I couldn't afford two working students.

I tore the label from the bottle of beer, rolled it between my fingertips, gazed out the kitchen window to where Dynamo grazed in his circle of tangerine light. Everything would be fine. I had Dynamo. I could make it with one horse.

For a little while.

Just beyond him, Mickey dozed.

Two horses, although Mickey was years behind Dynamo. Two horses would be better.

On the living room couch, Marcus rolled onto his back and yawned, a high, piercing puppy yawn. "I should be asleep, too," I told the beagle, but he was passed out again, legs in the air, ears flopped on the brown fabric.

I watched him snore for a moment and then wandered around the house, looking for something to do. My heart was still pounding with caffeine and adrenaline from wooing new clients, so falling asleep wasn't going to happen anytime soon. I flipped on the television, thumbed through a romance novel Becky had left, opened the freezer and searched for a carton of ice cream that did not exist. I paced. The double-wide felt very empty after having company so late at night. Outside the night grew darker, the shadows deeper. There was a rustle in the kitchen. A mouse or a palmetto bug? I'd rather not know.

The house was lit only by the blue of the television. And why blue, I wondered. There was nothing blue on the screen. Well. *I* felt a bit blue. I rubbed Marcus's spotted tummy and shook my head, trying to dislodge the melancholy feeling that was taking over. I had nothing to mope over. I had new clients. The barn was almost full. Dynamo and I were more than ready for the event this weekend. Sure, the house felt empty. But I was just tired, and coming down from both an emotional and a caffeine high. And I had horses to ride in the morning.

"Come on, Marcus," I commanded, but the beagle ignored me

and snored on, his black lips pulled down from his incisors to give him a ferocious, utterly out-of-character snarl. "Fine." I gave up and shuffled off to bed alone.

Then Thursday was gone, very suddenly, a haze of half-asleep chores and half-frenzied tack cleaning, and it was Friday morning, time to get Dynamo ready for the weekend of competition. I always took my horses to the showgrounds early, to settle them in, and Dynamo's nervous nature made this nonnegotiable. He had to have time to look around, eat some grass, and accept the new surroundings, or he would perform Lipizzan-worthy airs above the ground during his dressage test and we'd be disqualified for destroying the judge's gazebo.

I had Dynamo in my four-horse trailer by eleven o'clock on Friday morning (not bad, really) with all the hay and feed and bedding I would need for the next three days loaded up in the front. Dynamo gazed out through the bars on the window, his expression long-suffering after he stopped fussing over the snug plush-filled bandages on his legs and the bell boots wrapping all four hooves in heavy rubber protection. I told him he was lucky they didn't make bubble wrap in big enough sheets to wrap around his entire body. He sighed, nosing moodily at the alfalfa in his hay net.

Becky set off ahead of me with a few bags of shavings and Dynamo's water buckets in the back of her old sedan so that she could prep the stall before we arrived. I took one last look at the trailer, running my fingers over the hitch, the electric plug, the tires, the door latches, paranoid as only a horsewoman can be, and then hopped into the cab of my dually. It had seen better days, but my farm name was on its side over the silhouette of a jumping horse, and that in itself was a dream come true.

I always drove horses with the knowledge that I had priceless cargo, weaving around potholes, taking turns so slowly that a toddler could have stood up in the trailer, driving at the speed I preferred. Only a few of the cars that blew past me on the interstate honked, and only one driver gave me the finger, which I considered progress for humanity, and within an hour I had turned into the long grass-and-gravel driveway of the Sunshine State Horse Park.

Becky was smoothing out shavings in the little temporary stall we'd been assigned. Dynamo bulled into the stall with pleasure and she hustled out of the way, throwing me a glare as she went.

I ignored her. Dynamo was on his toes, ready for action, and I wasn't about to get into a fight with him. Horse show rule number one: never get into a fight with Dynamo.

"The stall looks good," I commented, unsnapping the lead and stepping out, fastening up the stall chain behind me. "Really nice."

It was perfect, in fact. Deep fluffy bedding, brimful water buckets, a net of hay in the corner to keep him from leaning on the stall chain and annoying the other horses walking down the narrow aisle.

Becky nodded, her jaw still tight. She had a thin face, with a sharp nose and a pointed chin, and she seemed to jut it out when she was angry with me, which these days was most of the time.

Then Dynamo, who had been snuffling around his stall, got down to the important business of throwing himself down and rolling in the fresh clean shavings, groaning with pleasure like a pig in mud. He rubbed his head back and forth in the bedding, pine shavings clinging to his furry ears, and looked generally like a clown. I shook my head.

But then I looked back at Becky and saw that she was watching Dynamo's stall ritual with something akin to pleasure. The first smile I'd seen in a month was slowly blossoming on her face, and for a startling moment, I thought she was going to laugh.

"He loves the stall, Becky," I told her. "Thank you."

Becky considered me, her mouth turning sour again. "You're welcome," she said offhandedly, as if her effort didn't matter, as if my compliment was unimportant. "I'll start unloading the trailer."

I leaned against the wobbly paneling of the stall, making sure that Dynamo settled down to eat his hay and relax, but I couldn't help but watch Becky from afar. She had a ruthless efficiency born of many years working with horses, but she did it without any sense of fun. Like me, she had never done anything in her life but work with horses. Unlike me, her parents had a small farm and she had ridden in her own yard, and done her own chores every day. When she'd come to work for me, it was her first time working for a commercial stable. It was a dream come true for her, the beginning of her life as a professional horsewoman, or so she had said.

And now, this bad-tempered robot?

She regrets coming to work for me.

I realized it with sickening suddenness, watching her labor to muck out the trailer, wiping sweat from her brow from inside the broiling metal box. She came to work for me and changed her mind, entirely, about being a professional trainer, about her life's ambition. All the plans she had ever made, wrecked by me.

I had made her rethink everything. Not just the work—although the drudgery of it, the long days, the endless chores, and the empty bank account to show for it all didn't help. But what she thought she knew about me. The things she'd heard. The trust she imagined I'd betrayed. Becky didn't just regret coming to work for me. She was having second thoughts about being a professional horsewoman, because if it meant being a person like me, she didn't want any part of it.

That's when I started to get angry.

She was always judging me! She thought I was an idiot who couldn't run my own life without resorting to lying and cheating. She thought she could manage my stable and my horses for me with her hands tied behind her back. Becky the great barn manager, who always managed to get the job done and *still* popped out when you least expected her, when you didn't want her, when you'd just gotten the set-down of your life from a trainer you'd trusted.

And couldn't she have supported me, that awful day? Standing by the trailer, Dynamo pulling at his hay net, while I was told that I wasn't good enough. Instead, she believed everything that trainer said. And from that day forward, Becky hadn't been my friend anymore. She'd been my disappointed, disapproving guardian.

I was so sick of it. Couldn't she let this go? Pause the act, have some fun, maybe crack a few jokes with me about the woman in the neighboring stabling tent who was raking up straw in nothing but a pink sports bra, a pair of low-rise riding breeches, and beaded flip-flops? Couldn't she offer to walk the cross-country course with me, so that we could stand in the ditch under the massive Trakehner and laugh and pretend there was no chance I'd be killed out there tomorrow? Couldn't she look around and see the gorgeous horses, the dedicated people, the accomplishment of all that hard work out there in the arenas and the fields?

Couldn't she just *talk* to me once in a while?

I mean, I was all about work, of course, but one of the pleasures of stable life was having friends to talk to. I knew this from first-hand experience. When I was a kid, I used to hear the other girls talking all the time. While I was mucking their horses' stalls.

And now I wanted that for myself. I deserved it, for all the years of hard work and sacrifice that I'd given to this life, and all the years of hard work and sacrifice yet to come. Couldn't I at least have a friend to talk to that didn't walk on four legs?

No. I had to make do with Queen Becky, who thought she knew everything about me.

I watched her, eyes narrowed, while Dynamo tore into his hay net and other competitors arrived, horses in hand, bringing their own working students, their own wheelbarrows full of tack trunks and hay bales.

She must have known she was being watched, but she just kept working. She brought over the wash buckets, the Rubbermaid container of sweet feed, the baggies of premixed supplements, one for each meal. I didn't make a move to help her, new and rude behavior for me, but she didn't say a word.

She was doing her job because she had agreed to do it, and she still liked getting riding lessons from me for free, but she didn't give a damn about me.

I felt like the working student at Laurie's barn all over again, beneath the other girls' notice.

10

AND THAT WAS the rest of my day. I stewed over Becky's efficiency like it was a slap in the face, and she just got on with things, ignoring me. She moved the truck and trailer to the distant parking field. She went to Publix and brought me back a Cuban sandwich, a bag of jalapeño potato chips, and a case of drinks for the cooler. She sat with me while I ate the sandwich, the chips, and drank two Diet Cokes, and she at least seemed to listen while I shared as much gossip as I had on the arriving competitors. She announced her plans to return to the farm at three o'clock so that she could start evening chores, leaving me here to babysit Dynamo until I finally got up the courage to leave him for the night.

She did her job.

But I didn't just *want* more than a hardworking groom; I *needed* it. I needed a friend—the human kind, this time.

Dynamo ran his muzzle through my ponytail, and his short-cropped whiskers pricked at my neck. I remembered sitting like this in the paddock those first early months we had been together, back when he refused to let me catch him, before he learned to trust me, to come to me. These had been his first daring touches, the beginning of our friendship. He was my first and only partner, and it had started with his warm grass-scented breath on my shoulder.

It still gave me the same sense of wonder, the shiver of goose bumps, that it had that first night.

It had been lonely growing up, the only working student at a barn full of girls my own age who didn't have to work for a thing. The only person I'd had any sort of relationship with was Laurie. Twenty years older than me, she had worked me like a dog and had taken advantage of me, that much was for sure. But even so, we'd had a closeness that the paying boarders and students had never been able to approach. Early mornings, long days, and late nights in the barn can bring two people together, especially when they feel united against clients who are forever complaining, forever demanding, forever trying to get something for nothing. We'd shared triumphs when we'd overcome some training problem, teaching a sales horse that a liverpool wasn't going to kill him, or some lesson pony that if he bucked off a student again, we *were* going to kill him. High fives, a Diet Coke at Laurie's kitchen table (that was where the Diet Coke habit started), an occasional McDonald's run in the gleaming farm truck, these were the markers that proved Laurie was more than just my boss.

I'd assumed that I'd have that closeness with my working students, as well. I didn't expect it to turn into contempt.

But then again, no one had ever told Laurie she was in over her head while I was hiding in a trailer tack room, listening in. Even if someone had done that, wouldn't I have sided with Laurie? Wouldn't I always have put her first?

I shoved up from the tack trunk. Time to get over it. Becky wasn't here and that cross-country course wasn't going to walk itself. Usually I enjoyed a good course walk. But somehow, this time, I didn't think inspecting my first-ever Intermediate course was going to cheer me up much. I looked down at the crumpled course map in my hands. There were a lot of scary jumps out there. Not many people would be looking at them alone.

Someone once told me event riders all tackled cross-country from a place of fear. I'd scoffed. But there might be something to that. We just had to channel our fear into cold, hard logic.

I leaned down and pulled on my green Wellington boots. There was a substantial water hazard out on the course, and I would have to go wading to see how deep the drop was. I put my game face on. There was an event to win.

An hour later, brushing sticky-wet hair out of my face, I leaned against a massive log and peered over its other side. Fence 12B was not messing around.

The water glowered back at me, barely bothering to reflect the blue skies overhead. I knew what was on the bottom—packed gravel atop a plastic liner to keep the pond filled throughout the event. But I couldn't see it. The towering slash pines in this highland section of the course dropped their needles into the water, staining it a dark, opaque brown.

And that dark water sure seemed to be a long way down.

I turned around and looked back at the skinny fence before the log—12A was a narrow little rowboat, oars stashed inside, with a red flag on the right and a white flag on the left. The poles that held up the flag looked to be no more than three feet apart—just enough room for a horse to jump through, if the horse was going dead straight and true. A feat in and of itself, before the three-stride gap to the looming log and its drop on the other side.

Of course, I didn't have to take it. I could take the long way around, canter off to the right, jump through a keyhole made of brush, and swing wide to splash into the water complex over a lower drop. It would be easier, and safer. But it would also take time. And I didn't want the penalties that would come with going over the allotted time limit. Every second counted, literally, and if I was to have a chance at winning this thing, I needed to be as clean as possible.

A team of several riders came up to the skinny, shook their heads, and walked over to the second option. *Go on,* I thought, leaning as casually on the log as I could. *Take the long option. You've got all the time in the world.*

I shoved off the log and treaded carefully through the close-cropped grass to inspect the skinny boat, walking the three strides between the two fences slowly, pacing off the distance, feeling the ground. The dry start to summer meant the ground was still hard, but even so, the soft sand underneath would be worked loose by many other sets of hooves before Dynamo and I approached this complex. Slippery sand and tight turns could be hard on suspensory ligaments and tendons, and I was more afraid of Dynamo's straining something than the short route through the water.

I nodded. Short option it was. Dynamo had never been a fast horse—I couldn't waste time.

Time for the next fence. I pressed my hands together, to stop them from shaking, and went on through the field. Fear, meet logic.

* * *

I was coming back into the stabling area, mind full of distances and speeds and takeoffs and landings, when Pete Morrison stepped away from the catering tent and took me by the arm. I stopped short and glared up at him, too astonished by his touch to even say anything. He took his hand away quickly, looking apologetic—as if he couldn't quite believe he'd done it. But when he spoke, there was an urgency to his voice that matched the concern in his eyes.

"Listen," he said under his breath. "You want to watch the skinny before the water complex. I don't think many people are going to get through the left-hand approach without wiping out. It's just set up for failure."

I felt a hot flush rising across my sweaty cheeks. I met his eyes, trying not to notice the way they seemed to set my heart pounding, and concentrated on how much I didn't like him. He had everything I wanted and then some, and still he asked for more. "I disagree," I said, and shrugged, as if his intense delivery meant nothing at all to me. "And why would you be telling me, anyway? I guess you're planning on taking the left-hand route, and you don't want to give up the half-second advantage you'll have over me if I take the long route? That's the *only* advantage you'd have!"

Pete stepped back, looking confused, and I felt a stab of guilt that was equally confusing. "No, that's not it at all. I just thought—I thought it would be . . . *sporting,* I don't know. From one competitor to another. We can get along and still be competitors, right? That's one of the things that makes eventing great. We're all in this together."

"You're not telling everyone, though," I pointed out. "You didn't exactly go stand up on the jump and announce to everyone that it was a terrible combination."

He blushed beneath his tan. "I just thought . . . Look, you got me. Ever since we were at Longacres—I just—you're very talented. And you care about your horses. I like that. I like *you*. Maybe some night we could grab a beer together."

"Oh no," I said, shaking my head, tamping down the surging feeling in my chest. No men for me—especially men who rode horses, and would always think they knew better than me. Even so, it took a moment for me to get the words of refusal past my lips. "I don't . . . No . . . I don't think so. Thank you. That's very flattering. Thanks. But—no."

"Why not?" Pete looked perplexed. "Is it because of the ACE thing? You were riding beautifully, if that's what this is about. You didn't deserve that gust of wind. I felt terrible about the whole thing."

"It isn't," I admitted, although I would have liked for it to be. The truth was, I didn't really mind that he'd beaten me for the grant—not at this moment, when he was standing so close to me, anyway. "I just don't do this sort of thing," I said weakly.

"What sort of thing—socialize with other humans?" He cocked his head to one side, like a horse who has heard a candy wrapper crinkle and can't figure out where it's coming from. "Drink refreshing beverages in the company of friends? Eat delicious food someone else pays for while they tell you what a lovely rider you are? Because that's what I'd like to do with you."

And that all sounded very nice. *But.* "Well—I mean . . ." I blinked, searching for words. "I work. I work hard. And I'm tired at night. I don't go out and drink. Or hang out with people. I just sort of fall asleep. Sometimes I don't even make it off the couch."

"That's too bad," Pete said. "Maybe sometime you won't be so busy, you can give me a call, then."

Wait a minute. I narrowed my eyes. "What's *that* supposed to mean?"

Pete actually took a step backward. "What's what supposed to mean?"

"You wish I wasn't so busy? Busy is *good*. Busy means I have *business*. I have sound horses in my barn who need to be trained. If I'm not busy, doesn't that mean I'm going out of business?"

"Whoa, whoa, whoa." He gave me a lopsided, apologetic smile and I almost liked him for it. "I don't mean anything like that at all. I see you riding straight to the top—you're a born competitor. I just meant . . ." He softened his expression, and the little blush returned to his cheeks. I swallowed and ignored the extra thump in my heartbeat. "I just meant, if you ever have an evening free, and you'd like to talk more . . . just give me a call."

I didn't have a ready response for that. What was I supposed to do? I had invested a lot of energy into disliking Pete Morrison. Him and his ACE win! Him and his new sponsorship! Winning things over me because he was a guy. And because he was luckier than I was.

But so is everyone, I reminded myself. *The trick is to succeed in spite of that.* But I wouldn't do it if I wasted time getting distracted by some rich kid who looked good in riding breeches.

"I feel like you won't be hurting for company after that ACE press release," I said. "Calling you eventing's most promising up-and-coming rider."

"Everyone there was promising. You, especially." He paused. "Also, I didn't know your name was Juliet."

"It's *always* Jules," I corrected him. "Juliet is a ridiculous name."

"It's pretty," Pete said softly. "It's romantic."

The perfect response, that smooth bastard. Dr. Em had been right about him. "I'm not, unfortunately," I replied, although the flush on my cheeks probably told him otherwise. "Thanks for the advice on the jumping route. And . . . good luck out there." The last words were nearly under my breath, but at least I said them.

And before he could say anything else to stop me, or brush my arm with his hand again, or do anything else to make me regret my prohibition on men, and on him in particular, I turned on my heel and started back for the stabling. The only male that mattered in my life was nibbling at his hay net back in the barn, and we had some communing to do before tomorrow's dressage and cross-country.

In the sport of eventing, the first phase of competition is the dressage test, in which a rider is expected to perform the nearly impossible trick of asking an incredibly fit and very enthusiastic horse to put his head down and behave himself like a gentleman (or lady) through a flatwork course of circles, transitions, and changes of pace, while a judge marks each movement on its quality and the horse's obedience. Dressage done right can be a joy to behold and an ecstatic experience to ride, but in all truthfulness, for most eventers, it is also just an experience to get through in order to enjoy the next two phases: the cross-country course, and the show-jumping course. Riders (and their horses) are not in eventing for the dressage. We are in it for the thrills that come after.

The Advanced riders were riding their tests first thing this morning. One might think that being at the top of the game could get you a nice late spot, so you could sleep in, have a cup of coffee, watch the news, mentally relax. But no, the big riders had to get up bright and early for their 8 A.M. ride times. So much for the privilege of being the best.

It was a little after eight and I had been at the horse park since six thirty, unable to sleep, nervous as a novice before her first Pony Club rally, but anxious as always to look the part of calm, cool, put-together professional. I took care of Dynamo myself, leaving Becky to deal with the farm, and then went to watch the dressage in my breeches and argyle knee socks, ratty running shoes on my feet in place of my polished dress boots. The morning humidity made my loose hair cling to my neck, and I wrapped it into a messy knot as I walked to the fiber-footing arenas where the dressage tests would be running all day long.

A noble bay horse was trotting around the ring looking like the very picture of patience. It was obvious from his wide eyes and working, open mouth that he didn't want to be there, but he, like his rider in a sober black coat, knew it was the price of admission for the fun to come. The same went for the handful of horse people standing around with arms folded or sipping at their coffees while watching the rounds. The only spectators were other riders like me, trying to fill the hours until their own ride times. There was a fence to lean on, and a few trees, but no seating or little grandstand like the show-jumping arena had. No one came for the dressage.

Later, of course, everyone would show up for the cross-country phase. The public areas would be crowded with 4-H kids and Pony Clubbers hoping to see their favorite riders, and Western riders in cowboy hats and boots who just wanted to see what the crazies were up to with their nutty eventing game. People who didn't event could never stop talking about how wild event riders were. How dangerous their jumps were. The huge log fences. The hair-raising twists and turns into dark paths in the woods. The drops into pools of water. The sheer *speed* on the long galloping lanes, where we would urge our horses into racing stride to make the optimum time. They didn't know they were missing out on the best feeling in riding. All they knew was brave horses and crazy riders made for some kind of spectacle, and Sunshine State's challenging course drew a crowd from around Florida.

But all that was later on, waiting for us this afternoon. During these Advanced level dressage tests, the real excitement was just beyond the quiet tension of the show ring, where the shenanigans were on in the nearby warm-up arena.

Riders there were putting their excited horses through their paces and dealing with all kinds of hijinks—bucking and sunfishing and rearing and bolting—*all* the good rodeo stunts. The merely nervous horses fed off the energy of the mostly naughty horses and behaved badly. The naughty horses fed off the energy of the nervous horses and become utter miscreants. It was one of the most dangerous places on earth, a warm-up arena full of fit, excited horses going every which way.

I watched the show for a few minutes, my eyes drawn away from the tense but obedient bay gelding in the arena by all that frenzied activity next door. A dappled gray startled at a butterfly, just like Twin One would, which in turn spooked a wide-eyed chestnut, who spun around on his hind legs, reared, and leaped forward, his rider clinging to the sparse tendrils of his braided mane like a burr tangled up in a tail. I smothered a laugh and looked back toward the competition arena. I wondered how long the bay gelding, who was standing stock-still for his rider's final salute, had been worked that morning. A seven-minute warm-up, or much longer? All of it would affect his energy and stamina on the cross-country course.

Then I noticed a lone rider near the in-gate, reins slack on her horse's lathered neck, gazing at her smartphone with a look of deep concentration. In all likelihood, she was studying the moves of her dressage test one last time. The quiet pair were utterly still, in stark contrast to the pandemonium in the warm-up arena.

Slyly, I cast my gaze just beyond the rider and nodded to myself when I saw the photographer lurking behind a tree nearby, surreptitiously snapping shots of the quiet rider's idle. She'd probably be on the cover of a magazine next month. The classic candid shot of twenty-first-century horsemanship. I fingered the ancient phone in my pocket. I needed an upgrade. I could use a magazine cover.

I tore my eyes away from the rider and watched a few tests from alongside the arena railing. Nearby, a knot of grooms, girls mostly my own age, had clustered. Identically accessorized with halters over their shoulders, carrots in their back pockets, and bottled water in hand, they whispered nervously during rounds, all the while keeping one eye on the current competitor and one on their own riders in the warm-up arena, waiting for commands.

The riders paused before they rode into the arena, kicking their feet free from their stirrups, waiting for the groom to run the cloth over dusty riding boots, sweat-foamed reins, saliva-stained mouths. A few pulled wet sponges out of buckets and rinsed the horse's mouth out, racetrack style. Whenever I saw a groom use this move, I watched their rider more carefully, suspecting they had learned to ride Thoroughbreds at the racetrack and brought this trick back to eventing with them. Thoroughbreds were my business, and anything I could pick up about the way older Thoroughbred pros handled their mounts would be of use to me in the future. I often suspected I should have spent some time at the racetrack before I set up my own business, but I was too impatient for that. Life was *now*. Eventing was *now*. I'd learn as I went.

When a groom was summoned, she did not return to the group; she stood nervously by the in-gate, watching her rider's test. A bad ride would mean a very long weekend for her. A good ride might mean a nice dinner tonight. Maybe the Cracker Barrel out by the interstate, before they drove back to their farm or settled in at the Ramada. It was a tough life waiting on a trainer. I didn't wish for a second that I could trade places with these girls and go back to that lady-in-waiting status, even if I was jealous of their camaraderie.

Laurie had offered to help me get a groom position with a trainer. "I can't guarantee it will be in Florida," she'd said. "But if you're bound and determined to be an event trainer, being a working student and grooming for a big-name trainer is the way to go."

I'd just spent nearly a decade as *her* working student and groom. Now she was telling me to go do it somewhere else? She had a lot of nerve, I'd thought.

"What am I going to do with another trainer that I haven't already done with you?" I'd asked indignantly. "I've trained dozens of horses, that you've sold on for a profit. I've taught some of your *advanced* students. I've gotten Dynamo all the way from racetrack-broke to competing Prelim—*alone,* after you've gone home for the night, after every other horse has been taken care of. I can do this on my own. I already have."

She'd shaken her head, and she'd sighed, and she'd said it was my choice in the end. "I'll send you clients if I think you can handle the horse," she said when I told her I was using my college fund to buy a little parcel called Green Winter Farm, and that I was moving to Ocala to start my own business. "I'll try to help, but you're a kid, Jules. Be careful out there on your own."

The horse in the ring swished his tail and kicked out his left hind leg when the rider's left spur touched him, asking for a flying lead change. The closest groom, a girl with dirt on the seat of her jeans and a big green mark on her sleeve that indicated the horse also bit and knocked people down, in addition to bucking in the dressage ring, put her face in her hands. She was as embarrassed as if she'd been the one to kick in front of the judge.

I'd come over hoping to engage in conversation with a big-name trainer or two, maybe be seen by a blogger from one of the eventing websites as I threw my head back in laughter at something that one of last year's Olympics squad had just whispered in my ear. Events were when old friends got back together, after months back at the farm, or on the road, and hugged each other and asked about each other's horses and exclaimed over their new riding boots.

But I didn't have any old friends to hug. Except for the chestnut waiting for me back at the stabling area.

I set off back for the stabling, anticipating a quiet hugging session with my favorite horse. But when I got back, the stables were anything but quiet.

I could hear the shouting from a distance, two girls shrieking at each other. Horses were peering from their stalls, ears pricked, looking for the source of the sound. It wasn't the sort of thing they often heard at home, since most of the fights between horse girls are too passive-aggressive for full-on shouting matches. Besides, shouting might spook the horses. But horse shows can spark a long-suppressed flame.

The first thing I saw as I turned the corner was that Dynamo's stable row seemed to be party central. People were standing all around the entrance to his aisle, knotted together in little groups, looking excited and disapproving and titillated all at once. In fact, I realized, my heart suddenly thudding with shock, the horse standing in front of the barn was Dynamo.

Why would everyone be staring at Dynamo? Had he kicked someone? Had Becky done something stupid, let him get too close to another horse? If he had kicked some big-name trainer's horse and done damage I was going to be sued out of business. I was going to be sued right back to my parents' house.

Then a groom in the crowd shifted to the left, and I saw that they weren't looking at Dynamo. They were looking at Becky and Lacey, who were facing off, fists clenched, in front of my superstar's astonished face.

11

CHEEKS BURNING, I set off to tear the two cats apart. The ranks were drawing closed as more and more horrified/delighted competitors and crew were stepping up to see the show, but with a little shoving, I made my way toward them. There they were: the two girls screaming at each other, and in between the two of them, standing alert, eyes warily on the loud humans, was my horse. My delicate, nervous, pride-and-joy, hopes-and-dreams horse. My heart. And his lead shank was gripped tightly in Lacey's hand.

What the *hell*? I stopped in confusion and a spectator stepped in front of me, blocking my view again. Someone muttered, "I'd hate to be the trainer at this barn," and someone else tittered.

"Girls!" I shouted, giving myself away as the unlucky trainer. There were wide eyes, heads turned in my direction, snickers and whispers. I ignored them. Dynamo was all that mattered.

As I pushed past the spectators, little groups of competitors and grooms carrying brushes in totes, wearing their uniform of breeches and knee-high boot socks, someone tripped on a bucket and fell back against me. I stumbled, lost my own footing, and lurched hard into a man ready for competition in full-seat breeches and black dressage coat. His arms went around me automatically, propping me up against his chest.

I glanced up and saw him looking down at me, eyebrows arched, and somewhere in my flustered, horror-struck brain, I recognized those familiar blue eyes. The sensation of being held against him was like a jolt of electricity right up my spine.

For the slightest of moments, I was frozen in place. I felt my lips fall open, though I had nothing to say. Then I turned back to the girls and the horse just a few feet away, and I forgot all about Pete Morrison and his stupid blue eyes. I was going to kill those girls.

Lacey and Becky saw me coming for them at the same time. They were a study in opposite reactions. Lacey looked measurably relieved, as if I'd right some awful wrong. Becky, on the other hand, looked dangerously furious, as if I had caused the whole mess in the first place.

"Take the horse to the barn," I hissed before either one could say anything. "That's enough for the peanut gallery, *children*."

Lacey nodded, still looking way too pleased with herself. It was obvious she had been banking on my siding with her, and that I had just confirmed it. Becky looked away from me, glaring at Dynamo's receding hindquarters before she followed them into the tent. I put my shoulders back and my chin up, a wall against the fascinated stares of the crowd behind me, and went after them.

There was virtually nowhere for a private conversation; the end stall I had been so happy to obtain kept us well within earshot of the people outside. So instead I just followed Lacey and Dynamo into his stall, gesturing with a tilted head for Becky to join us. She did so with evident unwillingness, and we stood quietly for a moment in the little ten-by-ten-foot stall, while Dynamo picked moodily at the bits of hay left in the corner. I took deep breaths, trying to quell the nearly insatiable urge to scream.

Finally, I was able to speak. "Okay, girls," I growled from between gritted teeth. "What the hell?"

And it all spilled out, first from the outraged Becky, then from the self-righteous Lacey, and finally from the two of them together, cutting each other off, bickering in tense, hissing voices. My own little den of snakes.

It all turned out to be a power struggle, as best as I could piece the two stories together. Becky had been sitting on the tack trunk in front of the stall, polishing my dress boots, and Lacey had shown up, said hello as she walked past, and taken Dynamo out of his stall without Becky's permission.

Becky recited the chain of events primly, her lips tight and her voice steady with conviction, while I shushed Lacey. Then Lacey went back in on the defense.

"He's not your horse," Lacey hissed at Becky. "I don't need your permission. And anyway, you were busy. He needs to be taken out of his stall, so what do you care if I walk him? It's good for him!"

Becky shook her head. "No, you can't just take him out. He's my responsibility. I'm the groom—he's *my* job—"

I realized, with a sinking sensation, that this was entirely my fault. I'd been bitching about Becky to Lacey for weeks. I'd been catty and rude, and stripped Becky of what little respect she was due as my working student. She'd been awful to me, that was true, but I was her boss. Wasn't I supposed to be the bigger one in this relationship?

I blushed to think of how badly I'd behaved, and I was thankful that the dimness of the tent hid the color in my cheeks.

And then, looking at Becky's pinched face, her downturned mouth, her angry eyes darting from me to Lacey, to Dynamo and back again, I felt rage rise up again.

Becky and her distant silences, her skeptical glances, her put-upon air, letting me know that she thought her boss was an idiot. Why did Becky get to call the shots? She thought she was protecting Dynamo, and me, but all she was really doing was bringing me down, reminding me that I wasn't who I wanted to be yet.

I walked out of the stall, and sat down heavily on the tack trunk out front. I leaned my head back, letting the stall bars cradle my scalp, and sighed. A glance to the right told me that the peanut gallery had gone back to their chores. The event must go on; ride times waited for no man. I closed my eyes. I had to ride a dressage test in less than an hour, and I was in no state of mind for such concentration.

Becky and Lacey came timidly out of the stall, their expressions now similarly worried and confused. Lacey wound the lead shank around her hand, coiling the leather in circles. Becky snapped up the stall chain behind her and put her hands behind her back, like a child waiting for a punishment.

I closed my eyes. "Lacey," I said woodenly. "You need to defer to Becky when we're at an event and I'm not around." Lacey opened her mouth to argue and closed it again when I frowned at her, thankfully copping on that I wanted her to keep quiet while Becky was around. "Becky," I went on. "You can't cause a scene in front of all those people. It was just Lacey. You should have waited for me and told me that you weren't comfortable with the situation. Or even texted. You made us look second rate."

Becky muttered something that sounded suspiciously like . . . but no, she wouldn't have said that. "Excuse me?" I asked, incredulous.

"I said, we *are* second rate!" she snapped, folding her arms across her chest. "We're not big shots. I've been working my ass off for you because you *might* be somebody someday, if you don't kill yourself and Dynamo first, but you act like you're winning at Kentucky already." She shook her head. "It's ridiculous. And it's *dangerous.*"

Beside her, Lacey's mouth had dropped open, and the coils of leather were falling from her arm.

I felt a pulsing in my forehead. Did she want to do this right now? Fine. "You work your ass off for *me*?" I stood up from the tack trunk slowly, eyeing Becky like a snake in the hay shed. "Are you kidding? Becky, believe it or not, you have it easy with me. You only work four days a week! No other trainer gives time off like that. And sure, yeah, I'm not a big shot. *Yet.* That's all about to change. And I need you on board with that. Because when we have a barn full of horses and we're competing half a dozen of them every weekend, you don't want to miss out because you weren't on my team when I needed someone. You got that?"

Becky paused before she nodded, sullenly. It was a long enough pause to tell me what I needed to know. I could see the decision in her eyes, in the set of her jaw: she had made up her mind before I even came back and broke up her stupid fight. Maybe even before Lacey had pulled the horse out of the stall. That was probably just the cue she had been waiting for. Well, that was just fine by me. But she wasn't walking out of here while I had an event.

"You have the weekend to think it over," I told her. "In the meantime, don't draw any more attention to yourself. We shouldn't be noticed anywhere but in competition. Got it? Please, the two of you, have Dynamo ready in fifteen minutes." And I turned and walked away before either girl could say another word. I needed a Diet Coke and a moment to run through my dressage test in my head. I wasn't going to let Becky take this event away from me.

I tried not to spare Becky another thought that weekend if I didn't have to. And I didn't, most of the time. She knew the routine and procedures of an event: when I needed a bottle of Gatorade, how to put on the ice boots after Dynamo's cross-country round, where in the trailer I'd stashed my black helmet cover after the last jumper show we'd gone to. Whenever I needed to throw my reins to someone, or whenever a water bucket needed filling, or whenever I realized I hadn't eaten a proper meal in a day and a half and needed a granola bar to stave off a fainting spell, Becky was there, silent and efficient as always, to make it happen.

Becky might have been good, but for all that, she still didn't give a damn about me, and I knew it. Lacey was my friend, there for everything else I needed, chattering when I needed a distraction and quiet when I needed to think. And oh, how I needed to think.

About how to liven up Dynamo's walk-to-canter transitions in the dressage test. About how to make it through the left-hand option of the water complex without finding myself with a mouthful of water or a handful of time penalties. And we *did* manage it, one of only six pairs who made it around that option fast and dry. Pete Morrison made it, too, which made me doubly suspicious of his warning not to try the fast route.

About how to get a clean round in the show jumping, the last phase at this event, and maybe, just maybe, move up in the placings. Tenth after dressage became fourth after cross-country, and suddenly I was within grasping distance of first place. I just needed the three riders ahead of me to make mistakes on their jumping round . . . and I needed to get around flawlessly. I gave Dynamo a sparing, careful warm-up, saving up all his energy reserves for the final test.

And when we did get that double clear round, cantering meticulously around the oval arena and negotiating the course of wobbly painted poles, so different from the logs and barriers in the great open stretches of field and twisty paths of forest that made up yesterday's cross-country course, it was Lacey that I screamed to as we went jogging out of the arena, the crowd clapping for the upstart newcomer who had just clinched the Intermediate Division blue ribbon on her first ride at this level. Unheard of, but that was what I was here for, the winner no one saw coming.

It was Becky who stepped up dutifully and clutched Dynamo's reins in one hand, hurrying with the other to loosen his noseband, free up his jaw, and improve his breathing. But it was Lacey who I leaned down to hug from the saddle.

There was no room for anything but jubilation after this weekend, after this ride, after those final moments aboard Dynamo, leaning down over his hot, wet neck, gloved hands pressing down on popping veins as he soared over the fences with such finesse, sitting back down in the saddle to bring his power and impulsion back under control so that we could wheel and be ready for the next fence without losing too much ground and racking up time penalties—he was a star, an absolute star, and he was *mine*. I found him, I saved him, I made him. And winning with him was so very sweet—I just wanted to share it with a friend.

So I turned to Lacey, hugging and squealing, while Becky silently offered Dynamo a drink from a bucket of water.

But as I straightened, out of the corner of my eye, I saw a familiar face, eyebrow quirked once again in my direction, as a man on a tall, liver-chestnut mare, red ribbon already in hand, watched my every move.

Hours after my greatest triumph to date, I was sitting with Marcus on my deck. A sadly neglected space, the broad wooden patio was really more of a storage area for my rusty grill, a few dead-looking turnout halters, and some water buckets with broken handles that I was sure I would find a use for yet. If I leaned forward and peered around the corner of the house, I could see Dynamo's silhouette when he leaned out of his stall window, watching his friends out in their paddocks. He was in for the night, legs done up in standing wraps and poultice beneath brown paper bags from Publix, on forced rest after the exertion of the event. He would rather have been outside, but that wasn't his choice.

He turned his head, and I saw his star in the moonlight, an irregular oval between his eyes, a jagged stripe down to his nose, shining iridescently beneath Florida's absurdly large moon. My heart rose into my throat at the sight of it. My sweet boy. He had done it. He had brought home the blue, proved his worth, proved our worth.

Dynamo turned his head back toward the paddocks and whickered, a lilting sound that carried through the humid night. A few horses out in the fields called back. Mickey, notably. I smiled. The gray horse was settling in nicely, his head wound scabbing over, his good spirits undiminished by the daily scrubbing and picking and anointing that he had to suffer through in the wash rack. I was growing so fond of him, and despite all my resolve to the contrary, I couldn't wait to get on his back. As soon as his head was healed enough for a bridle to go over his ears and sit on his poll, I was going to climb on board and see if he felt as smooth as he looked.

Maybe he'd be the next big horse. Maybe in two or three years, I'd have two big horses. Maybe I'd have three or four. We were going places. Today had cemented that. Today everyone had looked at me. Today everyone had wondered who the hell I was.

"It's beginning, Dynamo," I said into the night, but my horse was done socializing. He retreated into the darkness of his stall, back to his hay, or for a few hours of rest. I ought to do the same, but I was still too keyed up. I ought to get a beer, I thought, slow it down a bit. But I was comfortable. It was past the mosquitoes' bedtimes, the tree frogs' too. Aside from an occasional truck on the county highway beyond my driveway, there wasn't a single sound. I hated to break the peace of the country night.

Inevitably, though, my thoughts drifted to Becky. And then I wished I'd gotten up and cracked that beer.

Dynamo and I had done it, but Becky had done it, too. Should I have been surprised, that she hadn't stayed to celebrate the win with me tonight? She hadn't stayed to have dinner with me in months. And tonight, when she told me she wouldn't be coming back on Tuesday, either, I'd almost seen a ghost of a smile flit across her face. She'd taken the weekend to think about it, all right.

I stood up and went for the beer, the storm door creaking behind me. Marcus, tail wagging, followed at my heels. He brought a bone back out with him and we sat on the steps together. The night was not roused by my brief absence. A frog peeped lazily, a whip-poor-will from the pine forest across the highway sang out. I took a long pull from the bottle, savoring the icy bitterness against my throat, waiting for the bubbles to calm my overexcited brain, to give me a sense of perspective. It wasn't my fault Becky didn't like me, didn't believe in me, didn't need me. A few more gulps and I'd remember: I didn't need Becky. She was just the first in a long line of girls who would come and go, with their shiny new boots ready to be scarred and cracked, with their shiny new hands ready to grow callouses, with their shiny heads ready to be filled with all the horse care and riding knowledge I could stuff into them.

And she wasn't going to tell anyone about Sandra Holborn, and the signature. Even if she did, I didn't even care. I'd won at Intermediate, the first time out. People would probably be *more* impressed with me if they knew that I'd been turned away and wouldn't let that stop me.

Well, some people, anyway.

It was over now. Everything Sandra Holborn had said to me while I stood next to Dynamo, my hand on his neck, pressing against him for courage while she casually broke my heart. Telling me to get another opinion if I really thought I belonged in the ACE auditions! As if I had another two hundred dollars to drop on a riding lesson with another Advanced level rider. Ocala was full of them, but I didn't have the budget to bounce from trainer to trainer until I got the answer I needed.

I just needed one signature to get into the ACE audition, and she refused to give it to me. Based on a single moment in time, a few bad setups for jumps. No one had gotten hurt, and our ability should have been obvious. She'd been wrong.

I made it halfway down the bottle of beer, regarded it, set it down. The whip-poor-will had flown closer; it was in the turkey oaks on the other side of the parking lot now. *Whip-poor-will,* it called, and the little chirp the bird made after every cry was like a vicious little chuckle. Poor Will.

Marcus dropped his bone, hopped down the porch steps, ears flopping with every bounce, and went trotting off into the night, nose to the ground. The world just kept on turning when you were a fat beagle. He had never had much interest in Becky anyway, and the feeling had been mutual. What kind of horsewoman wasn't a dog person?

I looked up at the moon. The whip-poor-will relocated to beneath the stumpy orange tree at the far end of the house. His call was piercingly loud now. It was the sound of old Florida, the sound of my childhood. I wasn't nostalgic for much, but hearing that whip-poor-will made me remember nights just like this at the farm back in Punta Gorda, after I had taken a riding lesson and put the lesson pony away, long after the other girls had gone home. Laurie already in her house, done for the night. My bike leaning against the barn wall, near the empty picnic table where the girls cleaned their tack and ate potato chips and gossiped while I was mucking stalls. I'd been a little kid when it had all started. How old was I now? I could barely remember. Twenty-one, twenty-two? I felt like a hundred. And still too busy, and not good enough, to make friends with the people I wanted to like me.

And that look I'd gotten from Pete as we'd finished our round and clinched first place. So serious. What had *that* been about?

I finished the beer and called Marcus back to the house. God knew it was past my bedtime.

Once in the house, though, I felt restless all over again. I roamed around the living room, the kitchen, the office, peering into dark shadows, looking for things that weren't there. Marcus padded after me wearily, his jaunty hound's tail at half-mast, a look of solemn duty on his face.

I went to the kitchen window and leaned my head against the glass, damp with the air-conditioning's chill. The orange globe of the barn light illuminated Dynamo's empty paddock, and I knew what I needed.

In the barn, Dynamo was waiting for me, his ears pricked and his head over his Dutch door, silhouetted against the light. I savored his straight Thoroughbred profile, his sharp ears, his teacup chin, the way his forelock floated above his eyes. And then I walked up to him and let him sink his great head into my arms, pressing his forehead against my chest.

We stood like that for goodness knows how long, my cheek pressed close to his poll, the sharp hairs of his forelock scratching at my nose. He was warm, and alive, and real, the most warm and alive and real thing I had ever felt in my life. More than a horse, more than a person, more even than a faithful fat beagle—Dynamo was vividly himself, and totally mine. I closed my eyes, my fingers tingling along his cheekbones, in the soft fur beneath his jawbone, and felt him breathe against my stomach.

Finally, he let his breath flutter through his nostrils, gently signaling that the embrace was over, and carefully lifted his head from my arms. I raised my head and let him play his muzzle along my forehead, wiggling his upper lip along the loose locks of hair that had slipped from my ponytail, tickling at my skin until goose bumps raised along my neck and arms. I turned around and let him work his lips along my shoulders, massaging at my back and up to the nape of my neck, until the teeth came out and he began to nibble along my ponytail and pull at my T-shirt, forgetting that I wasn't a horse, too. When his teeth finally pinched a hunk of flesh

I jumped away with a shout, and Dynamo threw up his head as if he didn't know what to do with me.

I cupped his chin in my fingers and kissed him on his outraged nose. "I wish I was a horse," I told him. "We could groom each other all day long, and I wouldn't even mind if you bit me like that."

He whuffed hot horse breath in my face, and I laughed, feeling ten times lighter. "Why do I sit alone in my house when I have you out here to play with?"

Dynamo pulled his chin back from my hands and took a step back into the stall. Then he turned his head away from me, looked back out toward the paddocks where the other horses grazed, and whinnied. From the distance, I heard Daisy's lilting neigh in reply, and Passion's sharp, shrill shriek. A few others joined into the chorus, filling the night with rumbling horse song, and my smile faded just a bit. I folded my arms across my chest, suddenly feeling a bit of a chill in the damp night. "That's why," I said, nodding resignedly.

I wasn't a horse. No matter how hard I might like to pretend. But Dynamo was still my people.

I gave Dynamo a final stroke between the eyes, on his nobbly-edged star, and left him there in the barn. He neighed after me as I turned the corner. "You can go out with your friends tomorrow," I told him. "Stay inside tonight and rest." And I went back to the house and climbed into bed, to the infinite pleasure of Marcus.

12

LACEY HAD BEEN my sole working student for two weeks when it happened. The big moment—the one I'd been waiting for.

My phone was humming away industriously, wiggling its way across the kitchen counter as if carried away with its own importance. Lately, Lacey had been picking it up and pretending she was my secretary. She had a globe's worth of mock foreign accents, all of them equally pathetic, stored up for just this cause, and fortunately the poor quality of cell phone reception in the rolling hills of Marion County was enough to disguise the deception from our clientele who had actually *been* to some of these countries she was so glibly mocking.

But at this particular moment, she was busy at the stove, making us some eggs for our midmorning breakfast. Breakfast was a new word in my vocabulary. Apparently, it meant a meal you could eat in the morning to stave off starvation before your 2 P.M. lunch eaten standing up over the kitchen sink. Lacey had somehow managed to add it to my schedule, and I liked it. It wasn't the only change my new working student had brought into my life. The girl was efficient in an entirely different way from mirthless, nose-to-the-grindstone Becky. She got stuff done and she bossed me around to make it happen, but always with a grin on her irrepressible face. It was only 10 A.M. and somehow we were done with morning chores and I'd ridden two horses already. I was even toying with the idea of moving our morning start time to seven thirty. Lacey hated early mornings as much as I did.

"The barn sucks at seven," she would announce with her usual eloquence. "It would be better at seven thirty. When, you know, the sun is up?" And I had to admit, she had a definite point.

But we ended up doing more work in the heat when we started later, and I wasn't spending my day in the barn with a fan on me the way Miss Lacey was. I was out in the arena, under the full sun, wearing black riding boots and a black riding helmet. So the decision was still up in the air.

Now I snatched up the dancing phone and trilled, "This is Jules!" with all the pent-up glee of a woman who has done half a day's work and is about to be fed a hot breakfast that someone else has cooked for her.

"Jules! You sound *wonderful*!"

My overall sense of well-being was so great that I was only a little annoyed to hear Mickey's owner from Michigan on the other end. She called to check in on Mickey every few days, and I was running out of ways to say, "Mickey's just fine. Wishes he was working, though!" Couldn't the woman take a hint?

"Well, hello, Eileen, how nice to hear from you!" I said with exaggerated cheer, and by the stove, I saw Lacey's shoulders shaking as she suppressed her laughter. "I hope everything is good?"

As usual, I felt a pit in my stomach while I waited for her to say, "Just checking on my boy!" One of these calls might be to tell me she was moving Mickey at last. Eventually, she'd have to make a decision about his trainer. And what if it wasn't me?

"Jules, I have the most wonderful news," she said.

The pit in my stomach opened up into a massive sinkhole. The midsummer sunshine, dancing on the table between little fingers of palm frond shadow, seemed overly bright, and I found myself wishing for a nice gray rain cloud, bringing a washout, an afternoon in bed.

"Oh," I said. "Great."

"You won't believe it, Jules!" Eileen exclaimed. I held the phone a little farther from my ear. "I've just been talking to my friend Carrie. You must know her. Carrie Donnelly—"

"Carrie Donnelly?" I interrupted, unable to stop myself. "Carrie Donnelly who owns Donegal Seamus and Lucky You?" At the stove, Lacey stopped giggling and was standing utterly still over her smoking pan.

"Yes, that's her! What fun, do you know her? She was my roommate in college . . . we studied English literature at Sweet Briar. Total waste, of course, but we had the *best* time. This one time we snuck out to the stable after midnight . . . Oh, I won't waste your time. But she's a doll. You must know her. She's been in Florida every winter the past five years."

"I—um—we've met a few times . . ." I was lying.

"Oh, *good*, well, I was talking to her after your nice win at Sunshine State a couple weeks back—that was your first Intermediate, right? I thought so. Congratulations on winning your first time out at that level! And on such a great score! Practically unheard of! Anyway, Carrie and I have been talking about where to send

Mickey, and—oh, maybe I didn't tell you, but Carrie's actually his half owner, she's the one who first saw him at Turfway Park last fall—anyway, dear, we thought we might leave him with you. To compete this winter. Would you be interested in that?"

I was not breathing. My heart was not beating. And the phone was trembling dangerously in my bloodless fingers. I felt my mouth gaping open like a fish's, and Lacey had slowly turned around and was staring at me with alarm, the greasy spatula raised in her right hand. She should slap me in the face with it, I thought. Or crack me over the head with that cast-iron frying pan. Because this couldn't be true. And I knew it, and she knew it, so we were both trapped in the same impossible dream.

Carrie Donnelly, heiress to a food company fortune. Carrie Donnelly, the wealthy benefactress of three lucky event riders on the United States Equestrian Team. Carrie Donnelly, who not co-incidentally owned three of the top-ten event horses in the country. Carrie Donnelly, whose horse Donegal Seamus won the Kentucky Three-Day Event last year, whose horse Lucky You went to the last Olympics and brought home the individual silver medal, whose horse Lord Melbourne won the Advanced division at the Sunshine State event while I was busy taking home Intermediate.

Carrie Donnelly was half owner of a horse in my barn. And she was going to give the ride to me.

"Jules? Are you there?"

"Oh, I'm sorry, Eileen . . ." I tried to pull my thoughts together enough to speak a coherent sentence. Something dignified and pro-fessional, something that wasn't just *"Yippeeeeeee!"*

Lacey sat down across the table from me, dropping two plates of slightly burned eggs and jaggedly buttered toast between us. The plates clattered when they hit the wooden table, and I gave her a fierce look, trying to send the message, *Life-changing conversation going on here!* via furrowed eyebrows. She folded her hands in her lap obediently. We had gotten pretty good at mental telepathy.

I took a deep breath and managed to speak in a remarkably steady voice. "Yes, Eileen, I would love to take him on. I think Mickey's an amazing horse. He hasn't been doing anything but standing around and eating, but you can tell that he has a good mind and a great physique." *Physique.* Like he was a male model. Ugh. Could I not even speak properly now, like a horse trainer? But it was so hard to concentrate enough to even form words. My mind was sparking in every direction, like a transformer struck by lightning. I could practically see the blue and white explosions in whatever part of my brain was designated to picture the *Future* and *Possibility* and *Plans.*

And sweet, sweet *Ambition*, the fuel to every move I made.

"Oh, good," Eileen said, sounding relieved. "I'm glad you'll take him on." As if there was some possibility that I might have turned her down. Eileen lived in a fantasy world, and I envied her. "Well, I'll tell Carrie we're all set. I know he's been getting fat on you while we made up our minds, but this will be good. He needed that time off from the racetrack, anyway. His last race was in August last year. But he's been started over small jumps and he knows the basics, so you can start just as soon as you like and put him into competition when you feel he's ready. Send me the training contract and I'll get it signed."

Somehow, I managed to tell her I'd get right on it. Somehow, I managed to tell her thanks. Somehow, I managed to hit the End button on the phone with my trembling fingers. Then I set it down carefully on the table and looked at Lacey. She looked pinched and white, rather as if she might have stopped breathing some time ago.

"Thanks for the eggs!" I told her, and started dumping hot sauce on them.

"What's going on?" she gasped. "Tell me what just happened!"

I scooped up a bite and talked around my mouthful. "What did it sound like? These eggs are awesome. Bit burned, but I like the crispy parts." I spit out a shard of eggshell. That wasn't the crispy part I meant.

"It *sounded* like Carrie Donnelly bought you a horse to ride. Like Mickey is Carrie Donnelly's horse, which . . . that just can't be true."

"Why not? He's a nice horse. You've seen him move in the pasture."

"That's true." She considered this. "And you're always talking about how much you like him. I just never thought of him as . . . But how can you be eating *eggs* right now? This is incredible!"

"Sure is, and oh my *God*, Lacey . . . this is it!" I dropped the cool veneer, as fun as it had been to torture her, and threw down my fork, and we started dancing around the room, our feet heavy on the hollow floors of the double-wide trailer.

M Y printer was rattling when I came back into the house a little while later, drenched in sweat from riding the Twins and in search of Diet Coke to refill the tack room mini fridge. I went into the office and saw a cascade of paper spilling down from the printer and pooling on the moss-green carpet.

"What the hell?" I muttered.

"Look at it!" Lacey yelled from the kitchen.

I picked up a sheet and saw my email address at the top. "Are you on my laptop?"

"Yes," she said. "Someone has to keep up with your business."

I didn't remember giving her the password, but she'd probably leaned over my shoulder. I shrugged and picked up the rest of the printouts, studying them, and I couldn't help but smile.

It was Mickey's life history.

I hadn't known anything about him other than that he'd been a racehorse, and then hung out in Eileen's backyard for a while, her niece be-bopping around on him and jumping little crossrails, before she sent him to Florida to get serious. I gathered up the papers and spread them out on the cluttered desk, taking in the old vet reports, the racing record, the Jockey Club registration, the scanned photos of his clumsy first attempts at jumping fences.

For all the paperwork, the information was spare. His registered name was Danger Mouse; he won three races as a three-year-old, none as a four-year-old, and retired as a sound five-year-old. Now six, he was green as grass, but sound as a dollar. The paperwork assured me of that. My own knowledge told me he was possessed of the athletic potential and the mind to go to the top. To jump the moon. I studied the jumping photos, squinting at the bad print job, taking in his square knees, his tight fetlocks, his pricked ears, his eager eyes. And if my own knowledge wasn't enough to assure me, the bold signature of Carrie Donnelly on the scanned training contract certainly did.

For a few minutes I sat there on the stained carpet, looking over the forms and photos as if they held some key. I'd been given a gift, I'd been given a second chance after losing the ACE grant to Peter Morrison. Now I had to do everything right.

Outside, thunder rumbled, a low echoing growl that shook the windows in their frames.

I threw down the papers and ran back outside. I still had three more horses to get on today. And that didn't include Mickey. Not yet.

B ut it rained.
 And it rained.
 And it rained.

"A deluge," Lacey said morosely, letting the blinds drop back into place. She turned away from the living room window and threw herself on the couch. "We're going to wash away. Does this trailer float?"

"It's a mobile home, not a boat." I sighed, putting down an event calendar I'd been running through, trying to find a good show-jumping spot for one of the sales horses next month. August wasn't the best time of year to sell horses, but his owner had sent an email yesterday, and the tone had been a little antsy. She was tired of paying bills on a horse that was supposed to be selling for a profit.

Unfortunately, all of the horse shows right now seemed to have unpleasant names like "The Summer Sizzler." I'd done Sunshine State Horse Trials because it was the right time for Dynamo and I wanted to have him ready for the fall season, but it didn't mean I was happy about putting myself out there on a hot summer day with anyone else's horses. I didn't want to sizzle any more than they did.

And the usual heat wasn't anything compared to the soupy tropical mess we were getting this summer. After roasting through June, things had seemed marginally normal in July . . . and then it started storming nonstop.

"Soon we won't even be able to turn anyone out," Lacey grumbled. "The paddocks are a mess."

I chewed my lip. She was right about that. It had been raining nearly round the clock for seven days straight, and Florida seemed to be threatening to sink right back into the ocean from whence it came. The paddocks were looking more like ponds. Dynamo's hooves, which were prone to abscesses, weren't going to be able to take it. And I wasn't too thrilled with Mickey's hooves, either. A little flat and shelly, they were easily his worst feature. He would be just as susceptible to hoof infection as Dynamo.

"They're going to destroy the grass . . . we'll have nothing but mud," Lacey went on. "Not to mention white line disease from their hooves being wet all the time. Mickey and Dynamo already have such awful feet, this is going to wreck them."

"Why do the big horses have the bad feet?" I asked.

Lacey looked at me like I was an idiot. "They're *your* big horses. You chose them. Choose better hooves next time."

Fair enough.

I went into the kitchen to peer out the window at the paddocks. The rain was drumming against the glass, but through the streaming cataracts pouring down the panes, I could see that where the fields weren't underwater, they were colored jungle green with black splotches—the dark patches where hooves had torn up the grass, leaving only mud behind. To save the grass, the paddocks needed to be left to dry in peace.

But leaving the horses in would cost us, in shavings for the stalls, in hay to keep them busy, in time spent mucking out, in sanity for everyone. Stabled horses were more likely to develop ulcers and bad habits like wood-chewing, to say nothing of the extra energy and subsequent bad behavior when we were riding them.

Lacey joined me as a new, heavier squall came rushing in. Rain pounded on the roof above our heads, a roar of raindrops the size of quarters. If it stopped overnight and gave us a morning break, we'd ride between the puddles. But we were running out of room between puddles.

Two weeks ago, I had thought the coming fall would be my best season yet. Lacey on board, Mickey beginning his training, Dynamo fresh off his first Intermediate and feeling good. We'd compete this fall and winter all over the southeast, make our way to a two-star level, three-day event and bring home some bling. And then, finally, I'd start plotting our Advanced debut. But it was well into August and the monsoons were stepping up their game right when we needed to step up ours.

The entire farm needed to look its best. I was getting a few phone calls now, people who had seen me in the *Chronicle* and were shopping for a new trainer for the winter. A nice woman from Aiken, moving to town with her two young horses, seemed interested until she found out I was barely old enough to buy beer. And if I wanted boarders, I had more to do than just convince people to overlook my age. That was one reason I'd gone ahead and used some of the training fees Eileen was paying to hire a stall cleaner. Thank goodness for Manny. He wasn't afraid of spiders like Lacey and I were, mucked out quickly and efficiently, and brought a racetrack sensibility to the barn with him. The horses all appreciated him as much as Lacey and I did. The barn gleamed with cleanliness and smelled like Pine-Sol, and in this sport, hygiene went a long way. The horse world was happy to respect young trainers with money and flashy horses as long as they had a glitzy barn and shiny tack.

Clean was great, but sandpit paddocks and lakes in place of arenas were not going to advance my cause. I leaned my forehead against the cold glass of the window. It was always something in this business.

"This day's a wash," I said finally. "Look at the dressage arena. It could be a tourist attraction, like one of the springs."

"Come ride at beautiful Lake Dressage!" Lacey spread her arms wide like a presenter on TV.

I snorted. "Yeah, swim your horse to X, halt, salute the judge, empty your snorkel."

"Don't forget to call your farrier and ask for fins on the next shoeing cycle."

We giggled. Sometimes you just had to laugh it off.

But it was less amusing in the morning when I was forced to give everyone the day off. The dressage arena was soaked and the paddocks were nearly underwater. It was sunny at last, but so humid I felt like my lungs were filling with water. The sky was glistening blue, with cumulus clouds already lazing their way east, innocently fluffy. They'd be monster storms in a few hours.

We gave all the horses an hour each of turnout in the little round pen next to the barn. The deep ruts that ran along the wall were full of water, but the center was a high mound of sand, and the horses took it in turns to ignore the hay we threw out for them and instead run around like fools, splashing in the water and rolling in the sand, coming into the barn like they'd been out motor-crossing on dirt bikes. We had a farm of mud-encrusted grays where we once had chestnuts and bays. Even Mickey, who was close to white beneath his dapples, came in the same dark charcoal as the others. The wash rack drain choked with sand from spraying them down, and I had to pry off the cover and dig handfuls of dark muck. When we were through, the stable aisle looked like a particularly polluted beach, the kind where syringes and broken bottles tend to wash ashore.

"This is more work than riding them would have been," Lacey spluttered, spitting dirty water out of her mouth after Mickey shook himself off like an oversized dog, sending mud everywhere.

"I want to ride Mickey this afternoon, anyway," I announced. "I think the rain is going to pass us by this afternoon."

"Oh, the meteorologist has spoken!"

"Shut up, nag, I know plenty about the weather!" I gave her a friendly shove. "Look, everything is building up to the east . . . if it does rain, it won't be until late." I pointed at the midday thunderheads, their peaks reaching up toward the sun, so high that I could see ice crystals wafting down from their billowing heights. It was hailing somewhere over the Ocala National Forest, beating down on the fishermen and the four-wheelers and the Rainbow People in their tents, if there were any camping out there this time of year. "We get storms earlier when they blow out of the west. Don't you pay any attention to the weather?"

"Why are you going to hassle Mickey?" Lacey asked, ignoring my dig. "Can't we just go in the house and lay in the A/C until it's feed time?"

"We have to stop doing that."

"Oh, come on. I'm sure the weather will give us a break in a few weeks." Lacey's voice turned cajoling. "You're worn out, you could use the break . . ."

I shook my head. A break would be nice, but championships weren't won through naps. If they were, Lacey would be an Olympian. "No, he needs it. Come on, I need to be getting this horse going Novice level before winter. All we've done is light work. I'm thinking of taking him to Lochloosa Horse Trials in two weeks. He can do the Starter level, hop some little logs."

"*Lochloosa?* In two weeks? Are you crazy?"

"Because it's hot?"

"Because he's a baby horse you've only been riding for a few weeks!"

"He already knows how to jump. Any horse can do a Starter level event. All we have to do is get him going every day, work that fat off, balance him up with some gymnastics, and let him start looking around at the shows. I'm not saying he has to be competitive or anything." But naturally, I was thinking that maybe he would be. Lochloosa, which wasn't recognized by any national organizations, had some fantastic introductory fences for horses new to cross-country jumping. And it was never too soon to start winning classes.

"I think you're both going to work too hard," Lacey said firmly. She unsnapped the crossties from Mickey's halter and led him out of the wash rack. "It's still too hot and it's way too humid. The ground is probably like quicksand. I think you should just listen to Mother Nature and take it easy until this weather breaks."

I watched Mickey's hindquarters moving in rhythm, his catlike grace, his long easy stride, and admired the angles of his hocks and fetlocks. He left a pattern of wet horseshoes on the concrete aisle; his hind hooves reached ahead of his forehooves by a matter of inches.

Lacey was right, of course. Most days, the prospect of riding even here at home, let alone putting on the glitz in boots and breeches at any horse show, was appalling. If the weather didn't kill me, the vampiric mosquitoes, as big as hummingbirds, might. Lochloosa was along the edge of a vast swamp, and its bloodsuckers were legendary.

But now, with the pressure of having two potentially top-level horses in my barn, I knew I had to suck it up, get the tack on, and ride. I couldn't just give a good horse time off because it was hot out. I couldn't sit under the vent of the air conditioner and drink margaritas in front of the television because it was hot out. Not if

I expected to win this fall, when the big kids came back to Ocala to play. The best of the best wintered here. This was my chance to prep for the stepped-up level of competition.

"He has to be ready for Novice this winter," I told Lacey firmly. "He's not my horse, and he's not a pet. He was sent here to compete. If I don't do well with him, someone else will get him. And it isn't just him—Dynamo is going too. And anyone else we think could get a good placing and maybe sell this fall. We have to be at the top of our game by the time summer's over, not just getting started because we were scared of a little sweat."

Lacey latched Mickey's stall door, hung up his halter, and came back to the barn entrance. We were quiet for a few moments, watching the clouds. This past week, they had simply been sitting over us, drifting (that's weatherman-speak for *going nowhere*) and raining and rumbling and raining and rumbling and raining. It was new behavior in a previously predictable world.

"I have to be honest," I said eventually. "I can't really predict the weather like I used to. I don't know if it's climate change or what, but I swear it used to rain at three o'clock every day on the dot and this year that is just not the case."

"It's definitely getting weirder everywhere," Lacey agreed. "Also, I thought Florida had a lot of hurricanes?"

I considered this for a moment. We hadn't had a hurricane scare yet this summer. "Not a lot, I guess," I said. "But they're not usually a big deal here. More in South Florida, or the Panhandle. Just a lot of wind and rain, anyway."

"My parents didn't want me to move here because of hurricanes. Can I text them and tell them Jules Thornton said they're fine, actually?" She smirked.

"Yeah, you do that. We're all the way in the middle of the state here. Nothing to worry about."

Lacey nodded. "Thank God."

"But rain or not," I said, getting back on topic, "Dynamo and Mickey work every day. Nonnegotiable. Everyone else we fit in between raindrops and lightning."

We watched the clouds somberly for a moment, as Florida horsemen did every day from May to October, determining distances and movement, weighing our chances.

"I get it," Lacey said. "But I really wish it wasn't like that."

"Like what?" As if I didn't already know what she was going to say.

"So, I don't know, financial. Like he and Mickey are just an investment. They're big business, so everyone gets a day off but them. The weather's bad, but they have to work anyway. That's just a sad thing to say about a horse."

I sighed. The amateur's dilemma. Lacey was going to have to learn to make these decisions with her head, and put her heart in the back seat. "Those are the kinds of decisions you have to make if you're going to make a living with horses. They're horses, and yeah, we love them, but they're definitely investments and business deals. Some more serious than others."

"I know you love Dynamo, but do you love Mickey?"

I nodded. "I hate to say it, but I do. There's just something about him I can't resist."

"But you'll still treat him like he's just a big old business deal? I don't get it."

"What do you want me to say, Lacey? Horses have to pay the bills."

I'd worked this out in my head a long time ago, and if I was not thrilled with it, I'd rationalized it enough to get through my days and sleep through my nights. I thought that might be a line of demarcation, between the perpetual amateurs and the true professionals: the ability to conceive of a horse as an object, as a commodity, as a product, and yet still never forget that they felt pain or had very real emotions.

The folks that couldn't grasp that notion often fell into two camps—they either saw them as pets, or as fashion accessories. And the latter camp *really* pissed me off, even more than the coldhearted cretins who treated them as profit margins and tax deductions. A horse was not a status symbol. A horse was himself, and that was more than enough.

There was a dull rumble of thunder to the east. Against the blue sky and the blazing white of the midday sun, the sky over Ocala suddenly looked like a volcano had erupted, the storm clouds piling up on top of one another, tall and skinny and ominously dark within, like a little black dress laced with brilliant white cumulus.

I turned back to Lacey. "Do me a favor and tack Mickey up as fast as you possibly can." Lacey nodded and headed for the tack room to grab the saddle and bridle while I darted into the house for my riding boots and one more bottle of water.

There's a feeling you get when you're sitting so deeply in the saddle that you're part of your horse's back. It's a sinking and a rising, it's thrilling and meditative, it's sensual and otherworldly. Your legs are wrapped around his body, your calf muscles quiver against the long abdominal muscle that stretches from chest to flank, simultaneously lifting him into your seat and pulling your seat down into him, and you can feel your spine sync up with his spine, locking your motion together. His neck arches before you, his mouth is so soft on the bit that your fingers barely stroke the rein before he responds.

It's a oneness, a perfect sensation that negates all the heat, and the worry, and the exhaustion, and the loneliness, the sheer damn loneliness of it all, that you refuse to admit even exists. It's perfection, it's the whole purpose of riding, and it is fleeting.

Mickey gave me one perfect twenty-meter circle, perhaps a half minute, and it stayed with me for the rest of the evening, even when the rains fell, even when the lightning flashed, even when the rest of my day was washed away.

But, hours later, sleepless in bed, I was feeling the opposite effect. Perfect moments have their price: their absence reminds you of everything imperfect.

At night, I knew that despite everything I said, or did, or believed, I was lonely. And so I did what was becoming a very bad habit for a trainer who needed her sleep—I put my feet into a pair of flip-flops and went padding through the wet grass to visit with my horses.

13

LOCHLOOSA WAS HOT, so much hotter than I could have been prepared for, both in temperature and in competition. I guessed no one took the summer off anymore.

There were about fifteen other horse trailers in the big field where I was directed to park, mercifully on high ground so that none of us would get stuck in the muck of the flooded lowlands, and they were all huge rigs. Six-and even eight-horse trailers, and most of them packed to the gills with gleaming, sweating horses of every description.

A Clydesdale, white-feathered legs brilliant in the early-morning sunlight, was backed out of a trailer and into the dewy grass, only to be followed by a medium-sized paint pony, and then by a brown Thoroughbred with a head like an anvil and hindquarters like a Quarter Horse. Pony Clubbers milled around, children of all ages and a few teenagers, wearing brightly colored outfits advertising their stables and riding clubs. The only adults appeared as chaperones and riding instructors, and a few loners like myself, who were here with prospects in need of experience before the show season. I saw more than a few familiar faces as I looked around the showgrounds. I wasn't the only one who was putting training before comfort on this broiling hot day at the end of August. It meant I certainly wasn't going to win anything without effort.

Lacey took Dynamo's lead shank as soon as he came down the ramp and silently walked away with him, her hand loose around the flat leather so that he could turn his head and look around at his new surroundings. Her stiff shoulders and set jaw said it all: she wasn't happy that we were going to work the horses on such a brutal day. When she saw the forecast was for ninety-five degrees and only a slim chance of rain, she insisted we cancel our entries. But she was the student, and I was the trainer, so the show went on. "Bring back the registration packets!" I called after her, and she lifted a hand in acknowledgment without turning around.

Lochloosa Farm put on a pretty bare-bones show, with no stabling. I took Mickey down myself and tied him to one of the rings on the side of the trailer. He was anxious, swinging his head back and forth, whinnying for Dynamo, who had already disappeared in the maze of trucks and trailers. I hoped Lacey would come back soon. And I hoped she was up to today's challenges. Two horses weren't a lot to manage, but each had three phases to get to—and Lacey had never been my groom before. I was relieved, as I ran over the schedule in my mind one more time, that I hadn't brought any other horses.

I'd wanted to, but Lacey probably would have killed me if I had.

She'd been quiet about it, but it was obvious she still wasn't comfortable with how hard I was working Dynamo and Mickey through the summer months. There was a silent protest in her face when she tacked up the geldings these days, and I had caught her looks of reproach when she took my slick reins and ran a washcloth over their sweat-foamed faces after a hard ride.

And all of our rides were hard lately, I had to admit that. I was watching both horses carefully for some sign that they might need mental health breaks, but neither had given any indication of anything other than blooming health and happiness. Mickey's pale coat gleamed with well-being, Dynamo's chestnut flanks caught the sunlight with a metallic shimmer, and both horses' ears were always pricked and alert when they saw Lacey or myself walking around the farm. They were ready to work every day, no matter the soaring mercury or the sopping-wet air. But the overall philosophy was still weighing on Lacey, bringing down the chipper girl I had been so happy to have in my barn every day.

I told myself it would be fine—that everyone had to work through this sort of crisis when they started out in the business— loving horses and making a living with horses are not entirely the same thing. I just hoped she chose my team in the end.

M ickey hadn't been off the farm since he arrived back in June. And before that, he'd only been at Eileen's little farm. His experience with traveling was still 99 percent racehorse, and now he was definitely gearing up for a race. I looked at his sweating flanks and wide eyes with apprehension. "We can't leave him tied while we go to the dressage ring," I told Lacey.

"I'll take him for a walk. If you can handle your test alone."

"I guess I'll manage," I whined, trying to get her to laugh. But she just shook her head.

Mickey showed her his hindquarters but she slipped past him anyway, gave him an elbow in the shoulder to move him away from the trailer, and ran his chain shank over his nose. "Don't piss me off," she told him, sounding firm, but friendly.

I watched them walk off, Mickey dancing sideways on the end of his shank, Lacey ignoring his antics until he got too close to her, then giving the nose chain a quick yank. The pressure got his attention, and he would focus on her for a few moments before something else upset him, and then he'd start all over again.

They disappeared around a corner, heading for a shady area behind the trailer parking, and I let out the breath I didn't realize I was holding. Lacey was good with him. They'd be fine.

I hoped. I had to concentrate on Dynamo. We had a dressage test in less than half an hour.

"Dynie, you lovely boy," I crooned, running a hand down his sleek, wet neck. "Look how well behaved you are. You're my good, good boy."

The good, good boy ignored me and strained his neck to its utmost, trying to reach a few blades of hay that were poking through the trailer window. His lips clapped together just shy of the green wisps.

"Tragic," I told him, and jumped up into the trailer's tack room in search of his bridle.

"And here is the wonderful Dynamo," said a voice outside.

I poked my head out of the tack room and saw, between me and Dynamo, the rear view of a very fit man.

I might not have time for a dating life, but I could still appreciate a well-cut pair of breeches and good boots. That *Man from Snowy River* hat thing was really working for me too . . .

He took off his hat and rumpled his dark red-brown hair with one hand. Dynamo regarded him with quiet anticipation, hoping for a peppermint. But all I could think of was Dr. Em, trying to hook me up on a date with Pete back at the beginning of summer. Was that why he kept showing up? Did she tell him to try again?

Flustered by his unexpected appearance, I tried to stop my hands from shaking as I pulled down the bridle. The bit rattled against the wall, and Pete turned around and smiled with an *ah, there you are* sort of expression.

"Well, hello," he said.

"Hi," I said. I slid the bridle over my shoulder.

"The program still says Juliet, but I believe you said I had to call you Jules."

"Does it *really*?" I sighed. "I used to think that was some autocorrect error, but now I swear someone volunteering in the show office is trolling me."

"They're pretty brave, to troll you." His smile widened.

I smiled back, then frowned. What did he want? "I'm tacking up, so—"

"I just came by to say hello," Pete said, "and tell you Regina is still upset you beat us back at Sunshine State. I'd convinced her she was going to win, and she didn't appreciate it when I let her down."

"Did she buck you off?" I asked, slipping past him and going to Dynamo. My horse turned and ran his nose along my empty hand, hoping for a treat.

"She . . . considered it, let's say." He turned and eyed Dynamo, who had given up on any hopes of peppermints and was now cocking a hind leg, half-asleep. "Your old boy is going to have to wake up if he wants to beat the girl today."

"Oh! I guess you're in Open Intermediate, too?"

He shrugged. "Of course. We're going to see a lot of each other, you know. There are only so many Intermediate events to choose from."

He was right about that—most events only offered Novice through Preliminary. Lochloosa was the only schooling show with such upper-level classes in the area. "Is this the beginning of a beautiful rivalry?" I grinned, trying my hand at flirtation. Green, but game. And I really couldn't help myself. I hated him, of course, but . . . I *was* going to see a lot of him, and it wouldn't be the worst thing to have someone to talk to at events.

Pete chuckled. "Or something like that. Do you ever hit the jumper circuit? I could try beating you there, too, if you want."

"As hard as it is to turn down that invitation, I really only like doing three-phase events," I said, laughing. "Dressage-only days and jumper classes without getting to go cross-country just bum me out."

"Only here for the galloping?"

"Pretty much."

"I get that," Pete said. "You're in it for the thrill of it, right? You're an adrenaline junkie."

"No," I snorted. "Please. I just love jumping cross-country. I don't feel as connected with my horse in any other way. Dressage has its moments, but nothing compares to galloping over big jumps."

He considered me for a moment. "I think my grandfather would have said the same thing."

"It worked out for him," I said, thinking of his grandfather's gold medals. "Especially since back in his day they were jumping out of the sides of barns and galloping straight down mountainsides, right?"

"Yeah, it was a different time, thank goodness," Pete said with a chuckle.

I didn't know about the "thank goodness" part. I'd always

been pretty jealous of the riders in the fading photos from decades ago. The scarier the jump by modern standards, the more I itched to take it on. But eventing wasn't just about muscle and nerve anymore. "I said I'm not an adrenaline junkie, and I meant it," I said, "but the first time I took a half-broke pony cross-country schooling, I got run away with and accidentally jumped a couple huge fences and a Preliminary level drop, and my trainer thought I was going to die, but I just trotted back once I was in control and asked her when I could do it again."

Pete laughed so hard he bent over at the waist.

Dynamo turned and looked at him, eyes inquiring, hay poking out of his mouth.

"I was born into it," Pete wheezed, "but you were born *for* it."

I was pleased he saw things that way. "Remember that when I beat you later today," I told him.

"Listen," he said, straightening up and rubbing his face with one hand, still smiling. "I have a dressage ride to get to, and I'm guessing you do, too. But, in celebration of this rivalry, I say at the end of the day, the winner buys the loser a Coke." He paused. "Or Diet Coke?" He smiled at me boyishly.

"Don't worry about what I like," I told him. "You'll get your Coke after the show jumping."

Come on, Dyno, buck up!" I muttered. I pushed my hands toward his neck, freeing up his head to move forward, and squeezed my calves against his rib cage, hoping he'd pick up the pace and move more freely, filling in the loop in my reins. Nothing. His trot was more of a plod, and his canter felt like he wanted to pitch down onto on his nose.

The warm-up ring was pulsating with energy, horses flinging themselves around the arena, horses running away, horses throwing their heads up, mouths gaping, legs wild. But Dynamo remained dopily quiet, dawdling along the rail, while the traffic to the inside of the arena went spinning around us in fast-forward.

In the dressage ring next to the warm-up, the rider on deck ahead of me was trotting her horse around the outside of the low white chain fence. The rider in the arena was saluting the judge; her test was finished. I had about ten minutes before we were meant to go boldly down that center line.

And my horse was practically dead.

I shortened my reins for the tenth time; they were slick with sweat and hard to grip. My knuckles brushed against his neck and the heat there told me Dynamo was much hotter than he should have been. For the second time this summer, I feared heatstroke, and I wished Lacey would come to the rescue with a bucket of water to splash over his back, and a cool, refreshing sponge for his mouth. But she was off somewhere nursing her anger and keeping Mickey from having a nervous breakdown. "I'm sorry, Dynamo, but you'll have to wait until the test is over for a drink," I told him. "Let's go wait in the shade."

Standing under the tree near the arena entrance wasn't going to put any more energy on him, but if he wasn't feeling well, nothing would. I might as well let him relax and cool off a little. When he swayed into a halt, I felt a wave of dizziness. I put my hand to my forehead to try and ground myself.

A bell rang, and the rider on the bay horse went into the arena for their test.

The rider turned and flashed me a grin as he approached the in-gate, and I gasped in surprise. It was Pete, dapper in his white shirt and tie. We were riding without show jackets today, in deference to the heat, but he still somehow looked like an Olympian in the saddle.

He hadn't been kidding about Regina's will to win. The mare produced every movement in the test with character and expression. Her extended trot flung her forelegs out twice as far as her working trot. Her collected canter looked as though she was fully capable of simply launching into space, and only chose not to out of her own forbearance. She was exquisitely aware of her own power.

"Her jumping must be incredible," I told Dynamo, and a girl leaning against the tree looked up. She gave me a smile that was more of a smirk.

"It is," Becky said.

14

"MY DRESSAGE TEST could not have gone any worse," I snapped, cutting off Lacey before she could even ask. She stood still, Mickey pacing in a circle around her. I pulled off Dynamo's bridle and slipped on his halter. "Zero impulsion, horrible transitions. I don't know. I'm going to have to skip the rest of the event with him. Something's wrong. The heat has gotten to him, I guess." I ignored my own dizziness as I untacked Dynamo. I'd get over it.

Every time Mickey circled behind her, Lacey lifted an arm and let the lead shank pass over her head. She was too nice to tell me she'd told me so about the weather, God love her, so I didn't give her my usual fake horror story about the guy I saw who had his head cut off that way when a horse spooked and ran away.

"I don't think Mickey is going to make your day much better," Lacey said, and then added, "Oh! I saw Becky."

"I did too! She's grooming for Pete Morrison!" I wrenched

upward on the billets, loosening the girth strap. Dynamo pinned his ears and shook his head at me. God, he was pissed at me, too.

"Wait, you're joking!"

"Yes! Him!" I felt shaky with rage. First Pete came over and was a friendly distraction for no reason at all. Then I saw he'd somehow scooped up my former working student as his groom. Had she told him? Was he going to expose me?

"Well, what happened?" Lacey demanded.

"He had his horse in before Dynamo's round. Becky was by the ring. She literally said two words to me and then ignored me after that. She just went up to him when he came out of the arena and gave his horse a cookie, then she picked up a bucket with his name on it and walked away with him."

"So, nothing actually happened."

What did she want to happen? Becky was here. She'd quit working for me and now she'd popped up again a month later with Pete Morrison, who for some reason wanted to be my best friend. Becky wasn't going to be okay with that.

I stripped the sweaty saddle pad off Dynamo and tossed it through the open tack room door. "He's wringing wet. Please find a hose and give him a long, cool shower. I'm scared he's going to have heatstroke or something."

"We should take them both home," Lacey said, not moving. "This is too much for them. Too much stress for Mickey, too much heat for Dynie. Come on, Jules, let's just load up and go."

I shook my head. That would be nice, but there was no easy way out in this game. "I have to at least get on Mickey. He can't just show up, act like a freak, and then go home. He needs to understand that he comes to shows to work. And Dynamo needs cooling out before he gets in the trailer, anyway. Switch with me, please."

I reached out and she handed me Mickey's shank, wet with sweat from the pacing horse's lathered neck.

But Mickey was truly an emotional disaster. And an emotional horse is not the safest creature to handle. He clearly thought he was at the races, but none of his usual routines were being followed. Wheeling around, treading on my feet, swiveling his head every which way—it was all I could do to get the saddle on him. A young girl from the trailer parked next to mine, neatly dressed in buff breeches and a pink polo shirt with a jumping horse embroidered on the chest, came over and shyly asked if I'd like any help.

I eyed her warily. She was only about thirteen, but when I was thirteen I'd been riding dangerous auction horses, so age wasn't necessarily a detractor. "Promise not to get hurt, okay? Your mom will kill me," I told her.

Her French braid was already coming loose. She tucked a few extra strands of blond hair behind her ears and took Mickey's lead. She gave him a careful pat on the shoulder, and Mickey's muscles twitched in response. "You're Jules Thornton, aren't you?"

"Yeah, I am," I said, startled. I stopped pulling at the girth long enough to give the girl a look. "You know who I am?"

"You ride Dynamo," she explained. "I cut your picture out of my trainer's *Chronicle of the Horse*. I saw you win at Sunshine State in the summer, and at Rocking Horse in the open Prelim back in the spring."

"That's right." Hey, I had a fan. I'd be far more pleased if I wasn't so concerned about Mickey doing something stupid and killing her. *My one and only fan, Mickey, be nice*, I thought to

him, but he ignored my telepathy with finesse and pawed at the
ground impatiently.

"Who is this horse?"

"This is Mickey. Danger Mouse. Today's his first event."

"He's lovely," the girl said rapturously, and gave him a long
stroke on the neck. Mickey, quelled for the moment by her attention and touch, stood still. She looked him over carefully. "Where's
his forelock?"

"He cut it off on a board. It's growing back though. Watch
him," I told her. "His ears are still focused on the other horses over
there. If he moves, it will be sudden and fast."

But he didn't move. He was very good . . . unusually good. I
paused for a moment, studying him. I didn't like how still he was
standing. Thoroughbreds shouldn't stand stock-still, without a muscle twitching, ears pricked and eyes wide. They have a tendency to
explode out of such an eerie stillness. I'd seen it a few times, and it
was always scary. *Better hurry,* I thought, *before he tramples your
only fan.* I shook my head and hurried to get on my hard hat and
pull the bridle out of the tack room.

"Okay," I told my little fan. "Get the halter down around his
neck and buckle it there so we still have a hold of him. Perfect. You
know what you're doing!" Mickey's head free, his halter held by
her firm hand on his neck, I slipped the reins over his ears, then
lifted the bridle up in front of his face, opened his mouth with a
gentle thumb, slid the bit between his teeth, and then pulled the
bridle back, first behind one ear, then the other—

And he exploded like a firecracker, soaring straight up into the
air. The girl tried gamely to hang on to the lead shank but he was
too strong for her, and in an instant he had flipped over completely,
landing with a thud in the deep summer grass, waving his legs in

the air and swinging his head lethally from side to side, as violent as an alligator's tail. His jaw slammed into the aluminum wheel well of the trailer and left behind a dent and a smear of blood.

Before we could even register what was happening, before any of the startled horsemen around us could run to our aid, Mickey was leaping back up to his feet, the bridle hanging down to his hooves, and both I and the girl darted forward, snatching at anything—the reins over his neck, the dangling bridle near his hooves, the halter that was still buckled around his neck, hanging like a belt. Improbably, we both caught him, I by the reins and she by the halter, and we stood clinging on to the leather and the horse, while the horse stood still and trembled, his eyes dull, somewhere within himself. I watched him numbly, the refrain *Oh shit, oh shit, oh shit* running through my brain.

"*Ashlyn?* Ashlyn, what the hell are you doing over there?" someone was shouting furiously, and then there was a short, angry, sunburned woman in shorts and tank top running over from the neighboring trailer, despite the fact that she was surrounded by horses, a situation in which you never, ever run, and the girl handed me the halter guiltily, hissing, "Mom, don't run!"

The woman stopped a short distance away. "I've been looking for you and you're over here dealing with crazy horses? You have your own crazy horse to deal with, might I remind you!"

"I'm sorry, Mom, but that's Jules Thornton. She needed help. Her horse got spooked or something. He's not crazy!"

Great. Now everyone in the peanut gallery knew exactly who I was. Jules Thornton, rising star. Jules Thornton, up-and-coming young rider. Jules Thornton, Trainer, Endangers Pony Clubbers with Insane Horses. Jules Thornton, you know the one, she had the dueling working students back at Sunshine State?

I couldn't seem to avoid being the center of attention before I even kicked my feet into the stirrups.

"Do you need a hand?" a voice asked, and I looked through the crowd and bit back a groan. It was Becky, standing with her arms folded, a bridle slung over one shoulder, looking as triumphant as I had ever seen her.

"Becky—hey . . ." I felt myself blushing furiously and wanted to sink down through the grass, into the muck beneath, sink down through the dark sand and into the water table and flow away into the Everglades and never be seen again.

Becky strode over and took Mickey's bridle from where it was dangling from my hands, slipped it over his head and settled it snugly into place. The horse ignored her, his ears at half-mast, his eyes half-closed, and as she stepped back he let out a huge sigh, as if he was letting go of the tension that caused his anxiety attack in the first place.

"He's looking good. Too bad about the forelock." Becky turned to walk away. "Good luck with him," she called, not bothering to look back.

I watched her go as the little group of spectators dispersed, everyone back to their own horses and their own worries. People will tell you that they love horses because they are an escape from the worry of the real world, but the truth is that nothing is more worrisome than a horse.

At least Mickey seemed to have gotten himself together. I didn't know what happened, a spook, I guessed, but now he seemed quiet enough. Foolishly, without walking him out to see what I had, I put my boot in the stirrup and swung up into the saddle.

Immediately, I could tell he wasn't comfortable. I couldn't say that I expected a nice normal movement from him, but even so, his steps felt too quick somehow. He started bouncing across the parking field, lifting his legs in a gait not quite a trot and not quite a canter, but something infinitely higher and more buoyant than the two, and certainly nowhere near the quiet walk I would have preferred. He was growing more and more knotted up by the moment, working himself into a frenzy, and no matter how deep I tried to sit or how slowly I tried to breathe, he seemed determined to throw another fit. The worrisome bit was, I had no idea what the fit might be. He'd been so angelic at the farm. Was he a bucker, a bolter, a spinner? Or was the rearing and flipping act he'd just shown back at the trailer his favored method of rebelling?

Oh God, I hoped not. I sat down a little deeper, shoved down my heels a little deeper, and pushed my hands forward, trying to keep him from feeling too claustrophobic. *Forward*, I thought desperately. Not *up*. All I wanted was for him to relax a little, jog around the warm-up ring, and then I'd take him back to the trailer and get both horses home. I aimed for the warm-up ring and he pranced in its general direction. He had to end on a good note. However brief.

Then I saw a whole new problem to worry about.

A friend of Laurie's, Breeda Johnson, liked to say hello at events, and she'd left a note at the trailer saying she'd be waiting for me at the dressage arena, as our ride times were close together. Breeda was a respected rider and I'd been looking forward to seeing her and showing her how far I'd come since I was Laurie's working student.

I could see Breeda next to the tree where I'd run into Becky earlier, watching us with one hand shading her eyes, and I felt a sinking shame. This was going to get back to Laurie. She and Laurie would have a good laugh about Little Miss Jules who thought she was a big-time rider. I formed a game plan in my head: I'd go past Breeda with a big smile on my face. I'd laugh and call out that this silly baby was putting me through the business on his first time off the farm, but it sure was nice seeing her. I'd play it all off, pretend like Mickey wasn't actually scaring the shit out of me right now.

It was a good plan, but unfortunately, two things were standing in its way. One, Mickey *was* scaring the shit out of me, because he'd already proven that he was capable of losing his mind completely, and two, suddenly we weren't getting any closer to the warm-up ring.

Was it the little pavilion tent with the judge sitting inside that was freaking him out? Maybe the food truck parked nearby and selling iced coffee to the Pony Clubbers and their tired mothers? Either way, the more I asked for forward motion, the more he responded with vertical motion, until we weren't going anywhere at all. He was standing still as a statue once again, just as he did when we were tacking him up—his ears pricked, his head so high that I felt like he might smack me in the face with his skull, his body beginning to tense and shake.

Slowly, I wrapped my fingers in his thick gray mane, preparing my body for anything.

When he bolted at last, it was a leap worthy of a Lipizzan, or perhaps a deer. Hell, maybe a really athletic tree frog. First, he went straight up, his neck rising in front of me, and then launched forward, putting those glorious hindquarters to good use. I was flung backward, but didn't lose my seat and had just enough time to throw myself forward, grabbing hold of his neck, before he hit the ground and promptly did it again. Another rear, another leap—children were shouting, trainers were running toward us, dogs were barking—and as I kicked my feet free of the stirrups and leaped to the ground, hands fisted on the reins, I thought that I'd never been so embarrassed in my entire life.

And after the rest of this summer, that was really saying something.

Mickey yanked hard as he tried to throw himself forward again, but I gave a terrible yank on the reins, pulling his head to one side. Mouth gaping, he swung his body around and stood facing me, shaking, the red skin flaring from deep inside his nostrils, the lunatic rings of white sclera showing around his dark eyes. My mind racing, trying to think of what in God's name to do, I took a cautious step sideways, in case he bolted right over top of me, and jiggled the reins to ask him to move sideways, forward—anything but that awful stillness he seemed to be withdrawing into.

He moved—but not forward. He went up, and up and up—I remember watching, in a horror-struck sort of detachment, his legs pawing somewhere above my head—and then he went backward and hit the ground with a horrible thud, the stirrup irons clanking. I stared, reins still in my hands. *Flipped, twice in ten minutes?*

Breeda Johnson handed her horse off to a convenient Pony Clubber and came running over to us.

"What's going on?" she asked, brow furrowed. Mickey looked around, rolled over, and scrambled to his feet. He looked sick, as if the effort of his panic attack had given him heatstroke. There was foam on his neck, dripping lather at his mouth, a flooding patch of sweat between his ears soaking the bridle leather and darkening the thin hair where his injury had been.

"I don't know," I admitted. "I've never seen anything like it. He's flipping instead of moving forward."

She was looking at me with an assessing gaze, and I was waiting for that maternal tone, that implication that I didn't know much, hadn't been around long enough, wasn't good enough to be on my own, which never failed to outrage me, but instead she just shook her head. "I've never seen anything like it either."

A familiar face suddenly appeared behind Breeda. My stomach churned, but Pete Morrison looked neither patronizing nor amused, just concerned. "You might want to tranq him before you try to move him again. While he's still standing quietly."

"That's a great idea," I said. "There's a vial in my tack box . . ." I'd been wondering how I was going to move him again, even if was just to get him back into the trailer. A quick sedative was just the ticket. "The tack room door is unlocked—"

But Pete was already on the job, long legs flying across the grass, and I could see him rummaging through my tack trunk until he found the vial of acepromazine, plus a syringe and needle wrapped in a plastic package.

"Just enough to take the edge off," he said, pulling a dose from the upside-down bottle as he jogged back, and without pause stepped up to Mickey, pressed his fingers against his neck, and easily found the vein he was looking for. By the time he had pulled the needle out, a drop of red blood welling from the wound, Mickey was trying to step sideways, looking prepared to panic again, but Breeda and I both placed placating hands on his sweat-darkened neck, feeling the standing veins beneath the taut flesh and the slamming of his heart deep within his chest, and he stood quietly beneath our hands. Minutes passed, long and tense, but at last his wide eyes started to blink and his head began to hang lower.

"I think you can try walking him now," Breeda suggested, stepping back. I looked over at Pete for a second opinion, and he nodded, his expression tense.

It was a slow walk back to the trailer, our footsteps dogged by

Breeda and Pete, who were quietly discussing the various equine temper tantrums they'd seen in the past. I wished they'd just go away. The blush on my cheeks wasn't from the heat, and I couldn't quite keep my hands from trembling.

But Pete was in no hurry to leave me alone, stripping the saddle from Mickey's back without being asked and slopping a bucket of tepid water over his back. Breeda, evidently thinking I was in safe hands, excused herself and headed back to her waiting horse; she had a test to ride. I was left alone with Pete, who was handling my doped horse with practiced hands.

"We're going to have to team up to get him up that ramp," he announced, handing me the lead shank. "You lead and I'll push."

I sighed. He was right to assume I couldn't get the horse in the trailer alone, and God only knew where Lacey and Dynamo had wandered off to in their search for shade and cool water. It was galling to admit, but I needed his help.

We managed to shove and pull Mickey into the trailer and I slammed the stall divider into place, giving him four walls to lean upon. The trailer was like an oven. "I better get him home," I said to Pete's back. He was in my tack room, sliding away my old dressage saddle, which was already so beat up that it didn't look any worse for wear despite being flipped over on . . . twice.

He turned back and studied me. It was hard to remember to dislike him when he looked at me like this, equal measures of concern and respect in his blue eyes. It was hard to think at all.

"Are you going to be okay with him at home?" he asked seriously.

My defenses kicked in. I hated to be little-lady'd.

"We'll be fine," I announced, turning away from him and busying myself picking up a few bandages that had fallen out of the tack room. "Thanks for your help. I'll get him home just fine."

"I'd hate to think he'd pull a number on you when you get home. Are you far away? The ace will wear off pretty quickly. It's a weak drug."

Like I didn't know how acepromazine worked. What did he think, I was new to this game? Just bought a pretty horsey with my trust fund? "We're about an hour away, but I have my working student with me . . . she's just out with my other horse. We'll be fine."

"Oh, your new working student, of course," he said.

I narrowed my eyes, wondering what Becky had told him about me.

Lacey appeared suddenly, walking a lop-eared Dynamo. His coat was dry but his eyes were still dull and tired. "We getting out of here?" she asked, ignoring Pete. *Good girl.* I nodded, and she walked the chestnut horse up the ramp and into the back stall without another word.

"Well, thank you for your help . . . I better get this boy home and bathed, though." I helped Lacey close up the back ramp and slam the bolts home.

"Where's your farm?" he persisted, following me around the trailer. "I could come out and check on you guys, if you need more help with him."

There was a reason I didn't get involved with horse trainers, and this guy's clear lack of faith in my horsemanship was a galling reminder. I might not be able to stop myself from feeling physically attracted to him, but I could stop myself from acting upon it. I sighed. "We're west of Williston. Green Winter Farm."

"Wait, the famous Green Winter Farm?"

I gave him a side-eyed glance. "Are you making fun of me?"

"No, Green Winter Farm really was famous . . . and five hundred acres." Pete raised his eyebrows.

I snorted. "I have ten acres of it, I guess. There was a sign by the driveway that said Green Winter Farm and I kept it. Saved me some money."

"Before they numbered all the roads, 145th Avenue was called Green Winter Road," Pete said.

"You're kidding!" I stopped and looked at him, interested despite myself.

"It was like a massive ranch. Cattle, citrus, racehorses."

I imagined my farm, times fifty. "How do you know about that?"

"My grandfather's from here," he reminded me. "He told me lots of old Ocala stories before he passed."

"Well, at least I got the sign, I guess," I said.

Pete grinned. "I think there were like ten signs. One for each driveway."

"Oh, of course." I shook my head. "Well, anyway, that's where I am. But I won't need any help."

"Just—hang on. I could bring some dinner, we could chat, maybe figure out what set your horse off . . ." He gave me a wheedling smile.

"I gotta go," I said shortly. "But thanks."

Pete nodded as if he'd figured I'd say that. "See you soon, I hope," he said, stepping back and raising his hand. And as I started the truck and pulled out, slowly, so as not to jostle the two miserable horses in the back, I wondered what on earth he meant. Was he going to keep inviting himself into my life?

Did I mind?

15

"WHAT'S THE MATTER? You look sick." Lacey had just come inside from rinsing off the last horse of the morning. Now she wrinkled her nose at me as if already sensing contagious germs in her presence. Neither of us, for obvious reasons, was allowed to get sick. A barn full of horses waited for no man, rain or shine, sick or not.

I slid the phone across the kitchen table and tapped my fingers on the wood. "Sheila Burns is dropping me as her trainer," I admitted, not meeting Lacey's eyes. "And wants me to deliver the Twins to the new trainer."

Lacey went for the fridge to start our Diet Coke therapy. "She wants you to deliver them after she takes them from you? Bitch! What is she thinking? You told her no way, right?"

"Of course not, Lacey. She's going to pay me for shipping. I can't turn down paying work. Especially when I'm losing two clients in one."

Lacey smacked an open Diet Coke in front of me, ignoring the fizz that spilled over the top. I sighed and swiped at it before the soda could make more of a mess of the old table. "That's insane. You can pass up a hundred bucks. That's just a public shaming, to have to take them to the new barn."

I shook my head. I'd run the numbers in my head, over and over. Turning down a hundred bucks wasn't an option. Turning down twenty bucks wasn't an option, at this point. "Things are not great, Lacey. And losing two trainees just makes it worse. We're delivering the horses tomorrow."

"To who?"

"She said she'd text me the address."

We sipped Diet Coke and stared at the phone morosely.

Outside, thunder rumbled. Another afternoon beginning. September was the start of fall up north, but in Florida, it was just August Part Two.

"Already?" Lacey grumbled. "This lunch-hour rainstorm bullshit is getting old real fast, Mother Nature."

The phone buzzed its way across the table. I picked it up and studied the message. My heart sank to my toes. I swallowed hard and tried to ignore the prickling behind my eyes. I had to be a professional about this.

"Where to?" Lacey demanded, leaning forward.

"Pete Morrison's."

There was quiet for a moment. Thunder growled again, closer this time. "I thought you hit it off with him," Lacey said eventually. "At the event."

We hadn't been talking about the event of a few days ago, for obvious reasons. I was surprised she brought it up now.

"What made you think that?" She hadn't been around while Pete and I had been talking. The memory of that conversation made me feel warm somehow, even though the air-conditioning was going full blast. I almost thought that when we weren't competing, we could be . . . friends. But when weren't we competing? Even now, in between events, he was taking two of my horses from my barn. I shook my head at Lacey. "You're reading into stuff that isn't there," I said.

"You smiled at him." Lacey shrugged. "You never smile at anybody."

"I smile at you."

"Not that much, anymore."

They loaded nicely," Lacey offered, voice uncertain. Who could blame her? What do you say to break the silence, when your boss has to give up two clients because of her own spectacularly poor decisions?

I'd made a fool of myself at Lochloosa in front of God and the entire Florida eventing community, and word had gotten around. It had only been a few days, but an hour was all anyone had really needed. I had no doubt that there were entire websites devoted to my dunderheaded move with Mickey the Magnificent Flipping Horse, or Dynamo's evident heat exhaustion as I shoved him around the dressage ring.

I ignored Lacey's attempt at levity. I ignored a lot of things lately; there was really no other way to deal with things. And I had to concentrate on the road, besides—a perfectly good excuse for my rude silence, I was sure.

We were driving the truck and trailer around a particularly tortuous turn of the county highway, where all the engineering of man couldn't compete with the deep blue sinkhole spring that blocked the road's originally intended path. The sign for the spring, with its walking trails and scuba diving, had been the victim of so many hit-and-runs over the years that it was permanently twisted on its steel legs, the arrow to the parking lot pointing straight to the heavens.

This was northwest Marion County: limestone-rich ground, rolling hills like little Floridian mountains, with water gushing out of barn hoses so crisp and pure you could bottle and sell it—this was where the millionaires raised their blue-blooded horses. Movie stars bought hobby farms here, and Saudi princes built winter homes. The great Kentucky breeding farms had their southern training farms along these winding roads, lavish barns resting atop the live-oak scattered hills, hand-carved signs at their driveways, wrought-iron gates to keep out the sightseers.

I had been holding tight to the notion that if I played my cards right and worked incessantly, unceasingly, relentlessly, I might one day be able to afford an unattractive corner of land up here, something down two unpaved roads and on the far side of a swamp, perhaps, or something backed up to the interstate, by the time I hit forty.

Pete Morrison, damn him, was already here, and the knowledge rankled. "Born into eventing"—I'd laughed about it with him at Lochloosa, but it was true. And I resented him for it. He'd inherited a beautiful farm. He'd had everything handed to him. Wasn't Pete just like the girls I'd worked for at Laurie's barn, just another lucky one?

And it still bothered me that he'd been at the ACE auditions and entered my life at all.

He was the lord of the manor at this Millionaire's Row equestrian center, so what had he been doing at the poor-kids' convention, competing for that grant and sponsorship? Lacey would have told me to just ask him. But something in me was embarrassed to admit I even wanted the answer. He didn't need to know I was that curious about him.

"Or maybe they *didn't* load well," Lacey said coolly, clearly annoyed that I hadn't answered her. "What do I know?"

"Of *course* they loaded well," I burst out. "How long did I spend teaching them to load in the trailer? When they came to my barn they were so zonked out on tranqs they could barely stand up straight. Scared to death of trailers. But I fixed that." I shook my head, sick at the thought. All that work, all those hours lost. Pete would get all of the gains, and I would be left with nothing.

Lacey rested her cheek against the window and was silent for the rest of the trip.

And then we saw the sign.

It hung from an L-shaped post, elegantly carved wood with gold trim around a blue field. The letters were gold, as well.

"Briar Hill Farm—Peter Morrison Eventing," Lacey read aloud. She cast her eyes along the green hedge that ran for hundreds of feet on either side of the approaching driveway. "Is all this *his*?"

"Guess so," I said. I flicked on the turn signal. "Little Lord Morrison will be so pleased with his new horses."

"Oh my goodness," Lacey exclaimed rapturously as we turned into the driveway and came to a slow stop. Black iron gates rose before us, a trotting horse elegantly silhouetted across them. Through the bars, the driveway curved upward and to the right, and all that could be seen was four boards of black wood fencing, marching up the rising ground to meet the blue Ocala sky. "Is this Pemberley? I feel like we're going into a Jane Austen novel. Oh! He could be like Mr. Darcy!"

"He's like a king on a mountain," I grumbled as I rolled down the window and leaned down to the call box. I pressed the Call button and there was a mechanical ring.

"Briar Hill," answered a brisk, businesslike voice.

Becky. I swallowed, decided to play it off as if I didn't know her voice. "This is Jules Thornton, here with the Burns horses. We're at the gate."

"One moment," my former employee said without a hint of recognition, and there was a loud beep. "The first barn to your left, please," Becky instructed. "There's a loading dock—you can park just past that if you don't need the ramp." The call box clicked as she hung up.

She knew very well I didn't need a loading dock ramp. I looked over at Lacey in silence. She shrugged and looked away.

"Let's go," she told her reflection in the window, and in the trailer behind us, the Twins echoed her with a few impatient bangs and kicks.

"This is a load of crap," I told all three of them, and shoved the truck into gear.

The truck's engine was at a roar by the time we finished our ascent of Mini-Mount Morrison, and I was bitching not-quite-under-my-breath about the stupid egos of men that make them build driveways that go straight uphill, and how much gas I was wasting, etc., but when we reached the level ground and I got a chance to look around, I could honestly see why he—or whoever built this farm—had done such a thing.

If I had a piece of land like this, a long green ridge, crowned with massive live oaks that clustered around neat white barns trimmed in green, with a sprawling stucco house just beyond a brightly colored show-jumping course, and skirted on all sides with black-fenced paddocks and pastures that disappeared into the rippling folds of tree-lined hills, I'd build on the mountaintop, too. To be surrounded on all sides by the vista of rolling horse country—it felt as if we were somewhere in the Appalachians, but without the blizzards.

It was perfect.

And it was ridiculous bullshit. He had won a grant for promising young trainers who needed a boost just three months ago. All of that money I could have used . . .

"Damn him," I muttered, and Lacey just shook her head, clearly over me and my animosity.

"If we were friends with him, we could come over here and ride," she said. "Ever think of that?"

"Whose side are you on?"

"The side of getting good stuff from rich friends."

The first barn on the left was a gleaming white shed row, with green rails lining the breezy aisles, and horses leaning over their green stall guards, gazing fixedly to the right. Following their pricked ears, I saw a short man with a wheelbarrow heaped full of buckets, making his way from stall to stall.

"He feeds lunch," Lacey observed. "We should be feeding lunch. So good for their digestive system."

"We don't have time to feed lunch," I replied sharply, but I was only angry because I knew she was right.

The loading dock appeared at the end of the barn, and I swung the trailer around in an approximation of a U-turn, pulling it up in the gravel of the horse path next to the barn. Tree branches scraped the aluminum roof of the trailer and set Twin One, Avril, to kicking. I knew it was Avril, because I knew she hated every little noise. I knew everything about her, and her brother. And I was losing them.

I supposed I would have to be professional and tell Pete about her noise problem, that and her butterfly phobia. No one told me, of course—I had to figure out everything about those two silly beasts myself—but it was the proper thing to do, and it would make the horses' lives easier. It wasn't their fault Sheila Burns thought I was an incompetent nobody. The fault was mine. How had she put it? "A few of my friends called me after Lochloosa. They were a little concerned that you were in over your head with the young horses."

Exactly like that. I heard her voice over and over in my head, tinny through the cell phone. I would never forget those words. *In over your head.*

"Is that a butterfly jump?" Lacey hopped out of the truck and gazed excitedly at the neighboring show-jumping arena. On carefully raked clay, colorful fences that could have been stolen from a Grand Prix championship were set at careful angles around the ring. The butterfly fence was particularly impressive, with six-foot-high butterfly wings flanking rainbow-striped jump poles. It looked remarkably like the one I had crashed at Longacres.

"Avril's gonna love that butterfly jump." I turned away, about to go into the barn in search of Becky, when she appeared around the corner of the shed row, wiping her hands on her jeans. She looked tan and healthy and happy—the opposite, really, of how she'd looked at my farm. I wondered what happened to her summer-term classes.

"Jules!" she called out, seeming almost cordial. I blinked. "How are you?" Her gaze flicked to the left and her smile grew more fixed. "And hey, Lacey . . ." She trailed off.

"We're doing great, thank you!" I said brightly, more than willing to keep up the pretension of friendship, and Lacey mumbled something similar, but with less enthusiasm. She disappeared into the trailer tack room in search of lead shanks, and I was left alone, trying to keep things from getting too awkward. "Is Pete here?"

"Probably just on his way back," Becky said. She shielded her eyes and looked past the jumping arena, where the ground sloped gently downward into a vast pasture. "There—you see? He's riding up the hill there . . . out schooling a baby on the cross-country course."

Of course. I had to drive twenty miles and pay a grounds fee to school my horses on a cross-country course. Pete Morrison had his own course. "How fun," I said, declining to follow her pointing finger. If I could avoid seeing him at all, I'd consider this day half-salvaged.

"We can unload them, though. I have their stalls ready."

In response, Avril stamped restlessly and whinnied. Instantly, every horse on the property was shouting back.

"Let's get them out, I guess," I told Lacey over the din, and we pulled down the ramp and clambered inside to snap on lead shanks so that we could lead our old horses to their new stalls. Avril, completely worked up, nudged me hard in the chest, and I hauled back and whacked her with everything I had. When I turned around to lead her out, I saw Becky standing with her arms folded, head cocked, disapproving.

But who was she to judge me? I bit down on the inside of my cheek. This was all getting to be a little too much.

I was just preparing to turn Avril into a deeply bedded stall when the short Latino man we'd seen feeding lunch appeared out of nowhere, held up one finger, and crouched beside the mare to remove her leg wraps. His fingers moved like lightning. And I thought Manny was quick.

"Go, *sí*," he said as he hopped up, arms full of my leg wraps, and nodded toward the open stall.

"Thank you, Ramon," Becky said sweetly, but her triumphant smile was all for me. "Ramon's our barn manager," she told me from the stall door. "He's very good. Their legs will be perfect in his care."

She couldn't possibly be implying that I was hard on horses' legs. "Neither of them have had any leg issues." I tried to keep my voice even, but if Becky had been telling Peter that my barn had lameness problems, I was sunk. My business couldn't take another hit from bad gossip.

But Becky was wide-eyed innocence. "I just want you to feel good about Avril and Sam. I know you care about all the horses you have."

"You have a barn manager?" Lacey asked. "How many people work here?"

Becky shrugged. "Three people, I guess? Ramon and Mikey handle the barns and horse care, and then I help Pete get through his training and sales horses."

"We have a barn manager now, too," I said, giving Manny an unofficial promotion.

"That's really nice," Becky said sincerely. "Good for you guys."

Ramon hurried past us, and as one, we all turned to see the rider rounding the shed-row corner. I cursed my own heart for beating so fast when I saw him sitting his horse like a marble statue.

I turned my eyes away, and saw that beside me, Becky was watching the horseman with a rapt expression.

Ramon took the horse's reins, and Peter dismounted while the horse was still walking. His boots hit the dirt of the shed row with little clouds of dust, and he slapped the horse on the neck affectionately before he stepped back and let Ramon lead him on past. Why wasn't *Becky* taking Pete's horse? Wasn't she the working student? Wouldn't grooming his horses fall to her? The whole point of a working student, besides training them up to be good advertisements for your coaching ability, was to avoid having to pay for a groom.

Something was going on here.

And it was making me feel just a bit unwell.

Then Pete Morrison was standing in front of me and holding out a calloused hand, and his genuine smile made me catch my breath.

Dimly, somewhere deep inside, I thought, *Why are you so goddamned perfect?*

"Pete, it's so nice to see you again," I fibbed, but the words sounded so true I had to wonder if they were. Lacey thought we were friends. Maybe we were. I was starting to forget how friendship worked.

He nodded, eyes sparkling with pleasure. "Likewise. It's been too long."

It had been less than a week. I blushed. Suddenly, I realized that I owed him a Coke. I wondered if he'd mention it. I wondered if *I'd* mention it. I wondered if that would be weird. I wondered what I could possibly say to him that wouldn't make me sound like an idiot, and then I hated myself, viciously, without reserve. It was not a feeling I was used to having and it almost startled me out of my nervous silence.

But Pete had already turned to greet Lacey, and then he was off to look over the horses, his boots sinking into the sandy shed-row dirt. He was wearing swan's neck spurs, the brass buckles tarnished and the straps worn with age. His dress boots didn't have zippers down the back like most did these days. They were old guard, traditional riding boots, sunk into deep folds around his ankles, hugging his calves like a second skin. He had been wearing those boots for a very long time. He looked every inch a true horseman.

Damn you, I thought. *Why are you so hard to hate?* I usually didn't have any trouble despising my enemies. Despising enemies was sort of my hobby at this point. It fed my ambition, kept my dreams afloat through the worst of nights and the most depressing of bank statements.

He leaned over Twin Two's stall guard and peered inside. The chunky beast was already nosing around the hay in the corner. Nothing got him down for too long if there was food involved. Pete murmured, "Really top shape, Jules. I'm impressed—it isn't easy to keep horses fit in weather like we've been having this summer."

Becky suddenly darted away, ducked under the shed-row railing, and looked out at the eastern sky, shielding her eyes against the sun. "I'd say we only have another hour or so," she called. "It's going to storm again."

"Do I have another horse tacked?" Peter asked, attention diverted from my gorgeous horses and tip top conditioning work. Typical.

"Ozzie. Ramon has him ready—tied in his stall."

"Perfect," Peter replied, smiling at Becky, and when she smiled back at him I felt my insides twist.

Which was ridiculous, of course, because he was nothing to me but a rival, just a client-stealing, has-it-all, rich big-name trainer, and there was no reason at all why I should care if he shared a familiar smile with Becky. I was just angry that Becky had found such a happy home with him, after she had deemed me useless to her. I was jealous of Becky's shift in affections, if anything.

Not Pete Morrison's warm smile and twinkling blue eyes, not his strong hands or the muscles beneath those tan breeches and dusty black riding boots.

"We should hurry home," I blurted out, and he shook his head, looking back at me.

"There's no rush. The horse can wait a few moments. I wanted to show you around . . ."

"If there's rain coming from the east, we can get in another couple of rides, too," I said, shaking my head. "We're farther west than you. Lacey? Help me with these wraps?" I couldn't get away from that warm smile fast enough.

I muttered a flustered goodbye, ignoring his quirked eyebrow, and went racing down the shed row at a power walk, Lacey scuttling after me with standing wraps trailing from her arms. I flung the leads into the truck, hoping for a quick getaway, hoping to never run into him again, but by the time we had the trailer ramp fastened, he was at my shoulder. I took a deep breath and stood very still, willing him to go away.

"Jules," he said softly, his voice husky in my ear. I bit the inside of my cheek, the only way to stop from shivering with the goose bumps that fluttered across my skin. "Come on, Jules, I'm sorry about this. I didn't ask for these horses. And I did suggest she leave them with you."

Had he really?

I turned, slowly, and took a step backward to widen the gap between us. But the trailer was just behind me, and my back was against the hot metal. I had nowhere to go. Pete stood inches away from me, looking down with concerned eyes, his helmet unbuckled and the strap hanging past his chin, smelling of horse and sweat and leather, and looking every bit a horseman's horseman. My heart fluttered, and in my mind I cursed it.

"I promise that I never meant to take your clients. If I can send business your way, I will. You're a good trainer. You're a horse-woman. I saw the way you handled Mickey last weekend. That wasn't easy, but you got through it."

"You helped," I admitted, then bit my tongue so I wouldn't say anything else. He didn't need more credit for being great. He didn't need more of *anything*, judging by this farm.

"I was your backup, that's all."

I looked at the ground, at the trailer, anything to avoid gazing back into his serious, entreating expression. He made me want to drop my defenses. I couldn't think of anything more dangerous. "Well, thanks," I said. "And this does leave me with some open stalls, and I'm always looking for prospects. So if you hear of anyone . . ."

"Next time someone offers me a nice amateur project, I'll give them your number," he said. "You're really good at training the packers. That's good money, too—"

"Packers?" I snapped, flicking my gaze back to meet his. I was finally able to look at him without feeling my insides tremble. Because he'd just insulted me, and that was something I felt more than capable of dealing with. "I'm not here to specialize in breaking in robots that anyone can point and shoot at jumps, Peter Morrison. Might I remind you that I have *two* upper-level prospects in my barn? Between Dynamo and Danger Mouse, I have five-star horses in the making. You know what?" I shook my head. "Fine. Send me packers. They can pay for my vacations."

His face fell. "I didn't mean to say that you aren't good enough, Jules," he said, shaking his head in apology. "I just think training solid, safe horses for amateurs is your niche right now. You'll climb, I have no doubt. But—I know where you're at right now. Can I offer advice? As someone who's been there? Hell, as someone who is there, right there with you?"

I tightened my jaw. "Sure," I answered, because there was no way out of it.

"Slow down." He put a hand on my arm. I felt goose bumps rise obediently, as if my skin had been longing for his touch. I would have liked to have shaken him away, but my arm would have none of it. "I know what you're doing. I know you're in a rush. Don't be. Enjoy the levels, take it easy. You say packers pay for your vacations, Jules, but come on, let's be friends and let's be honest with each other. When's the last time you took one?"

I ground my teeth, but he had me. I hadn't been on a vacation since my mother dragged me along on a spring break cruise when I was eighteen. My grandparents came. There had been a faux-Broadway show and a dinner dance with a big band and more drunken college students in one place than the Swamp parking lot before a University of Florida home game. I'd missed an event I'd been aiming for with Dynamo. It was the worst. I remembered the disappointment, wandering around the ship, missing my horse, feeling completely unable to have fun, to talk to anyone, to connect with anyone. And then, there it was again: that awful, sinking, lonely feeling, the one that hit me in the middle of the night and kept me awake until I went to the window to watch Dynamo, the one friend I could always count on.

Pete was still talking. "Don't kill yourself. Go slow, learn, let it come to you. And in the meantime, make a little time to enjoy yourself, okay?"

I started to speak, to tell him that he was right, I should work less and play more, and I should start by having dinner with him, or at least buying him that Coke I owed him at the country store down the road, but a rumble of thunder distracted us both, and as we broke away from each other to gauge the storm's progress, I saw again the perfection of his farm: the trim barns, the tidy arenas, the rolling fields. And I remembered that he had it all, and I was barely hanging on.

"You expect me to take it slow?" I snapped. "You didn't get

all this by going on vacations. We are ambitious people, Pete Morrison, and what you have—I will have. I will never stop working until I do."

He looked at me sadly, suntanned skin crinkling around his eyes. "I see that," he said softly.

16

DR. EM DIAGNOSED Dynamo's listless behavior at Lochloosa as heatstroke and told me to go easy on him until the weather broke. Which might be in a month, or in three months. I thought of the event dates written on the calendar for the next six months and bit my lip.

The Lochloosa weekend had utterly ruined my life. It was Friday. In five days I had lost two horses, received three cancellations from scheduled barn tours with prospective clients, ridden exactly no one, and demolished a case of beer and a bottle of cheap tequila. It had been a long five days.

She didn't find anything new with Mickey. "Just his hooves," she announced, stepping back and putting her hands on her hips to regard the gray horse, who was standing quiet as a saint in the barn aisle, having submitted to her pokings and proddings and flexions for the past twenty minutes. "Those flat feet of his. We already know they need to be fixed. I'm not sure your farrier has a handle on things yet."

"He hasn't had any abscesses," Lacey said, rubbing his face and spilling short gray hairs all over the front of her black tank top. "But they still hurt him?"

"There's white line disease going on here, and here," Dr. Em said, picking up his right front leg and pointing at two deep grooves along the inner ring of the hoof wall. "It's partially from all the rain and mud. You can soak it in vinegar and this packet of meds they sell at the feed store. I'll write it down for you."

"I'll take care of it," Lacey said. "We'll fix him." She had gotten really attached to Mickey after Lochloosa, as if his incident of psychotic behavior confirmed her worst suspicions that I was overworking him in the name of winning at all costs, and she was his only hope of friendship. She didn't know I came out in the night and hugged him in his paddock, and told him I loved him, and that someday all this hard work would be worthwhile. And I wasn't going to tell her. What kind of a softy boss did I want her to think I was?

"But his feet shouldn't make him flip over," I told Dr. Em. "Or blow up like he was doing. That's mental."

"I think it *could* be his feet, though," she said. "Maybe he's panicking about working on sore toes. I'd say they're fine now, but if he's always had flat feet, he might have a memory. Horses get stuck on memories of pain sometimes." Dr. Em rubbed her forehead, as if she wasn't quite sure of what she was saying. It would be easier if horses could just tell us. There would be fewer guessing games and false starts. I gazed at Mickey, and he gazed back at me with soft brown eyes. There was no sign that he'd had a panic attack at a horse show and made me look like a total hack.

"I thought he was reliving a racing day," I told her.

"Well." Dr. Em shrugged. "Either way. It could have been a sore day at the races for him."

Lacey patted Mickey's neck. "We'll fix your feet, buddy," she told him.

"And then again, he could just be overtired," Dr. Em told me later, over our ritual of cold Diet Cokes at the kitchen table. "He could be a little sour, and the prospect of strenuous work was too much for him. You said you think he expected to race, after all. You could get that kind of big reaction with these ex-racehorses for the first few outings. Especially if they had any pain issues while they were racing."

"That's true." I ticked my fingernail against the cold soda can. "To be honest, I'm really worried that if he's not ready to compete this winter, I'll lose him. There are expectations here. If not spoken, implied."

Em nodded sympathetically. "He's a Donnelly horse, right?"

"Yeah. And Donnelly horses win. You don't see the failures. She doesn't tolerate failure. She moves the horse."

Dr. Em looked over my shoulder, studying the fridge magnets from pizza joints and feed stores, avoiding my eyes. "That's a risk you have to take," she said finally. "I don't know that Donnelly will pull him right away, just because you can't get him through Novice by the end of the winter."

"Every other rider she supports already has an international agenda," I pointed out. "She isn't going to sit around and wait for me to learn to ride her horse. She'll expect me to provide results as long as the horse is sound." I paused. "He needs a break before we try to show again, right? A mental health break, while we get a handle on his brain?"

"Oh, for sure. He needs to let go of the tension from the weekend. You wouldn't want to just start taking him off the farm again right away."

"He needs an injury, then." I rapped my knuckles on the table. "Know what I mean?"

"You want me to forge something?"

"No, I want to ride him all afternoon until he bows a tendon for real," I snapped, fresh out of good mood. "Come on. I want you to write something down that gives him time off. As much as you think he needs. Heat in his knee. Something minor, but it will give him a couple weeks off. A month. Something to explain the time off to the owners, and his bad behavior. In the meantime, I'll be giving him a very gentle remedial education. Catch him up a little on the basics. Maybe we went too fast," I conceded. "So this will buy us some time."

She drummed her fingers on the table. *Dah*-dah-dah, *dah*-dah-dah, *dah*-dah-dah. A cantering horse. I held my breath, waiting for her to decide.

"I can do that for you," she agreed finally. "Heat in the knee, some tenderness in the suspensory region. Nothing conclusive on ultrasound. Time off, poultice and standing wraps, light turnout always in boots. Easy enough to explain with that angle on his hooves, anyway—he really could strain the suspensory ligament without too much effort."

I let loose my pent-up breath, relief flooding through my limbs. "Thanks, Em . . . for real."

She shrugged. "We do what we have to do. And listen—do all that stuff anyway. Poultice him, turn him out in boots, give that vinegar potion time to work on his hooves. I can't say he isn't feeling some discomfort from that hoof angle. Maybe change your farrier."

"And light work?"

"Yeah. I'd say you can still work him. Just do exactly what you said, work on the basics. Give his brain some time to catch up with his body."

Fair enough, I thought, nodding in agreement. "About Dynamo . . . how easy is easy?"

"*Easy*. Like, walking, until the humidity drops below sixty percent or the temperature drops below eighty . . . whichever comes first."

"That's not happening any time soon." The misery came creeping back.

"Early morning or late evening, if you walk," Dr. Em said thoughtfully. "Put him up in the bridle for some lateral work, just walking but you can work him good, then a half hour of free walk for a cool-out. Keep him sweating. If he stops sweating, we're sunk. You see anything, put him on dark beer and a sweating supplement." She paused, considered. "Put him on dark beer now, anyway."

I nodded fervently. I'd do anything to keep him sweating. Anhidrosis ruined good horses, especially in Florida. You saw them forgotten, in the corner stall of training barns, the stall with the most airflow, three or four fans trained on them as they heaved their labored breaths, unable to keep themselves cool in the summer heat. It was devastating and unpredictable, and all we could do was keep them fit and hope for the best.

Dark beer wasn't cheap, unfortunately. Nothing in this business was. "The fall season feels like it's pretty much shot." I slapped my hands on the table, feeling defeated. "I can't keep Dynamo in shape for Intermediate if he's not doing conditioning work. We're going to lose all that progress."

She shook her head. "Nope. But you can bring Dynamo back into fitness when it cools off. Show him at Preliminary again this winter. By the end of the season you could be back in Intermediate. And you have plenty of sales horses to work on in the meantime, right?"

"Yeah," I said. "I haven't sold a horse in months, so I have plenty to show this fall."

She grinned. "So, that's something."

"I know . . . I just . . . I want to keep moving up, Em, you know? I want to climb, not stick around at Prelim and try to sell adult-amateur horses."

"That's where the safe money is, though."

She was right. The bombproof packers went for big bucks. "No glory, though."

"No," Dr. Em agreed. "Listen, I have another appointment. Thanks for the drinks. And hey—" She paused and ran her finger around the water ring on the table. "I work with a lot of big trainers, Jules, you know that."

I nodded. She wasn't boasting, it was the truth.

"I just have to tell you . . . people are talking. I saw you lost two horses to Morrison, too. So listen, Jules, slow down. Okay? Just, do the amateur horses and do them well this winter, and next year come back out swinging. Dynamo and Mickey will appreciate the slowdown, too." She grabbed her truck keys and headed for the door. "I'm sorry to preach," she said as she was leaving. "But you're my friend, right? I want you to be aware. Just—take it easy."

The storm door slammed behind her.

Lacey was informed of Mickey's supposed injury, in case she answered the phone when Eileen called for one of her constant check-ins, and I spent an hour teaching her how to apply poultice under standing wraps. "The brown paper soaks in the bucket while you slap the mud on, and then you wrap the wet paper around the mud to keep it damp all day. And then cotton bandages over top to hold it in place."

"Why are we doing this if he's not really injured?" she asked.

"Support, in case he has any soreness, and it backs up our claim if anyone comes out here and sees him."

She shook her hands, which were already covered with clay. "Jeez, this is messy."

"You get used to it."

There was clay everywhere when we finished, white and gooey and smelling deliciously of menthol. Marcus came over and sniffed at the gobs of clay on the barn floor, then sneezed. Lacey inspected her hands again. "I look like a mummy."

"Wait until it hardens on you."

"At least it's cool . . ."

"Spearmint and menthol," I mused. "I want to take a bath in it."

Fake injury or not, Mickey was enjoying the attention. He closed his eyes and let his head hang off the crossties while we fussed over him. Lacey giggled and kissed him on the nose. His ears flopped but he didn't move. Then she straightened and looked around. "What's that sound?"

I held up a finger and listened for a moment. "That is my weather radio," I said. "Be right back."

It was a tornado warning for the rural town of Fort White, miles away from us, but even so, I came back to the barn with a new worry. The northwestern sky was dark, with white fingers of cloud stretching out ahead and flickers of lightning flashing from heavens to earth like curtains of electricity. It didn't look like our normal afternoon storms. It looked like something more powerful, something worth hiding from.

"We're going to have a tornado?" Lacey asked nervously when I relayed the news, trotting after me as I led the way to the paddock where we had set up a few jumps. "Should we be out in this?"

"No," I said. "But I just want to drag these jump standards together and lay them down flat."

"In case what?"

"In case the wind knocks them over and breaks them." The wind knocked down jump standards all the time, but if there was real force in this storm, they might shatter.

"What if the wind picks them up and throws them into the barn?"

I didn't answer. What if? You could spend all day answering that question. I did what I could.

In the end, there was just a lot of wind and rain and lightning, not that different from any other day in summer, and I managed to ride two horses while Lacey fed dinner, the eastern sky yellow and flickering as the storm blew out its fury across Ocala and the national forest and the beaches far to the east.

But the evening was a little more tense than usual. Lacey felt unsettled by the tornado warning, and that night she found a television show called *Surviving the Storm,* which she watched with rapt attention. She turned to me when it was over.

"Did you know that September is the most serious part of hurricane season?"

I nodded without looking up from the game on my phone. Floridians knew that from birth. Lacey, on the other hand, was from Pennsylvania.

"Where will we go in a hurricane?"

I considered her question. In southwest Florida, where I'd grown up, we'd had a few hurricanes roll through. Flooding was the big thing, sometimes wind, always power outages. Laurie never evacuated, of course; she had the horses to take care of so there was no running away. My parents didn't, either. We just rolled down the hurricane shutters, made sure the generator was gassed up, and filled the bathtub with water.

I told Lacey about that and she raised her eyebrows. "You drank out of the bathtub?"

"No," I said. "The water was for flushing the toilet."

She made a face. "Let's at least stay in the barn if there's a hurricane," she suggested. "We can pee in a stall and pretend it's a horse show."

"That's a good idea. At least the barn is concrete block." My double-wide wasn't exactly hurricane-shelter rated.

She bit her lip. "So are you sure hurricanes aren't a big deal?"

"Sure, of course. I grew up in Florida. They're like big thunderstorms." I studied Lacey's nervous face. She had grown up in the north, where hurricanes were something you saw on the evening news, full of wreckage and reporters trying to stand up against howling winds. They weren't all like that. But the ones that were . . . well, what were the chances that would happen here? We weren't on the water like Punta Gorda. "I do have a prep kit. Want to see it?"

Lacey nodded.

Out in the tack room, I pulled a heavy rubber container out from behind a wooden trunk I'd scavenged from one of Laurie's former students, sliding it across the sandy linoleum floor with a scraping noise. Marcus wagged his tail, snuffling at the lid as I yanked it off the bin. "Get out," I told him. "There's nothing dead in here for you to roll in." I hoped so, anyway. I did a quick recon for dead mice and giant spiders, and then motioned for Lacey to come and take a look at the contents. I might not have a plan for myself, but I was pretty proud of my horses' hurricane supplies.

Bound in neat bundles with orange baling twine were piles and piles of luggage tags, spare leather halters, bags of braiding bands, yarn, roles of duct tape and packing tape, plastic gallon-sized bags, scissors, and permanent markers. Lacey peered in, pawed through the stacks, and finally shook her head. "I don't get it. What's all this for?"

"The luggage tags have the farm address and my phone number on them," I explained, picking up a bundle of the leather tags. "The braiding bands are for braiding them into everyone's tails. Extra leather halters in case someone doesn't have a leather halter when there is a storm coming in. Can't use nylon in case it gets caught on a broken fence or something—we need breakable halters. We write our phone number on paper and then use clear packing tape to wrap it onto the halter cheekpiece. And even if they lose their halter on a tree branch or something, at least one of the luggage tags will stay in."

She nodded. "So . . . they stay outside in a hurricane?"

"Depends on how strong it is. Big one, yes. In case the barn collapses."

"But . . . *we're* in the barn."

I pointed to the helmets hanging next to the tack room door. "Good news—we already have head protection."

Lacey put her face in her hands.

"It's really unlikely that we'd have a bad hurricane," I offered.

"We're right in the middle of the state. Storms are really weak by the time they get here."

She nodded slowly, reaching down to rub Marcus behind the ears as he sidled up against her. "Do you promise?"

I grinned and sat back on the cold floor. "Yes. I promise. No bad hurricanes will get you, or our farm."

17

I WAS SITTING on Mickey in the dressage arena, waiting for something to happen.

Fortunately, nothing was happening. My goofball gray hadn't given me another fit since he'd come running backward out of the horse trailer after Lochloosa two weeks ago, and now, the first time I'd been on him since the whole affair, he was acting as bored as a lesson pony. I dropped my feet from the stirrup irons and twisted my ankles in slow circles, loosening up the tense muscles in my legs. I'd been prepared for the worst, but Mickey evidently saved his worst for public performances. Which made the whole behavior problem rather harder to diagnose and solve.

A car door slammed behind us. Mickey started a little as I whipped around in the saddle. Unexpected guests were unusual here.

A battered SUV had pulled up in the parking lot and a tall figure was walking toward me. I saw Lacey come out of the barn, get a good look at the man, and back off a little. I assumed she didn't know him and picked up my stirrups, prepared to put on my professional face and send this guy packing. Every now and then we felt a little exposed, being two girls alone in the countryside.

But there was something familiar about this guy's walk . . .

"Morning, Jules," he called, and I realized, with that curious mixture of elation and panic I felt whenever I saw him, that it was Pete Morrison.

"Morning, Pete," I replied, keeping my voice steady, but I didn't bother to move Mickey. I let Pete come to me, picking his way around puddles and slopping through the deep wet sand of the arena. Mickey watched his approach with pricked ears but didn't move. I couldn't help but be pleased to be sitting on the problem horse with loose reins and slumped shoulders, now that a rival trainer had come to gawk at him. And I had no doubt that was why Pete Morrison had driven all the way out to West of Nowhere, Florida, on a perfectly good morning for training.

"So this is Danger Mouse at rest!" Peter announced as he reached us. Mickey flicked an ear at him and sighed: *So bored*. I could have kissed the horse then and there.

"This is him!" I smiled and gave Mickey a pat on the neck. "A few days off to settle, and now he's begging to work."

"Time off can do wonders," he agreed. "Becky says hello, before I forget."

"Becky?" I scowled, caught myself, and tried to just look inquiring. "How is Becky?"

"Oh, she's fantastic," Pete said eagerly, and I fought to keep my expression interested. "Such a hard worker. And I can't believe she's managing to get her degree as well. Doing night classes in the fall term now, after working with me all day! More dedicated than I'd ever be for school!" He laughed.

I did not.

"Well, Pete, I was just hopping off Mickey here. It's been his first day under saddle for a while, like I said—we gave him some time off to regroup. I'm afraid we're not riding anyone else today. It's getting hot." I picked up the reins and gave Mickey a little nudge, and set off walking toward the barn.

"Taking it easy with this never-ending summer, then?" Pete didn't seem at all dismayed that we were done working; quite the contrary, he began walking alongside us, swinging his ball cap by his side, right into the barn. I slid off the horse in the shade of the barn aisle, and Lacey silently stripped the tack, giving me little sidelong glances all the while, before taking Mickey off for his bath and leaving me alone with Pete.

"Listen, Jules," he said once she was gone, his voice low and earnest. "One of the reasons I came round was to see how Mickey was doing, and he looks really good—"

"Thanks . . . we work really hard on our horses, Pete. It's literally all we do." I unbuckled my hard hat and shook out my sweaty ponytail. Pete did not look at all put off by my red face and drenched hair. I supposed he was used to sweaty horsewomen. Of course, he spent most of his day being drenched in sweat, as well. We had that much in common.

"That's what you told me. But you ought to get out more," he suggested, grinning. "Go have some fun without horses."

This again? I forced a laugh. "No such thing. I know exactly what I want, and this is where I'm going to get it, not out at some country bar."

He followed me into the tack room, and I could feel his gaze on the back of my head as I moved around, hanging up tack, straightening straps and gear. "Why did you come here, Pete?" I asked him.

"I was in the neighborhood."

"Looking at a horse?"

"A really cute one," Pete said.

"Did you buy him?"

"He didn't pass the vet."

"I hope this isn't one of the horses you were planning to pass on to me."

He laughed. "No. I'm keeping an eye out for a *sound* horse for you, I promise."

"You'd better." I sat down on a tack trunk, suddenly at ease with him enough to ask, "Why did you go for the ACE grant?"

He raised his eyebrows. "The same reason you did," he said. "Money and a sponsored horse. Who can turn that down?"

"You're a millionaire," I said.

Pete snorted. "Is *that* what you think?"

"I've been to your farm, remember."

"Trust me, Jules, it's complicated. And I'm not a millionaire. I promise you that."

"Fine," I said. "You're a multi-thousandaire. I'm still mad at you for beating me for something you didn't need."

"You have a pretty nice place here," Pete said, folding his arms and looking around. "Maybe *you're* a secret millionaire."

"Oh, if only." I shook my head. He wasn't going to be honest with me about it? Fine. It didn't matter anymore. I had Mickey, didn't I? "Okay, so you didn't buy the horse. And you haven't found one for me yet, which, you're slacking off, buddy. What's next?"

Pete looked at me for a moment. Then he said, "Next, I take you out to dinner."

I shook my head, startled. Where did that come from? "What?"

"Come on. We're practically the only living souls in Ocala right now. The show circuit won't pick up for another month. There's just enough time for us to go out and have a nice conversation before everyone comes back and the town's bursting at the seams again."

I peered at him. He was serious. "Why?" I asked, suspicious.

"Because I like hanging out with talented, dedicated equestrians?"

Hanging out. So . . . he was not asking me on a date.

"And also," Pete said, flicking his gaze to the floor for a moment, as if embarrassed, "because ever since I saw you kissing on your horse at Longacres, I've had a little crush on you."

My heart did a pointless flutter that just made me mad at myself.

"Say something, please," Pete said. "I'm dying here."

"No," I said. "But thanks."

Pete sighed. "Why not? I thought we were friends."

Were we friends? I wasn't sure. We were friendly sometimes, sure, and I liked being around him sometimes, definitely—but he also kept taking things from me without permission. Money. Horses. Working students who swore they were leaving the business thanks to my bad example, and then went to work for him instead. Maybe we were friends despite all that, I'd have to think about it. But dating took things a step too far. Dating would give him a feeling of power over me I couldn't live with.

"I can't go out with you," I said. "I don't date horsemen. Like, as a general rule." The words felt sticky coming out, like they didn't want to leave my mouth. But it was true. I'd told Dr. Em the same thing at the beginning of summer. Apparently, she hadn't passed that on to Pete.

"What?" He looked genuinely baffled. "Who else are you going to see around here?"

"I don't date anyone. Like I've said a hundred times, I'm just focusing on horses. Becky should have told you that," I added.

He lifted his eyebrow in that familiar angle. "Becky's my groom, not my dating coach."

"Well, then, I'm telling you now. I don't have time for anything but horses. I'm concentrating on my career."

He turned away and gazed into the barn aisle. I felt bad for embarrassing him by saying no, but then again, I hadn't asked him to come by unannounced and drop a bombshell on my head, either. That was all his doing.

"I have to throw lunch hay," I said, to give him a reason to leave.

But he followed me down to the hay stall, and hooked a bale of hay by its orange twine binding before I could reach for it, slinging it into the wheelbarrow for me. I could feel Lacey's eyes on us, as she leaned out of the wash rack to see what we were up to.

"Thanks," I said, annoyed. "But I've got it. You can head out."

He handed me his pocketknife while I was still hunting for the steak knife I used to cut open bales. I took it grudgingly. Lacey must have let the knife fall between the hay and the stall wall again.

"Look, Jules—" Pete began.

The hay bale split open. I handed back his pocketknife and pulled the baling twine out, looping it into a big knot and hanging it over a nail already festooned with loops and loops of orange twine, my emergency supply for fixing just about anything that broke around the farm. "*What*, Pete?"

"Is this about Sheila Burns's horses, or the ACE grant, or what? Which one can I make up to you? I'm not sure where to start."

I hefted the wheelbarrow and backed up. He moved aside quickly and followed me up the barn aisle.

"It's about eventing," I said shortly. "I'm focused on where I'm going. And I cannot let anything get in my way. I don't think you have to work as hard as I do. Maybe you don't get it, because you've been given everything you need."

He held out hands for hay and I gave him two flakes, nodding to Dynamo's stall. He nudged Dynamo's head aside and threw the hay on the floor inside. "I don't have it as easy as you think," he said.

I handed him another flake of hay. "You've got the farm on the hill in Reddick. You've got the big horses, you've got a sponsor. You might not have made an Olympic team, yet, but you're already a big name, and you know it. Give the pony a half flake, please."

He obliged, pushing Passion's block-head out of the way so that he could get the hay into the stall.

"I want the farm on the hill, Pete," I went on. I threw hay into Mickey's empty stall. "I want the big horses, and I want the sponsors. That's what I came here for. And I can't stop until I've got it. Can't mess around, can't go on dates, can't think of anything else. I feel like you should understand that, if you're struggling, too. Which I seriously doubt, but, whatever you say."

He turned to me, but he was quiet. It was like he was inviting more, like he wanted me to keep going.

But I was done. I'd said all that mattered. And I was afraid if he kept watching me like that, he'd get me to admit something I wasn't willing to say, not even to myself. That I liked him, that if there was some reason why he felt compelled to seek me out at events or when he was in the neighborhood, well, I kind of felt it, too.

I looked back at the empty wheelbarrow. "Thanks for helping," I said at last. I turned around and pushed it back to the hay stall.

"You're welcome," he said.

Lacey had been grazing Mickey outside while he dried from his bath. She waited until Pete's SUV was gone before she walked the horse back in, his shoes clip-clopping on the concrete aisle.

"What was that about?" she asked, once she'd put Mickey away.

"Oh, Becky says hello, apparently," I said, as if that was the whole point of his visit.

"Ugh, this Becky thing is so awkward. What else did he want? He didn't drive out here and follow you around for that."

"He asked me out."

"And you said no," Lacey said, shaking her head like I'd made a mistake. "Why? Because he's rich? Because rich boyfriends could be handy around here."

"He *says* he isn't rich," I scoffed, and Lacey snorted. "But that isn't the only thing."

I leaned over the stall door and rubbed Mickey on his damp neck, feeling the tautness of his skin beneath his gray coat. He felt healthy and fit; his break had been good for him. "Dating a horseman would be the worst. He'd second-guess everything I did with a horse. I mean, really, he said one of the reasons he came over was to see how I was doing with Mickey. I know he wanted to see if I could handle this horse or if I'd given up yet. And it would be like that *all the time* if we were dating. I couldn't deal with that."

"So all horse people are just like, completely unacceptable to you? Are you going to stay single forever? Can I live in your house with you until we are old spinsters?"

"Sure. Or maybe I'll find some nice accountant or something."

"An *accountant*!" Lacey screamed with laughter. She clutched at her chest dramatically and flung herself around the barn aisle.

I watched, arms crossed, until she subsided. "What's so funny about that?" I demanded.

"Look around you," she gasped. "What accountant would ever put up with a horse trainer? You don't even get much more than a fifty-cent ribbon for winning a three-day event that costs two hundred dollars just to enter! This is the most uneconomical job in the entire world. The only thing you could do to make yourself be less attractive to an accountant would be to literally burn dollar bills for a living."

"You're probably right. But you get my point, right?"

"Yeah." Lacey sobered up and gave me a pointed look. "I get it. You don't want anybody telling you you're wrong."

Y*ou don't want anybody telling you you're wrong.*
    Lacey's words stuck with me all day. She fell asleep on the couch and snored away while I listened to the afternoon rain beat on the windows and thought about it. Well, of course I didn't want anybody to tell me I was wrong, I reasoned. Who would want that? And what kind of relationship would two horse trainers have? I could just imagine our dinner conversations.

"Well, I had a little trouble with the chestnut mare today."

"Did you try her in a new bit?"

"Yes, Pete."

"Did you try longeing her?"

"Yes, Pete."

"What about leg yields? Try those?"

"Yes, Pete."

"Do you want me to get on her?"

"Go to hell, Pete."

I simply couldn't deal with it.

There was only room in a relationship for *one* expert. That much, I was certain of.

What I was supposed to do with all those tingles and trembles and goose bumps whenever he came into my field of vision, that was an entirely different question.

18

THE WEATHER RADIO woke us both up from a fantastic afternoon nap, blaring through the double-wide like a harbinger of the end of the world. Lacey was up first, bounding into the kitchen to slap the message button. The robo-meteorologist, popularly nicknamed Igor for his mechanical Russian accent, started droning away. I looked out the window, bleary-eyed. The sun was shining, not a cloud in the sky. I furrowed my brow.

"Marion County, Citrus County, Levy County," Igor recited, like a chant, midway through a message.

"What's he talking about?" I asked. "Do you see anything out there?"

Lacey shook her head. "No idea. It looks like the storms passed us. Sky's clear."

That's what I thought, too. I got up slowly and gave Marcus a rub on his belly. The beagle flapped his tail against the ground. He was thrilled that we'd joined him for an afternoon nap. It was a beagle dream come true.

"*Hillsborough County, Pinellas County . . .*"

"That's not even close to here," I said. "That's Tampa Bay."

"Maybe the radio's broke," Lacey suggested.

"*A hurricane warning means that hurricane conditions are imminent and precautions should be taken to protect life and property.*"

I jerked my head around to look at the radio. "A *what* now?"

Lacey looked at me with wide eyes. "Is this a test?"

"It must be a test." I picked up my phone and saw the long line of messages crowding the screen. HURRICANE WATCH. HURRICANE WARNING. SPECIAL WEATHER STATEMENT. "Uh . . . is your phone . . ."

And then my phone rang, scaring me half to death. The number on the screen didn't help much. "Jesus Christ," I said. "My mother."

Lacey was looking at her phone. "Jules? It's a test, right?"

I answered the call.

"I know you don't pay attention to the weather," my mother announced briskly, without greeting. "That's why I'm calling you."

"I don't . . . what?"

"The *weather*, the *weather*. You know, rain and wind and bad things? There's a hurricane watch, that's what."

"I think it's a warning," I said, confused. "Where did this come from?"

"There's a warning for Tampa," she corrected. "It's just a watch for your neck of the woods. But you're next."

I rubbed my face. The last time I'd seen the tropical forecast, some weak storm had been heading for Louisiana. That had been two days ago, and since then, I hadn't given it a second thought. "What happened to New Orleans getting this thing?"

"Low pressure. Change of plans. Act of God. Something. You better go get supplies. You have a plan for the horses?"

"The same as always, I guess, the same as we did when that storm came through when I was in tenth grade. Phone numbers on halters, luggage tags in their manes, turn them out—" I paused, feeling shellshocked. "Is this thing going to get bad?"

"They're all bad now, Jules."

"Right."

"The Weather Channel is sending Jim Cantore to just north of Tampa. It's a straight line from him to you."

Well, that wasn't good news.

"Okay. Fine." I was not ready for this. That's what I didn't say. "We can handle it," I said instead, because I had to.

"You going to stay there?" she asked.

"In the barn. It's cinder block . . . there are shutters we can close, and we can stay in the tack room." I looked up at Lacey, who was still standing in the kitchen, watching me with big eyes. Poor northern girl. For me, having grown up with the summers of nerves and free hurricane-tracking charts from Publix and the big storms that knocked out power for months on end and missing school for "hurricane days" (much cooler-sounding than snow days), I felt that familiar swirl of adrenaline and fear. It was not unlike reaching the top of a roller coaster's highest tower. *Something bad could happen! We could be in serious danger! Wow!* But having my own farm sort of took all the fun out of bad weather now.

"I'd tell you to get the hell out of town but it's too late for that, 75 will be jammed." My mom honestly sounded as if she was having a good time. She *liked* catastrophes—that must be where I got it from. They broke up the monotony of the workday, they gave her something to organize. She ought to have run the Red Cross or something. "Listen, call if you need anything. I'm going to go make sure our storm shutters are working. Bring your weather radio out to the barn with you today. You'll want to know if things change.

And you better go to the feed store and stock up. If the power's out, there's no gas, and if there's no gas, there's no shipments."

"It's fun living on a peninsula," I said.

"A blast," she said dryly, and hung up.

I went to the kitchen and gave Lacey a friendly pat on the shoulder. "Well, this is interesting."

Lacey didn't look up from her phone. She was scrolling through miles of weather news. "Why didn't we know about this?"

"We were busy?"

"It could start storming tomorrow night!"

"What else is new?" I tried to keep my tone light. "It's always storming."

"Jules." Lacey put down her phone and looked up at me. "What do we do?" She was genuinely afraid.

I wasn't. My nerves were singing with anticipation. I realized that I'd been looking for something major to occupy me all summer, something bigger than schooling horses, and this hurricane was hitting all the right buttons. "Supplies first, then batten down the hatches. Gotta stock up on feed . . ." *Along with the rest of Ocala,* I thought. It was going to be busy out there. "We better divide and conquer. You go to the store. Look for shelf-stable food and bottled water. If anyone loses electricity for a month, it'll be us."

"A *month*? That can happen?"

"It happened to some people when I was in high school. We didn't have power for three weeks at home—it was worse farther out in the country. I'm not saying it's going to happen here, but there's definitely a precedent."

Lacey's mouth was open and perfectly round. I suspected this was what hyperventilating looked like and initiated damage control.

"Listen," I told her in the most reassuring tones I could muster.

"It will be fine. Most hurricanes are just big, annoying thunder-storms that don't want to end. They take forever and you get bored waiting. Then you have to go outside and pick up tree branches and other people's garbage that blew onto your property. They're more of a pain in the ass than anything. Let's just . . . we'll flip on the TV real quick and see what we're up against. Maybe it's not as bad as my mom is making it out to be. Remember, the other night, this was just a tropical storm heading for Louisiana."

Lacey turned off the weather radio, silencing Igor as he ad-monished residents not to drain their swimming pools, and made a beeline for the living room.

If I was looking to comfort Lacey with the Weather Channel, I was looking in the wrong place. The TV network was wall-to-wall red alerts, storm warning graphics, and beachside reporters. I winced when a meteorologist appeared on-screen alongside the fishing docks of Cedar Key, the little gulf island about an hour to our west.

"And of course we're just at sea level here and a direct hit from a major hurricane would cause catastrophic flooding," the meteorol-ogist was explaining, with an enthusiasm that I found questionable. "It's entirely possible that at this time tomorrow, this entire scene around us will be underwater." She smiled beatifically at the cam-era. All around her, car doors slammed. People were getting out. The water flapped lazily against the boat ramp in the background, the gulf stretching out in a big, drowsy sweep of green water.

When the screen cut to a reporter at a frantically busy Home Depot in a Tampa suburb, I had to call a halt to the disaster porn. It was time to go join the panicking masses. "Lacey, you're going to have to take the car and go to Winn-Dixie or Publix in town. Not Williston. And don't go to Walmart, whatever you do."

"Why not? It's bigger."

"Precisely why it's the first place to get cleaned out."

In the office, my sleeping computer suddenly came awake and started dinging with incoming messages. Probably boarders wanting to know what was happening with the horses. I sighed. "Head out, Lacey. It's going to be insane out there. I have to email these people real quick or they're going to freak out about their horses."

Lacey snatched her keys and rammed a ball cap over her messy ponytail. "If I have to go to the store, where will be you going?"

"Feed store. We need to load up on grain and hay. If the interstates get blocked or flooded, there won't be any deliveries."

At the feed store nearest to us, there was a line of trucks half a mile long, hazard lights blinking along the sandy shoulder of the county highway. I grimly joined the queue, flipped on my own hazards, and leaned back on the headrest, allowing the truck to crawl forward every few minutes. The tires bumped over discarded Coors Light cans. The local NPR station reporters talked about hurricane evacuation zones, bare grocery store shelves, traffic jams on the highways leading away from the coasts. They talked about rapid intensification and worst-case scenarios. They talked about inland wind damage and flooding rains.

"Are hurricanes worse now than they were ten years ago?" a reporter asked a meteorologist.

"Ken," she said, "statistically, they're worse than they were five years ago. If you think you know what you're up against because you're a longtime Floridian, please take a moment to look at this with an open mind."

I wasn't loving this report.

It took nearly forty-five minutes before I reached the parking lot, which was oddly empty. I recognized the cars of a couple of the regular employees, but no one else, just the line of trucks heading forward into the loading area. Where was everyone? A salesgirl came up to my window and I hit the button to lower the window.

"Howdy," she said. Her face was red with heat beneath her ball cap, which advertised a brand of horse dewormer. "Loading dock service only. I'll take your feed order. Need anything from inside? Buckets, halters, meds?"

"I'm good." I asked for my usual high-energy feed mix. "Maybe thirty bags?"

"I got five," she said, scanning her legal pad, which was scrawled over with crossed-out items and tally marks. "I can round off the other twenty-five with senior feed. It's easy to digest so you shouldn't have any colic trouble if you switch 'em."

"Yeah, that's fine." I guess I was lucky I'd gotten anything more desirable than the store-brand feed, Lucky's Pride Horse Pellets.

She picked up a walkie-talkie and relayed the order to the loading bay, including the color and make of my truck. "Any hay?"

"What do you have?"

"I got plenty coastal. I got three dozen O and A, some peanut, some hun'erd pound timothy and alfalfa . . ." She trailed off.

"Ten of the hundred-pound T and A," I decided. I didn't have that kind of cash in the bank account, but I couldn't take chances with other people's horses. If we got cut off from civilization for a week or more, and the paddocks were flooded, I had to have hay for them.

"That it?"

"That's it." I fingered my credit card.

She wrote down my account information to ring up later, presumably when they ran out of feed and finally had a few free moments, and waved me forward to the loading dock. The truck groaned as it was assaulted with more than a ton of feed and hay. Days like this, I was extremely happy to have shelled out the extra bucks for the heavy-duty shocks on the truck. I was able to shuttle enough fodder back home for a week at an elephant farm.

I ended up wasting another twenty minutes' worth of diesel, idling in line at the gas station, but in the end, I somehow managed to wedge two cans of gasoline into the back of the truck along with the grain and hay. It wasn't really enough to keep the generator going for long, but if we lost power, it would let us cook something on the tack room hotplate, make some coffee, charge our phones. I shook my head at how outlandish these plans seemed. Nine times out of ten, nothing happened but a little wind and rain. I hoped we were still on number seven or eight, at least.

And sure, maybe next time I'd pay more attention to the weather. If I'd had any inkling there was a storm heading this way yesterday, I might have waited in much shorter lines.

When I got back to the farm around five, the sun was still hot and blinding in the western sky, not a storm cloud to be seen. *The calm before the storm,* I thought grimly, and turned the truck around to back it up to the barn aisle.

I blinked when I saw Manny sitting in front of the barn drinking a Corona. He didn't usually hang around when he was done with the stalls in the morning, because he drove down the road to Marchwood Thoroughbreds and fixed fences. With one hundred acres and nearly as many head of crazy little Thoroughbred babies crashing around, they had a lot of fence work to be done. He was usually gone by 10 A.M.

"Hey," I said, getting out of the truck. "Everything okay?"

Manny gestured upward with his Corona bottle. "Sky look pretty today."

I looked at the fluffy white clouds dotting the brilliant blue sky. "Yeah. One day without a thunderstorm, I guess."

"Gonna be hurricane, radio say. I come over to see if you need help getting ready. My other farm's all set."

I felt unexpected tears prick at my eyes. Who else around here would do that for me? I had no one to help me but Lacey, and she was half-panicked and ready to flee for home. "Thanks, Manny. I really do need some help with this hay."

He nodded and put down the beer bottle. Manny was the definition of small but mighty, and he hefted the huge, hundred-pound hay bales with popping biceps. I knew those muscles were exactly why he wore tank tops all the time. He thought Lacey and I appreciated the view. I did—the view of them doing work I couldn't manage on my own.

When we were finished, the feed room was heaped with sacks of grain, and the hay stall was piled high with new bales. It felt reassuring. Even if there wasn't a hurricane coming, I always felt safer and more successful when I had a full load of hay and feed in the barn.

Manny settled back down on his railroad tie and popped the cap from another Corona he'd fished out of a cooler in the bed of his pickup. I handed him a crumpled twenty that I'd had wadded up in my truck's cup holder, waiting for just this kind of occasion, and he pocketed it with a nod of appreciation. Then he waved his bottle at me. "Help yourself."

I didn't usually sit in front of my barn and drink—not exactly the image that I wanted to portray—but it didn't seem likely that any prospective clients were going to arrive unannounced the day before a major hurricane was predicted.

"Thanks," I said, and reached into the cooler for a dripping bottle of my own. We sat on the railroad tie and looked at the sky.

The sun was slowly sinking behind a growing shield of high clouds, and a breeze had mustered a little energy from the west, making the early evening feel almost pleasant. Manny was quiet, sipping his beer meditatively, and as I began to down mine, I noticed that my own brain slowed down and things began to feel a little less manic. Sure, we were in for a big storm tomorrow night, but honestly, what were the chances it would be some sort of record-breaking calamity? Everyone was just being extra cautious, and so was I. It was good horsemanship to be prepared.

We were still sitting in silent companionship, watching the darkening skies and their promise of future violence, when Lacey came back. She got out of the car slowly, and without saying a word, lifted her eyebrows at Manny. He nodded and she reached into the cooler. I got the distinct feeling that those two were on friendlier terms than they let on.

She sat down heavily next to me and twisted the cap off with her own work-roughened hand. When Lacey first came to ride with me, she'd had a manicure, and always wore gloves. It was pretty funny to think about now.

Just now, though, she didn't look like she wanted to be reminded of how silly her simpler life had been. She looked like . . . well, like she just went to a grocery store before a hurricane strike. Marcus appeared from the barn aisle and padded over to her, putting his head on her knee. She sighed and stroked his ears.

"Was it bad?" I asked sympathetically.

I had to wait for her to take a long, deep swig from the bottle before she would answer.

"Retirees and rednecks on a rampage," she said finally. "Overturned displays in the aisles. I had to step over broken wine bottles to get to the bottled water. An old woman in a motorized shopping cart rammed me when I tried to pull the last twelve-pack of Zephyrhills off the shelf. I thought she broke my ankle. So we're drinking store-brand tap water during the apocalypse, sorry. And eating five-dollar organic sunflower-seed bread, so I hope you like it. That's all that was left."

"I thought the Winn-Dixie in Williston would be worse," I said regretfully. "That's why I said to go to Publix in town. It's less isolated, there's more options."

"Well, you're the boss," she said, taking another long slug off the beer. "And you've lived here longer. I did get some shelf-stable food, and I got us a steak for tonight—no one was in the meat section."

"No one wants to buy meat in case the power goes out," I said. "It's grill night in Florida, emptying out the fridge."

"What else needs done here?"

"We have to go out and drag everything that's loose back into the barn—the jump standards, the dressage letters . . . everything."

"The horses will be out in the paddocks during the storm?"

"Yup." I'd had plenty of time to think about it, sitting in the truck and listening to the weathermen and reporters. The winds, should the center of the storm pass over us, would be well over one hundred miles an hour—enough to threaten the barn roof. We could cover ourselves with blankets if the roof started to go, but the horses couldn't. So they'd stay outside, and we'd all just have to hope no one was hit with debris. The idea made my heart pound faster, but it really was the safest way for them to weather a big storm.

"Should we top off the water troughs?" Lacey asked.

"I don't think that the outside water supply is going to be a problem."

We sat and watched the western sky, where lower clouds were

starting to boil up—the wet tropical squalls approaching the coast hundreds and hundreds of miles from the center of the storm. Ten minutes passed, twenty, and eventually there was no denying it—the beers were gone, our slight buzz was already waning, and there was still work to be done. I retrieved a few bottles of Gatorade from the tack room fridge to keep us going, and offered Manny another twenty bucks, a pack of hot dogs, and a case of water if he'd stay and help us move the heavy wooden jumps inside the barn. He smiled and nodded. I had no idea if he had his own family, his own place—anyone or anything to shop for before the hurricane—but he seemed content to stick around and help us out, and I was thankful.

Dragging the jump standards into the barn frightened the horses, and soon they were all jumping around their stalls, snorting and carrying on, looking at the once-familiar jumps like they were an alien invasion. Halfway through, I told Lacey to grab lead shanks and we turned everyone out early, so that they could run around the paddocks like idiots, drunk on fear of change and the unmistakable threat in the atmosphere.

To the west, the evening sky grew darker still, and the thunder was a low, continuous rumble. Occasionally the sound grew so deep it settled in my chest and hurt my eardrums, like standing against the speakers at a concert. From the house, we could hear the weather siren squealing constantly, the off-kilter tones of the weather bot listing off warning after warning for towns just to our west, north, and south. A tornado warning in Otter Creek. Hail in Dunnellon. Flood advisories for Alachua County. Excessive lightning and wind gusts in Bronson. Reminders of the hurricane warning, over and over again. But the swath of fertile oak-lined hills from Ocala to Williston still lay dry and in shadow.

"Is this the hurricane?" Lacey asked fearfully, watching the lightning flash in the distance.

"Just a line of storms kicked up with extra tropical juice," I said. "Normal."

"None of this is normal," she muttered.

"Welcome to Florida."

We were oiling the chains of the garage doors that theoretically pulled down over the aisle entrances, hoping we could coax them down when the weather turned bad, when I heard a car pulling into the gravel of the parking area. I went to investigate. Becky was getting out of her little car, eyeing our row of Corona bottles perched on the railroad tie like the aftermath of a relatively tame frat bash.

"Becky," I said, trying to disguise my surprise. "Long time no see," I added, by way of a greeting.

"Pete sent me over, to see if you were okay before the storm. It looks like it's really happening—I heard it on the radio while I was driving over . . . seventy-five percent chance the eye will pass right over us here."

"Yeah, I heard. The weather radio won't shut up."

We both surveyed the dark sky, then Becky looked back at Manny's truck. "We got all our things inside and the horses ready . . . so we thought of you guys, just the two of you . . . but I didn't realize you had help. Whose truck is that?"

"Manny's . . . he's helping us."

"Manny?"

"Our stall guy."

"Oh, that's nice." I could hear the quiet disbelief in her tone—*How can they afford someone to muck stalls?*

"What about you?" she asked, changing the subject. "Where are you going to ride out the storm?"

"The tack room," I said, shrugging it off like it was nothing. "We're going to close the doors to keep the wind from going down the barn aisle—and close the shutters on the stall windows. We'll be fine in there."

"Will you? Do you think the doors will hold up against a category three storm? That's like, a-hundred-and-twenty-mile-an-hour winds, at least . . . if you lose the doors, you'll lose the roof."

"It's the best option we've got," I insisted, annoyed. "We can't leave. What if we couldn't get back? I have a barn full of horses to think about—and most of them don't belong to me."

"Yeah, true. We have twenty in our barn . . ." That was unnecessary, I thought. "But the house is pretty new. Up to date on all those hurricane codes. We'll be in there."

She glanced at my double-wide.

I didn't reply.

Becky took the hint. "Okay, well, if you're okay, I'll head back now. Let Pete know you're all set. And don't hesitate to call if you need anything."

"Yes, thank you very much for coming . . . Seriously." I escorted her to her car, hastening her departure.

Lacey came out of the barn as soon as the car disappeared over the hill. She had probably been hiding just inside the end stall, listening to our every word.

"What did *she* want?"

I felt way too tired for this. "Can we not have this rivalry thing, please? Or at least let it go while we're planning for the end of the world? I don't have the energy to deal with hurricanes *and* high-school jealousy. Okay?"

Lacey was taken aback. "Sorry," she said, clearly hurt. "Manny says the doors are all set."

"Oh, thank God. Let's go eat. I'm losing my mind with this. I need meat."

Lacey nodded and headed for the house, ready to take on her duties as my personal chef, but I hung back for a moment, looking at my shuttered barn and my empty arenas. Without jumps and dressage letters, the riding arenas were just big patches of irregular sand rectangles, waterlogged and pitted with puddles. The farm looked desolate already, even with the horses turned out and settled down to graze, their tails whipping in the stiff breeze. *We should have brought them back in,* I thought, and then I felt overwhelmed by the futility of it all, the constant life-and-death situations that living with horses brought down on my shoulders. Inside in the storms tonight, outside in a hurricane tomorrow—make it make sense. Anyone. Please.

Manny came out of the barn and got into his truck. He waved out the window, then flicked on the windshield wipers. A few drops of rain stained the ground at my feet. The first squall was blowing in.

"I'm not ready for this," I said, looking around. And then I squared my shoulders, put my chin up. "But that's okay."

I knew I was going to be drenched to the skin if I stayed out any longer, but still I stood in the coming storm and stared, until my eyes blurred and I couldn't see anything at all anymore. My farm, my start. My horses. My Dynamo, my baby. My Mickey, my big chance. They would be turned out in the storm, while we huddled inside, and hoped, and prayed.

Make it make sense.

None of this made sense, when you came down to it. The horses, the jumps, the dressage, the sacrifice, the money and the sponsors and the everlasting circle of training and cleaning and laughing and crying. Nothing *had* to make sense, though. It all just was.

"I love you," I told the farm, the horses, the barn, the oak tree whipping in the gusts.

The heavy rain was marching across the paddocks, a swiftly moving wall of water obscuring the tree line beyond the mares' pasture, and I ran for the house before it could touch me.

19

OUR DINNER THAT night was tense.

We ate in the living room, the TV set to the local news. The networks had all suspended the usual reality shows and crime dramas for as much on-scene reporting as possible. The weatherman on my favorite local news channel had rolled up his sleeves and taken off his tie, which was a sure sign of impending doom. His name was Frederick Lewis, but a few hurricane seasons ago, a particularly cataclysmic year seemed to unhinge him, and he was now known by local wags as Freak-Out Freddy.

Needless to say, Freak-Out Freddy's outbursts made his channel the highest-rated station in any sort of weather calamity. There were entire YouTube channels dedicated to chronicling his on-air panic attacks. He was our buddy in storms, though. Freak-Out Freddy got it. Storms were just a little crazy, and he responded by going a little crazy, in kind.

The storms that had been hovering nearby all evening finally began crashing around our ears as we worked our way through our supper, and in the premature darkness Lacey blended up mudslides and we laughed nervously at the interviews with panicked tourists evacuating from Tampa-area hotels, and shook our heads at the fifty-mile backups on interstate 75. The weather radio continued to squeal its alarm at regular intervals, announcing flooding on the Rainbow River, a tornado near Morriston, nickel-sized hail in Reddick. It felt like the hurricane was here already. But this was just the warm-up act.

My ears pricked when I heard Igor mention Reddick and I sat up on the couch, dropping my paper plate from my lap. Marcus slithered down from the cushion next to me, wagging his tail as he went to work on the steak juice, but I ignored him. I was thinking, involuntarily, of Pete Morrison, hoping he and his horses and yes, even Becky, were safely indoors, away from the bruising, cutting hailstones. I glanced at Lacey, as if she might have noticed I was thinking about Pete, but she was fixated on Freak-Out Freddy as he illustrated, with a homemade computer graphic, how the cumulative effect of more than four hours of hundred-mile-an-hour sustained winds can easily tear the roof off a new house built to the latest hurricane codes.

Her eyes were like saucers.

"No more TV for you," I suggested.

"I need to know this stuff!"

Lightning flashed outside the windows, and the thunder rattled the floor of the trailer, reminding me that Pete wasn't really the one in a precarious situation here.

"The bad stuff won't come until tomorrow," I told Lacey. "We can relax tonight. You can study building codes all day tomorrow, if you want."

Lacey shook her head and gestured to Freddy. "We have to listen for tornadoes tonight, he says."

"We have to listen for tornadoes every night," I said. "That's just a fact of life. That's why I have a weather radio."

"It's more likely with a tropical band spiraling onshore," she parroted.

I sighed. "Freddy would be proud. You stay up and keep watch if you want. But I'm going to bed."

In the night I woke up to the sound of wind; the trailer was creaking and groaning as gusts hit the southern frontage. A few small branches from a nearby bottlebrush tree pinged against my window. I went to the window and looked out at the paddocks. In the orange glow from the streetlight, Dynamo stood with his tail to the wind, grazing as if nothing was going on. It wasn't raining anymore, despite the howling wind. A plastic bag from heaven knew where went scudding through the grass between the house and the barn, and Dynamo started, trotting a few paces, before he came back to a halt and put his head down to graze again. I leaned against the window a few more minutes, feeling it vibrate with the wind, but he didn't spook again and I figured if Dynamo could have a normal night, I should be able to manage it, too. I sighed and climbed back into bed, wiggling close to Marcus. He sighed and licked my nose before going back to sleep.

The next morning was cloudy and windy, with occasional bursts of rain slapping against the windows. The outer walls of the huge hurricane, though its center was still way out in the gulf, were coming ashore and rolling up the coastal plain toward our farms and homes. It was knocking on our door.

Lacey was standing at the living room window, holding back the blinds with a shaking hand. "What do we do now?" she quavered.

"Bring the horses in and feed them breakfast, then throw 'em back out," I said pragmatically, pulling on rubber boots. "No work today."

As if doing any sort of riding would have been possible in the squalls. When faced with the horses' kicking, bucking, galloping, sliding antics, even my determination to keep a stiff upper lip took a blow. They'd gotten amped up this morning.

"This isn't good," I had to mutter, as a wild-eyed Dynamo came lurching up to the fence line, sliding up to the gate and ripping up a six-foot section of sod in the process. Everyone else was in the same sort of hysteria. The farm was in an uproar.

"Can't we just leave them out?" Lacey suggested. "I don't think skipping breakfast would hurt them today."

I shook my head regretfully, watching the horses spin and cavort. "I wish. But we have to tag them."

Eventually, we got the whole crew into the barn without anyone getting loose or kicked or bitten or trampled upon. Mud-spattered, the horses ate their breakfast in huge, fast bites, turning in anxious circles to look out their windows, oats trailing out of their mouths and leaving sweet molasses trails in the stalls for the ants to delight in later. Even Passion, who never found anything more interesting than food in front of his face, managed to make a mess of both his stall and his handful of feed.

Getting manes and tails tagged while the horses were leaping about like startled gazelles wasn't the easiest of tasks either. It took Lacey holding a chain shank over Mickey's nose, warning him to stand still or *else,* to braid a luggage tag into his dark mane. Even gentle Monty needed a stern reminder to be still while we were working on him.

We wrapped the cheekpieces of all the halters with duct tape and wrote our contact information on the tape, and then everyone got kicked back out to the paddocks.

Horses never appreciate a change in routine, any more than they did the scent of the storm in the air and the blasts of hot humid wind. So once they were out again, there was a lot more running and squealing and bucking and farting. After Mickey's particularly crazed gallop ended in a sliding stop that nearly threw him back on his haunches to avoid crashing into the fence, we filled a wheelbarrow with hay and tossed piles into every paddock, and they settled down for the unexpected treat.

"What now?" Lacey asked. She had been asking "what now" constantly since the first news of the storm yesterday morning and it was starting to make me a little crazy. I didn't *know* what now. I had never done this before. Sure, I'd been through hurricanes before . . . but then, I had always been the working student.

Being the boss during a natural disaster wasn't exactly easy.

"We cook a good breakfast while the power is on," I announced after a few moments' thought. "Then we move my bedroom TV into the tack room. *If* we have to evacuate to the barn, we can watch TV as long as we have power."

"Freak-Out Freddy will be with us."

"He'll keep us safe." I grinned.

But Lacey was already looking back at the horses. "Will they be okay, seriously?"

I looked out at the horses, nose-deep in hay while the wind fluttered their manes and tails. They *had* to be okay. These horses, and this farm, were all I had. I knew the wisdom was to keep them outside. I knew all the reasons. But I still hated doing it.

"Just fine," I said with a bravado I didn't feel. "Hurricanes are always a major letdown. Big thunderstorms. The annoying part is losing power. But we're set for it. We'll be fine in the tack room, it will blow through by tomorrow morning, and then we'll go bring the horses in and feed them a late breakfast."

I wish it had happened the way that I had said it would happen. For a while, it did. The storm blew in, first with squall line after squall line, every twenty minutes or so a new microburst whipping across the farm, blasts of wind-driven rain like a hailstorm of pellets beating furiously against the windows, only to subside nearly immediately back into half-hearted drizzle, or even just dark skies, with only that warm, humid wind as evidence that there was something different in the air. And the clouds—the low, racing clouds scudding past the higher ones, which moved grandly and with grim purpose above us, spinning to the southeast as the distant eye of the storm slowly slid northeast.

Of course, it was that contrast in direction, the northeast march of the storm and the southeastern crawl of its lower decks of clouds, that would cause all the problems.

We sat in the house at suppertime, the horses in the wet fields sedated with more hay, and ate hamburgers and French fries and watched as Freak-Out Freddy loosened his tie and rolled up the sleeves on his dress shirt. There were little white spinning graphics on the radar images, indicating possible tornadoes. There was one near Cedar Key. Then one down near Inverness, to our south. Then one in Orange Lake, to our northeast. We were surrounded by vortices within the vortex.

A branch from the bottlebrush tree hit the living room's picture window—a big branch, a sizable portion of the tree, in fact. We turned and watched the smashed petals of the pink bottlebrush flowers ooze down the glass with the streaming rain.

"It's about time to go," I told Lacey.

She put down her soda and looked at me. "Go?"

"To the tack room," I said. "Look." I put my finger to the glass of the television, right on top of one of the spinning circles. It was just to the west of us, near Rainbow Lakes. "This is all around now. Any one of these could be a tornado. This is just a trailer—it doesn't have to be a big tornado to wreck the house. That's why we have all that food and gear and the TV in the tack room, Lace. Let's just go out there, bolt the door, and be safe. Look—" I pointed to the big glass windows of the living room, shaking as a violent gust of wind hit them. "We don't even have boards on the windows—a branch could fly right through one of them. The tack room has a storm shutter on its window and the door is steel. Let's just go out now, okay? It's going to happen sooner or later anyway."

Lacey sighed and got up. "Let's do this."

It was about seven o'clock, and the sun was still out on the horizon somewhere, maybe in South Florida where it probably wasn't even cloudy, but it was gone from here without ever having shown its face. The world was draped in a dark, haunted-mansion kind of dusk. The fields on either side of the driveway shimmered with floodwater, green grass covered with black reflections of the darkened sky. Water below and water above. Only the driveway looked familiar, glinting through the gloom like a white ribbon, its gravel track raised above eight-foot-deep ditches on either side, dug out by the original owners, who had surely been in some doozy storms of their own.

Marcus came to my side, tail wagging, and I snapped a stray lead rope to his collar. "No wandering," I told him, wagging a finger. "We have to stick together."

We grabbed raincoats and went running through the stinging pellets of rain and the strangely warm wind, still tingling with the sunshine from above and the bathtub temperatures of the Gulf of Mexico, and then we were flinging open the side door to the tack room—the barn doors were already down and bolted—and lurching inside. With a struggle, I shoved the tack room door shut again and slammed the deadlock home. The steel door felt reassuringly strong. The accordion shutter had already been rolled down over the small tack room window, and the room, though dark, felt safe and a little cozy, with its comforting scents of leather and neatsfoot oil.

Lacey switched the little TV on immediately and Freak-Out Freddy was back in our lives. We had underground electric along the driveway from the main road—an unusual luxury from a forward-thinking previous tenant—and I had high hopes that we might hang on to electricity and the TV signal for a while. It was reassuring to know exactly what was going on out there, instead of just having to listen to it.

And it was getting loud. The noise of a hurricane is indescribable until you've heard it; after, you can never forget it. The sound of shopping cart wheels on the polished concrete floors of Sam's Club never failed to remind me of the weird moaning of the wind outside my parents' cinder block house. Dropping a pile of books on the floor at the library one day, I'd been reminded of the bang and clatter of branches and unknown objects on the roof, walls, and storm shutters. So far, all we heard was the moaning of the wind and the staccato bursts of rainfall, but I knew that the truly ghostly sounds were still to come.

We'd already laid in provisions, so I pulled out a bag of potato chips and went over to the washtub sink to mix a couple rum and Cokes. Lacey needed all the mellowing that she could get. Riding out hurricanes traditionally meant drinking parties. There was nothing else to do. We watched Freak-Out Freddy gesture frantically at the screen as he relayed reports of a waterspout moving onshore in Aripeka.

"That's a long way from here," Lacey ventured.

"Unfortunately, the storm is moving northeast, and Aripeka is southwest," I said. "It's north of Tampa."

"Oh," Lacey said glumly, and I thought perhaps I should have left her knowledge of Florida geography where it was, happily in the dark.

"And this cell right here," Freak-Out Freddy intoned, pointing to a spot on the map that pretty much correlated exactly with where we were sitting, "is ripe to produce a tornado, in fact I'd say there's already a tornado on the ground, but it's very hard to tell because during hurricanes, tornadoes jump up and down, they come and they go so rapidly—"

There was a sudden *bang* on the storm shutter. Lacey and I both spun around and stared at the dark window, but of course, it was covered by metal and there was nothing to be seen.

Bang.

I felt a numbness spread across my body. It was here.

"What's that?" Lacey ventured, voice quivering.

"Branches," I answered uncertainly. "Shingles. Fencing."

"The horses . . ."

"Yeah."

We were pretending to be secure in the barn, yet we hadn't trusted the barn enough to leave the horses in it. I told Lacey that we could survive a roof collapse, hiding under pillows and horse blankets. The horses would panic, tear down their stalls, kill themselves to escape. We left them out to take their chances and hope that the wind didn't start throwing bits of tree and structure and fence at them.

As it was doing now.

The banging went on and on, and the wind rose to that frantic moan, like banshees howling just outside, and the steel door of the tack room began to shift back and forth with little thumps, as the deadbolt caught it each time, wiggling in the lock, and the rain was beating against it with such force that water began to trickle through the jamb, and Lacey was curled up in a corner of the couch, clutching a blanket to her chest, eyes round with fear and horror, and Freak-Out Freddy was bellowing *"Hunker down if you're in Williston, right now, our friends up on the Nature Coast are really in for a beating now, the eye wall is nearly there and it's going to pass right over Williston in about half an hour . . . Remember not to go outside if the weather lets up, because it will start again without warning once the other side of the eye crosses you. You will have to be in a very specific place for the rains to stop at all, just hunker down, stay close, if you lose power get that battery-powered radio on so that you can be informed"*—a disembodied arm handed him a sheaf of paper—*"Folks, here's a confirmed tornado on the ground west of Williston, it's been seen by weather spotters on Highway 326 and it's moving northeast very quickly"*—he wasn't taking a breath and the storm was hammering at the barn, and the building was creaking and groaning and the wind was moaning on and on and on, and Lacey was starting to cry and I curled up around her, but I wasn't her mother, I wasn't even older than she was, and I couldn't comfort her either because I was realizing that this was it, this was the worst case, this was so far beyond anything I had ever experienced before, and with a great shrieking groan the roof began to peel away and rain was falling down on our heads, the lights were out and the TV was off and Freak-Out Freddy was long gone, and I was pulling her under the couch cushions, pulling horse blankets down over us, hoping most of the roof would stay on, wishing wishing wishing it had just gone like I said it would—

And then the squall passed, very suddenly, and the rain let up, and I looked out from beneath our little fort of sofa cushions and horse blankets. The wall between the door and the window was open to the air, the steel roof above us had peeled back like a tin can, and the drywall had soaked through and collapsed in the same instant that the roof gave way. There was a pile of wet white stuff in the corner, bits of the ceiling like snow draped across the tack trunk that sat there, and the rain was pattering down on it, spreading white goo across the tile floor in a growing puddle.

I didn't move for a long time.

Lacey was crying, face buried in the blanket, and we were both wet and smelled of horse, which really wasn't that different from usual, and I was just thinking that maybe we should get into a stall down the aisle somewhere, away from the damage of the roof, when I heard a noise outside. A diesel engine. A slamming car door. And then—

"Jules? *Jules?*"

Lacey snapped her head back and I jumped up, slipping out from under her, and ran to unlock the deadbolt. I stepped out into the wet, cataclysmic world, my boots crunching on the twigs and branches of what used to be my beloved oak tree. Now it was split and collapsed across the yard between the house and the barn. There were headlights in the parking lot and then I saw Pete Morrison, waving a flashlight and looking frantic.

20

"PETE! OH MY God, what are you doing out here?" My words were a little slurred and it occurred to me that I might be slightly drunk. I looked around wildly and saw that the roof of the barn had come to rest against my truck and trailer. Jagged sheets of metal trembled in the wind. "Shit," I whispered. We were trapped here until I could free the truck. And I was strong, but I didn't think I could pull half a barn roof away.

"Came to check on you," Peter said roughly. "And your student—is she here?"

Lacey came out, trembling, a polar fleece sheet wrapped around her. I could see the name embroidered across the blue cooler in bright yellow script: *Margeaux*. "That's Margot's cooler," I said, and she smiled in a dazed kind of way.

"I love Margot."

"You girls can't stay here," Pete said impatiently. "Get in the truck."

"We have a truck," Lacey said. "And a car."

I tugged at Margot's cooler, directing Lacey's attention to the barn roof that had decided to eat our vehicles.

"Oh."

"We need to go, now," Pete said.

Obviously, Pete was insane. "I can't leave. I have horses to take care of!" It occurred to me that I hadn't heard a sound from the horses all evening. Not a whinny, not a hoofbeat. What did that mean? Were they just out there with their tails to the wind? How did a horse even turn their tail to the wind when it was swirling around at a hundred miles an hour?

"You've got to," he declared in that same rough voice, as if he had been expecting trouble from me all along. "That barn isn't going to survive the other half of the storm. It's coming. We'll be right in the middle of it."

"What about the horses?"

"Your life has to come before theirs," Pete said.

That sounded kind of crazy, but at the same time, I knew he was right. "Maybe it won't be as bad," I said, looking around. "There's probably a stall here that still has the roof on—"

"Look at this," Pete said, shoving his phone at me. "Look at that radar picture. See the eye? We're *in* it. Do you know what a lucky chance that is? We've got a clear path to Reddick. If I floor it, we'll make it."

I looked at the radar picture, and I swallowed. The eye was wide, full of dry air as the hurricane began to crumble away from its source of energy in the Gulf of Mexico, but the squall lines on the western side were illuminated in bright oranges and reds, easily as dangerous as the ones that had rolled through a little while before. The ones that had just ripped the roof from over our heads.

Do you know what a lucky chance that is?

Pete didn't know about my bad, bad luck, though, did he?

"You shouldn't have come," I said. *Why* had he come?

"I had a premonition you'd need help. Now, get in the truck."

"A premonition? You could have died—"

"I still can, and so can you!" Pete turned on his heel. "Let's go."

I was feeling a bit dazed by the whole situation, and suddenly couldn't think of a good reason to decline his forceful invitation. There was probably nowhere to ride out the rest of the storm, and if it was half as bad as what had just rolled through, we really were risking our lives staying in this barn. I looked at Lacey and she nodded in the direction of the truck. "We should go," she said. And then: "I'm going."

Lacey set off for Pete's truck, leaving me to either ride it out alone, or come along.

I went along.

I clambered into the back seat after Lacey and looked back, unable, unwilling to close the door. Peter did it for me. Everything felt too sudden—I didn't have time to make a proper decision. The tack room door waved gently to us in the soft humid breeze; the ripped tin can of the roof wiggled back and forth above. Lacey took deep sobbing breaths, and I could barely see out the rain-riddled windows to try and assess the damage to my farm. The only saving grace was that there were no loose horses running around. And where the hell was Marcus?

That's what was missing.

I smacked the door latch and flung myself back out into the starry night. "Marcus! *Marcus!*"

A horse whinnied in the distance, and someone else returned the call. They sounded remarkably calm. All was well in the horse world, apparently.

Lacey was beside me, her hand on my arm. "We can't stay here."

"Are you *joking*?" I whipped around and fixed her with an icy stare. She quailed and stepped back. "You want me to leave my *dog*?"

Peter was out of the truck now, looking furious. "What the hell are you doing?"

"My dog," I snapped. "Marcus, Marcus, come, Marcus!" I wished that at some point in the past few years I had spent a minute or two teaching Marcus to actually listen to me. But I trained horses, not dogs. "Marcus!"

Peter swung his flashlight around the property, illuminating the pools of floodwater rippling in the breeze. "Look for his eyes."

We looked, but there were no green flashes, nothing to indicate my dog was out for his usual evening sniff. It wasn't like Marcus to wander; he was too lazy for that. So he must be—"He's under the house," I realized suddenly. "Oh, sweet Jesus."

I was terrified to go under the house. I wasn't afraid of much, but I was claustrophobic as hell and the crawlspace under the trailer was one place where my courage could not take me. But Marcus loved to go down there, and on the few occasions when weather had spooked him, that was where he hustled his fat little beagle self.

"Where does he get in?" Pete was all business.

"Under the front porch, by the steps—" But Pete was already running, the flashlight's beam bouncing off the house wall and dark windows as he splashed through the puddles in his Wellingtons. I took Lacey's elbow in cold fingers, forgetting that I'd just given her a glare I reserved for my worst enemies. "He's going to go under the house?"

She didn't try to shake me off. She just watched as Pete disappeared under the front porch, the flashlight, feeble now as its battery began to die, glowing through the wooden lattice around the deck. I thought of the mud and the bugs and felt my knees grow shaky.

There was a shout and a yelp, and I tightened my grip on Lacey's arm. And then he was emerging, dragging a shrieking beagle by its scruff.

"He's hurt!" Lacey put her hands to his mouth. "Oh my God . . ."

I felt dizzy. I was going to faint. I closed my eyes.

"Shut up! Shut up!" Pete was shouting. "You're fine! Shut up!"

"He's not hurt," I realized, and my heart started beating again, blood flushing my face. I was hot all over, but I was so relieved I nearly burst into laughter. "He's just being his whiny asshole self. Marcus, *shut up*!"

The dog went on yelping, twisting at the end of Pete's fisted grip on his scruff. He really was too big to be held like that, I reflected. But it was better than being abandoned under a mobile home during a hurricane.

"Here's your dog," Pete announced when he reached us, shoving the wet, muddy mass of dog into my arms, and I took him gratefully. Marcus whined once more for good measure and then settled for licking my wet face. I took the sloppy love, but my eyes were on Pete.

He looked back at me for a long moment, and then broke away, turning for the truck. "We have to get out of here."

I looked back at the dark paddocks. "Shine the headlights that way before we go."

He turned the truck around, avoiding a pile of roofing material, and flicked on the high beams.

I counted horses, looking back at us with pricked ears. "I think that's eleven," I said.

"I think so, too," Lacey murmured. She wrapped her arms around Marcus. "They look okay."

"We'll come back for them tomorrow," Pete promised. And he threw the truck into reverse, spinning us around.

The dually engine roared as we went flying over the debris-covered roads, splashing through giant puddles that threatened to overtake entire valleys, and part of me was urging him on, seeing the wind start to pick up in the trees outside, the rain starting to beat harder and with more determination on the windshield, and the other part was thinking with desperation of my horses, out there in the fields, beneath those stormy skies, and how would I ever get back to them? The roads were being washed over, the squalls rippling the clouds behind us were felling trees across the drives and the highways, and I would be separated from them for days.

Anything could happen. I had to get back.

But that wasn't going to happen now. Behind us, the storm must have already hit the farm. The barn would lose the rest of the roof. Ruined. Ruined. All of it. The house could easily be destroyed as well. Homeless, barnless, maybe horseless.

It was a half-hour drive to Pete's farm, all thirty minutes of it frantic, listening to the warnings on the radio. We shouldn't have been out, and it was a wonder we didn't have to swerve around more than three downed power poles, more than half a dozen toppled trees. Grimly determined, his jaw set, Pete never turned back from a flooded low spot, no matter how deep the water looked. The truck was made for this sort of heavy-duty evacuation drama. Freak-Out Freddy would have torn off his shirt and started jumping up and down on it if he had seen what we were doing. But I had a strange trust in Pete. And, for the first time in my life, I was tired of being in charge.

The driveway to Pete's farm, elegantly long, shaded by oak trees in the southern plantation style, was a threat to life and property now. The trees were flailing dangerously by the time the truck went roaring beneath them, branches slapping against the windshield.

Pete swore. "This place will never look the same."

"I'm sure it's been hit by hurricanes before," I said. Some devil inside me was still determined to play it off, like this storm was just like all the other ones, instead of a monster that had just demolished my life.

"Not like this. This is one for the record books. And we're out driving around in it like a bunch of crazy people." He pulled the truck up before the house. All the storm shutters had been rolled down, so that the big sprawling ranch looked like a pastel-painted bunker. I felt relief just looking at the house. Beneath the stereotypical Florida palette of candy-shell pink, it was a fort of concrete blocks, standing firmly against the wind.

"A house made of concrete, with more concrete poured down the middle of the blocks," he announced, hauling my door open. "It's like the blockhouses they built at launch pads. You could survive Godzilla in here."

That was a weird choice of impending disasters, I thought, but he was dragging us inside before I could reply. Even so, we managed to get soaked in the few short steps to the house. He slammed the door shut on the storm, turning the bolt and locking it all out, and I turned to see Becky, standing in the hallway, holding out fluffy towels.

Lacey's eyes grew wide as she reached for a towel. I could tell she was already wishing her eyes weren't so red and her nose wasn't so snuffly. *Sucks to be crying in front of Becky like this*, she was probably thinking. I had to agree.

"Thanks, Beck," I said, taking the towel. "It's chilly in here." I dripped a puddle onto the tiled floor. Marcus ran his tongue over it, disgustingly, and I gave him a nudge with my foot.

"Peter keeps the air turned down so low," she said, with a side-long smile at Pete. "I'm always telling him it's too cold for me."

I felt sick as the realization washed over me. She wasn't just riding out the storm in this house. *Becky is living with Pete.*

Was she more than his groom?

And what happened to his big old crush on me? I felt oddly offended. No, I hadn't wanted to date him . . . but that didn't give him permission to get over me, either.

Okay, you've officially lost your mind, I told myself.

Lacey was giving me little nervous glances, as if she was afraid I was going to say something inappropriate, but she was reading the situation all wrong. I wasn't angry that Pete wasn't into me anymore—well, that wasn't the only thing I was upset about, but I still wasn't sure why that was a problem—but I was *furious* that Becky had so easily insinuated herself into his life, into this beautiful farm and this beautiful house, while the rest of us had to work for what we wanted.

I had worked every day since I was just a kid. I gave up everything for a chance at being a trainer, and here was Becky, the absolute antithesis of the exhausted working student killing herself to get a shot at the top, handing out fluffy towels as the hostess of a Millionaire's Row farm. I had ten acres and an almost-certainly-collapsing barn, a double-wide trailer that probably wasn't there anymore, a dressage ring and some show jumps (maybe, if they were retrievable from beneath the debris). Until tonight, I'd had just enough to get by. Meanwhile, Pete had everything I could ever dream of and he still would, tomorrow. And here, enjoying it all . . . Becky.

Who was looking at me as nervously as Lacey was, as if she could read my confused thoughts.

The only one in the room who looked quite comfortable was Pete. "Come in and get some dry clothes," he said, evidently at ease now that he wasn't driving through a major hurricane, and we all filed into the house, while the storm outside began to hammer at the steel storm shutters again.

21

THE TRIP TO Pete's had taken thirty minutes, but the trip back to my farm the next morning took nearly two hours.

We weren't supposed to be on the roads at all. The sheriff had declared that the entire county was a disaster area, so everyone should please just stay at home and let the authorities get on with their cleanup. But Pete just looked at me and shook his head—he knew we had to go back.

Horsemen don't leave their horses, and I'd already been gone too long.

Officially, though, there was a curfew that didn't lift until 9 A.M., meaning we had to stay put or risk a ticket. I fell asleep around five o'clock, as the storm sounds began to wane and the wind stopped howling around the corners of the house, and when I woke up at seven, Becky and Pete had already gone outside to deal with their horses. I opened the front door and Marcus trotted past me to sniff around the wet front yard. In the distance, I saw people leading horses into the barn.

Lacey hadn't slept. She was still shaking from the night before, but I gave her coffee and a handful of mini Reese's Peanut Butter Cups that I found in a pantry. "Breakfast of champions," I said when I presented it to her in the living room, where she was still parked in front of the television. The sheriff was warning people to stay home and respect the curfew.

"Thanks," she said weakly, and sure enough, the combo of black coffee, milk chocolate, and the (probably-imagined) protein from the peanut butter brought her back from the edge of madness. It freshened me up as well. Looking around, I decided this was the perfect time to get a look at the house without anyone around, and get a better picture of just who Pete really was. The walls were covered with pictures: cross-country photos, steeplechase photos, hunting photos. It was exactly my style of decor, and I peered at the living room pictures eagerly, hoping to see some evolution of Pete's riding career.

But on closer inspection, none of the pictures in the house seemed to be of Pete. They were of his grandfather. He was an older man in the first picture I looked at, but his face grew younger as the pictures turned from color to black-and-white. In a large photo at the end of the hall, bathed in watery light from a window, he stood on a podium with his hunt cap under his arm, bald head gleaming in a bright southern sun, smiling as he accepted a medal. I studied his face. He looked an awful lot like Pete. I put a thumb over his head in one of the jumping photos, and the equitation could have been Pete's.

"You inherited everything," I muttered. "Even talent."

I turned my head and saw the open door of Pete's bedroom. There was a framed photo on the bedside table. I could just make out a horse's pricked ears and long profile. I crept into the room, hoping no one caught me snooping, but too curious about who Pete kept next to his pillow at night to pass up this chance.

The photo was of Pete, standing beside his mare, the lovely Regina. I picked it up gently, surprised that it wasn't a competition photo, the two of them leaping over some huge fence together. Instead they were captured in a moment of stillness, Regina saddled and bridled, Pete in his jacket and helmet, waiting for results or watching a fellow competitor. Both of them were concentrating very hard, the mare gazing forward with wide, bright eyes and pricked ears. It looked as though whatever they were watching had them both captivated with equal intensity and passion.

There was something about the picture that I loved, something about Pete's connection to his horse that appeared otherworldly, beyond the reach of ordinary horsemen. I gazed at it for longer than necessary.

And then Lacey came into the hallway, looking for me. I whipped my head around, feeling foolish, and she laughed.

"Whatcha lookin' at?" she asked in an exaggerated voice.

"Just these pictures . . ."

"Of Pete."

"Only the one. All the rest are of some older guy."

"You *like* him! Admit it."

"I do not." It was getting very sixth grade in here.

"You like him, you like him, you like him . . ." Lacey, apparently fully recovered, danced around me in a little shuffle.

"Well, he's living with Becky, so probably it wouldn't matter."

Lacey stopped dancing. "Are you sure?"

"She said last night that Pete *always* keeps it too cold in here for her."

"She could be coming in here to work in the office, or have lunch," Lacey pointed out. "Or else she has a bedroom here as part of her pay. Like I do with you?"

"This place probably has a barn apartment," I grumbled.

"Where his barn manager probably lives," Lacey said. "Anyway, how could he go from crushing on you to being into her? You two are, like, dead opposites."

"Maybe that's why," I mused. "Maybe Becky is a nice alternative to a bitch like me."

Lacey thought about it. Finally, she nodded. "That's gotta be it."

The front door slammed. "Breakfast time!" Pete announced.

In the kitchen, Pete was still wearing his muddy muck boots, and Becky was wrinkling her nose at the filthy tracks left in his wake.

Prude, I mouthed to Lacey, and she stifled a giggle.

Pete looked up questioningly.

"Are all the horses okay?" I asked.

"Not a scratch on them," Pete said. "Wish I could say the same for some of my trees."

"You have plenty of trees," Becky said.

Pete shrugged. "You can never have too many trees. I like riding in the shade."

I thought about my sunny stretch of heaven. My best shade tree was destroyed last night.

Breakfast turned out to be microwaved Jimmy Dean sausage biscuits. They tasted fantastic but slid down greasily and sat unhappily with the Peanut Butter Cups. I nursed my stomach with more coffee. I supposed I was a little hungover—Lacey and I had gotten really drunk at some point last night, right before the barn started to tear apart.

The barn would be gone. The barn would be gone. I had to get that into my head.

And the house, most likely.

But not the horses. I had to believe they were fine. And they were all that mattered. I put down my empty coffee cup. "It's nine o'clock," I said.

"Are we ready to go, then?" Pete asked.

Becky hopped up. "I'm going to go help Ramon with the horses," she said.

Pete looked at me. "We'll call her to come over if we need anything."

"Bye, guys, good luck," she called, practically running for the door.

I raised my eyebrows. "She's in a hurry to not help us, huh?"

"Ramon's the only one in the barn," Pete said. "Mikey stayed home with his family. She's just making sure he doesn't have to handle everything on his own."

"Sure," I said. "But seeing as your place looks virtually undamaged, and mine is probably destroyed . . ."

"We appreciate all your help," Lacey interrupted, giving me a sidelong glare. "Really. And I know it was a luxury to be here and have the TV and know what was going on, because they're saying on the news that like eighty percent of the county lost power."

"I don't remember the last time I've had the TV on for such a long time," Pete said. "I usually ignore it. Too busy."

"We leave ours on even when we're not in the house," I admitted. "But it's just background noise. When I lived alone, it was nice to pretend there were other people around. Farms get lonely." Hearing myself, I shut up quickly, wondering where all that was coming from. Must be the exhaustion talking.

Pete looked sympathetic. "At least you two have each other for company. That must be nice."

"Well, we're not together," Lacey blurted out. "If that's what you were thinking."

Peter burst out laughing. And after an embarrassed moment, Lacey and I did too. How else could you react to that?

"And, you have Becky living here," I said, pulling myself together and touching on the subject I couldn't leave alone. "So that's nice for you guys."

He frowned. "She's only been in the house a few days—her apartment had a leak, which is probably ten times worse now. And anyway, she tends to keep to her side of the house. There's a guest suite over there, past the garage door. Practically its own place."

"So you and Becky aren't—" Lacey said questioningly.

"Oh, no." Pete glanced between the two of us, then flicked his gaze away from mine.

I cast a furious look at Lacey. She looked back, clearly hiding her *I told you so* grin. I could tell by the dimples in her cheeks, even though she was covering up her lips with her coffee mug. Pete was looking fixedly at the remote control, as if he couldn't place just what it was for. And I realized that we'd just reopened the topic of my turning him down. *Nice work, Lacey.*

"So we're going to go back to the farm," I declared, to change the subject. Pete nodded, and we all got up to find our boots.

Outside was bewildering. We were driving roads that had become unrecognizable overnight. The trees had been battered by the wind, so even the ones that survived the storm were stripped bare. It was as if every tree had been suddenly transported into winter. Their leaves and needles, twigs and branches, were scattered across the ground in every direction, crunching under the truck tires. The unlucky trees that had been damaged bore great slashes of white in their brown trunks where the winds had torn them apart. The branches and trunks that had snapped off across the roadways brought with them great tangles of electric wires—still live and dangerous, for all we knew.

The damage was tremendous and terrifying. A massive live oak had fallen through the center of Derby Run's magnificent training barn, crushing the shining copper cupola that had crowned the central rotunda. The four-board fencing that ran all along Silver Tree's road frontage had completely collapsed.

"Where are their horses?" I wondered aloud, and Pete shook his head. "Hope to God they're in back pastures," he said, "and not running around the roads somewhere."

We didn't see our first loose horse until we were well west of town, but then we all gasped. Along the verge on either side of the county highway, an entire herd of horses was moving purposefully north, some of them snatching mouthfuls of grass as they went, others breaking into a jog as those behind them goaded them forward with teeth and pinned ears. A few wore mud-encrusted nylon halters; one had a half-broken halter hanging from his neck, dangerously close to his legs. I pictured a fine bone stepping into that unforgiving nylon strap—we all did, I'm sure—and shuddered. The rest of the horses were bareheaded.

"No identification," Pete said slowly, stopping the truck for a good long look. "They could be from anywhere. Just a bunch of loose horses in a county full of horses."

I thought of my own horses and swallowed, unable to speak.

For a half mile more, the scene around us was one of utter devastation. It was a shattered landscape, as if a bomb had gone off. The fences were all flattened, and horses wandered the grassy median of the deserted highway and jogged across the asphalt lanes. Horses tripped and hopped over the massive trunks of felled slash pines as they continued on their journey to destinations unknown. A few had scratches and scrapes but most were untouched by the storm, and they moved with purpose. The primal herd instinct to just keep moving had taken over their brains once the fences were out of their way.

We were silent and horrified, passing through the wreckage of a once-familiar enclave of farms. And then, suddenly, it all went back to normal, or as close to normal as the landscape could possibly be after a hurricane. The truck tires were still grinding across the carpet of branches, leaves, and pine needles, but the fences were upright and there was only the occasional snapped-off tree. Here and there we'd see an old single-wide trailer that hadn't survived, its insulation and linoleum hanging out of a gaping hole in its side, like organs slipping out of a death wound.

"Crazy," Pete managed, but Lacey and I sat in dazed silence, unable to think of anything but what might be waiting for us as we drove closer and closer to home.

And then we were there.

There was a tree over the entrance to the driveway. A tree. Over my driveway. And on top of my sign, my antique "Green Winter Farm" sign, the wooden post poking out like flattened roadkill.

Pete put the truck in park and we sat morosely on the branch-strewn shoulder of the road.

The fences were up. At least, the road-frontage fences were up. But these weren't my pastures. My farm was a furlong down the blocked driveway, hidden behind a low rise that was picturesque any other time, and positively diabolical now.

"We'll have to climb over the tree," I said decisively, impressed with the steadiness of my voice. It in no way matched the bone-deep trembling in my limbs. I climbed down from the truck and the others followed after in silence.

The day was turning bright and blustery, the spinning clouds left over from the storm pulling away rapidly, and we walked up my rutted, flooded driveway beneath a gleaming morning sun. I guess I could have chosen to take the sunlight as a good omen, but it all just seemed so inappropriate—the way it highlighted the white gashes on the oak trees, the way it sparkled in the deep puddles in the driveway. We didn't need a spotlight thrown on the difference a day and a hurricane can make.

At the top of the rise, Lacey simply started to cry, and I bit back my own howls with difficulty. *Just things,* I told myself, and forced myself to look past the devastation to the paddocks. The horses were grazing, right where I'd left them, like it was just another morning. Exhausted relief trickled through me like cold water down my spine.

I did a quick count—everyone was present and, judging by their colors, they were all in the same paddocks where I'd left them. A minor miracle on the best of days.

Sometimes that's all you can hope for with horses, that you get out of bed in the morning or come home from a trip to the store, and they're exactly where you left them. That same philosophy, times a million, applied after a hurricane.

And that was it, that was all that was right.

The bottlebrush tree had been stripped to twigs; all the leaves were gone, the red flowers torn away. Sad, but that was nothing. The lovely old oak tree had come down between the house and the barn, harming nothing but itself, but the pine tree at the far end had come down right on top of my house. Or what was left of my house, anyway, after the storm had stripped its roof and blown out two of the thin, metal-skinned walls. From where I stood, still a good distance away, I could see my bedroom scattered across the lawn. My blue sheets were vivid on the green grass; my pillows were piled up against the wall of the barn. The whole stretch of yard between the house and the barn, and the parking lot as well, was strewn with pink insulation and white sheets of paper. I fixated on the paper for a moment. How could I have had so much paper?

The barn still had four walls but it, too, had lost its roof—that first peeling panel in the tack room had been the beginning of the end. The metal had been wrenched up, sheet by sheet, until all the roofing lay scattered in the swampy pit of my dressage arena or across the parking lot. The wind had come in and shoved out all the shutters and one of the garage doors from the inside. The left-over pieces of wood and metal, mangled and cracked, were left to rattle in the stiff gusts of wind.

I'd lost everything that didn't whinny.

We walked closer and saw that beyond, behind the wreck of the house and the barn, the fences were nearly all intact. I hadn't lost my paddocks or my horses. But that was all. I kicked something and looked down—some of the crumpled paper. I picked it up and typewritten words jumped out at me.

—The hindquarters are engaged and the back lifts, creating impulsion and collection simultaneously. The horse is now ready to—

It was a page from one of my books.

All that scattered paper was the stripped pages of the training books from my shelves.

I scarcely noticed that it was Pete who put his arm around me, or that it was Pete whom I had collapsed into, biting back suffocating sobs, or that it was Pete rubbing my back and resting his stubbled chin on my head. My farm, my farm, my farm—I'd fought for this farm, fought my parents for it, fought the naysayers who called me a trust-fund baby, fought everyone to get my barn and fill its stalls with clients and land my sponsored horse and now . . . nothing.

"Nothing," I murmured, and scraped fiercely at my eyes. "There's nothing left."

"The horses," Peter murmured against my hair. "You've got the horses. They're all on four legs, and everything else can be replaced. Come on, honey, you know the rest can be replaced. But you can't replace the horses."

He was right.

I looked up through my tears, seeing through blurred eyes the dark bay and four socks of that silly mare Margot, the sparkling red chestnut of my darling Dynamo, the little brown pony's body and well-bred head of Passion, the big gray flash of my greatest hope, my Mickey. "The horses," I whispered.

"Come on, honey, let's go down and check out everyone, make sure they're all okay."

And with his arm firmly around my shoulders, Lacey trailing behind, we set off down the hill.

There wasn't any cell phone service. The towers were probably in crumpled piles of metal all over the hillsides of Marion County. Horses were probably trundling through them, getting caught up in the wires that were never there before.

Don't think of it.

We ended up driving back to Pete's farm to pick up the trailer and a chain saw, some lead shanks and spare halters.

"It's going to take all the daylight we have left to get the tree cleared and a load of horses back to the farm," Pete predicted, looking up at the cheerful sun. It was nearly 2 P.M. and for once, there wasn't a cloud in the sky. The day after a hurricane can be disconcertingly dry. On one hand, the clear skies are a blessing for people trying to clean up. On the other, there's a distressing lack of normalcy. Nothing looks the same, and even the weather is behaving strangely.

It was hot—late September, dry and sunny, and the temperature was around ninety degrees. I reflected on the supposed joys of an upstate New York summer. It was probably so cold folks had to blanket their horses at night. What utter bliss, I thought, managing to forget that I started to shiver uncontrollably the second the temperature dropped below seventy-five.

Lacey reminded me. "You, up north? You'd freeze to death." She laughed, and it was the first time any of us had laughed all afternoon. I couldn't help laughing with her, which was impressive, considering that I was holding a section of log for Pete while he sawed through it, chopping up the beautiful live oak that had previously shaded the entrance to my driveway. Beneath it, once we rolled the log aside, were the shattered remains of my signpost. Peter picked up the antique sign that had swung in the sea breezes for five decades.

"This is salvageable," he said. "Just needs a touchup on the paint." He set it gently against the paddock rails. "Would hate to lose such a piece of history. That's the last Green Winter Farm sign on this whole stretch of road."

I remembered—he had told me there were once ten signs, one at each driveway. "I'll fix it," I assured him. "It can go on the insurance bill."

"Well, at least you have insurance," he said matter-of-factly.

"I'll bet you a lot of these people don't, or at least nowhere near enough, and they're just going to be wiped out. It'll be a smaller business from here on out."

I didn't tell him that it wasn't very good insurance. I was fairly certain that I was wiped out, too. But I had to push that thought from my mind. As long as I had the horses, I wasn't completely out of business—not yet, anyway.

It was late afternoon before we managed to get the trailer up the driveway and parked in a relatively dry spot. Lacey and I had already discussed who could travel together: Mickey, Dynamo, and the two boarders from Orlando would go in Pete's rig. The other trainees could go in my trailer, which had been mercifully spared significant damage, once we dragged the roofing metal away from it.

"The layups can come tomorrow," I announced, trying to sound cheerful. "Nice and easy."

I left the others to load the horses while I went scouting around in the wreckage for things that could be salvaged. I had put a lot of things, like photos and my computer, into waterproof containers bought for just this situation. I managed to fill up the tack room of my horse trailer with the detritus of my life. Well—I didn't quite fill it up. I stood back and looked at the rubber bins. A tack room in a horse trailer. That's what I had to show for my life.

And the horses.

Lacey was poking around the barn's sodden tack room when I finished rummaging through the trash on the lawn, stepping through soggy piles of drywall that were drifting across everything like newly fallen snow. "The stuff in the tack trunks is fine," she reported. "And the saddles . . . we can probably save the saddles and bridles. I mean, we just need to oil the crap out of them." She brushed her hand over a show helmet, the soft fabric covering soaked through with rain and coated in drywall. "This, though . . ."

"Another night won't hurt, then." There was some stamping from the loaded trailer behind us. "Let's go. The kids are getting impatient."

The horses left behind whinnied frantically to the chosen ones in the trailers, and I sent Pete on down the lane with his load while Lacey hurriedly threw grain and hay into the paddocks and I went down the row with Betadine and antibiotic ointment, playing triage nurse. No one was seriously injured, but everyone had at least one mark from airborne branches, or bits and pieces of people's houses and barns. I lingered over Jim Dear, who had a long, clean laceration along one shoulder blade. It probably could have used stitches, but there was no one to sew them in. I had to be content with disinfecting the wound and then anointing it generously with goop from the antibiotic jar. "You'll be okay," I told him when I was through, offering him a cookie. "I'll come back for you tomorrow, and we'll see if we can't find a vet."

Jim Dear snarfed down the cookie and looked for more. "You'll be fine," I reminded him, and threw him another cookie before I went to the next paddock.

At last, everyone had food and water, and their few cuts and scrapes were treated. I could leave.

But I hated to do it.

I stood looking at my house for a few long minutes. It wasn't exciting living in a double-wide, nothing to write home about, except when it was your first place of your very own. I went from my parents' house to this place without any of the usual in-betweens, no college dorms or shared apartments.

Lacey stood next to me and we regarded the wreck of our home with dry eyes. We were both all cried out.

"We can get the other things out in the morning," she offered. "It won't rain tonight, anyway, and things can't get any wetter."

"Yeah," I agreed. "Tomorrow morning." And I turned my back on my house. *The* house. I would have to stop thinking of it as "my house." It wasn't anyone's house anymore, just rubble to be cleared away with a bulldozer and a dump truck.

Lacey climbed into her car, running her fingers over the deep gouges in the metal left by flying branches and bits of my—*the*—house. The back windshield had an impressive crack running from side to side. "Don't hit any bumps," I suggested, as if that was an option on the tree-strewn roads.

The horses in the trailer were whinnying and stamping and generally making a ruckus, but the horses left behind were content with their sweet feed and hay. And that was just it, I thought. They had somewhere safe to spend the night, they had food and water, they had each other.

And I would have to learn to be just as content. At least for a little while.

Still, I wished I had Marcus with me, or Lacey, anyone to talk to, anyone to stop me from feeling so alone. Just me in my truck, the horses in tow behind . . . at least I had them back there. And that, I thought, pulling slowly onto the county highway, was what I had to remember. Always, every day. I didn't know where I was going to live, or where I would keep the horses, or where I would train from, in the coming weeks and months. I didn't know how long it would take to fix the place up, get a new trailer on the property, put a new roof on the barn. I didn't have any answers, and it was killing me. But I had the horses. And that was going to have to be enough.

I sighed and shifted in the truck seat, sitting up a bit straighter, and flipped on the radio. A press conference with the governor: he was speaking about protecting life and property, about sending in the National Guard. Someone asked about a lack of drinking water. The governor said he would be sending out task forces to assist with the recovery. Water tankers, MREs, the Red Cross. Lines for gas, price gougers would be prosecuted, limited supplies, stay off the roads.

A disaster, I thought, looking at the stripped trees along the road. It was a war zone out here. I slowed the truck to avoid a long roll of unfurled insulation, neon pink and gathering pine needles and oak leaves, that had come from some manufactured home much like mine. I should figure out a way to build a barn apartment, I thought. Stop living in a tin can that could blow apart in the next big gale. Put on a better roof with hurricane clips, and climb up under the eaves every night to sleep above the horses.

It would be nice to be closer to the horses. In the winter, when they were inside at night, I would hear them snorting and whinnying, I'd hear if anyone kicked the wall or grew restless. I could peek down at them from windows above the barn aisle.

But there wouldn't be room for Lacey to live with me up there. And there was one thing I knew now: I wouldn't be able to bear living alone again.

22

THE ANNEX BARN at Pete's farm was tucked away in a hollow be-tween two of Marion County's beautiful rolling hills. Its aisles were walled in with cinder block, an old-fashioned design, with high, glassless windows cut into the walls for light. It was dim, and a little airless. But from the central entrance, which ran straight through the barn and cut it in two halves, you could look out and see the green pasture sloping down to the ivy-covered walls that hid the farm from the county road. It was high enough to make a Florida-bred like me feel a bit dizzy.

But this was what made Marion County the greatest place in the country to breed horses. (Kentucky could try for the title all they wanted, but Florida horsemen knew the truth.) These rolling hills were supported by a thick layer of shaky, porous rock called Ocala limestone. And that limestone fed the land so that it grew beautiful trees, lush grass, and exquisite horses.

Even though the farm was carpeted with leaves and broken branches, you could see that Pete's farm was breathtakingly beautiful, a chunk of the most expensive land in this part of Florida, and now I was living on it.

For the first three mornings at the annex, it was all I could do to get to work and not stand staring, open-mouthed, at the yellow sun rising above the curling morning mist, bathing the lowlands before me in shimmering veils of cloud.

But I did get to work, because that was the only thing keeping me sane these days.

While we had been picking up the horses from my farm, Becky had been busy preparing stalls in the annex, efficient as ever. The barn was dark and cobwebby, her efforts not extending beyond the bare bones of bedding and buckets, but the horses didn't notice poor housekeeping, snorting with pleasure at their new bedding and rolling rapturously in the fresh shavings. Lacey stood before the open stall fronts, which had only stall guards instead of doors, and laughed at them, while I decided to start pulling my earthly possessions out of the trailer tack room and carrying them into the barn's concrete cubicle of a storage room.

A few giant spiders hovered in the uppermost corners of the room, which normally would have sent me racing from the barn and down the hill. But today spiders didn't seem to matter so much. I ignored them, and they ignored me. I figured if I was in and out of the tack room enough, they'd eventually move away, up into the dark rafters. It didn't seem worth all the screaming and swatting with brooms that I usually put myself through. There really wasn't any more cause for drama in life, after a hurricane had blown away my past, present, and future.

You can stay as long as you need to," Peter assured me over dinner that night. We were working our way through an impressive platter of barbecued chicken he'd made on the big gas grill on the back patio. The back patio that lined a sparkling in-ground pool, of course. Well, it was probably sparkling, on better days. Today it was filled with leaves and a few branches from a nearby oak tree that hadn't fared very well in the storm. The pool, and the patio, and the commercial-class grill all went firmly into the "con" column in my mind, where I was trying to work out whether or not I still despised Pete for being a rich trust-fund baby. But there was the feeling I had whenever he walked into the room, the shiver that went up my spine, the flip-flop of my stomach, the slight dizziness. None of these things sound nice, but they weren't as bad as they sound.

I kind of liked them.

Kind of wanted more of them.

I was watching him now, as he rubbed a piece of bread around his plate, sopping up the leftover puddles of barbecue sauce. He had a stubble on his face after the long day, and the overall effect was a very alluring ruggedness. His reddish-brown hair fell in a fringe over his brow, and he pushed it behind his ears reflexively with his clean hand.

"You ought to take a pair of horse clippers and give yourself a haircut," I said, and then blushed instantly. What was he going to think about me making comments about his appearance?

That I liked him, that's what. I felt my cheeks grow hotter yet.

But Pete just smiled at me, and the warmth of his eyes, from across the table, was like a caress on my flushed skin.

Becky snorted. "He never bothers with a haircut, he just complains about hair in his eyes. Pete just likes complaining."

Pete put his hand on his heart and looked wounded. "Me, complain? I haven't said a word about anything! I've just been eating my chicken over here."

"You don't need words to complain," Becky retorted. "It's in your mannerisms."

"You should listen to her, she's an expert on this sort of thing," I drawled.

Becky shot me a look, her pale eyebrows knitting together, and there was an uncomfortable silence. Next to me, Lacey gave me a shove in the side that nearly made me tumble out of my chair. Pete rubbed his face wearily, and I considered how nice it would be if the earth would open up and swallow me whole.

Everyone ate in silence for a few moments. Then Becky stood, dish in hand. "I'm going to bed," she announced.

"Goodnight," Pete said, standing up. What century was this? I looked at Lacey, eyebrows raised. She shook her head slightly. *Don't make a scene.* But Lacey misjudged me. I wasn't going to make a scene. I already regretted every single thing I'd said. My new goal was to remain utterly silent, starting now, until we moved back to our own place.

Becky disappeared into the house, her back stiff and her jaw tight. Judging me, as usual.

"I think I'll turn in, too," Lacey said, glancing at me. "Can you behave yourself alone, Jules?"

Pete snickered.

"I'll try," I said. "But no promises."

"So, you and Becky don't get along," Pete said once we were alone. It felt like he'd been waiting to say something.

I looked at him. "You're a regular Sherlock Holmes."

"What happened?"

"You mean, between when she quit working for me and started working for you?" I took a long swig of iced tea and wished it were something stronger.

"No, I know exactly what happened then," Pete said seriously. "She quit working for you, wasn't around horses for about five days, and ran into me hanging up a flyer for a working student at the Tack Shack. She practically begged me to hire her. Said she'd messed up at her last job and she needed a second chance."

My eyebrows practically lifted into my hairline. That didn't sound like Becky at all. At least, not the recalcitrant, pissy Becky I had known for the past few months. The one I had met originally . . . maybe. "And you took her on based on that kind of credential? She screwed up at her last job?"

Pete laughed. "I wasn't impressed by her wording, no." He reached for another piece of chicken. That man could *eat*. "It was when I asked her who she'd worked for, that she caught my interest."

I narrowed my eyes.

"Not that I wanted to steal your student," he said around a mouthful of chicken. "It's that your horses always looked perfect. Turned out immaculately. I didn't know what happened between you two personally, but I knew she did a great job with your horses."

Well, this was true. But still.

I looked down at my plate, the barbecue sauce congealing. Beside me, Marcus panted, fully aware that there were forbidden chicken bones just waiting to be stolen, chewed into bits, and thrown up later in my shoes. I put my hand on his head. Disgusting darling dog. At least Marcus was honest with me.

"She did a great job with your horses, and you obviously trusted her," Pete went on. "That was a plus in her column, since you wouldn't let just anyone around your horses. I know you love them all."

I waved a dismissive hand. "I love Dynamo," I said. "But I know better than to fall in love with every horse in my barn."

"I think you *do* love them." Pete leaned back in his chair, studying me with something like mirth in his eyes. "You try to hide it, but I think the little girl who loved ponies is still in there. I see her sometimes, when you flip back your ponytail and give your horse a kiss on the nose."

"You see me as a little girl?" I raised my eyebrows.

"No—no—" he backtracked quickly. "I see you . . . I see you as a horsewoman."

I smiled. That was more like it. "Go on."

"A horsewoman who devotes herself to her craft, and to the happiness of her horses." Pete smiled, returning the favor, and I felt warm inside. "A horsewoman who doesn't care about her own comfort, as long as her horses are fed and safe and bedded down in at least twelve inches of shavings."

"Especially if someone else paid for those shavings," I amended, my smile turning into a grin, and Pete laughed.

"Stay as long as you like," he repeated. "But try not to bankrupt me while you're at it, or I'll ration your bedding!"

"You wouldn't dare."

"Try me." Pete leaned forward, and I felt my heart quicken. His eyes lost their mischievous gleam, replaced with a look altogether more hazy, more mysterious, and I knew what was going to happen, and I closed my eyes and gave in to it, accepting it as one of the crazy, terrible ideas that sometimes you just have to surrender to—

And then a crashing and shattering sound sent me flying out of my chair, banging my forehead into Peter's chin. He recoiled backward, hand to his abused jaw, while I spun around and faced my very, very, very bad beagle, who was slinking away with a chicken bone in his mouth, the broken plate he'd knocked down in pieces behind my chair.

I t took me a few days to start riding again. I felt so drained after the days spent on moving horses, rummaging through the wreckage of the farm, and trying to get through to an insurance agent, that I just didn't have the energy to get in the saddle. Lacey held down the fort in the barn, mucking stalls and doing the chores. I checked everyone after morning feeding and then left her to it, so that I could get back to the business of cleaning up my life.

But it wasn't going so well. The insurance company was backed up for weeks, and they had no one to send to the farm to do an assessment. I told a tired-sounding agent that she didn't need much of an assessment—the guts of the house were strewn across two riding arenas, the barn roof was torn off and lying in the parking lot—but she insisted that nothing could be done until someone had taken a look at the damage firsthand. And that wasn't going to happen . . . she paused, and I pictured her eyes skimming through a spreadsheet of red ink and crossed-out days . . . until the beginning of October.

"*October!*" I cried.

"Assuming we don't have any more severe weather," she said, sounding pessimistic.

I thanked her, ended the call, and leaned back in the leather office chair until I felt like I could face the outside world without bursting into tears.

It took about twenty minutes.

I walked down to the annex in my riding boots and a pair

of spare show breeches I'd kept stored in the trailer tack room, stepping around leftover puddles in the gravel drive. The weather had changed dramatically from summer to autumn after the hurricane—now it was hot and dry, with a yellowish hazy sky in the afternoons. I missed the shade of the clouds, and the thought of my dressage arena drying out at last, now that I couldn't use it, was incredibly frustrating.

The annex was a broodmare barn, a holdover from the property's early days as a breeding farm. It didn't have its own arena, which meant I was going to have to ride back up the drive, about a quarter mile, to use Peter's riding arenas. If I was going to get back to a normal workload with each horse, Lacey would have to bring horses for me to ride, and take the worked ones back to the barn.

It sounded pretty fancy, really, having a valet bring me my horses. I smiled to myself. Lemonade, please, and lots of it. I had a bumper crop of lemons.

Lacey was finishing up the stalls when I came into the barn. Dynamo, in his customary spot by the center aisle, was the first to see me. He trumpeted a whinny, and Lacey popped out of Passion's stall, brushing hair out of her face with dirty hands. "Look at you coming down to the barn in the middle of the day!" she said with a grin.

"I finally got through to an agent." I gave Dynamo a rub behind the ears. He lipped at my ponytail. "And they said they might be able to assess my claim in October."

Lacey leaned her pitchfork against the wall. Passion promptly stuck his head over his stall chain and knocked it over. "You little shit," she snapped, straightening it up again. And then, to me: "That's weeks away. Can we do anything in the meantime?"

"Not a thing. But even if we could, there's no one available to do any clearing. If their phone works, they're already out on jobs. And most of them don't have working phones. There's blackouts all over the place."

"I heard on the radio. We got lucky here."

I forced a smile. "We did get lucky," I admitted, although at the moment it didn't feel like it.

"So you're in boots. Who do you want tacked up?"

"Mickey," I said immediately. "And after I've been gone about half an hour, bring me Dynamo. Then we'll work our way through the rest of the bunch. You can ride Margot later, too."

Lacey brightened at the thought of riding her favorite. "You got it," she said, and pulled Passion's stall grill shut. He squealed in protest and went darting around his stall, kicking the wooden boards that lined the concrete walls. "You can ride that mess later too, okay? He needs a job. He's been making me crazy since we got here."

"If I have to," I agreed. "Last pony I ever take in."

"Amen to that."

Mickey and I made our way through the sunny afternoon by darting from shady patch to shady patch, longing for the overhang of the next oak tree before we had even left the last. The gravel driveway was mostly cleared of tree debris from the storm, and the black-board fences were only sporting a few raw yellow replacement boards here and there. All in all, Briar Hill had fared well.

But Mickey wasn't happy about being here, and he wasn't happy about this ride; his head was held high and his neck was already darkening with sweat. I sat deep, my fingers loose on the reins, resting gently on his withers. I didn't want him to feel claustrophobic and rear up as he had done at Lochloosa. But he was making me nervous, and by the time we neared the cluster of buildings where the arenas were situated, he was already starting to feel explosive. I tried slow breaths, sinking heels, a deep seat, anything I could think of to help him relax. "Come on, Mickey," I whispered. "We have to do this right. We have an audience now."

We came up to the in-gate of the big jumping arena and Mickey stopped at the entrance, his breath coming hard and loud. There were two riders in the ring, Pete and Becky. Pete was cantering a leggy chestnut toward a gymnastic setup at the far end; Becky was sitting still in the center of the ring, reins loose on a sweaty dark horse, head turned and watching me. I thought I could see the smirk on her face from all the way over here. "Let's go, Mickey," I chided. "Get on into the ring." I gave him a nudge with my calves, then a fairly solid kick with both heels when he failed to acknowledge me. "Get up, now!"

He gathered himself, prancing a few nervous steps, and I instantly threw myself forward, arms around his neck, when I realized what was coming. It was a good thing—Mickey went straight up, head to the sky, and he was a tall horse. I saw the ground slipping away beneath me, felt my saddle sliding down his back, and then as he began to sink toward the earth again he leaped forward, a huge convulsive flight like a novice attempting a capriole. He landed on all fours, braced like a frightened dog, and I kicked my boots free of the stirrups and leaped to the ground.

There it was, the dull, glassy-eyed look; the red-rimmed nostrils; the foamy sweat rising up from behind the bridle straps. I tried to move him forward, and he trembled and refused to move.

Oh my God, I thought. *This horse is completely messed up.*

"What happened?"

I turned around. Pete was walking up slowly on foot. He'd given the reins of his horse to Becky and left them both at the other end of the ring. His face was concerned. I hated that he was seeing me like this again: a novice, an amateur, unable to figure out the tremendous horse I'd been gifted.

But I didn't have an answer for him. I just shook my head.

He paused a few steps away, looking the horse over with an expert eye. Searching for clues: pain signals, twitching muscles, anything that might give it all away. Nice try, Pete, but I'd already been there.

"What happened?" he asked again, stepping back. He hadn't seen anything. That meant I hadn't missed anything. I couldn't imagine dealing with him if he caught something I hadn't. The shame of it would make living here impossible.

"The same thing that he did at Lochloosa," I explained, voice gentle to avoid setting the horse off again. But Mickey was in a world of his own; he wasn't paying attention to me or anything else around him. He had gone completely inside himself. "He decides he won't go forward, he rears and plunges instead, and then he just withdraws into himself. It's like he can't deal with stress."

"Well that can't be right," Pete said, furrowing his brow. "He was a racehorse, wasn't he?"

"Maybe that's the problem. Maybe he can't figure out why he isn't a racehorse anymore."

"I could see that if he was bolting and challenging other horses, but refusing to move forward . . . that's kind of the opposite response, right?" He stuck his thumbs inside his belt loops and fixed his gaze on me, his eyes full of concern. "I've never seen anything quite like this."

"I have no idea what to do about it." It was nice to be able to admit it without worrying he'd show me up.

"Well, a vet checkup for one thing," he said seriously. "A complete exam, radiographs, the whole nine yards, to make sure that it isn't a pain response." Peter looked downward at Mickey's legs again. "His hooves are very flat, aren't they?"

"He gets treated regularly for white line," I said defensively. "My vet says they're fine."

Pete nodded slowly. "Have you had X-rays done of them, though? Just to see what's going on in there?"

"I haven't." And just like that, a terrible fear unfurled in my stomach. "What are you thinking?"

"I'm thinking," Pete said thoughtfully, approaching the horse slowly and crouching down beside him, running his finger along the sloping curvature of Mickey's forehoof, "that every step might cause him pain, and he doesn't know how to deal with it when he thinks hard work is ahead." He looked up at me. "Like a race."

We stood still for a few moments, watching the heaving sides of the catatonic horse.

I met Lacey on the drive, halfway back to the barn. She was riding Dynamo, who looked surprised and delighted to see Mickey. Mickey, sedated with a dose of ace borrowed from Pete's tack room, picked up his head slightly and regarded Dynamo with a woozy, drunken expression. Lacey looked from the horse to me, horrified. "What the hell happened?"

"He had another fit," I said. "He's not right." I led the swaying horse past Dynamo. "You can take Dynamo up to the ring and jog him around on a loose rein," I said over my shoulder. "Loosen him up a little. I'm going to call the vet and see what we can do about this guy."

"You want *me* to . . . Okay. Okay. Be careful with him."

Behind me, Dynamo's hooves picked up the tempo again on the gravel of the drive. Lacey may have been shocked that I was allowing her to hack Dynamo, but not so shocked that she hadn't jumped at the chance. It was a big deal, the day your trainer let you hack the big horse. And with Mickey an unstable mess, Dynamo's spot as my big horse seemed pretty secure.

I rubbed my hand cautiously along Mickey's sweaty neck, feeling the salt prickle the myriad cuts and fissures in my work-roughened hands. He didn't react, just plodded along with heavy-lidded eyes. His nostrils, still pink around the flared edges, dangled close to his hooves. I watched them, chewing at my lip. They really were flat and wide—were they worse than when he had come to Florida, more than three months ago now? Had the farrier some-how overlooked the way the hooves were flaring out? I liked my farrier—Ronny was fast and reliable, and he didn't charge me very much. Using an old racehorse blacksmith from way back was one of my How to Stay in Business tricks. You found one of the old guard that still charged forty bucks for two shoes and got the job done in fifteen minutes, and you clung to them tightly. I couldn't possibly afford one of these guys who charged two hundred dollars and spent an hour and a half on each horse.

Mickey stumbled, picking up his forehooves delicately as he stepped on a rough patch of large paving stones, and his eyes widened for a few moments.

And so did mine.

That was it, then. Pete was right. The words were bitter as poi-son. The horse's hooves were a mess, he was in pain, my cheapskate farrier was making things worse. Every time he faced a new situation, Mickey remembered that going to a new place, with new horses, meant going out to gallop. And he just couldn't face the pain.

"You poor thing," I told Mickey, and his left ear flicked in my direction. "You poor bad-luck horse. To get sent across the country to some schmuck like me, who can't even figure out that your feet hurt without having some guy she hardly knows explain it all. She should have sent you to someone who knew what the hell they were doing. I'm just going to ruin you. On accident, you know, but still. After I fix your feet, I'll probably mess up something else."

"That's not true."

I jumped and turned around. Mickey came to an obedient halt next to me. "Everyone needs a second pair of eyes, Jules."

I kicked at the gravel, not even thinking about the scuffs I was leaving on my show boots. "I should have seen that his hooves were flaring out so far," I muttered. "Look at them. The quarters look like duck bills."

Pete came up to me, his own scuffed boots dusty with sand from the arena. He reached out his hand and gripped my shoulder, and the sensation of his touch rippled through my body like electricity. "Sometimes things happen beneath our nose, and we're too close to the problem to really see it," he said gently. "It's happened to all of us."

I was standing a little too close to him to think clearly, or I might have asked him for an example, challenged him to come up with some way in which he *wasn't* perfect. Instead, I just drew a shuddering breath, looked longingly at his lips, and kept my own mouth shut.

Next to me, Mickey stood quietly, blinking, waiting to continue his walk to the barn. The September sun beat down, and we stood there, not speaking, for longer than we should have.

Pete reached up and brushed a drop of sweat from his brow. "It's hot," he said huskily.

"I have Diet Coke in the barn," I offered, my voice a ghost of itself. "If you want to cool off."

"I'd like that," he said, and when I turned and started walking, tugging at Mickey's lead shank to bring the horse along, he came up next to me, his hand brushing my side. I closed my eyes momentarily, to stave off the vertiginous dizzy excitement his touch aroused in me, and in doing so, stumbled into a deep puddle left over from the hurricane. He grabbed my elbow before I could go to my knees in the brackish water, and when he pulled me upright, I was against his chest, my eyes glued to his. Mickey, may the eventing gods bless him, stood still again.

"Hello," he murmured, his voice rumbling against my chest. "Jules, I know that you said you don't date horse trainers, but . . ." He trailed off, his eyes searching mine.

I thought I would explode. "But what?" I whispered desperately.

"Just let me see if I can change your mind," he growled, and with that his lips were on mine, his hand pressing my body hard against his, and with a sigh of pleasure that came all the way from the soles of my boots, I slipped my hand into his damp hair and pulled him closer still.

23

THE WORLD OUTSIDE was no more orderly than the world inside my head—or inside my horse's head.

While I was sitting in the cobwebby tack room of the annex, hoping to heaven that Eileen wasn't going to flip out over the four-hundred-dollar blacksmith bill I had just sent her for Mickey's reconstructed hooves, Ocala remained locked in a tailspin. There were no working traffic lights in town. There were entire highways still shut down. There were lines at suburban gas stations, where shellshocked residents slowly shuffled to Red Cross tents to pick up their MRE rations. The tornado that ripped apart my farm was not the only funnel cloud to spin down to earth during the hurricane. Other sections of the region had been hit just as badly—and even far worse.

I didn't see much of it. With my horses and my remaining possessions finally recovered and stored safely in the barn around me, I had no reason to go back to my farm. I couldn't fix it up on my own.

So I stayed at Briar Hill, among my horses. I didn't leave unless I absolutely had to buy groceries. Or toothpaste, or deodorant. The horses' supplies were delivered—this close to town, you could have luxuries like free feed delivery. It was a different world than life on the fringes of horse country. It was nice, really. A girl could get used to this, especially if she was interested in becoming a shut-in.

And I had decided this was the best course of action.

After all, my life had gotten out of control, I reflected, shifting on the tack trunk lid where I had perched. I still had no desk, no chair, no calendar with show dates circled. My old desk and chair were flattened beneath a section of roofing. My old wall calendar, with all my ambition written across it in slanting marker, was scattered across the fields. I could have gone to the office-supply store and bought another of each, adding an inconsequential amount to already daunting credit card bills, and admit that I had to start my life anew.

But I wasn't ready for that yet.

Mickey's hooves were fixed, although patched here and there with yellow chunks of plastic filler, and I could ride him lightly around the arena now if I avoided the hard gravel of the driveway on the way there and back. Pete's farrier had looked at his hooves and then me with cold eyes. "Who's your farrier?" he'd growled, and when I told him he grunted and shook his head. "Let him touch your horses again," he'd warned, "and I won't clean it up for you next time. This horse has been in pain for a long, long time."

I hadn't known, and the enormity of that kept me awake at night for weeks afterward. How could I not have known? Wasn't I a trainer? Wasn't I a horsewoman?

We learned from our mistakes, though, and I wouldn't make this one again.

Meanwhile, Mickey went back into work. I could trot him in twenty-meter circles, riding the swing of his stride, and try to concentrate on pushing him into the bridle and the bend of his spine around curves. And sometimes, I succeeded.

Until Pete came into the ring.

Still, I didn't let things go any farther than that one, knee-trembling kiss. The fact was, whenever I was away from him, whenever my mind could turn over rationally and coolly, the way that I liked it, I knew that playing around with Pete was a fool's errand. And so I avoided him whenever possible.

I crossed my legs on the tack trunk lid, put my hands under my thighs, sighed. I was wearing jeans—it was a cool night, the very first one of fall. Cool to me, anyway—I doubted it was cooler than seventy-five degrees outside. But still, the weather was changing, the seasons were turning, and it looked as if I would go on living at Briar Hill forever. Which made the whole situation with Pete rather worrisome. What if we had a fight? A lover's quarrel? I'd be out on my ass, up shit creek and without a paddle, that's what.

Lacey said that was ridiculous because Pete was obviously in love with me and would do anything for me. I told her, good-naturedly but seriously, that she was an idiot. In love with me? Prickly, hateful, chip-on-her-shoulder Jules Thornton? Even if Pete claimed that he was initially attracted to me because of the way I adored my horses (and the way I looked in breeches, he always added), no one could ever claim that I was good company.

And I wasn't in love with him. Because that would be ridiculous.

And no matter how much I enjoyed his company, or the thrill

in my spine every time I rounded the bend in the barn drive and saw him riding in the arena, or the electric memory of that kiss, he was still Pete Morrison, who had beat me for the ACE grant when it was obvious he didn't even need it. *Why* had he done it? Other than telling me things weren't what they looked like, he hadn't given me an answer. He was hiding something about this farm.

Which I supposed was fair, since I had my own secret about the ACE grant. Who knew that one attempt to get ahead would leave us in such a complicated position? With Becky sitting smack in the middle. I'll bet she knew Pete's secret, too. She somehow had the dirt on both of us.

The tree frogs in the lower paddocks began to chirp their night-song. It had gotten dark while I was sitting in here, trying to avoid going back to the house. I got up and wandered aimlessly around the darkening tack room, unwilling to flip on the light and startle the spiders I knew had already begun to climb from their hiding places. The letter I'd thrown down earlier was still in the doorway, pages luminescent blue in the dusk-light outside the barn.

While we appreciate the extraordinary circumstances you've found yourself in, we will be removing our horses Saturday morning. Please have their files in order to send along with the van driver. We hope we can work together in the future when your facilities are repaired. Sincerely, David and Maggie Wilkins

I stepped on the paper, leaving a boot-tread across the typed letters. In the pasture beyond the barn, Maggie and Dave's pretty Hanoverians grazed with my other horses. In a few nights they'd be grazing in Orlando. I hoped they liked fireworks every night. It was a shame. They'd been fun to ride, and I didn't say that about every horse I got on.

I considered whether or not there was tequila in the kitchen of the guest suite. I thought perhaps there was. And so I started the long walk home.

A few margaritas later, I was ready to get some answers.

I got up from the chair where I'd been drinking for the past hour and started looking around for my flip-flops.

Lacey was eyeing me warily from the other side of the sitting area, where she was curled up on the sofa with a riding magazine. "Where are you going?" she asked, voice suspicious. As well she should be. Neither of us ever went anywhere after seven o'clock at night.

"Talk to Pete," I muttered. Where were those flip-flops? I knocked over a cluster of old umbrellas leaning haphazardly in the hall closet and found a bridle, two riding crops, and, beneath it all, my flip-flops. "Gotta talk to Pete. It's time."

"Time for what?" Lacey put down the magazine and got up. She was wearing her usual evening attire, a pair of gym shorts and a tank top. "You can't go bother him now. It's late. And what would he think, you getting drunk and then banging on his front door?"

"He'd think I want him," I slurred, laughing. "He'd think *booty call*!"

Lacey crossed her arms. "Only if you want him to think that." She lifted an eyebrow.

I stared at her, delighted. I'd never seen her do that before. "You look exactly like him!" I declared. "That's his move!"

Lacey's jaw dropped. She looked down and I followed her line of sight to the empty pitcher next to my chair. "You drank all of that?"

I nodded. The room nodded with me, furniture wiggling and waving.

"Oh, no," Lacey said, and just like that she had darted past me and was blocking the door. "You aren't going anywhere."

"Yes, I am." I giggled, and put on my flip-flops. I shuffled toward her, arms out. *"I'm a zombie! Grrrrrr!"*

"Jesus Christ," Lacey said, obviously not as amused as I was. Or maybe she was afraid of me. Maybe I made a very convincing zombie. "You're wasted."

"I am," I growled. "I'm wasted. Move or I'll eat your brains." I plucked at the straps of her tank top.

"You know what? Fine." Lacey ducked under my outstretched arms, shaking her head as she went. "You want to get us kicked out of here? You want to be homeless? Fine. I don't understand you anymore. I don't know what's coming next, but I'm not sure I'm going to be here to see it."

I remembered her words later, improbably enough. But at the time, all I knew was that I was free to march over to Pete's door and bang on it.

Or come as close to marching as one could, wearing flip-flops.

The fall night was scented with jasmine or some other tropical plant that had been enjoying the long summer. I'd never had the time or patience to find out what flowers were called what, even though we lived in a state of eternal blooms. I crossed the little courtyard between the guest suite and the side door of the main house, noticing that the kitchen light was on, shining yellow on the pebbles beside the path stones. Instead of going around to the front door, I just waltzed up to the kitchen window and peered in.

Pete was sitting at the kitchen table, a thick book open in front of him, finger marking a spot on the page as he reached for a glass of red wine.

How sophisticated. My mother drank wine.

I rapped on the window and he started, nearly dropping the wineglass. He looked up at the window, his eyes widening when he saw me. And then he flipped the book over and got up. I looked at the title. *The Elements of Classical Dressage.*

We had the same taste in books, anyway.

"Jules?" He stood in the pool of light from the open kitchen door. "Have you given in to your raging desire for me at last?" He grinned.

"I need to talk to you," I said, admiring how steady my voice was.

"Did something happen?"

"No," I said. "Maybe. A while ago."

Pete cocked his head, and a lock of his red-brown hair fell over his shadowed eyes. I felt my stomach turn over—damn, he was sexy. The rich bastard. "Come in," he said, stepping back and holding open the door. "Before the mosquitoes eat you alive."

I settled into the couch in the big living room and declined the offer of a glass of wine. I might have been wasted, but I knew enough to not pour wine on top of tequila. Plenty of other bad decisions to make tonight. "I have to ask you something," I said, laying my head back on a plush cushion. Such a nice couch. "I need to know why you went for the ACE grant."

Pete blinked. "I went for it because I needed it."

I sat up a little too quickly and needed to take a minute to stop the room from spinning. Then I waved my arm around the living room, which was nearly as big as my old trailer had been. "You live in a mansion on a hundred-acre farm! You *needed* it? Let me help you out with words, Pete. *Need* means if you don't have it, something bad will happen. You'll fail. You'll die if you don't get it. Excuse me, Pete, but it looks to me like you already have it."

I threw myself back on the cushion. The tequila was starting to make me sleepy. That was no good. I needed energy if I was going to have my say and then get the hell out of his house without looking like an idiot.

Pete just shook his head and looked down at his wineglass. When he finally spoke, his voice was tight. "Jules," he said slowly. "I only own a few things in this world besides my clothes, my tack, and Regina."

"A few hundred acres, you mean."

"*No*. I don't own this place. How could I ever afford a place like this? This belongs to my grandmother—my grandfather made her swear not to sell *if* I could make it onto the United States Equestrian Team." He swallowed and turned his head, looking at one of the myriad black-and-white photos on the walls. I chewed at my lip, starting to understand.

"She hates horses," Pete said after a quiet moment. "He had a bad fall, and broke his hip, and never really recovered. She was angry at him for riding at all—he was in his seventies. But it was all he had ever wanted to do."

I could understand that. I leaned forward, resting my elbows on my knees, and waited while Pete worked out the words he wanted to use. My head wasn't spinning so much, my eyes weren't so heavy. I wanted to know. I wanted him to tell me everything. I wanted to understand Pete Morrison in a way I had never wanted to understand anyone. If I was honest with myself for just twenty seconds or so, knocked all the ambition and jealousy and rage out of my heart just long enough for a few moments of clarity, I'd know—I cared about Pete Morrison in a way I had never cared about anyone.

"She told me to give up eventing and stick to dressage," he said.

I remembered our conversation back at Lochloosa. He'd said he was born into eventing. "But you're an eventer like your grandfather and that can't be changed," I said. "You can't just change disciplines because someone said you have to."

"Right, and so I have two more years, by her calendar," Pete went on. "Two more years to get into team competition."

"That's—a big ask," I ventured. "Even if you had a really good winter and stepped up in spring, the chances of being asked to join any team trainings are—"

"Slight, I know," Pete said grimly. "We're hardly the only ones trying to get there. I thought if I had a second horse at Intermediate, that would give me a better chance."

"The ACE horse," I said, understanding at last.

"Exactly. Leo. He's a lovely horse. But he's had trouble with the heat this summer." Pete rubbed his forehead. "So that puts us behind going into winter . . . and I only have him for this season, anyway."

"You'll catch up," I said. "Two horses are better than one." Like I was always telling myself, two was a chance.

"I hope so, Jules."

"And what's her plan, if you don't make the team?" I asked.

"She wants to sell the farm," Pete said bleakly. "She wants rid of this place so badly. She blames the farm for everything that went wrong in her marriage, even in my grandfather's dying."

I felt my mouth fall open. Sell *this farm*? A person would have to be crazy.

"And so if I don't make the team, and she wins, I can either give up eventing or find some other way to support myself. I'll have to find a farm to rent, with enough facilities to keep the clients I've got . . . and they won't be happy with a little place after Briar Hill

Farm has spoiled them. They come here and they see the tree-lined drive and the cross-country course and the show jumps and they think *that's horses*. If I had to downgrade to a little barn with a few jumps, I'd lose at least half of them, even though I could make it work." He looked at me, blue eyes flashing. "Like you make your place work."

For a moment, I was held captive by his gaze, and downright flattered by his words. *Like I make my place work*. And then I remembered. "Pete, I don't have a place anymore." The words were like a knife to my heart. "I'm as bad off as you. If the insurance doesn't come through, I'll be bankrupt and homeless. And even though you've taken me in, I just lost two more clients over this. No one thinks I have any stability. At least you have a safety net for another two years. You could build up a lot of business in two years' time."

Pete smiled sadly. "You have a safety net for as long as I do, Jules," he said. "Don't call yourself homeless again. I won't let it happen."

I smiled and tried to take a lighter tone. "So, two years, huh? We have two years to become top international riders and make the US Equestrian Team, and then you get to keep your farm and I get to be your tenant for good?"

"You'll have to start paying me rent once I'm your landlord and not just the benevolent trainer helping out a colleague."

We were gazing into each other's eyes at this point, enchanted with each other, alcohol bubbling up in our bloodstream and assuring us both that we were much wittier than we actually were. And there's really no telling what might have happened if Lacey hadn't come storming into the living room looking for me, apologized to Pete for my rude behavior, and dragged me off by the elbow.

I looked over my shoulder, though, as I went obediently with my working student. And he was watching me, that eyebrow of his quirked, those lips of his curled up in a quizzical smile. And I knew I was in serious trouble.

Which is why, after Lacey went to bed, I went straight back to that kitchen window and knocked again.

24

HOW LONG DID it take Ocala to recover from the storm? Depends on who you asked. Some people said a month. Some said six. For some, the Ocala we knew never came back.

A bulldozer cleared away the wreckage of my farm, and *my* old Ocala was gone forever. There was just enough insurance money to pay for the final destruction of my house and my barn. The fences still (mostly) stood though, and the arenas were good, so somebody could move in and start over again on the bones of my old farm.

But it wouldn't be me. I had no more money, and no choice—the red-and-blue realty sign was put up where the old Green Winter Farm sign had stood for generations. The real estate agent sunk her signpost right into the same hole in the ground.

I took the farm sign back to Briar Hill with me and stowed it in the tack room. Maybe it would come in handy someday. Or maybe I'd give it to the new farm owner.

I wasn't the only one bidding farewell to my dreams. Half the properties in Ocala seemed to be for sale, in earnest this time, and not in the usual "let's see if anyone will give us a boatload of money for this" manner that had always characterized Marion County's largest and grandest farms. Leighann "Your Dream Farm Awaits" Anderson stopped sending me weekly emails asking about Passion's sale prospects; she was too wrapped up in taking photos of stallion barns and gourmet kitchens.

Ever hovering on the edge of bankruptcy, the hurricane pushed the horse industry straight into the abyss. Beyond the wrought-iron gates and rubber-paved, horse-safe driveways were shattered fences, boarded-up windows, and roofs covered with blue tarps. The roofs that weren't missing, anyway. There wasn't enough money to replace the roofs. Or, if there was, there weren't enough workers to do the jobs. The construction industry was booming, as the lucky few with the credit or the insurance money to pay were lining up to have their shattered homes put back together.

The rest of us just put our soggy, ruined dreams in trash bags and drove them to the county dump.

It didn't sting quite as much as it could have, though. Because, well, because of Pete.

And I wouldn't have had Pete in my life if it weren't for the storm. Yes, I needed a barn collapsing around me during a cataclysmic cyclone and a subsequent domino effect of business and personal disasters to push me into admitting my feelings for Pete, but what could I say? I've always been difficult.

And when Pete tried to help me with Mickey, he found out how difficult I could be. I wasn't ashamed to push back when he questioned me in the arena. I spent a morning toiling with Mickey's trot-canter transitions and came out feeling sweaty and discouraged, only to have Pete think it would be a good idea to insert a suggestion about encouraging Mickey to pick up the canter when *he* felt ready for it, not when I did.

"Right," I scoffed, "and I'll just accept the penalties for going off-course in the dressage test. Great plan, Pete."

Oh, Pete. He let it go, and when he wasn't pretending to be my trainer, things were so good. Briar Hill Farm became our bubble, as the last days of summer faded into the cool nights of autumn, and the puddles around the pasture gates slowly dried up.

A good-morning kiss when we came down to the arena, tipping our hard hats back so that our lips could meet without the ritual clacking of the hat brims. Lunch in the kitchen, stretching out our tired feet, freed of boots for a few minutes, while Becky excused herself to her own apartment and Lacey watched us twinkle at each other with a mixture of envy and disbelief. Evenings . . . evenings that weren't sprawling on the couch and watching TV until I fell asleep, we'll say, and leave it at that. He made me happy, in every way, and I made him happy, too.

But when he tried to critique my riding, I drew the line. We could be friends and lovers, but we weren't going to coach each other. When I wanted coaching, I'd ask for it.

Pete, however, couldn't seem to follow my rule. Every time he came into the arena while I was arguing with Mickey, he had something to say about it.

Like the day I spent half an hour trying to get Mickey to put a precise number of strides before a fence. The horse jumped long, every time. And though he did it handily, it wasn't good enough for me. Why wouldn't he wait until I told him to jump?

I wasn't in tune with this horse, I thought, looking down at Mickey's bobbing head. I wasn't getting him. And it was really worrying me.

Pete had an opinion, of course. "It's really important that you stop disciplining Mickey when he tries to make his own decision, and instead encourage his assertiveness and independence. No matter how annoying you find it. Do you know why?"

"Because it will make his sweet widdle heart happy?" I asked, not too tired to be snippy.

"Because it will save your neck one day on the cross-country course," Pete said, ignoring my attitude. He dropped his feet from his stirrups and slumped a little on the gelding he'd been riding. "One day you'll be in a sticky spot and not know what to do, and he'll make the decision for you. Because he likes to do his own thing and not wait for you. But you have to encourage that behavior now, not punish him for it."

"I thought that was bad," I said, frowning. Laurie hadn't liked it when I let a horse decide where to take off before a jump. She insisted that a horse ought to listen to his rider, first and foremost. "One day, that horse will decide to put in two strides where he ought to do three, and flip over a log and kill you," she had told me after a particularly fast cross-country round on a young Dynamo. "*You* tell him where to put his feet. *You* know best."

Pete quirked his eyebrow skeptically at my explanation. "Who knows best about where to put his feet? You or him? Let me tell you a story. I rode this horse of my grandfather's, Wazzoo, when I was a kid. He was hard to work with, but he could save your life. He once slid down a slope going to a water complex. A four-foot log like a redwood just three strides away. I could have reined him back and sat him on his hindquarters to stop from crashing. I could have spurred him to take two big strides and just leap it. I knew there wasn't a third option—there was nowhere else to go. But Wazzoo knew the third option, and he decided to take it—three tiny strides and a bunny hop over the log. Nearly straight up in the air and his hind legs scraping the log on the way down. All I could do was stay out of his way. He saved our asses that day. If we'd hit that fence, we would have flipped right over it."

"Did you win the event?" I asked, just to annoy him for being so *right* as usual. Obviously winning wasn't the point of such a story—living to tell it was.

"As a matter of fact, we did," he said, beating me again.

"So you're telling me, let Mickey jump how he wants." I was skeptical, but I had to admit that Pete's story had legs.

"For now, for the little jumps. Later, when you're doing the bigger fences, you'll have enough partnership through your dressage to understand each other without getting too pushy." Pete patted his horse on the neck. "I mean, what's the worst that could happen? You're jumping two-foot-three. He's not going to flip over."

He had a point.

I just hated being reminded that we were still jumping baby novice jumps. October was rolling on, and now that Mickey's hooves were put back together and his training was back in full swing, I wanted to start thinking about entering events again. It was time to put the memory of Lochloosa behind us and start getting some show-ring mileage.

There was just one problem with this plan: there weren't any events.

"'Holly Hill regrets that their Fall and Winter Horse Trials will be canceled this year due to substantial storm damage to the cross-country course and grounds,'" Pete read aloud. It was the first of many postcards flooding the big cast-iron mailbox at the foot of the drive. A photo of a leaping horse on the front, an apology on the back. And I morosely drew more and more Xs through the plans optimistically jotted onto the big training calendar in my tack room. I'd finally bought one, and now it was just bringing me down.

Every morning in late October, the dawn gave way to a cloudless sky of unrelenting blue. The weather was unseasonably sultry. The horses were hot, we were hot, everything was hot. It was ten o'clock in the morning and we were riding up on the rise behind the arenas, with Marion County spread out below us in a scatter of farms and jumps and training tracks and, farther on, the interstate and retirement homes and shopping plazas that kept the other half busy while we were riding and flinging manure. People joked now that the blue tarp was the state flag; they dotted the roofs of barns and houses and businesses alike. I blew a cloud of gnats away from my face and wondered if everything was over.

"Eileen called me this morning," I said. "She wants to know if we're going to fit in a full event schedule this winter. Apparently two of Carrie's riders aren't even coming back to Florida this season."

Pete ran a hand along Regina's neck. "I've heard from a few friends that they're staying in Southern Pines this winter."

"What if there aren't *any* events?" I'd asked Lacey the same question, back in the barn, but she hadn't had an answer. Somehow, I thought Pete might.

"I don't know," he said. "We can go to South Carolina, or Georgia. We'd go for one or two big events in the season, anyway."

"I don't know about you," I said, "but I just don't have the budget to ship out of state and pay for gas and stabling all season long. One or two events in a winter is a lot different from one or two events a month."

"I don't have the budget either," Pete said.

Of course he didn't. Funds were tight and growing tighter. Hay and feed and bedding had doubled in price since the hurricane.

Feed stores, crunched by defaulting accounts as more and more farms went under, were putting up signs: NO CREDIT. Skinny horses in failing fields were being shipped to auctions in Georgia and Tennessee and never coming back. With the winter show season appearing to be canceled, business as usual was out the window.

"I heard the equestrian team training sessions are staying in Aiken this winter," Peter said glumly. "Not a single date scheduled for Florida."

I looked at him. That meant even if he managed to impress someone enough to get an invitation, he'd have to travel to South Carolina. One more roadblock in his quest to save the farm.

And as for me? I couldn't imagine a way to feed all my sales horses through another season. Jim Dear and Margot and Daisy and the rest of them . . . all hungry mouths who were supposed to be sold to the winter riders.

"We'll just have to pick and choose carefully, get the most bang for our buck. If we sell anything this winter, it won't be in Florida, I can tell you that much." Pete looked over at my gray horse, who was blissfully relaxed after our jumping session, neck stretched out long and ears flopping sideways, concentrating on nothing at all. He had appreciated my change in riding from the get-go, and I'd had to admit that Pete had been right. "But you can't take this horse on the road for his first outing, Jules. Too much stress, and we still don't know how he's going to react to a change in scenery."

I remembered. Just getting him home from Lochloosa had required heavy sedation. Not to say that he'd react just as badly, or that he couldn't be brought back to earth, but if he did, and we couldn't—no, an overnight show was out of the question, at least for the first trial.

"Fine, but what if there's nothing here all winter?" I asked.

"Pete, the owners will never go for his missing the entire winter season. They'll lose confidence and move him. And you have to be in the same boat with some of yours. We're both too new at this to get away with skipping a season. They'll expect us to pick up and go to Southern Pines or Aiken."

He nodded thoughtfully. "They've been more than patient but that can't last forever. You're right—they won't stand for a winter off."

"So what will we do?"

"We hope, I guess. We wait and see. Someone will have something."

And then, after waiting a few restless weeks, even sending in reluctant checks, postdated, to an event in South Carolina, Lacey retrieved the mail and came into the kitchen bearing the first cheerful postcard of the season. "Look at this!" she crowed. She handed it over.

It was me, galloping at Sunshine State on Dynamo, in the picture that had made *The Chronicle of the Horse,* my hand patting his neck in a *good-boy* gesture.

Nervous, I flipped the card and stared at the curving script.

"Read it aloud!" Pete said, squeezing my shoulder. Lacey was laughing with delight and impatience.

"'We're excited to announce,'" I read in a trembling voice, "'that Sunshine State Horse Park will be running its *full calendar* this winter, thanks to our devoted volunteers . . .'" I trailed off and looked around the room. "You guys," I said wonderingly. "We're going to make it."

25

THE LOW-HANGING NOVEMBER sun made the morning feel like late afternoon, casting deep shadows across the tree-lined stables as we unloaded the horses at Sunshine State a month later. Dynamo stepped out of the trailer like a lamb, looked around, and sighed gently, before consenting to be led to his stall by Lacey. Somehow the turmoil of the summer had done wonders for his nerves, as if teaching him that he would always have a safe landing somewhere, and he had become the picture of the old campaigner. I watched him walk away, heart swelling with the mixture of love and pride and fear that accompanied me every time I brought Dynamo to an event.

Mickey came out of the trailer in a rush, his hooves slithering across the matted floor, and his first steps onto firm ground quickly dissolved into a rear, standing up on his hind legs in trembling excitement. I stepped back to escape the reach of his pawing forelegs, shaking my head as the leather shank slid through my fingers. "Come on, man," I snapped. "Not this shit again."

Pete looked on from inside the rig, waiting to bring down Regina, who was being her usual regal princess self. "You need a hand?"

I waited for Mickey to come down to the ground before answering. "I have him," I said stiffly, but when I tried to move the horse forward, he went up on his hind legs again. I ground my teeth together and brought all my weight down in one hard *snap* against the lead, driving the chain shank down against his nasal bone. Mickey flung his head from side to side, furious, but brought his forelegs down to earth. I gave him another shank for good measure, and he snorted and actually swatted the air with his left foreleg. I jumped back, startled.

"That was nasty," Pete observed.

I glanced around. Two horsemen walking their own horses past were watching us, eyebrows raised. Judgmental snots, I thought. Like their horses had never pitched a fit before.

"I've never seen him do that before," I said, but already I was remembering the way he had lifted his left foreleg and held it out when he first arrived in Florida. I had thought he was planning on pawing. It hadn't occurred to me that he might have been a striker at some point in his previous life.

That was really frightening. Colts often decided to "slap," as Laurie used to call it, and it was of prime importance to break that dangerous little habit the second it cropped up. Nothing could ruin your day quite like a striking horse. And by "ruin your day" I meant "split your skull."

"You okay?" Pete asked again, and I realized I was staring at Mickey instead of getting a move on. Inside the trailer, Regina stamped a hoof, politely, to let everyone know that the princess was getting impatient.

"I'm fine. Let's go, Mickey," I said firmly, and started walking. To my relief, the gray horse began walking too, falling into stride next to me. The chain was loose over his nose, the shank loose in my hand. We were going to be okay, I thought. We had this.

And then he started jogging beside me, jigging nearly straight up and down. His neck was arched and his profile was nearly vertical, as if he was trying to duck behind the chain over his nose, and his breath came hard and fast. He sounded like a horse at a full gallop. I glanced over his neck and saw the veins standing out under his taut skin, the sweat beginning to darken his coat. I was walking next to a pressure cooker that was about to blow.

Luckily, the barn was just ahead, and I managed to get Mickey into the dark interior of the temporary stabling before he was so worked up that he couldn't move forward. In the claustrophobic confines of the tent, he seemed to shrink, and by the time I got him into his stall and turned around to face the door, he was practically slinking along, his head held low, his eyes wide and shifting like a frightened dog's.

I removed the chain and carefully backed out of the stall, latching the door and giving it a little jiggle to test its security. Temporary stalls were made to collapse flat for storage and transportation. I would have given anything to have put my time bomb of a horse into a solid wooden box stall.

Pete came in with Regina, who was surveying her surroundings with a sort of detached interest. Her lead was loose in his fingers, and I watched them pass to the next stall with a sense of jealousy. In Regina, Pete had the perfect partner—she was endlessly talented and completely in love with him. I had Dynamo's affection, but my horse had to work so much harder to give the same level of athleticism Regina performed without mussing her hair.

And I was less and less certain I was going to get Mickey through Novice, let alone to the top of the game.

Pete closed Regina's door and watched her for a moment. The mare did a walking tour of her ten-by-ten space, put her head over the door and looked up and down the narrow little aisle, and then sighed and went to her hay. Next to her, Mickey was walking in a circle, the thick curls of wood shavings rustling around his hooves, looking as if he wanted nothing more than to escape and run all the way home.

"He wasn't like this when I got him," I said despondently, and Pete came over and put a hand on my shoulder.

"He's still thinking about pain."

I considered this. "How can we make him forget?"

"You have to prove to him that it won't hurt to work hard, and that other things might be worse." Pete paused. "Someplace away from prying eyes."

Mickey leaped away from me the moment that I mounted, and I hit the ground hard on my back. The wind knocked out of me in more than one sense, I just stayed there, lying in the dirt. I wasn't thinking about any potential injury or the serious risk of a thousand pounds of horse and hoof waving above me—I was thinking that I was a failure. And when Mickey's hooves finally did hit the ground a few inches from my head, and Pete was grabbing his reins and shouting, and Lacey was kneeling next to me and gabbling about nothing at all, I was thinking *I can't ride this horse*. And when I snapped out of it and Lacey suggested that I had a concussion and Pete was all for shining a flashlight in my eyes, I was thinking, *I have to ride this horse now*.

You have to get back on the horse after you fall, that's what they all tell you, and that's not just a saying, it's God's honest truth. You have to get back on, or the fear eats you up from the inside out.

So that's what I did. I waited until the buzzing in my ears was (mostly) gone and the black spots in front of my eyes were (mostly) vanished, and I marched right up to that damn horse, snatched the reins from Pete's reluctant hands, and swung up in the saddle before Mickey could do boo about it. The entire time I was thinking *I loved you so much, from the moment I saw you, I knew we were going to have something special, and just because I didn't know your feet hurt once, doesn't mean I have to be punished forever.*

"We have to work this out, Mickey," I told him aloud, just before I nudged him forward and Pete jumped aside and Mickey took one of his flying leaps, me clinging to his mane like a little kid on a pony ride, my heels jutting down from the stirrups somewhere near his heaving shoulders.

He hit the ground and I smacked him with my jumping whip and he did it again, of course, because I hit him with a whip that was only there to gingerly ask for more, not to punish, and his leap was harder to stick this time because I only had one hand on the reins. The other was somewhere behind me, held out for balance as if I was going down a steep drop on the cross-country course. The third time he actually groaned, as if he couldn't believe I was making him do this again and again, and the fourth time he crumpled to his knees and remained there, half on the ground and half standing, until I climbed out of the saddle. I tugged on the reins. "Come on, Mickey, for God's sake," I said, not above pleading with this horse.

Mickey responded by lying flat out in the dirt, his polished gray coat spoiled by the sooty-black Florida scrubland sand, and

I wondered if maybe I had more than a concussion after all, and I was imagining all of this.

Mickey groaned again and closed his eyes.

"Jules, are you okay?" It was Pete, closely followed by Lacey and Becky. The girls looked horrified, but Pete had an expression of scholarly concern. "What's going on here?"

"Well," I said. "I'm okay, but I think my horse is broken."

Pete looked down at Mickey and shook his head. "Son of a bitch."

"What do we do?" I had to stop myself from wailing.

He took the reins from my unprotesting hands. "We break the habit once and for all," he announced. "That's why I wanted someplace remote. We can't disturb the rest of the event."

All of us looked around; we had trekked to a distant corner of the horse park, a clearing in pine woods that were crisscrossed with trails for recreational riding. There was no one in sight.

"What are you going to do?" I asked cautiously, feeling a sudden sense of foreboding. I thought we had sought out a secluded space to spare embarrassment when Mickey behaved like a criminal. I hadn't considered that Pete might have some sort of training method up his sleeve that he wasn't proud of. How could I have? Pete was the most caring, gentle horseman I'd ever known. I looked at him, the tension in his shoulders, the fist on Mickey's reins, the tightness of his jaw, the sheer ruthless determination in his eyes, and I saw a Peter Morrison I'd never seen before—and that I found a little frightening. "Pete?" I asked again, voice tremulous. Beside me, Lacey plucked at my sleeve. "What are you going to do?"

Pete turned his head slowly and looked me in the eye. "Something I learned from my grandfather," he said. "But you aren't going to like it." He took the jumping whip from his boot and eyed it.

The whip was made by a racing company—it had a wide, padded piece of leather on the business end. Jockeys rode with stirrups too short to kick on their horses, so they needed a whip to act as their leg aid.

It wasn't supposed to hurt. Just encourage.

Pete cracked the whip across his own hand, so hard the slapping sound made me jump.

"Pete!" I was shocked. Beside me, Mickey looked up, his eyes round.

"It stings," Pete said, flexing his hand. "But it doesn't really hurt. Remember that."

I opened my mouth and found that I didn't have the words to reply. I was trying to imagine a world in which Pete did something cruel to a horse, and I was failing. I started to step forward, to take the reins back, to tell him to cool down first, but before I could make a move, Pete gave Mickey a smack across the chest with the whip. Astonished as the rest of us, Mickey scrambled to his feet in a second. He stood facing Pete, his nostrils and eyes wide with surprise.

"You see," Pete said—to Mickey, not to us. "You're already thinking about me instead of your problems."

Mickey took a step sideways, his eyes glued to Pete, and swished his tail peevishly. Then his ears flattened to the sides, and that dull expression filtered back over his face. "Pete," I said urgently, "don't stand in front of him, he's going to jump again—"

Pete took a step *toward* Mickey instead, yanking the reins beneath the horse's chin, and said, "Back up!" When Mickey didn't move, he gave him another thunk across the chest with the padded end of the whip. Mickey darted backward, his eyes alive again, and this time Pete went with him and didn't let him stop, clucking his tongue and yelling *"Get on! Back up! Get back!"* as he insisted Mickey back right across the clearing. Mickey's eyes were fixed on Pete, his hind legs backpedaling as fast as he could make them go.

I'd never seen anything like it.

"What the hell is he doing?" Lacey breathed, staring at the scene with her mouth wide open. "Is he crazy?"

Becky just pursed her lips, as if she was trying to parse the reasoning behind Pete's behavior.

But there couldn't be any sort of reason here, could there? What on earth did he mean to accomplish by backing my horse around and around a clearing no larger than a small dressage arena? Mickey was tiring; sweat was darkening his neck and he stumbled once or twice, his hind legs exhausted with the effort of backing. His ears flicked back and forth, trying to keep tabs on what was behind him. "Go on, get back!" Pete told him, again and again. "Keep moving, get back!"

I balled up my fists.

"You should stop him," Lacey cried. "You have to stop him!"

"No," Becky said softly. "He wouldn't do this to be cruel."

"It doesn't matter, Becky," I told her stonily. "He had no right to take my horse and behave like this. This is my horse. He can do whatever he likes with his horses. But he shouldn't have touched mine."

Becky looked at me, that old familiar measuring gaze that always found me wanting. "You couldn't fix him," she observed. "Why can't you accept help from someone who can?"

Across the clearing, Pete finally let Mickey stand still and they were like two statues facing each other, both heaving with exertion. Mickey's eyes were locked onto Pete's. He was present at last.

I thought I understood what had just happened, but something larger—my resentment—was overruling that side of my brain.

"You've never been able to admit that you need help," Becky went on, her voice faintly mocking. "You've always thought that you know everything. Why would a girl your age know everything, Jules? What kind of inflated ego do you have, anyway? Even Pete takes riding lessons and goes to clinics when he has some spare cash. Everyone else in this business understands that they can never stop learning. Everyone but you. What did you do? You *forged a signature to get ahead*! And that's why you will never succeed. And that's why I gave up on you." She paused. "And if you march over there and take those reins, Pete will give up on you, too."

Lacey was staring at us. *She knows now,* I thought, suddenly resigned. I tried to think of a way to explain.

But just then Pete turned away from Mickey and started walking toward us, with the gray horse following him wearily. The change in my horse was so remarkable, I forgot about Lacey and Becky. I just waited for Pete, while inside my head, two rivals battled it out.

He had no right.

He fixed your horse.

I put my hands behind my back so that he couldn't see they were still clenched into fists.

His eyes searched my face as he approached, and I thought he might apologize when he realized how angry I was. But he just said: "Get on the horse now."

Getting on the horse was the last thing I wanted to do. "I'm not getting on him like this."

"Just get on the horse, Jules, for God's sake. Get on and walk him around." Pete threw the reins back over Mickey's neck. "Here, I'll hold him for you while you mount."

Mount that horse again? Even though Mickey's expression was alert and present, I still didn't trust him. "No, you do it," I challenged Pete.

Pete shook his head. "I'm not getting on him. This is your horse."

"After you did *that*?" My angry side won out, despite the rational side reminding me that Mickey's expression was clear and interested for the first time since we'd arrived. "You broke it, you bought it! Get on him your damn self. I'll even hold the reins for you." I stepped up next to him and clutched the reins in a fist, just below his hand.

Pete looked down at me. There was sweat running down his face, cutting dirty paths through the dust layering his skin, and his eyes were fierce and angry. I probably looked much the same, but somehow it didn't stop a quiver of excitement from running up my spine.

"Dammit, Jules," Pete growled. "You think I'd put you on a horse I'm scared of? I can't get on him, not without eliminating *you* from competition, remember?"

My heart sank as I remembered one of the simplest rules of eventing: only the registered rider could get on the horse at the showgrounds.

Once again, Pete was protecting me. If I had a horse left to compete, no one could say we'd broken any rules.

Time to see what he'd left me to ride.

I took one more look at Pete before I stuck my boot in the stirrup, making sure he had a firm grip on the reins, and then I swallowed my nerves and swung into the saddle.

Mickey stood still.

I gathered up the reins in my hands, holding them gently between forgiving fingers, and waited for Pete to step back, out of the way. Just in case it happened again. And really, I had no reason to believe that it wouldn't. Even so, I whispered, "Please don't be broken, Mickey," one last time, before I nudged him gently.

And Mickey walked forward.

Hesitantly, and with ears uneasily cocked toward me, he walked. He didn't jump, he didn't leap, he didn't bolt.

He walked, four hooves flat on the ground.

I rode Mickey back to the stabling area without much incident. Indeed, by the time we got there, he felt more normal than ever. He was doing the things you'd expect of a young horse at a show, looking around with interest at other horses, spooking at plastic bags, walking at a good gait, head bobbing and ears pricked.

He felt exactly as he should.

And I was deeply confused about what had just happened. Using whips and forcing a horse to back (something that was very hard on both their bodies and their minds) were not in my play-book. I carried a dressage whip for flatwork training and a jumping whip for fences, but that was just for asking a horse's body to move in a certain way, whether it was to flick the hindquarters over in a shoulder-in, or get a bigger jump over a particularly wide oxer. It was never for physical punishment.

Although a whack for refusing a fence wasn't out of the question, Laurie had always taught me that it was more important to convince a horse he *couldn't* refuse a fence, rather than punishing him after the fact. Once a horse knew he didn't have to jump, she'd explained, there was always the possibility that he'd add up the action and the punishment in his mind, and decide he didn't really mind the punishment. (This was especially true of ponies, of course.)

When I combined the perplexing training technique of threatening Mickey with a whip to back up, alongside the visual of *Pete* doing it, I was utterly confused.

Had he revealed himself, completely out of the blue, to be a horse abuser? He'd taken it upon himself to teach my horse a lesson without my permission, which in and of itself was a high crime. And he'd done it in such a way that I was wondering if I even knew him at all.

And most confusingly of all . . . it worked. *Why?*

These were my thoughts as I rode back to the barn on a high-stepping, bright-eyed Mickey, who seemed to be completely over the entire event, as if none of the drama, from his arrival this morning to his leaping stunt and subsequent punishment this afternoon, had happened at all.

Becky and Lacey were already back at the barn, having taken the golf cart that Pete brought to shows in the back of his truck. They peeked out of the stable aisle, whispering to each other as I rode up, and I blinked to see them in cahoots. I hadn't seen them working together since the fight here at Sunshine State over the summer. Months ago. A lifetime ago.

Lacey came out of the barn and took Mickey's reins as I pulled up. "He looks much better," she offered, patting the horse's wet neck. "Did you work him?"

"I just walked him," I replied shortly, slipping out of the saddle. "He'll be sore behind from all that backing. Can you give him a liniment bath?"

"Sure." Lacey rubbed Mickey between the eyes while I pulled off his saddle and pad. The horse closed his eyes and appeared to enjoy the attention. I just shook my head. I didn't know what to think. About any of it.

I took the bridle when Lacey had put the halter around his neck and lingered for a moment to make sure she didn't have any trouble getting it over his nose. "Jules," Lacey said, "did you really forge Sandra's signature?"

I sighed. "Yes."

Lacey shook her head. "You're crazy, you know that?"

"I couldn't afford another training session, Lacey. She told me to go ride with someone else like I just had two hundred bucks lying around. No one was going to find out. There are way too many Advanced level riders here for anyone to go checking up and ask her about it."

"Is there anything you *wouldn't* do to get ahead?"

I shrugged. I thought I'd been pretty clear with Lacey about who I was, all along. "I probably wouldn't murder anyone," I said after a moment.

Lacey snorted and gave Mickey a peppermint. "That's a relief."

"Is Pete back yet?" I asked, trying to keep my voice casual.

She shook her head. "He didn't want to ride back with us. He said he'd walk. Haven't seen him."

"Probably just out on the cross-country course," I said, and carried the tack into the stables to be wiped down and returned to its trunk for the night. I thought about going to look for him, but I couldn't figure out what I'd say when I found him. Bitch him out? Ask him what the hell he'd been thinking? Thank him?

Never date a horse trainer. I'd given him my trust and he'd returned it by deciding he was the one to train my horse, and by completely unorthodox methods, to boot. I couldn't even imagine what might have happened if someone had seen that go down. Nothing good, that was for sure.

I decided to beat it back to the farm, and hole up in the guest suite before he got home. I definitely wasn't ready to see him yet.

He knocked that night around seven. Not late, but I was in my pajamas, curled up on the couch with a pillow in my arms, watching a video of dressage tests from last year's Kentucky Three-Day Event. Other riders could afford to train with five-star riders as their coaches. I had to content myself with watching the masters on my television.

Lacey, reading at the kitchen table, looked up. "Pete's at the door," she observed.

"Yup." I didn't move.

"You aren't going to let him in?"

"Nope."

Lacey got up with a huff. "You can't lock out your landlord, Jules," she said, exasperated, as she unlocked the door. "Jules is being a baby," she told Pete.

"Thank you," I said, not looking away from the TV. A horse performed a jaw-dropping extended trot across the diagonal. I watched the rider's legs and hands, trying to memorize angles and motion so that I could replicate it while riding Dynamo tomorrow morning.

"Solivita is a gorgeous mare," Pete said, slipping past Lacey and into the living room. "Regina doesn't like her."

"Well, she isn't here, she's in Aiken, so Regina is in luck." I paused the video and glared at Pete. "Why are you here?"

He quirked his eyebrow, and I wanted to slap it off his handsome face. "I think we have some things to talk about."

I shook my head. "Not tonight. Not before the dressage. I have too much else to think about."

Behind him, Lacey disappeared down the hall and into her bedroom. I heard her door click shut. Pete glanced after her and then back at me. "Are you going to refuse to talk to me all weekend?"

"Probably," I admitted. "It would make things easier for me."

"And what about me?" His voice grew tight. "How do you think it will go for me? Or is icing me out your winning strategy?"

I stared at him. His face was deadly serious—which meant he really believed I was capable of something so devious. Did he know me at all? "I can't believe you'd accuse me of that," I said slowly. "I can't believe you'd think I'd do that to you."

"I don't know what to think," he snapped, his rigid composure breaking. "I made your dangerous horse walk around the show-grounds like a puppy-dog today, and all I get is a door in my face. Who knows what you want out of this relationship? Maybe you just want to get back at me for beating you after all."

I jumped up, dropping the pillow to the floor. "How dare you? Who the hell do you think you are? You take my horse from me and beat him in circles, and call that fixing him? Without permission, without invitation? What would his owners say, if they found out? My boyfriend beats my horse at an event and I can't even stop him? Are you joking?" I choked on the tears thickening my throat. I'd never been so angry and I'd never been so hurt and I'd never been so confused in my entire, desperate, hard-luck life. I let one person get close to me and this was the misery I got in return?

He opened his mouth to defend himself and I threw the heart of the matter at him. "You could have gotten me eliminated to-day. You could have gotten me kicked right off the showgrounds.

I trusted you the way I've never trusted anyone and you broke that trust. You almost ruined everything!"

Pete's jaw dropped and he stared at me as if he'd never laid eyes on me before. "Is that what this is about? Getting caught?"

"It's about the *event*," I snapped. "If we'd been seen—if anyone reported us—they would have asked us to leave so fast. I thought you needed this event. You certainly said you did. You know that I do. Unless—" I paused as a hideous new thought entered my mind. "You wanted to have me ruled off the grounds."

Pete looked at me as if I had kicked his dog, and my stomach lurched. His face told me, beyond a shadow of a doubt, that he had never tried to sabotage my chances at the event. I'd gone too far. I held up a hand, trying to wrap my tongue around an apology, but it was already far too late.

Pete spun on his heel and went out the door, slamming it behind him.

I sank back down onto the couch, trembling, and picked up the pillow from the floor. I squeezed it against my chest, hard, and willed myself not to cry. *Big girls don't cry. Boys don't cry.* All the old lines from all the old songs that said to suck it up. I wasn't in this game to find love. I was in this game to find success. And I was right to be angry, when the person that I loved endangered my shot at success. Maybe not on purpose, but still . . .

I was so busy trying not to cry, I didn't notice that the word "love" had entered my ever-chattering internal monologue. I didn't notice until Lacey came into the living room, an hour or a lifetime later, and sat down on the couch next to me and ran her hands down my tangled hair, over and over, like a woman soothing her horse. I didn't notice until she said: "He's in love with you." And then I started to sob, because it was all going so, so wrong.

26

MY DRESSAGE RIDE on Dynamo was at 8:40 A.M., which was ungodly early if you asked me.

No one did, of course.

It would have been hard for anyone to have gotten my opinion, anyway, because I wasn't speaking to anyone. No one who spoke English, that is. I talked to Dynamo and Mickey nonstop.

"Mickey, darling boy, I need you to be lovely for me this afternoon," I told Mickey at four o'clock in the morning, when I gave up trying to sleep and drove to the showgrounds. Mickey dug his nose into his timothy and ignored me. Just as well—I didn't need to bother him for his dressage test until after ten, and that was six hours away. I turned instead to Dynamo, who was watching me with bright eyes.

"You will be lovely for me, I know that much," I told him, and he nickered. I was exhausted and emotional, but I knew a feed-me nicker when I heard one. I gave him a flake of alfalfa and watched him dig into the leafy greens, utterly content to be near him.

The barn started to wake up around five, when other trainers with early rides started showing up—or their working students and grooms, in most cases—to get horses fed and cleaned up. There was plenty to be done between breakfast and showtime. Braids had to be fixed, socks had to be scrubbed. Before too long the breakfast nickers had been replaced with the sounds of electric clippers and swearing grooms. "Stand up! Be still! Knock it off! OUCH!"

Dynamo was chestnut, with only white on his face; I got lucky there. All he needed was a grooming and a polish with ShowSheen. Mickey was another story, but since I had Lacey coming later, I wasn't concerned about all the greenish manure stains that would need to be scrubbed out with alcohol and a washcloth before our dressage ride.

"We have ages," I told Dynamo, and he shoved his nose against my chest and asked for more timothy. Might as well keep him happy.

Becky arrived at the stabling around six thirty. She paused outside Dynamo's stall, eyeing me while I combed out Dynamo's tail. We hadn't spoken since her little speech to me yesterday, and I purposefully ignored her for a few minutes before my own impatience caught up with me and I asked her what she wanted.

"Did you already feed Pete's horses?" she asked. "They're not beating down the door asking me for breakfast."

"Oh, yes. I had to," I said. "They were very jealous of my horses."

She nodded. "Thanks. That will let me get rolling on Regina's white, then." Regina had three white stockings, flashy and beautiful and filthy every morning. "These early dressage times can suck it," she said, pulling a bucket and washcloth from a tack trunk in front of Regina's stall. "Enough to make me go back to school full time."

I was so surprised that Becky was making conversation, I almost didn't answer her. "Are you going to finish your degree?" I asked finally.

"I am," she said, rummaging for the rubbing alcohol. "But I might change it to equine business management. Stick to running barns, ride one or two of my own horses on my own dime. I still want to compete, but I don't know that I want to train." She turned to face me through the bars of the stall and smiled. I stopped brushing Dynamo's tail, astonished. "You work so hard," she went on. "And so does Pete. And for no thanks at all. Your horse could be taken away at any moment. I've been thinking, watching Pete work his butt off just as hard as you, the constant fear of losing it all . . . I guess I get it, Jules. Why you are the way you are."

I stared at her.

Becky kept going. "I've learned a lot from both of you, but I think what I've learned most of all is to appreciate how hard trainers work, and for how little thanks, most of the time." She turned back to her search for rubbing alcohol, and I went back to pulling the comb through Dynamo's luxurious red tail, utterly lost for words.

I couldn't get out of the barn before Pete arrived, as much as I would have liked to. Around seven, when I figured he'd be rolling in, I started to throw tack on Dynamo. I knew it was too early to get on him, but I thought we could just hack out, take a look at the warm-up ring and the dressage arenas, and generally relax. He preferred to be out of his stall, after all, and it would do him good to have some time to chill out while other horses were warming up for their tests.

When he was saddled and bridled, I put his halter back on, tied him to a stall bar, and asked Becky to keep an eye on him while I went to change into my good clothes. She nodded, a little smile playing on her lips as if she knew exactly what I was trying to do, and I took off down the stable aisle.

And nearly ran smack into Pete, strolling in with a box of coffee from Starbucks and a brown paper bag that was greasy with pastries.

I looked up at him and he looked down at me, and neither of us said a word. I saw his jaw set into place, the way that it did when he was angry, and that told me all I needed to know. This wasn't going away. I ducked under his arm, bumping into the bag of pastry, and took off for the horse trailer to wriggle into my show breeches alone.

I felt his gaze on my back all the way there. But when I reached the trailer and turned around, there was no one in the stable aisle at all. He had gone on with his morning.

"And so will I," I told myself.

I was struggling with my hair, which did not want to be confined into its hairnet, when there was a rap at the metal door. I whirled around, expecting Pete. "Come in!" I called. I just wanted him to apologize for taking my horse without my permission. That was all I wanted. Everything else I could forgive. As weird as his training method had been, the worst of it was really the visual. No one had been hurt. Startled, yes, surprised into a complete life-change, for sure—but not hurt. So I could forgive him the moments of training—but not that he'd done it without asking. I couldn't live like that, with someone who thought they knew better than me.

My heart thudded as the door opened, and skidded to an awkward, off-center halt as Lacey stepped up into the tack room. "You can't get dressed on your own, silly," she said affectionately, reaching for my hairnet. "Now turn around and let me fix this mess."

I handed over the hairnet and elastics and obediently turned around, letting her experienced fingers loop my messy hair into something tidy that could be hidden under a riding helmet. Then she turned me back around, maneuvering me by the shoulders as if I were a little girl, and straightened the pin on my stock tie. "Want your jacket on?" she asked, once she had stepped back and given me the once-over.

"Just my sweater right now," I said, and she nodded.

"I'll bring the jacket to the ring along with the bucket and the towel."

"And some Gatorade."

"And some Gatorade," she promised. "Do you want to look over the test again?"

"No, I know it." I'd read it over and over again, all night long, when it was obvious I was never going to fall asleep. Enter at A, working trot. At X, halt, salute, proceed at collected trot. At C, track left. From H to P, medium trot. At P, collected trot. K–E, shoulder-in right. I could recite it in my sleep, if I ever slept again. "Come at eight, okay?"

"I'll be there." She hesitated. "Pete's ride is at eight thirty, you know."

"I know."

"Are you going to talk to him beforehand?"

I shook my head. "Today, I'm just going to compete. When he's ready to apologize, then we'll talk."

Lacey nodded slowly, which meant that she didn't agree with my logic, which meant that she didn't think it was going to happen, which meant that my world slid a little farther toward the precipice. I swallowed and pulled on my hoodie, zipping it up to keep my white shirt and stock tie spotless. If I could hold it together until I was mounted on Dynamo, I could hold it together through the day. Barely.

"I'll be at the barn with Dynamo," Lacey said, heading out of the tack room.

She paused just outside the door and peeked back in. "Hey, Jules?"

I turned. "Yes?"

"Are you mad at him for what he did, or are you mad that he could have gotten you in trouble?"

"Are you serious?"

Lacey held up her hands. "I don't know with you anymore."

"I didn't show up to get eliminated for abusing a horse, Lace."

"Do you really think it was that bad?"

I shrugged. "It sure *looked* bad. Does it matter what I think? Everyone thinks I'm insane anyway. That I don't know what I'm doing. They look at Mickey and they remember him trying to kill me at Lochloosa. They see someone chasing him backward with a whip at his next event? Yeah, combine those two things, and it's that bad."

Lacey furrowed her brow. "Okay, public perception—I get that. But you—do you think Pete would abuse your horse? He must have had a reason for what he did, right? Why don't you just ask him what it was all about?"

I sighed. "You ask him, Lacey, if you really want to know. I can't think about Pete right now."

Lacey shook her head at me, clearly disappointed, and walked off. I closed the tack room door behind her and turned back to the flimsy plastic mirror hanging on the wall. I inhaled, filling my lungs with air until there was no more room. When I exhaled, my breath was one word.

Win.

We were loafing under the oak tree near the dressage arenas. Taking a little break to watch the first few rounds felt indulgent and wise, as if we were on the other side of the divide from the horse-and-rider team we'd been back in June, new at this level and still uncertain. The first Intermediate riders were beginning their tests, and an energetic warmblood was carting his rider around the arena while a sleepy-looking spotted horse trotted around the exterior path, getting ready for his turn in the spotlight but not getting particularly worked up about it. I watched the rounds with my feet out of the stirrups, reins loose on Dynamo's neck. He knew how to do the test, and I knew what I had to do to get him through it. The kind of elevation and self-carriage required at this level was not easy for him, and I wasn't going to tire him out before the judge even got a look at him. We'd do a quick, solid warm-up before the test, and go in fresh as daisies. That was the plan, anyway.

I looked at my little silver watch, the one I saved for dressage, when I wanted to look classy. It was eight fifteen. There was no sign of anyone from Briar Hill—not Pete, not Lacey, not Becky. I was starting to feel nervous. What if something had happened back in the stable? What if Mickey had done something stupid? What if one of Pete's horses had acted up?

Then I looked over my shoulder and saw Lacey and Becky walking together, deep in conversation. Both had leather lead shanks and halters slung over their shoulders, both had buckets with washcloths and bottles of Gatorade, both were the pictures of happy young grooms off to help their trainers, and I nearly looked at the sky to see if any pigs were flying by. Instead, I just waved hello when Lacey looked up. She waved back. Becky glanced up and smiled, a genuine smile, and I had the confusing realization that even while my unexpected relationship with Pete was collapsing around me, my old friendship with Becky, if not exactly rekindled, might just be possible again.

And this was why I preferred my horses to people. Horses were never this complicated, even when they confounded you.

Lacey handed me up my bottle of neon-blue Gatorade. "Pete's on his way over. He just wanted to do a couple transitions and some shoulders-in, he said. Regina works best fresh."

"That's our strategy too." I took a gulp of Gatorade and wished it was caffeinated. My stomach was too nervous for coffee, and I was starting to feel the effects of my wakeful night. Then I saw Pete riding over on a high-headed Regina, his hands light and easy on the reins, and my anxious stomach flipped. I handed the Gatorade back hastily and concentrated all my efforts on not fainting, or being sick, or whatever trouble my body seemed to have planned for me. Just seeing him made me shake.

Lacey followed my gaze and gave Becky a tap on her shoulder. Becky waved goodbye and went running over to take care of her rider, who appeared to be studiously ignoring me. The harder I looked at him, the more he seemed to stare off in another direction. I put my face down on Dynamo's neck to hide my flushed cheeks. His hot flesh was a comfort, his solidity, his familiarity—he was my rock while every other relationship I had was shifting around me.

The silence between Pete and me continued through the dressage tests and the time in the stable afterward, while Lacey and

I rinsed off Dynamo and he and Becky rinsed off Regina right next to us.

Our test had been good, although I feared it wasn't good enough to put us in the top ten. I hadn't liked our first canter transition very much, and judging by the way Dynamo had pinned his ears and stuck his nose straight out, he hadn't liked it much either. We recovered, and my legs were now aching with the effort of putting him back together. But I was afraid the damage had been done.

I thought Pete and Regina had done beautifully, though Pete told Lacey that he thought Regina was too fresh. Maybe Pete and I were both suffering from shaken confidence after yesterday. I didn't know anymore. I just wanted to get through the weekend in one piece, so that we could talk this thing out, and get going wherever it was we were going. Upward, I hoped. Whether it was together or separate, I really couldn't say.

I hoped it was together.

27

STANDING IN MICKEY'S stall, I rubbed the horse between his dark eyes, running my hand up the gap where his forelock should have been. There was a little fuzzball springing up from his poll, right between his ears. It wanted to stand straight up and looked more like an untidy bridle path than a forelock, but it looked as if a replacement to his shorn locks was coming. I was aware of how fortunate I was that he had come through the scalping incident without a scar. My first stroke of good luck? Or had I been having good luck all along, and never even noticed?

I pulled a dark blue bonnet out of the tack trunk just outside his stall door and held it up for him to inspect. He ran his nostrils over it and snorted. "It will bring out the brown in your eyes," I told him. "And hide what you did to your face."

I was nervous about riding him. I couldn't pretend not to be. But we had a dressage ride to get through. So I tied him to the rail and tacked him up.

Pete looked over as I led Mickey out of the barn. He was grazing

Regina while Becky gave Vanellope another stocking scrubbing with the wash pail and a bottle of whitening shampoo. She stopped what she was doing and watched us walk by, her hands stained purple with the soap suds.

I ignored them. I just wanted to get mounted, and get out of here. I threw the reins over Mickey's ears, gathered them at his withers, and said a silent prayer to the eventing gods. Then I added a silent plea to Mickey as well, just in case that whole "horses are psychic" stuff was for real: *Please don't be a freak. Please be the horse I know you can be.* I lifted my foot toward the stirrup—and felt a touch on my shoulder.

"What." I didn't turn around. I was facing my saddle, the black leather gleaming a few inches from my nose.

"If he does anything at all, get off him and back him up," Pete murmured in my ear. "Break the cycle. Ten steps. Fifteen. Until he will walk forward gently. You can do it quietly now, and it will work."

I swallowed hard, and then nodded.

"You'll do it? Promise me."

I nodded again, and brushed his hand from my shoulder. I heard him step back.

"Thank you," he said. "Good luck."

I mounted, and Mickey took a few dancing steps before he consented to walk, spritely and high-headed, but definitely a walk. I let out a harsh breath that I'd been holding without realizing it, and guided him toward the warm-up ring.

I backed him exactly one time. As we neared the dressage arenas and warm-up, Mickey began to jig sideways and wring his tail, slashing it against my boot. First one side, then the other—*swish swish swish*. When he began to grind his teeth and lift his head so high I found myself looking between his ears to see where we were going, I knew I was in trouble.

We were in trouble. We were a team in this, even if Mickey didn't quite believe it yet. I gathered my reins closer but kept my fingers loose. "Easy, son," I whispered, hoping to see his ears flick back to hear me. "Relax, buddy boy." His ears remained fixed forward, glued on the scene ahead.

And it was a rather more chaotic scene than it had been earlier. The lower-level horses were not so composed as the upper-level veterans, and there was plenty of bucking and spinning and rearing and bolting going on in the warm-up. Worst of all, just beyond the dressage there was a view of the starting box, where the earliest cross-country rides were already getting underway. The air was crackling with the tension and excitement and nerves of several hundred worked-up horses.

Mickey began to bounce up and down like a rocking horse, unfortunately with the same amount of forward motion. I dropped my hands, spread wide, past his withers, hoping to bring his head down. He only arched his neck in response, tucking his chin close to his chest, and I felt him bring his magnificent hindquarters beneath himself, preparing for his one special trick.

And before I could really think about what I was doing, I had kicked my feet free, slipped from his back, and was bunching the reins in my fist, slapping them against his chest. He groaned at me, picking up his right foreleg, and I flung the loose end of the reins at his forearm like a barrel-racer gunning her horse for the finish line. "Don't you dare slap at me!" I roared, and several Pony Clubbers manning the nearby tack-cleaning tent turned their heads, mouths perfect Os at the prospect of fresh carnage from the famous Jules Thornton.

But it was too late to worry about the peanut gallery now. And not having any tricks in my arsenal but the one Pete had used yesterday, I gripped the muscle of his chest and squeezed. *"Back. Up. Back up!"*

And Mickey backed.

Ten strides, fifteen, twenty—I lost count. I just backed him up until I could tell by his expression that he was more worried about what was behind him than what was in front of him. And then he was more worried about *me* than anything else. His eyes were focused on me, his left ear trained on me, his mouth open and working. He was hoping and praying to whatever gods the horses prayed to that I'd stop and go back to being nice.

So I did.

Mickey stood still, his sides heaving, working the bit anxiously in his mouth. Foam dribbled down to the ground and spattered the toes of my boots, but I wasn't worried about losing the sheen on my boots. I watched his closest eye, the way it was fixed on me—not on the other horses, not on the chattering people, not on the fluttering canvas atop the tack-cleaning tent. *Me.*

"Can we do this?" I asked gently, and put my hand on his damp neck. Mickey chewed on his bit in response, saliva spilling over the metal.

Good enough.

Heart in my throat, willing my hands to be still, I sprang back into the saddle, found my stirrups, and asked him to walk on.

Neck arched, ears on me, hooves careful, Mickey walked.

I held the reins gently, waiting for my heartbeat to slow down to a more natural rhythm, and let Mickey choose a slow pace toward the warm-up.

* * *

We were leaving the dressage arena, both feeling a little wiser and a lot older, when a voice startled me. "Jules! Jules Thornton!"

I turned quickly in the saddle, causing Mickey to shy a little from my sudden movement. I tightened the reins and pressed my hand on his neck to calm him. It had been a tense dressage test, with one exciting moment when he decided that the fluttering flowers in front of the judge's gazebo were going to eat him, but we recovered, and I now had an idea of just how good his pirouettes would be someday. We might not bring home a ribbon this weekend, but at this point, walking normally was a win. Everything else was gravy.

"Jules, over here!" A woman extracted herself from the little grandstand and came jogging over to meet us. She was plump and red-faced and wearing a massive floppy sun hat that Mickey at first regarded as a second coming of the gazebo flower monster. But she held out a carrot, the kind with the green leaves tasseling from the top, and the horse graciously changed his mind. The woman unbuckled his flash noseband and was handing him his carrot before I could say a word of protest. And then a second woman, greyhound-slim and athletic, with a graying ponytail and a face I knew from a hundred magazine articles, joined her, and I realized with a jolt that I was looking down at Mickey's owners.

The round woman gave Mickey an enthusiastic pat on the neck and beamed up at me. "Oh, Jules, I can't believe you have him at a trial already. This is just fantastic. I'm so proud of him!"

I opened my mouth, but no words came out. Which was just as well, because Carrie Donnelly spoke next, and I would have died if I'd interrupted the undisputed queen of eventing. "Fancy footwork when you first brought him out. Did you learn that backing-up trick from a cowboy?"

My face flooded red. "No, it was just—he had a bad habit of plunging and bolting—"

Carrie smiled. "I wasn't criticizing you. That was really very clever. Reset his entire mind and focused him completely on you. I love a Thoroughbred, but every now and then you run into one that fixates on some past experience and it's dangerous until you get their heads back to the present." She gave Mickey a rub, then ran her hand up his head and flipped up the ear bonnet. "Forelock's growing back, I see. Good! I think you two are a nice match."

Eileen, pulling more carrots from her voluminous handbag, nodded enthusiastically. "Oh, they're just adorable together," she announced. "Here, Mickey, have another carrot."

I was dying to get back to the barn, to tell Pete that it had worked, to apologize. But Eileen and Carrie had other plans, dragging me from friend to friend while they showed off Mickey. I smiled and shook hands with two dozen riders and owners, all prominent eventing people I had seen from afar and longed to meet and schmooze with, but now my heart wasn't in it. I just wanted to talk to Pete.

By the time I got away from the socializing and made my way back to the barn, Pete was already out on Regina to warm up for her cross-country run.

Lacey was sitting on the tack trunk in front of Dynamo's stall, going over my cross-country saddle for any signs of wear we might have missed in the ten thousand inspections before. She looked up as I led Mickey into the barn, and hastily pushed the saddle aside so that she could hop up and take his reins.

"I was there to catch him, but you were so busy with those ladies, I didn't want to interrupt," she explained, looking guilty.

"Settle down, you're fine," I said, unbuckling my hard hat. "Where's Pete?"

"Gone for his next ride with Becky. I saw Mickey go like an old pro. That was crazy good, Jules." She kissed Mickey on his nose, and his nostrils fluttered in response. "Such a good boy!"

"It was crazy good, considering he was about thirty seconds from trying to kill me on the way over to the warm-up." I rummaged in the cooler for a Diet Coke. "Pete's trick worked," I added as casually as I could. "Shut the whole nonsense down. It reboots his brain or something."

Lacey shook her head while she fumbled with the bridle straps, Mickey's curious lips wiggling after her fingers and making the operation difficult. "Craziness," she managed to say.

"I know." I took a deep swig of soda. Caffeine bubbles popped in my sleepless brain. I had a lot more day to get through. "I have to talk to Pete about it. And apologize," I added. "That's going to suck."

"It's worth it," Lacey said, sounding pleased. "But you really don't have time now. We have to get you and Dynamo ready for cross-country."

And it was a mark of Lacey's efficiency that twenty minutes later she had Dynamo and me kitted out in our protective boots and safety vest, respectively, ready to go onto the cross-country course and tackle the Intermediate course we had won nearly six months ago.

"Good luck," she said, slapping my boot at the in-gate to the warm-up arena. "I'll be near the finish line."

I was busy looking around at the other riders. "Do you see Pete?"

Lacey shook her head. "Hey, Jules? Pay attention to your ride. There will be plenty of time to talk to Pete afterward."

I laughed. "I can't believe you have to tell me that."

She rolled her eyes. "Jules in love is actually more annoying than ambitious Jules. I can't believe it."

I leaned down and gave her a cuff on the side of the head. Dynamo side-stepped, throwing his own head. "Literally everyone is telling you to focus right now," Lacey smirked, letting go of the reins. "Go get 'em. Eventing before boys."

I nodded in agreement. "Eventing before boys." I had about twenty minutes to get Dynamo's muscles warmed up before we went out there and tore up the cross-country course. This was what we showed up for. This was why we got up in the morning. I grinned at Lacey and shook out my reins. "Here we go!"

I remember it now in slow motion, as if that's how it happened. We were galloping, of course, but we were galloping in slow motion. We jumped the eighth fence, a straightforward ditch-and-wall, but we jumped it in slow motion. We landed and turned toward the drop into the forest, a dark wall of trees one long gallop away, where the woods nearly concealed a tall hanging log with a slippery gravel hill on the other side, sloping dangerously down into the wooded portion of the course, but we made the arcing turn in the poison-green grass in slow motion. The ambulance went racing past us, but somehow that, too, was moving at a rate much more slowly than real life. There was no siren—I remember silence.

And then the jump judge was running toward us, walkie-talkie in one hand, red flag waving at us in the other. "Hold on course, hold on course!" she must have been saying, but I couldn't hear her, I don't remember her voice. It all happened, but it all happened so slowly.

And then it all happened so fast. I looked past her, to the forbidding darkness where the ninth fence was, and saw the ambulance pulling to a halt, grass flying from its back tires. And I kicked Dynamo into a full gallop, my spurs in his sides, my elbows out like a cowgirl, and we went flying past the jump judge and tore down the galloping lane at racing speed, my heart in my throat, my horse at his utmost.

Because Pete was the rider in front of us.

28

THE EMTS WHIRLED as we came slipping and sliding into the forest, plunging down the side path that had been built for the course-walkers, and the jump judges, and, of course, the EMTs themselves.

"What the hell, hold back, hold back!" one of them shouted, holding up his hands. "You have to get out of here! We have a rider down!"

I ignored his protests and looked past him to see the cluster of paramedics, the empty stretcher, Pete on the ground in his green-and-blue colors, splayed on his back. Just behind him, a scared little Pony Clubber with a walkie-talkie and a nicer horse than she'd ever touched before was hanging on to Regina's reins, too confused to remember to always walk a hot horse. I jogged Dynamo right past the EMT and did the unthinkable without thinking.

I slid right off his back and abandoned him.

A dismount on the course was the same as a fall: elimination. I didn't care.

I shoved past a paramedic, who looked at me as if I had produced a jar of leeches and started chanting, and knelt down next to Pete. His face was white, smeared with a streak of blood and dirt where he had scraped along the gravel of the hill—he must have been dragged for a stride, I thought desperately, to have ended up down here. I glanced back at the hillside and saw the broken stirrup leather in the scuffed gravel and my stomach lurched. I didn't look at his legs. I was too thankful that his head seemed to be intact to wonder too much what had happened to the rest of him.

I laid my lips along his cheek, close to his ear, my hard hat rapping against his, and his eyes opened abruptly, wide and unfocused. I drew back so that he could see me. "Pete," I whispered. "Goddammit, Pete."

"Miss," the paramedic said impatiently. "Miss, I need you to give him some room. We need to make sure he can be moved without risking further injury."

Pete's eyes roved around my face and slowly focused. I waited, breathless, for something to happen. Anything at all, just to let me know he was okay—

He groaned and closed his eyes again.

I shook my head, a million terrors crowding out any sense, and I leaned forward, shoving away the interfering paramedic with one horse-strong arm, and pressed my lips to Pete's dry ones. What was I doing? True love's kiss? Playing at fairy tales?

Wasn't a girl who lived only for her horses living in a fairy tale every day, anyway?

Which was why I didn't faint dead away when I felt him lift his hand and slowly, gently, stroke my arm, the only part of me that wasn't covered by a body protector or a hard hat. There was some mystical part of me that had never grown up, through all the bitterness and all the brittleness that the struggle to get here had imparted upon my spirit. And I knew then that the place I had wanted to get to, the place that I had fought for my entire life, had abruptly changed addresses.

People came and cleaned up after us, and got the show back on the road. Pete was loaded into the ambulance, a lingering smile on his lips as he waved goodbye to me, just before the scowling paramedic slammed the door. The jump judge offered to take Regina back to the barn for me, another Pony Clubber arrived on a four-wheeler and took over her post. The broken stirrup leather was retrieved, the scary scuffs in the gravel where Pete had been dragged and ultimately fallen were hastily raked over. We started walking through the woods to find the trail that cut back toward the starting box and the stabling area.

"You could still show Mickey." Becky caught my arm. "You're only eliminated on Dynamo. And that was a good dressage test. I mean—you really pulled him together. Whatever that trick was, it worked. The cross-country course would be great practice for him."

"Becky," I said, suddenly curious. "Have you ever seen Pete do that before?"

"Fall off?"

"No—back a horse up like he did Mickey."

"Oh." She thought. "No. I've never even really seen him hit a horse. Not the way he hit Mickey to get him started. It startled me, I have to tell you. But he must have had a reason. Pete wouldn't abuse a horse."

"No, he wouldn't," I agreed. "But I just don't know why he

thought to do it. Carrie said something about Thoroughbreds fixating on things in the past, though. Does that sound like something?"

"Oh, and Pete figured out how to shake him up," Becky suggested. "Pete has said before that horses replay old situations in their heads. They get upset, they go back to the last time they got scared, and they replay that scene over again. Like a stuck tape. They don't always realize that things have changed, that it's not so bad anymore."

I nodded, chewing at my lip.

"So he had the pain issue, right?" Becky went on, warming to her subject. "The farrier said it probably went way back. So maybe when he was racing, his feet hurt. And he arrived at a new place, thought he was going to race, and panicked. And so it continued, even after his feet stopped hurting him. And he had to be reminded: hey, wake up, it doesn't hurt anymore. He was too far into his own head, worrying about problems that weren't even real anymore. He needed a big shock to help him snap out of it." She gazed out at the horizon, clearly taken with her theory.

"That makes so much sense," I said.

"Right?"

It was all coming together now . . . the weird way Pete had adjusted Mickey's attitude, and the way the horse responded to me when I did it, too. And yet, he'd still broken my trust by taking the lead when Mickey was *my* horse.

Becky turned back to me. "He's been trying to figure out what was wrong with your horse since Lochloosa," she said. "He said a horse like that could make your career, and he wasn't going to hesitate if he came up with a solution. Even if it made you mad. And it did, didn't it?" She grinned. "It's making you crazy."

"No," I snorted. But I had to look away from her, and Becky knew me well enough to guess why.

"When Sandra Holborn told you to go home, practice over smaller jumps, and try again, you lost it," Becky said. "You couldn't take her advice, even though she *clearly* knew better than you."

Everything she'd told me had basically been what Pete had said months later, all that stuff about doing the work instead of letting my horse make all the decisions. Sandra really had been right. "So?" I asked. "What about it?"

"I just think if you fixed Mickey out there this morning, you're learning to take advice from someone who knows a little more about it than you," Becky said, shrugging. "Color me impressed."

I looked at her for a moment. "Are you saying I've grown?" I asked.

"That, or you just found the only person on earth you're willing to learn from," she said.

"Don't get used to it," I told her.

Becky rolled her eyes. "Listen, are you going to finish this event or not? Because you need to get back to the barn and prep Mickey for jumping."

I tried to imagine myself going back to the stables and tacking up Mickey, jogging over to the warm-up arena and putting him around the course as if nothing had changed. I couldn't do it. There were things I needed to talk about with Pete, and they couldn't wait.

"I'm withdrawing," I told her. "I need to be with Pete. Can you girls get them home all right?"

Becky nodded, and in her eyes I read something that might have been respect. "Go."

For the first time in my life, I'd found something more important than an event.

29

SPRING WAS ALWAYS a fleeting thing in Florida, and despite the optimistic name of the event, the Lochloosa Spring Fling was already feeling more like the July event we'd nicknamed the Lochloosa Hellfire Inferno. The April sun was fierce, and the fluffy white clouds dotting the North Florida sky were just pale imitations of their UV-blocking summer cousins, providing next to no shade. But it was the last big event before the season ended and the migration to Virginia, Maryland, and New England began in earnest. Just us Floridians would stay behind, whether we were native, like me, or adopted, like Lacey. Sticking it out in the heat and the humidity, the rain and the thunder, hoping for a break from the hurricanes, planting our roots deep in the sandy soil. They'd be back in the fall, and we'd be waiting for them. Tougher and tanner and ready to go.

Mickey pulled at the reins, yearning to eat a palmetto bush a few steps away, and I straightened him out so that I could see the dressage arena a short distance away. Pete was riding his new filly in her first test, and she was skipping her way around the arena with nervous energy. Pete sat still, right in the middle of the action, refusing to argue with her. He flexed his wrist, which still ached sometimes from the fracture he'd sustained at Sunshine State back in the fall. He was lucky that was all that he'd broken.

It had been a crazy day, one I hoped we never repeated. Of course, the odds were not in our favor, not if we insisted on galloping horses over immoveable objects. But maybe the next time one of us ended up in the hospital, I didn't have to make it so . . . *emotional*?

I was a snotty mess by the time I got to Pete's side. A nurse, leaving his bedside in a white room with a curtain down the middle, put his hand on my arm and told me to relax. "He broke his wrist, not his neck," he told me. "We're just watching him awhile to rule out a concussion and then you can take him back to the farm, honey."

I couldn't tell this nurse, who was already raking his gaze down my dirt-streaked riding clothes, that my upset was about way more than broken bones. So I shrugged and nodded and wiped my nose on my sleeve. He let go of my arm and disappeared into the hospital bustle.

Which left me alone with Pete.

Our eyes met and we both said, at the same time, "I'm sorry."

He grinned nervously. "Do you think we could start this day over?"

I snorted. "I would prefer it just ends and never happens again, if that's okay."

"That's fine. I was just looking for a do-over where you weren't mad at me, and I wasn't on painkillers the size of a bute tablet."

"I wanted to talk to you before the cross-country," I blurted. "Becky explained—I mean—we talked about why you did it. With Mickey. I think I understand the idea behind it."

"But I shouldn't have done it without your permission," Pete said.

I wiped at my eyes. The tears weren't flowing anymore, but I still felt overwrought. Prickly with fear and exhaustion and all the detritus of the day. Pete apologizing was just about all I could take. I said, "I wish you hadn't. But—I think I understand why you did it, too."

"I didn't want to see you get killed."

I cracked a nervous smile. "Kind of ironic that you're the one in the hospital, isn't it?"

"Jules," Pete said, rolling his eyes, "if we're going to event together, there are probably going to be a fair number of hospital visits in the future. I've already had three doctors tell me to give it up. One of them told me I should try motorcycles instead. And you know what ER doctors think about motorcycles."

"A *motorcycle* to replace a horse?" I was incensed. "What the hell?"

Pete laughed. "Exactly."

"No one gets us," I said, taking his unbandaged hand. "Or the reasons why we do the things we do. I always said I'd never date a horseman—"

"I remember," he said dryly.

"But no one else would ever understand me," I finished.

He gave my fingers a little squeeze. "I won't try to train your horses for you, although I can't promise I won't interfere if I'm worried about you breaking your neck."

"I'll try not to put you in that position," I said, but we were both grinning at that because of course it was going to happen. Again and again.

I could have left things there, but Pete had just apologized for trying to keep me alive, which was decent of him, so I felt like I owed him a little something, too. And even though I still didn't think there was a thing wrong with it, I said, "I forged Sandra Holborn's signature to get into the ACE scholarship."

Pete looked at me for a moment. His eyes widened.

"What?" I asked, annoyed. If this was how he was going to take confessions . . .

Then he burst into laughter. Loud, over-the-top laughter that filtered into the busy corridor outside. The nurse poked his head back in. "We okay in here?"

Pete, still laughing, waved him away with his bandaged hand.

I took my hand back so I could fold my arms across my chest and glare at him. "Why is that so funny? I made a *confession*."

"But did you actually ride with her?"

"Yes, of course I did! But Sandra didn't pass me because of a few silly things. I couldn't afford any other lessons, so . . . I took a chance and faked it." I paused. Suddenly, in the cold light of the hospital room, forging that signature didn't seem like such a great idea. Had it changed anything for me? I'd kept things going without the ACE scholarship, after all. "No one would have found out," I hedged, but what if someone had?

Maybe I shouldn't have taken that chance.

"I'm glad you did it," Pete said.

Or . . . "Really?"

"I fell for you at ACE," Pete reminded me, his eyes twinkling. Or maybe it was just the fluorescent lights sparkling in his eyes. "So maybe you were meant to be there. So I could meet you at just the right moment."

"Don't try to make this about you," I told him, but inside, I was melting a little.

"It's not about me," Pete said. "It's about us."

A few minutes later the nurse came back, saw me kneeling on

the bed next to Pete so that I could kiss him properly, and instructed us in annoyed tones to please sign the paperwork and get out of his hospital.

Back at Lochloosa, my phone buzzed and I pulled it from the pocket of my breeches. A text from Lacey. She was bringing Dynamo over to the show-jumping warm-up. We had our jumping round right after my Novice dressage test on Mickey. His last one, I hoped. We had been schooling Training level cross-country jumps back at the farm, and I was ready to move him up. But during our phone consultation last month, Carrie and Eileen had reminded me to take it slowly, waiting until he was absolutely ready. And then added that they were thinking of sending me another young horse. I couldn't ask for better owners. "Taking it slow" was new to me, but I thought I could learn to enjoy it.

The gray horse shifted beneath me, cocking one hind leg to rest it. His nostrils fluttered in a little sigh, and he shook his head to dislodge a fly. All the tiny twitches and movements that are naturally part and parcel of a horse "standing still," barely noticeable anymore after years in the saddle. I could still remember, if I tried, the feeling of terror, the shriek that escaped me, the first time five-year-old me sat on a pony and it shook off a fly. Now, all those twitches were part of my second skin, an extension of me.

Pete came riding up, smiling broadly. He was evidently pleased with his ride. He'd picked up the little bay filly for free over the winter from a breeding farm that was closing down suddenly. We both had a few new prospects we'd acquired this way—free young horses were a dime a dozen in Ocala these days, and not just unsound ones who needed a layoff or veterinary work before they could be put back into training. The recovery from the hurricane was barely a recovery at all: it had left its mark everywhere. Foreclosures—my own farm among them—were so common there was no shame in admitting it, and trainers who had once proudly run their own properties were banding together, sharing barns and houses, much as Pete and I had done.

Although admittedly, not everyone shacked up quite as thoroughly as we had.

"How was she?" I asked, eyeing the wide-eyed filly, who was snorting at a palmetto frond lying in the sandy path. She had never been to a show before, and she was certain that Lochloosa's sun-scorched fields and oak-shrouded dressage arena were hiding monsters.

"Fantastic," Pete said, even as she wheeled and threatened to rear. He slackened the reins and gave her a good kick in the ribs, which sent her ducking into Mickey for reassurance. His bulk absorbed the impact of her little frame without complaint, and he nudged her with his big head, nearly knocking her over. "I mean, before that," Pete went on, grinning. "Keeping Mickey away from the ring was the way to go. She was able to concentrate on her work. Even got her leads." He patted her on the neck and she sighed, chewing at her bit. "You did a nice job starting her."

"She's a good girl," I agreed, ignoring the compliment and focusing on the horse. I still wasn't good at taking compliments. Or advice. But I was working on it—when the compliments or advice came from Pete, anyway. "She's getting way too attached to Mickey, though."

"One thing at a time," Pete replied. "There's no rush. If she can go around the ring without him, she'll figure out the rest in time."

In time. There's no rush.

Learning to slow down, appreciate our time together . . . That was another lesson I was working at every day.

We sat quietly together, our horses napping, our knees touching. The dressage tests in the distant arena wore on with an unendingly hilarious lack of finesse or precision. A pigtailed girl with hunter-ring ribbons bouncing on her shoulders went slogging earnestly through her own version of Novice Test A on a bored school horse, ending with a proud salute to the judge, who maintained a straight face with a prowess that spoke of many years' practice. He knew: everyone has to start somewhere.

"You're on in ten minutes," Pete said eventually, checking his watch. "After the next ride, take him and jog around the arena while the rider before you goes. Just loosen him up, don't ask for anything precise. Once you hear the bell, take him in at the same easy trot—don't change a thing. Pick him up after the salute. As soon as you salute, it's all business, okay?"

"I really appreciate you explaining that to me. Is that how dressage tests work? We trot around the arena while the other rider is in the ring? Are you sure? I don't want to get in trouble. If only I'd done this before!"

Pete stuck out his tongue at me. "You have one last chance to win a Novice championship on this horse. Try not to screw it up."

I grinned.

The next rider entered the arena, a middle-aged woman bouncing along on a broom-tailed Appaloosa who lived with a happy disregard for the basic tenets of dressage, his nose straight in front of him as if there was a carrot dangling before it.

I leaned over and kissed Pete. He sat back on his little filly and smiled at me. "Go get 'em, love," he said. "Or I'll have to do it for you."

I scowled. "Always a competition."

"You started it."

I picked up the reins and awakened my drowsy gray horse with a little squeeze of my calves. He picked up his head willingly and we stepped off for the dressage arena. We'd do our test, and I'd hop off and ride Dynamo in the show-jumping. Then I'd get on a project horse, Virtuoso, for one last dressage round before his new owner took him home tomorrow night, and, finally, watch Lacey ride Margot in her test. It had been a long, hot morning, and there was a long, hot afternoon ahead of me. But I was ready for it. This was my life. These horses, this land, this brilliant blue sky. And that man sitting back there behind me, believing in me as I believed in him, while we strove to be the very best. We were ambitious as hell, and there was not a thing wrong with that.

The bell rang.

Rising trot, halt at X, salute the judge.

Acknowledgments

I couldn't write about horses if I wasn't immersed in the horsey life. I was born to be an equestrian, and thank goodness my parents came to understand this phase was not going to end. Thanks, Mom and Dad, for riding lessons, for horses, and the whole circus that came with it. From Land of Little Horses to Kentucky Horse Park, and from my first handwritten horse stories to the Eventing Series, it all started with your support!

My amazing husband, Cory, thank you for enabling my craziest equestrian dreams, handling life because clearly I cannot do life and also write books, and simply being the best person. My genius son, Calvin, thanks for being extremely understanding and practical about a family that does things like work at racetracks for six months or move to the country to homestead with horses. I love that our family life is stuffed full of horses and books, and I'm excited for many more of both in our future!

Equestrians are often loners but we still love to get together and talk horses, and we are a generous bunch, too. To my friends Jessica Horne and Alyssa Nebus-Weihe, thank you both for bringing Ben and Manny into my life so that I always have four-legged inspiration just outside my back door. I am lucky to live near Ocala so that I can be part of the eventing community and I have to thank the people who help me stay close to the action, even if Ben has decided he is not an event horse: Rachel Killian Kuntz for all the wild rides (more to come!), Cassi Cameron-Dukes for teaching me whatever volunteer position I feel like learning at our local events, David Taylor for being the kind of reader who says hello at every event, and all the volunteers and competitors I've chatted with or latched onto at events.

As for my cohost and equestrian partner in nonsense, Heather Wallace, we haven't stopped talking since the day we met, and hopefully we don't stop anytime soon, since podcasts kind of depend on talking. Thank you for being the very best work wife anyone could ever have.

I have been writing and publishing alone for a long time. So I am deeply appreciative of the teams that have stepped up to join me on this journey. We were nearing the end of edits on this book when an email came in for "Team Eventing." I looked at all the names on the send list and realized what an amazing, huge team this really was, and I felt lighter than I had in a long time. Riding is more fun with friends, and it turns out publishing is, too.

So thank you, Team Eventing, for the incredible care and cheerful emails! The enthusiasm of everyone at Flatiron Books made me feel so welcome and valued, and I couldn't be happier to be part of this family. I am flattered and delighted to have been welcomed by this team. I am so thankful for the thoughtful editorial work by Megan Lynch and Caroline Bleeke (who makes me feel like a champion even as she draws a relentless line through my longer sentences), and privileged to work with the Flatiron family, including Jon Yaged, Mary Retta, Maris Tasaka, Nancy Trypuc, Marlena Bittner, Malati Chavali, Emily Walters, Ryan T. Jenkins, Eva Diaz, and Keith Hayes. Thank you all!

Lacy Lynch, the agent that put this team together: thanks for appearing in my life and turning it upside down in the best possible way. I frequently see authors asking, "How did you choose your agent?" and the answer that comes to me is, "Well, do you feel like you've known her your entire life? Then that's your agent!" I am so lucky and joyful that we get to take this trip together. Thanks to everyone on the team: Ali Kominsky, Haley Reynolds, Dabney Rice, and Rebecca Silensky—when I see your names in my inbox, I know everything is going to be just fine.

So many amazing readers have supported my work over the years. I am forever grateful to all of you! Along with the readers are the writers and booksellers who have become my friends, book event partners, and all-around besties. To Lauren O'Connor, a fellow horsewoman, thank you for being a champion for my stories and everyone at Briar Hill Farm. To Jessica Burkhart, thank you for so much advice and hand-holding via text. And thanks also to Susan Friedland, the queen of Chincoteague; Jean McWilliams, of Taborton Equine Books; Martha Cook and Rebecca Didier, of Trafalgar Square Books. Horse book girls, unite!

ABOUT THE AUTHOR

Natalie Keller Reinert is the award-winning author of more than twenty books, including the Eventing and Briar Hill Farm series. Drawing on her professional experience in three-day eventing, working with Thoroughbred racehorses, mounted patrol horses, therapeutic riding, and many other equine pursuits, Natalie brings her love of equestrian life into each of her titles. She also cohosts the award-winning equestrian humor podcast *Adulting with Horses*. Natalie lives in north Florida with her family, horses, and cat.

www.nataliekreinert.com